JIMMY MACK
Some Kind of Wonderful

John Knight

Published in 2017 by FeedARead.com Publishing

Book and cover design by John Knight. Final interior by the author.

A CIP catalogue record for this title is available from the British Library.

Dedicated to my wife Julie and daughters Emma and Kimberley-Joy.
Amandi donum est

"What's meant to be will always find a way."

PRELUDE

One Fine Day – The Chiffons (Stateside SS202 –1963)

Saturday 27 July 1963

Effy sat cross-legged on her bed, gazing out of the open window. A Penny Catechism lay unopened beside her on the white counterpane. The lyrics of *One Fine Day* by The Chiffons, diffused by a tiny red transistor radio, pervaded her thoughts. Surely she wouldn't always be invisible? Surely one day he would notice her? When he did, would he want her for his girl? Somehow, someway, Effy Halloran was going to make James MacKinnon hers one fine day.

CHAPTER 1

Stubborn Kinda Fella – Marvin Gaye (Oriole 45-CBA 1803 –1963)

Saturday 10 October 1964

So these were Mods. Like the ones who had battled it out with Rockers last May on Brighton beach. The national newspapers had been full of it. Seeing these Mods on their scooters left Mack feeling stunned and excited. Only one word summed them up. Cool. Seriously cool.

Two days earlier he had turned fifteen. Walking down Godwin Street, trailing his mum at a teenage-safe distance, he saw the Mods ride past. He had almost frozen midstride at the sight. It was a cold, crisp yet still sunny afternoon. They were heading downhill in the direction of the Co-op department store. The same direction he was heading. His mum had given in, agreeing to buy him a Dansette record player on a proviso: that she accompanied him to buy it. It was the alternative late birthday present he wanted. Getting it had taken much frustrating persuasion. Why he couldn't use the radiogram in the front room was quite beyond his mum's understanding. It had cost enough. Why wasn't it good enough? Why did he have to have a gramophone in his bedroom? Gramophone? Well, he'd thought, I ask you? This was the Sixties. Nobody used wind-up gramophones any more. Talk about a generation gap. Dad had the final word. Not to mention the cash. The record player was about to become reality.

As much as Mack was anticipating the Dansette, when he saw the Mods go past on their scooters he was transfixed. They were an amazing sight.

For a moment it was as though he were experiencing an epiphany on the road to the Co-op. Right then, right there, he knew. He had to get a scooter. He had to be like them, the epitome of cool. His conversion was complete. He was determined to be like them when he turned sixteen.

Their scooters were moving works of chrome art. Rear-view mirrors sprouted in profusion. Extra spotlights festooned on the leg shields glinted in the pale sunlight. Mack knew little about scooters but what he saw was, he imagined, something akin to falling in love. The last of the Mods turned left at the lights into Kirkgate, looking awesome in a French beret and aviator

2

sunglasses. A paisley cravat and an olive-green US Army parka completed the ensemble. These guys were the business and they knew it. It was all style: style that was smart and sharp.

Waiting for the traffic lights to change Mack watched them parking their scooters.

Some experiences become deep-seated memories, unforgettable turning points in life. Everything that happens has a cause and serves a purpose. In less than two years, on this same spot, he would deal his own brand of vigilante justice on an attempted rapist.

Mum prodded him back into the real world as the traffic lights changed.

"Young tearaways." Jane MacKinnon had noticed her son's interest in the Mods and their scooters. "They're nothing but troublemakers disturbing the peace by causing fights. I don't want you associating with youths like that, James. I've heard they take drugs, too."

"They're not doing any harm, Mum." Mack found himself defending the Mods. "For a start, we're a long way from Brighton and Margate so I doubt they would have been down there. They're only local lads."

As he crossed the road he could see his mum's disapproval.

"Besides," he continued, "they're too interested in looking smart to go causing trouble. Those scooters look fantastic."

"All the same, James, I don't want you getting any ideas about scooters or Mods. It's bad enough your brother with his motorbike playing at being one of those Rockers."

How little his mother knew about Adam. He didn't play at it!

"So it's okay for Adam to be a Rocker who might go beating up Mods?"

Jane MacKinnon gave him a frosty knowing look. She was well aware it was a possibility she could not discount. Adam was like human barbed wire, doling out incessant emotional pain to his parents.

Schoolmates knew James MacKinnon as Mack because MacKinnon was a mouthful, and James was too posh for Bradford lads. Mack was easy on the tongue and ear. Jimmy, he found acceptable. But he preferred Jim. Jim sounded stronger. Neither Jim nor Jimmy was acceptable to his parents. At home it was always James. No one ever called him Jim, though he'd tried to get it accepted. Only Mack ever caught on as a nickname.

The Co-op was a 1930s building on the corner of Sunbridge Road. It was a less pricey department store than Busby's, although nowhere near as upmarket as Brown & Muffs. The Co-operative gave customers dividends, something the other snooty stores didn't. Mack and his mum went through a side entrance and down the long wide stairs into a huge basement sales area.

Tucked into the corner to the right of the stairs was the electrical goods department. Mack loved this place. It was a teenage boy's dream haunt. Most Saturday afternoons he would go just to look around. On display were reel-to-reel tape recorders, record players and transistor radios: items he coveted. There were also selections of records for sale but nothing he found interesting. It was mum and dad type music for those with ghastly tastes. Crap LPs by the likes of the Black and White Minstrels, Liberace and Semprini. On Sunday afternoons his dad would sometime play his Semprini LPs. This guaranteed self-imposed exile to Mack's bedroom. The Tubby Hayes Jazz recordings were okay, though not to his mum's taste – which was why Mack suspected his dad played the jazz LPs so they left him alone.

What Mack wanted was a stereo system that he'd read about in one of his dad's magazines. The Stereo 20 would have been the business with its 10 watt per channel output. Mack's dad planned to get one someday, although the price being what it was, it wasn't going to happen any time soon. The priority of a new motorcar topped his father's shopping list. Stereo was not an option. It was 1964. Mono sound was the inexpensive choice when it came to buying a record player.

Jane MacKinnon had to have the last word with her son as she paid for the Dansette. "You'd better look after this record player. It's an expensive purchase. Your father must have lost his marbles giving you the money to buy it. He's become far too soft with you of late."

"Yes, Mum. Of course I'll look after it. You know I will."

"And I don't want you playing it so loud that I can hear it downstairs. Do you understand?"

"Yes, Mum." He sighed.

"It's bad enough with your father listening to those expensive records on the radiogram," she muttered. "I can't believe he paid 32s 6d for that last LP. To say the Scots have a reputation for prudence – he's profligate when it comes to buying records."

"They do give him a lot of pleasure, Mum. It's not as if he smokes or goes to the pub. It's his only pleasure apart from going to the footie." There he was defending his dad now. "And didn't he take you shopping to Leeds to buy you a new hat, coat and two dresses this summer?"

4

The words elicited a tight-lipped smile as Mum admitted the truth of her son's words. Half an hour later Mack was the proud owner of a brand new mono Dansette in red and cream livery. Humming and hawing over the different prices, the salesman had offered his mum HP terms. She refused, paying with the money his father had handed over to her. Jane MacKinnon did not believe in Hire Purchase. Hire Purchase was debt, and debt was something she didn't tolerate. As she was always fond of telling Mack and his brother, "Never buy what you can't afford to pay for there and then." Given his dad's line of work, HP was definitely not even a consideration. The MacKinnons were quite well off.

The record player was a hell of a weight to carry, so they took the No. 8 trolley bus home. Mack's delight was such, he wouldn't have minded if it had weighed twice as much. He would have carried it all the way.

From being a kid he had been mad keen on music. That had never changed. Some of his earliest memories were of songs and music played on the radio. He could still hear in his mind Eddie Calvert's trumpet on *Oh My Papa* and Johnny Ray singing *Walking in the Rain*. Later on Nancy Whisky's *Freight Train* fed his love of listening to music. So, too, did Johnny Duncan's *Last Train to San Fernando*. When he was eleven he'd heard The Drifters' *Some Kind of Wonderful*. This awoke a serious interest in soulful sounds. It became the first record he ever bought. It remained his favourite version until he heard Marvin Gaye's rendering a few years later.

What had fired Mack's imagination was the sound of Marvin Gaye, an American singer. When he heard *Stubborn Kind of Fellow* played on an open market stall he knew he had to buy it. A week later he bought the record with his pocket money. The yellow cover displaying the word "Oriole" introduced him to the Motown sound. Over the next weeks and months he hunted out more records by artists like Mary Wells and The Marvelettes. Whenever his parents were out he would play his small but growing record collection. Not that there were many occasions when he could do so. Getting the Dansette was about to change all that. Next week he would have enough money to buy a copy of The Supremes *Where Did Our Love Go*. It had reached Number Three in the Top Twenty.

Today the afternoon was complete as his brother and father were out. Mum would let him get on with it. Whilst he was upstairs she would be busying herself preparing the evening meal. He'd overheard Adam saying he was off to a mate's house to help fix a motorbike and he wouldn't be back for tea. As for his soccer-mad dad, it would be five o'clock before he returned.

Robert MacKinnon spent most Saturday afternoons down at Valley Parade watching City play. Given the club's poor performances, Mack couldn't understand why his dad supported them. No doubt he would return home grousing. As usual this would be about the manager needing sacking. There would be the usual full-scale inquest, delivered with Shakespearean passion, extolling the on-field doings of Roy Elam. Then other team members would be denigrated for under-performing. The studied angst of wondering why they had let "Bronco" Layne go to Wednesday would surface. City had received a staggering £26,000 record-breaking transfer fee for his services. As a bank manager, the finer points of this financial transaction seemed to elude him. Mack's headmaster was also called Lane and nicknamed "Bronco". So the tired, lame joke about why would you want a headmaster playing for City ended up being repeated over and over again.

When they had lived in Halifax Mack remembered going to watch Halifax Town at the Shay. Soccer never appealed to him after that visit. It had been a cold, joyless, rainy afternoon that he hadn't enjoyed in the slightest.

He unpacked the Dansette. Having fitted a three-round pin plug, he was almost ready to put on the first record when Jane MacKinnon came upstairs to check his wiring.

"Yes," she confirmed, when she'd seen the brown, red and blue wires in their correct positions. "It's safe. You can screw the top on. Now let's check it works. If it doesn't, it will have to go back."

"Mum, you know I can wire a plug. For goodness sake, I'm fifteen. Dad showed me how to do it when I was eleven. Don't you trust me to do it right?"

In an instant Jane experienced her moment of truth as a mother. Her son's words were those of a young man who was no longer a boy.

"It does no harm to double-check. I don't want the guarantee invalidated by you doing something wrong." There was sadness in her voice as she spoke and a look on her face he found inexplicable.

Everything worked.

"Don't play your records too loud." It was less of a warning reprimand and closer to an adult request as she left the room.

"Yes, Mum. I heard you before. I'll keep it down."

It was going to be a great afternoon. Juke Box Jury would be on television with David Jacobs reviewing the latest releases. At last Mack was in his own personal heaven listening to the sound of Marvin Gaye. As each treasured single went on the turntable his thoughts kept returning to the Mods. The afternoon became a haze of musical fantasy. Mack imagined himself on a scooter riding alongside those guys.

CHAPTER 2

Just One Look – Doris Troy (London HLK 9749 – 1963)

Sunday 11 October 1964

Sunday meant going to Mass. Except for Adam, the whole family attended nine o'clock Mass at St. Patrick's Church. The weekly ritual was the same. No one had breakfast apart from Adam, who seldom rose before ten. Breakfast took place when they returned home. There were few things Mack envied about Adam. Not going to Mass on Sunday was definitely one of those. Staying in bed until midday was another.

"Are you going to communion today?" Jane MacKinnon asked, knowing full well what her son's answer would be.

"No, Mum," came the sullen reply. "Not today."

It was the same question every Sunday morning, with the same response.

"Let the lad be." Robert MacKinnon defended his son. "I'm sure he's not committed any mortal sins. He's old enough now to decide for himself. Though I do think you should make more of an effort."

Mack had no intention of making an effort. He had his own reasons for not taking communion. Doses of catechism lessons had made him question his beliefs. His pastime during Mass was watching the Hallorans traipsing up to the communion rail. It was the highlight of an otherwise boring forty-five minutes. The sight of the seven sisters trooping out of the pews made his day. In age and alphabetic order they led him into an avalanche of impure thoughts. Mack's rampaging teenage hormones conflicted with his Catholic upbringing. The hormones always seemed to win out. At night the sisters were a magnificent source of sexual fantasies. Getting an erection in church was wrong, somehow, but he couldn't stop it – no more than he could stop thinking about sex. Since God knew his every thought he was certain to be bound for purgatory, if not hell and eternal damnation. Ending up blind like Little Stevie Wonder or Ray Charles was another possibility. He suppressed a smirk at the idea.

"James?" His mother gave him a strange questioning look. "Jeopardising your immortal soul is no light matter. I hope you took note of what your father said."

"Yes, Mum, I have. And you're right. It's nothing to smirk about." No, he hadn't given his immortal soul another thought. Nor was there the possibility that he would. The Hallorans remained foremost in his thoughts.

This Sunday turned out no different from the previous one. It was yet another rerun of impure fantasies to keep from a priest's confessional. Watching the sisters walking up the aisle in their demure dresses was heaven. It had nothing to do with religion whatsoever. His parents were already behind Mr and Mrs Halloran on the way up the aisle. The Hallorans led the holiness charge to the altar rail. Not that it was an undignified race, even though Mack chose to see it that way.

These days he got the looks from his parents as they rose. Shaming him for not going to communion with them like a good little boy. No doubt over Sunday lunch he would receive yet another lecture. The usual blah on how he was jeopardizing his immortal soul. Nothing – but nothing – was going to interrupt his furtive viewing of the sisters. Not even the loss of his immortal soul. Those minutes spent in blissful contemplation were worth the telling off. What colour knickers did each of the sisters wear? Did they wear roll-ons or suspender belts? What if they wore the big pink bloomers favoured by old women? Now that was a turn off! The thought ended up speed-edited out of his daydream. As each sister went to the communion rail and returned, Mack performed his catwalk audit.

Aileen was the eldest, in her early twenties, and she worked in a bank as a teller. She was much too old and a bit too austere for his taste. Then there was nineteen-year-old Bridget with the big boobs. With sexy stocking-filling calves, she was an awesome-looking woman. She worked as a secretary for a local solicitor somewhere in the city centre. Too old once again, but then there was this appeal of the mature woman. Caitlin was eighteen and as flat-chested as Bridget was big. She had a fine behind that swivelled as she sashayed down the aisle. Deidre was the freckled-faced seventeen-year-old best described as the family twig. The gossip mill rumoured that she had ambitions to go to university to study medicine.

Mack had to admit he found it hard to fulfil any sexual fantasy with Deidre. Sexy was not a word that fitted her. The horn-rimmed butterfly-style glasses did little to enhance her appearance. All in all she hardly conjured up an image of a sex goddess cum femme fatale.

9

Ellen Halloran was another matter. Mack found her one of the sexiest of the sisters. Of them all, she was the one who made the most frequent appearances in his mental sex movies. Beyond his reach, the sixteen-year-old guaranteed the hardest fastest spillages.

Fiona was Mack's age. Like her sisters, she had long strawberry-blonde hair. Expressive green eyes and an almost elfin like appearance gave her an angelic look. She possessed a beatific expression like the one found on the female saints' statues in the church. There was not much shape to her figure. Even so, Mack found it uncanny how he was so taken with her. It was hard to think of her in a depraved way. She was the one who always looked him in the eyes as she pitter-pattered back from the communion rail. Fiona Halloran made him feel guilty. It was as though she could read his mind, going by her expression. Of course, he rationalised; it wasn't possible to read his thoughts. And yet there was some kind of deep attraction to her. Of all the sisters, she had the firmest hold on his imagination.

The last was thirteen-year-old Grace. The dark coppery mane was so different from the strawberry blonde of her sisters. She was far too young for any dirty deed thoughts. Though covered with freckles, she possessed the Halloran feminine attractiveness. Grace must finally have shattered Old Man Halloran's dreams of a son. Still, he and his wife had proved themselves the best of Catholics. No finger-pointers could taint their reputation with insinuations of family planning. Either that or Mrs Halloran's womb had finally given up. The burden of introducing more females into the world must have proved too much. Or had she tied a knot in his manhood? The thought made him smile as Fiona Halloran returned from the communion rail to her pew. His unintentional smile went down well. She glanced away, her shyness evident, with a faint smile of her own. That came as a surprise to him. Still, it didn't mean anything, did it? All the sisters had attended or were attending St. Joseph's Girls' Grammar School. As a grammar school reject, Mack knew there was little or no chance of having any contact with her.

Resuming his train of thought, Mack mused that they made a fine posse of womanhood. To be sure, to be sure: he enunciated the words in his head in a mock Irish accent. Arranged in age and alphabetic order the sisters appeared so disciplined. Alphabetically named, too. Now that was so weird: Aileen, Bridget, Caitlin, Deidre, Ellen, Fiona and Grace. What had possessed the Hallorans to name their daughters in alphabetic order? Then another thought crossed his mind. What if the sisters ever learned what he had done to each of them in his bedroom fantasies? They would gang up on him and cut his meat and two veg off. Now that was a terrifying thought. An image formed of the sisters holding him down as one of them wielded a kitchen knife. His mother broke this unpleasant daydream with a not-so-gentle prod to the ribs.

"James," she whispered. "Remember where you are. God is present. Stop grinning like a Cheshire cat."

Mr Halloran had dealings with Mack's dad through the bank. Yet the two families didn't know each other on a social basis. Mack suspected that, unlike the musical, there were no seven brothers for seven brides. Then again, Mr Halloran was the chief man of the local Opus Dei. If there was one thing Mack's father detested it was Opus Dei. The name of the organisation made his hackles rise. Some of the things he had to say were not at all pleasant. "Fascist origins," his Dad muttered whenever he heard Opus Dei mentioned. It was bad enough his Mum's involvement in the Mothers' Union. At least she leaked occasional interesting snippets of information about the Halloran girls.

At the end of Mass Mack made his usual practised getaway. There would be the usual minor scold for doing this but he didn't care. He had no time to waste. Driven by ulterior motive he always left before the Hallorans.

Dipping their hands in the holy water font, they made the sign of the cross. There was almost a kind of saintliness about the sisters as they left the church. Like the call of the communion wafer they did this in age and alphabetic order, much to Mack's amusement.

The sisters congregated with military precision. Standing to attention beyond the convent door they exchanged pleasantries with congregation regulars. Chorus-like, they echoed, "So nice to see you, Mrs Flaherty," or to whomever happened to be passing. Mack grinned, wondering if they practised the unison greetings at home. Today was different. An unwitting event unfolded – another turning point in his life he would never forget.

The two youngest sisters were paying him attention. Red-headed Grace kept nudging her sister. Fiona pretended not to look at him but was actually doing so. Blushing, she was trying to maintain a studious, serene, disinterested face but without success. Despite her shyness, she was looking at him. Without a doubt he was the object of her attention. It felt as if she was doing this in a deliberate attempt to attract him. Sensing this was somehow special, Mack delighted in being the object of her attention. A strange feeling, thrilling in the extreme, surfed through him. His heartbeat almost exploded in the shock of the moment of realization. Being a typical gauche

11

teenager he didn't know quite what possessed him. Locking glances, he winked at her. Fiona's cheeks blushed an even deeper tint. Witnessing what transpired, Grace cupped her hand to her mouth, suppressing laughter.

"Did I catch you winking at one of the Halloran girls?" Grace hadn't been the only one to see him wink. His dad had seen it too. His mum was busy doing her Mothers' Union bit with Mrs Halloran so she missed the exchange.

"I was only having a joke, Dad," he muttered unconvincingly, feeling his face reddening.

Something in his relationship with his father was about to change. Robert MacKinnon allowed himself an appreciative beaming smile. It was his way of signifying he was revelling in the moment.

"A bit young for courting yet, James. Still," he added with a hint of teasing, "she is a bonny looking girl. Could make a fine daughter-in-law in time when you're both a bit older, eh?"

Hearing his dad saying this made Mack groan. His cringe gland went into overload. He pleaded, muttering with embarrassment, "Dad!"

Putting on a Yorkshire accent masking his Edinburgh Morningside accent Robert MacKinnon joked, "Not ta worry, lad. Sithee I'll say nowt to yer Ma about this."

After a pause he added in a more sombre manner, "Make sure you don't let Old Man Halloran see you winking at one of his daughters. He keeps those girls well regimented. Too well regimented for their good, I suspect. I'd rather not have a conversation with him about you courting one of his daughters."

"Courting? We're not living in the eighteenth century, Dad." It was so obvious. His father was having fun at his expense. Courting might be a bit strong but there could be nothing wrong in having a girlfriend at fifteen, could there?

"Well, I'm glad I could have these words with you, son. At least now I know my lad likes girls and isn't a teapot. Quite a relief, young James, quite a relief." A hearty pat or two on his shoulder followed.

Mack found himself taken aback. A teapot? What on earth did his Dad mean by a teapot?

Grace's cheeky grin confronted him. Each moment of his and her sister's discomfort enjoyed to the full. Well, she at least had found the innocent incident entertaining. Meanwhile Fiona had turned to face the convent. No doubt she was wishing she would find herself swallowed up within the convent's confines. Mack had to turn away to avoid Grace's eyes. As he turned, so did Fiona, now appearing more composed. Their eyes met. She gave him such a beautiful smile his pulse began to race again. In those couple of moments their fates joined. Their lives were about to change forever because of a simple wink.

Mondays to Fridays the car remained bonded to the tarmac outside their front door. Robert MacKinnon had bought the Ford Cortina for £550. Every Saturday Mack washed and then polished it until it gleamed. Whether it needed it or not was immaterial; his dad took pride in the family saloon. On a good day he could see his face mirrored in the metalwork. Mack had to clean the Cortina as one of his household chores to earn his weekly pocket money, a lavish 5/6d. During the week, he also did a paper round, netting himself a further 3/6d. The total came to 9 shillings. Mack considered this a more than reasonable amount of money. Next summer, when he was sixteen, he intended to get a Saturday job and earn even more. He loathed doing the paper round but did it out of necessity. It was possible he might get lucky in the school holidays and find a well-paying part-time job to replace it.

Today the Cortina had done its church run. Instead of heading home it was heading in another direction.

"Aren't we going home?" Mack asked. As usual, he was in the back seat.

"No," replied his father. "We've had an invitation from your Aunt Ellen to come over for Sunday dinner. We can have some toast when we get there to tide us over."

"Great!" Sundays were boring beyond belief. This was a welcome way to break up that boredom. "Isn't Adam coming?"

"Seems he has other plans today." There was terseness in Robert MacKinnon's voice. "His motorcycle and his friends appear to be more important than family these days."

"Goodness knows what he gets up to," added his Mother with more than a hint of sadness. "I can't seem to communicate with him anymore. At times he's like a complete stranger, not my son."

An uneasy silence followed his mother's admission. Adam had become especially difficult and morose of late. He had never been easy as far as Mack remembered. But he wasn't going to let thinking about his brother spoil today.

13

"I could have gone to the same school as Tom." Mack changed the direction of the conversation. He was aware Adam was a major pain in his parents' life. "We may even have been in the same class."

"Don't you like going to Edmund Campion then?" his father asked.

"I like it well enough. It's a good school but it's in Bradford, not Halifax. Besides, I would have been able to see Tom and my aunt and uncle more often."

Visiting his aunt's was always a delight. Aunt Ellen was his father's sister. Mack adored her. She was his second mum. He also shared a close relationship with his cousin. Tom Catford was a month older than Mack. Not only was he a cousin – he was his best friend.

Before Mack's family had moved to Bradford the two had been inseparable. They had played together from when they were babies. Aunt Ellen had looked after him as if he were her own when his mum was at work. Adam, a few years older, had already gone to Infants school, never figuring in the picture as such. When the time came Mack and Tom even went to the same primary school until the MacKinnons moved to Bradford. After the move his mother stopped working and became a housewife now that his father had a top job.

Mack hated Bradford. Not only had he had to move to the city, he was also taken away from Aunt Ellen and Tom. For Mack there was nothing redeeming about the city. Apart from the centre it was a drab, cheerless place. Streets leading into more streets and even more streets, going on and on. It was an ugly sprawl with some hideous rundown districts off Lower Manningham Lane and around Lumb Lane.

Leaving Halifax had been a terrible experience for Mack. Not only had he left Tom and his aunt there but also all his school friends. And he missed his trips down to the old market in town with Tom.

"I wish we still lived in Halifax." Mack found him self speaking his thoughts aloud again. "I miss the place."

"Unfortunately, James, work means we have to live in Bradford," Robert MacKinnon responded. "I know you and your mother miss the town but there's nothing we can do about it. My job is a high-paid one and it means we can afford a better standard of living than if I had stayed."

"That's life, James. We had no choice," added his Mum in a wistful voice. "We did love it in Halifax. Your father and I have many happy memories of our time there."

Halifax was much pleasanter: a cleaner place, even if there were no electric trolley buses. It was Mack's hometown. Whenever he could, he took the bus to Halifax to meet up with Tom. Sometimes his mum went to visit at the weekend to have a good chinwag with his aunt. When his mum went, he went too. Mack looked forward to those outings more than anything. He and Tom would go out and disappear for hours if the weather was good. If the weather was bad they would hole up in Tom's bedroom and read American comics. When Tom came over they did much the same, but Bradford was nowhere near as much fun. His cousin always brought a pile of second-hand DC and Marvel comics with him, although now they were getting older that had dropped off. Instead of comics they shared an interest in pop music. This revolved round the latest issue of the NME or Melody Maker. Mack couldn't wait to tell Tom about his new record player. Would Tom know what his dad had meant about not being "a teapot"? Mack was still clueless about its meaning.

The journey took about thirty minutes, the roads being almost empty on Sundays. Mack's dad always took the Queensbury route. Without fail he reminded them that Boothtown was where the inventor for cat's eyes for the road lived. Dad delighted in pointing out where Percy Shaw's house stood. This always happened going out – never on the return. Mack suspected his father did it on purpose to be annoying. Today, for the first time ever, there was no mention of the fact.

The Catfords lived in a terrace house on Wyvern Place off Albert Road. Located at the end of Hansom Lane near the outskirts of town, it always seemed tranquil. Uncle Phil and his wife were not as well off as Mack's own parents but they had a comfortable home. For Mack, it was his second home. His aunt always gave him a big hug and a kiss when he stepped through the door.

Both families got on well. Mack's mum and dad were older than his aunt and uncle, but not by many years. Dad was five years older than Aunt Ellen, although Uncle Phil was only two years younger than him.

Tom's Dad was a regular joker who enjoyed poking gentle fun at his son. This seldom went down well with Tom. Tom had a serious grievance about his forename. Whenever father and son had a spat, the matter of the naming arose. Tom insisted that his dad's choice was deliberate, picked to cause him problems. According to Tom, Uncle Phil had known full well he would have the mickey taken out of him at school. This was why the young Catford had to put up with "Tom Cat". Not to mention coping with the

15

inevitable cat jokes and other feline-related ribbing. It was a sore point with Mack's cousin, but a fist-sore face for those who made fun of his name.

Aunt Ellen's Sunday roast beef dinners were something special. Yorkshire puddings were huge, perfect and mouth-watering. Mack's mum's puddings tended to turn out on the soggy side. Food piled high, the teenagers ate plateful portions rivalling their respective fathers.

After dinner Mack and Tom went upstairs. Tom's room was a total tip in contrast to his own. Clothes were strewn all over it, and piles of comics, magazines and books took up most of the floor space. For a bedroom bigger than Mack's, somehow it managed to look smaller.

"My dad said a funny thing to me today. He said he was glad I wasn't a teapot. Have you got any idea what he meant?" asked Mack.

Tom rolled his eyes, feigning disbelief. "God, cuz, you are gormless or what? Teapot's a slang word for a Homo. Don't tell me you didn't know?"

Then, as if to reinforce his explanation, Tom queried, "You do know what a Homo is, don't you, cuz?"

"Yeah! 'Course I do! Blokes who fancy other blokes."

"In one, my son, in one," replied Tom. "What made him say that? Doesn't sound like something your dad would say."

"He caught me winking at a girl outside church this morning. He thought it was ha-ha funny." Mack tried to make it sound trivial.

"Oh, aye? Tell me more."

"There's nowt to tell," Mack replied, knowing full well he had aroused Tom's curiosity. "Dad went on about courting and stuff."

"No, you dope!" Tom pressed on with a sly grin. He meant to prise information out of Mack. "I meant who's this bird you were chatting up?"

"I wasn't chatting her up. We never spoke. Never said a word. In fact, I've never spoken to her. She goes to our church along with her sisters. Anyway, she's one of these grammar school girls. I can't see she'd have anything to do with me."

Tom's face took on a look of disgust. "Bloody typical. I get that from those snobby lasses who go to Crossley & Porters. They don't have time for us secondary modern lads. Fair pisses me off."

"So you've been trying to chat lasses up as well, have you?" teased Mack.

"Yeah," replied Tom, trying to be dismissive. "Been down to Palin's in town with some mates from school."

"Palins? What's Palins?" asked Mack, puzzled.

16

"Nowt for young ones." Tom began the tease. "Especially if you're from Bradford."

"Aw, come on, Tom." Mack stretched out the words in mock disbelief. "What's the big secret?"

Tom's grin broadened. After a moment's pause, with an expression masking embarrassment, he continued, "It's a dance hall in town where they play pop music and you can meet girls."

Grinning, Mack pretend-punched his cousin on the shoulder. "Quite the hound dog, eh? I ought to call you Casanova. Go on then, what have you been up to at this spot? Dancing?"

Mack could see Tom was dying to tell all. As usual his cousin was dragging it out, dangling the information like bait, as though it were some irresistible titbit of arcane knowledge for the uninitiated. Which, of course, it was. When it came to knowing about girls his cousin had the advantage over him.

Tom leaned forward and in his best blackmail voice whispered, "Only if you tell me about this girl at church first."

"You're a right one, you are." Mack feigned mock disgust at the blatant blackmail attempt. "Seeing as it's you, I'll tell you."

Mack's description of the sisters trotting out to communion made his cousin laugh. Tom hung on every last word with the kind of shared humour both enjoyed.

"So is she good-looking, this Fiona?"

"She's pretty." A mental image of her formed at that moment. "Yep. She's pretty, I have to admit. Actually, she's gorgeous. Trouble is I'd never get a chance to talk to her. Anyway, why would she want to have anything to do with me?"

Tom laughed and said nothing for some seconds before asking, "Then why did she give you the eye my son, eh? Why did she blush and turn away? She must fancy you. Going by what you said happened, she must definitely be into you. Gerrrrrin, my son!"

"Oh! And I suppose you're every girl's dream answer, are you? Know what's going through their minds, do you?" Mack answered before Tom could say another word. "Like I said, I don't how I could meet her. We don't go to the same school or anything."

"Do you know where she lives?"

"Why?"

17

"Why not wait outside her house? Follow her when she goes out. See where she goes. Chat her up if you get the chance. You never know, she might have to do an errand for her mum or go to the local library or something."

Mack had to admit his cousin made sense.

"Anyway, lover boy, now it's your turn. Spill the Heinz." It was their slangy take on spilling the beans.

"I've got a girlfriend," Tom blurted out, unable to confine it to himself any longer. "She's called Val and she comes from Mytholmroyd. Guess what?"

"No, what?" gulped Mack, somewhat staggered

"I've snogged her!"

"Bloody hell, Tom! You never!"

It was a surprise but also not so surprising. In many ways his cousin seemed so much more mature than Mack. Then again, Tom was always so sure of himself. There was never a lack of confidence in either of them.

"What's more, I copped a feel of her jugs, too."

"Bloody hell, you never!" Mack found himself repeating, the revelation taking him by complete surprise. "Go on, pull the other leg and ring Quasimodo's bells."

"No. Straight up. She let me. She 'frenched' me, too." Tom enjoyed the moment watching his cousin's electrified expression. Mack's face looked as if he had shoved his fingers in a wall socket.

"That's disgusting. You mean she actually stuck her tongue in your mouth?"

"And tickled my tonsils when she did it."

"Piss off!" Mack burst out laughing. "Now I know you're kidding."

"No, honest," continued Tom. "I mean she did french me and her tongue went in all the way but the tonsils bit was an exaggeration. Mind you, she couldn't have been too far away from them."

"What's she like?" Mack asked, intrigued about who this wanton creature was and how Tom had managed to get so far.

Tom was only too willing to tell all. They had met when he went down to Pearl Palin's with some of his school friends. When the truth finally came out the story differed. It appeared a girl had approached one of his mates. Words to the effect of "my friend fancies your friend" had been passed on. Tom had been duly informed. Looking across the dance floor, he'd got his mate to act as a go-between with an affirmative answer. It had

18

been so simple. Or at least Tom made it seem like that, though Mack reckoned Tom had missed out on some of the fine detail. Such as his cousin crapping himself as it all happened. For all of Tom's bravado Mack was certain it must have been a damn sight more nerve-racking than he made out. It was hard not to feel envious. Even at school Mack found it quite a struggle coping with the girls in his class. He had to admit he fancied more than a few of them but he struggled when it came to talking to them. They seemed so giggly, different, almost alien.

He found himself thinking again about Fiona. She was pretty. No. She was gorgeous. No. Not gorgeous – she was beautiful. What if she did fancy him? How alien could she be? Surely no more alien than the girls in his own class? How was he ever going to strike up a conversation with her? More to the point, how was he ever going to meet her other than at church after Sunday Mass? It was going to become his mission to meet her somehow. He needed to take Tom's advice.

"Now then, cuz." Tom broke into Mack's daydream. "Have you still got your collection of comic books?"

"Why?"

"I told this guy you had all the No. 1's. Fantastic Four, Green Lantern, Spiderman and so on. He was wondering if you wanted to sell them. I said I'd ask when I saw you."

"Nope. I sold them when I was hard-up. Took them down to the open market a while back. There was this record I wanted. I reckon one day I'll regret it," sighed Mack. "Be my rotten luck if in future they were worth something."

There was a pause. "Oh, hell! I forgot to tell you," added Mack. "I got the Dansette!"

CHAPTER 3

Great Balls of Fire – Jerry Lee Lewis (London 45-HL-S 8529 – 1957)

Sunday 11 October 1964 – Later

Rescuing the Dansette Mack hurried back to his bedroom. He was none too careful about removing Adam's records. What he had seen was unbelievable. There was an almighty shouting match going on downstairs. Sunday evening was turning into a less than pleasant experience. Returning earlier than usual, he and his parents had found the house full of Adam's Rocker mates and their girls. Infesting the lounge, living room and kitchen, they were swigging beer and smoking. They were committing the ultimate sin in a no-smoking near teetotal household.

Mack had known straight away that there was a problem as they drove up to the house. The space in front of their home had a dozen or so motorbikes taking up the parking place. To say his parents were angry was an understatement to end all understatements. They had demanded to know what was going on and where was Adam? They had received their answer with chortling, sniggering, and fingers pointing upstairs. Robert MacKinnon made it clear the partying was over and they should leave. Fast. His father's choice of no-nonsense nautical-blue terminology impressed Mack. His commanding presence made Mack realise for the first time why his dad had been a naval officer.

Adam was upstairs using his new Dansette. It was worse still when his mum and dad walked in on him. They caught their son in mid-flight ecstasy with his Y-fronts down. In fact, not even with them on but stark bollock naked. Adam was panting with some girl under him, groaning, with her legs spread wide. Mack had snatched a quick eyeful of the action. Cursing, his naked brother had leapt off the bed and slammed the door in their astonished faces.

Much later Mack would see the musical funny side. It was the less than romantic sounding Rocker "fave rave" blaring out of his Dansette that did it. As Adam was caught *in flagrante delicto, Great Balls of Fire* was playing on automatic repeat. In years to come Mack would whistle the tune in his brother's hearing and then burst into song with gusto, enjoying

20

winding Adam up. But at that moment Mack was far more concerned about whether there was any damage to the stylus or the speaker.

The shouting match increased. Mack heard nothing but raised voices. It sounded serious. He opened his bedroom door and went to get the Dansette back from Adam's room. It was then he caught sight of the girl who had been the object of his brother's lust exiting the bedroom on tiptoe. Dressed in a black roll-neck sweater and jeans, she looked familiar. The phrases "jaw dropping" and "heart stopping" came to mind as Mack recognised her. This was as dazing as it could get. Mr Opus Dei would freak out if he found out. It was his daughter, Caitlin Halloran. Mack watched her trying to make a silent getaway down the stairs. The creaking stairs betrayed her efforts. Everything went completely silent as she reached the hallway. Did Mack imagine it? He thought he heard his mother gasp. What followed was audible.

He heard his mother exclaim, "Young woman. How could you behave like a common hussy? What would your parents say?"

Something resembling the plaintive mewing of a cat was the response. Mack heard no more. The lounge door closed and then voices became raised again. His mother sounded as if she were crying. So did Caitlin Halloran. Mack was tempted to go down and watch the further unfolding of the drama but then he thought better of it. Sometimes it was better to stay out of the way, and now was one of those times. He was, after all, not his brother's keeper when it came to something like this.

Adam, three years older than Mack, was a Rocker. Motorbikes were his passion. Life was about going out with his mates. The first thing his brother had done after starting work was to buy a 1953 ex-GPO BSA Bantam. This still had the big ugly steel leg protectors when he bought it. It cost him £15 and a guitar he never managed to learn to play. Not a bad trade with one of his workmates as it turned out. The BSA must have been lucky for Adam. He passed his test the first time within three months of getting on the sprung saddle. He made a Triumph 650SS his immediate buy, using money left to him by his grandfather. That had upset their mother. The Triumph had immediately elevated Adam to local Rocker stardom. The leather jacket and helmet emblazoned with skull and crossbones completed the image.

Sundays were for getting out of bed late. Sundays were for going out with his mates on a run. Trying to hit speeds of 100 mph or doing the ton on a bypass was the great adventure. After which stopping off at some greasy spoon cafe for a few hours followed. His parents had no idea what doing the ton meant. Had they known, they would have had coronaries. Nor did they know about jukebox racing. Setting off at the start of a record on the cafe's jukebox to reach a predetermined spot and return before the record finished. According to those who had brothers in the same gang, Adam was the man. Mack thought it wiser not to enlighten his parents. It was one of the few favours he did his brother. It was also a favour to his parents. Sometimes ignorance was a form of discretion. This evening ignorance was no longer possible.

The sound of the front door slamming made Mack head for the window. It was dark but the streetlights illuminated the motley crew of Rockers. Almost as if to mentally pinch himself Mack double-checked that it really was Caitlin Halloran. Indeed it was. She looked to be in floods of tears but he couldn't be sure. It was difficult to make out under the streetlight. Adam was kick-starting the Triumph but for once it didn't fire straight away. It seemed to take forever before the motorcycle finally decided to spring into life. The others followed suit, starting their bikes with a veritable roaring cacophony. Then they were gone into the night. Adam didn't come back home that night or the next. It would be days before he did.

Some while later – Mack wasn't sure how long it was – his father came into his room. Looking collected and calm, he said nothing to Mack but sat down beside him on the bed. It was obvious he wanted to say something but he was mulling over what and how to say it. Mack sensed the usual certainty and surefootedness that defined his father were missing. Robert MacKinnon appeared lost for words. Finally he spoke.

"Listen, James." There was a long pause as he weighed his next words. "Your brother has done a stupid thing. Whatever happens, you mustn't say anything about what you saw this evening. Especially about the Halloran lassie."

"You mean Caitlin?"

"Yes. Caitlin."

"Okay, Dad. Not a word. Zipped lips."

There was another, longer, awkward pause. It seemed that his father was wrestling with how to proceed. Mack kept quiet, his heart thumping, not sure if it was excitement or some other emotion.

"It would ruin her reputation if it got out. I can't imagine how her parents would take it if it came to light. Do you understand what I'm saying, James?"

"I think so, Dad."

22

"And it could be worse if she were to become pregnant." His father uttered a low sigh and then, after a further brief pause, continued. "Your brother has behaved in an irresponsible way. A bad way if I'm honest. You see, James, if she became pregnant your brother would have to do the decent thing by her. He's too young and immature to be a father and a husband."

Mack wanted to laugh. It wasn't so much what his father was saying: that was fair enough. Imagining *Crumplestiltskin* pushing a pram around and wearing a studded leather jacket was priceless. How he kept a straight face Mack was unsure but he did. There were a few moments of silence as he regained a degree of composure. Then, surprising himself, he blurted out, "God, Dad, what on earth did she see in my spotted 'oik' of a brother? I know he's my brother but she could have done so much better."

This took his father by surprise. It was an unexpected response from his youngest son. He had a strange look in his eyes as he studied Mack. "Why would you say that? You can't be jealous?"

"No. Not at all, Dad. I don't fancy her. It's not what I meant. She's a bit too old for me, isn't she? But it doesn't make sense, her and him. Yuk." Mack gave a pretend shudder.

There was another longish pause. "Your grandfather didn't think so much of me when I married your mother. James, there's no accounting for what makes them attracted to one another. Who knows? In all honesty, I don't. I've known the Hallorans ever since we moved to Bradford. I've seen those girls growing into young women. They are a decent, moral family governed by strong religious conviction. They would be even more shocked with their daughter's behaviour than we are with Adam's. I have no idea why or how they got together. Like you, I'm baffled. At least with Adam we understand why he is as he is. We expected too much from him and it was more than what he was capable of doing. But he should have respected her and not led her into... well, you know what. You're old enough to work out what they were doing."

Another longish pause followed before he continued, "He must have lured and pressured the young woman. I hope to God he didn't force himself upon her."

Was his father suggesting Adam was a rapist?

"But Dad, it takes two," Mack began. "It's not like she didn't know what she was doing. What I mean is she must have agreed to... if you know what I mean."

MacKinnon senior said nothing for a while. "You're right, of course. I don't believe he forced her. I couldn't believe it of him. It takes two. The church views carnal relations outside of marriage as sinful. I know your brother's faith has lapsed. That could yet change and one day he could return to the church. But it's surprising the Halloran girl would succumb to carnal temptation. And yet..."

"And yet?" Mack prompted.

"And yet her parents may have tried to impose their faith on their daughter with too much zeal. Whatever the cause both Adam and Caitlin may now have to deal with serious consequences. Let's hope he took some precautions."

"But supposing she tempted him a bit like Eve in the Garden of Eden?"

Robert MacKinnon confronted his son with his most serious bank manager face. "Yes, that might have happened too. James, I won't try to make you promise not to do the same as your brother. We should not seek temptation. Being men, we have urges leading us into temptations that are best avoided. It was that kind of temptation that brought original sin upon us. I hope as a good Catholic you avoid such temptation, whoever initiates it. But if you don't, then please think of the consequences for the girl. I'm sure you understand."

It was strange hearing his father say these things. It sounded peculiar. Later it would all make a great deal more sense. As it was Mack was experiencing a major system shock. This unexpected father–son exchange was novel. His father's frankness was like this evening's events. Extraordinary. This was new territory where Mack became aware his Father was a man as well as a parent. In those few moments he realised that in life there were some things you couldn't laugh off or joke about. His father was treating him as an adult. This had never happened before. Neither was the realization he was no longer a kid but on his way to being a grown up. Today's events somehow marked the end of childhood. Mack was closer to his father than he had ever been. Life was changing. The meaning of what it meant to be a father had started to crystallise. Yet he sensed there was something much deeper behind all this. His father was taking the whole matter far better than he would have expected. In time Mack would learn why.

"Come on, son. Let's go down and see if your mother has calmed down. Get some supper, eh? Best if you said nothing and pretended you didn't see anything, okay?"

Mack nodded.

His mother was sitting at the kitchen table and it took no genius to work out that she'd been crying. Mack could see the tracks of her tears in her makeup. She was rocking forwards and backwards as though this comforted her; it was an almost imperceptible action. At that moment Mack shared in his mother's pain, experienced her disappointment, and understood its impact. Adam's actions had tested her faith and maternal love. He overheard her saying, "It's history repeating itself, Robert, isn't it? Is God punishing me?" He watched his father put his arm around his mother and whisper in her ear. This seemed to bring some momentary solace.

Many months later he would remember her words. He would learn there were other reasons for his mother being upset and his father so calm. Tonight must have capped it all. Worse still, it had taken place in her home. It was a desecration, a sacrilegious act and a violation of her home by her eldest son. He could relate to that. Adam had a way of violating. Beyond this was the physical violation of spilled beer and scattered cigarette butts. One of his bastard Rocker mates had dared to grind his cigarette ash and stubs into the carpet. Mack helped his dad to tidy up. In fact, the two of them did their best to clean up the damage to the carpet so the worst didn't show. His father's only comment was that Adam would be paying for any damage.

When Mack slid between the sheets thinking over the day's events he could only wonder at how crazy it had all been. This morning Caitlin had sashayed down to communion and taken the holy sacrament. Then later in the day she had committed a mortal sin by having sex with his brother. The thought of his brother doing it with her was a bit of a stunner. There was a word for the way she acted but it eluded him for the moment. A word that had arisen in a religious instruction class summed up her actions. He couldn't bring it to mind. Then the theology kicked in. Damned.

Damned for all eternity, according to what the Catholic Church preached. Somehow it didn't sit right with Mack. How could it be so wrong? For doing something that was natural for all creatures except humankind? Then what about his father saying he hoped Adam had taken precautions? Contraceptives were unforgivable in the eyes of the Church. Then Fiona drifted into his thoughts and he wondered, was she anything like her sister? Well, he was nothing like his brother so she was bound to be nothing like her sister. He found himself stiffening at the thought of her. The morning's events were still etched into his mind.

He could picture her outside the convent with her younger sister, blushing as he had winked. Her parting beguiling smile was still fresh. Tom was right. She must fancy him. Girls didn't look at you that way and blush, nor give you those kinds of smiles unless they meant it. What had she been wearing? He couldn't remember. It annoyed him. One thing was certain. Mack could not stop thinking about Fiona confirming that she felt a serious attraction to him. As he was slipping into sleep the annoying word he couldn't recall came to mind.

Hypocrite. Caitlin Halloran was a hypocrite. Pretending to be something she was not. That was it. A "whited sepulchre" was the phrase in the Bible. The word hypocrite had surfaced at the time. Supposing they had done the deed already? That would mean… well, whatever that would mean.

Then it occurred to him. He was a hypocrite as well. He went to Sunday Mass with his parents but he didn't actually believe the Church's guff. At least Adam was honest in his own way by not going unlike himself. Mack relished watching the Halloran sisters walking down the aisle. Then in an instant of clarity it came to him. She was the reason. It was Fiona he looked forward to seeing on Sundays. He still went to Mass for no other reason.

Then another thought surfaced. Would Caitlin walk down the aisle next Sunday having repented of her mortal sinning? Or would she sit glued to the pew and not move? Would she even dare to go to the Saturday teatime confessional to recount her deed to the priest? Odds on she wouldn't dare confess to her sins to the Canon. Mack had heard him going ballistic in the confessional railing throughout the church. There was always the possibility Caitlin might not even show at Mass. Next Sunday would reveal all, but tomorrow was another day. Drowsing, he knew it was back to school for another week.

CHAPTER 4

Cupid – Sam Cooke (RCA 1242 – 1961)

Monday 12 October 1964

Mack's mind always drifted on the school bus. Locked in reveries, his mind mixed free-flowing memories from the past with the day's events. He found it strange how unconnected thoughts and memories streamed together. He was on his way into the city to pick up a new single he had ordered from Wood's record shop. This was something he did so often that it was almost like clockwork.

Mack enjoyed school. That was a fact. He liked the teachers and he liked most of his classmates. He had no regrets about going to the secondary modern. Blessed Edmund Campion was less than two and half years old, having opened its doors in September 1962. It was one of three new Catholic secondary moderns built in Bradford.

There was nothing much he disliked about what they taught, except for "RI" or Religious Instruction. In his mind, it wasn't so much religious instruction as religious indoctrination. Still, religious instruction was what they did in Catholic schools. This did not happen over the road at Rhodesway. Then again Rhodesway was a non-denominational secondary modern with token RE lessons.

Despite the rivalry between the two schools Mack had no problems with Rhodesway kids. When he took the city centre bus after school to hunt for records he was usually the only one from Eddie Campion. Not that he had anything to fear, since by reputation he was well respected. There had been occasional fights between the best fighters from each of the schools. His reputation as a top-dog brawler was well known in both schools. Hardened by encounters with his older brother, Mack had no fear of getting stuck in with his fists. Most avoided getting a beating when confronted by him. A menacing cobra-like stare, an aggressive posture and a growl intimidated them. He had Uncle Phil to thank for that. The memory was as fresh as today's events.

Uncle Phil had taken Tom and himself aside when they were much younger. He was the one who had imparted fight wisdom. It had been

27

almost biblical in its delivery. In a warped kind of way it had seemed as though it were gospel.

He had begun in a cautionary, even apologetic tone. "Now, I know your mum and dad wouldn't approve of what I'm going to tell you, James. In fact neither would your aunt. But when it comes to a punch-up you could both do with a bit of man advice. Believe me, there might be times as young men when this advice might come in handy. So, as your uncle, I'm going to give you this advice, Mack. As for you, young Tom, the same applies."

There was a longish pause before he continued. "You should avoid trouble if you can but if you can't… remember there is only one rule. Do unto others as they would do unto you… but do it first and do it bloody quick. Forget about the niceties of Queensbury rules. There's no etiquette when it comes to street scrapping. In a brawl anything goes except using knives or anything resembling a weapon. Weapons are guaranteed jail time. So don't use any kind of weapon or object. A kick in the balls makes sure the fight will be over before it starts. Failing that, give them a Glasgow kiss or a Barnsley tap-dancing lesson."

"What are they?" Tom had piped up.

Lowering his voice, Tom's dad continued. "Listen and learn. The Glasgow kiss needs perfect timing and coordination. It's a head butt."

"What's a head butt?" Mack had never heard either expression before.

"Yeah, Dad. What is it?" echoed Tom.

Dropping down to his son's level his father performed a slow-motion demonstration. "The one thing you need to remember is your forehead is aiming at their nose. Not their forehead. Do it wrong and it will hurt you as much, if not more, than the other bloke. As for the Barnsley tap dance, it's a kick to the shin. If you're quick do it to one and then as they howl in pain do it to the other. With luck they'll end up on the pavement and you'll walk away. But remember. Never kick or hit a man when he's down. If he gets up… well, that's a different matter."

The highlight of the day had been the careers interview. Mack planned to stay on into the Fifth Form. If the did well enough he could go into the Sixth Form at the Grammar. Sitting extra O and A Levels could lead to better future prospects.

Partway through Mr William's math lesson he had found himself summoned for his career's chat. Math was his best subject; he had learned more from his father and was way ahead of the rest in his group. Most in the class were not exactly good at the subject and found it a struggle. So it was no great loss to get called out.

It was not the Career Teacher he'd been expecting. Instead it was someone from the Careers Service. Inviting Mack to sit down, he introduced himself as Mr Wain. It was grin-suppression time. Mack could make out the man's name as Mr S. Wain on a file even though it was upside down. What was it with people's names? S. Wain as in swain? Swain sounded familiar. Familiar or not, he soon found himself interrogated about his future career aims.

"You appear to be a bright pupil according to your Career Teacher's report. You could do well if you stayed on in the Fifth Form." Mr Wain paused for a split second. "So have you given any thought to staying on? Have your parents said anything about staying on?"

Making a conscious effort not to say swain, Mack said, "I want to stay on, Mr Wain. My parents expect me to stay on."

"Have you given any thought to what you want to do when you leave school? An apprenticeship?"

It was tempting, so tempting. So tempting he almost said he wouldn't mind getting an apprenticeship in Taxidermy. Then he thought better of the idea.

"I'm not sure yet, Mr Wain. I want to sit some GCEs and CSEs and do well enough that I could get a job in a bank." Mack didn't want to work in a bank. It was the first job that jumped into his mind: something his dad wanted him to do.

"Well, you realise you need to get some top O Level grades to do that, don't you, young man? Few secondary modern pupils achieve those grades. GCE O levels are usually a prerequisite. You'd be better setting your sights lower."

Mr Swain was so condescending that it made Mack's hackles rise. He wanted to tell Mr Swain that his father was a bank manager, so he already knew the qualifications for getting a junior position. Instead he said nothing.

"As you're quite good at maths you might like to consider being a wages clerk. Or working in the accounts department of a mill. Anyway, as you plan to stay on we could have a longer chat about it when you're in the Fifth Form." Then Mr S. Wain or Swain wrote something down and the interview, such as it was, ended. A strong urge had been there to correct Mr Wain. It was math, not maths. So much for the career advice offered. Working as a wages clerk in a mill office? He had to be kidding. Whatever

Mack ended up doing, it wouldn't be working as a wages clerk anywhere, especially not in a textile mill. As he left the room he wished he had mentioned taxidermy instead.

Mack had already looked into career opportunities on his own. Visiting the Central Library and the one on Carlisle Road he had researched careers. Still clueless, he had no idea what he wanted to do. He had thought of joining the Royal Marines or the Air Force and then thought better of it. Getting killed for Queen and country did not appeal. He had already lost two uncles in the war.

Playing it safe and going to work in a bank like his father sounded deadly dull. The pay was good especially if you got extra banking qualifications. You could even rise quite high to become a bank manager some day like his father. Knowing this did not enthral him at all – even though, as his father kept informing him, you got a good pension with the bank when you retired. Pension? It was the last thing Mack was worried about at fifteen.

All the things he fancied doing appeared unrealistic, beyond his reach. Becoming an airline pilot sounded exciting. But how on earth did you get to be one after going to a secondary modern school? You had to go to a grammar school and then to a university to get a degree to get a top job. It seemed like failing the Eleven+ condemned you to apprenticeships. Or working in dead-end jobs without prospects. Mack wasn't going to let it happen. His brother had taken that route and what a messed-up individual he was turning out to be. As for having sex with Caitlin Halloran – where would that end?

Mack's reveries stopped as the bus finally arrived in the city centre. His trip to the Wood's turned out to be disappointing. The ordered record had not arrived. But with luck, the assistant informed him, it might be in tomorrow. To make sure she suggested he return the day after.

Mack browsed through the deletions box but found nothing to tempt him. After several minutes contemplating the dire selection he made for the door. Stepping out into Sunbridge Road he was greeted by a chirping cacophony of girls' voices. As he emerged from the shop doorway Mack encountered the harbinger of his fate.

"Oi! James MacKinnon!"

Mack turned in the direction of the voice. A gaggle of half a dozen or so schoolgirls in St. Joseph's uniforms were standing nearby. With berets perched near the backs of their heads, they could have passed for extras from a St. Trinian's movie. Standing centre stage was Grace Halloran. She must have spotted him leaving the shop. All he could do was to give a wry smile. Raise his hand in acknowledgement. Then attempt to walk away in the opposite and wrong direction as fast as possible.

"Hang on! Don't walk away!" He heard her call after him to more accompanied giggling.

The word "damn" almost escaped his lips. Had he written it he would have added five exclamation marks at the end.

Mack found himself looking down at the diminutive girl. The deep copper-coloured hair flowed out from under the blue beret. The sensible coat almost buried her and the satchel appeared overloaded.

"It's Grace." Mack paused before continuing. "Halloran?"

How feeble that sounded in his head.

"Ooooh," she cooed. Her face lit up in the mischievous smile he had come to recognise over all those church Sundays. "So you know who I am?"

"Yeah," he replied, taken aback by her forwardness. "Yes, 'course I do. I see you and your sisters most Sunday mornings at St. Pat's."

"You don't live far away from us, do you?" she pressed him. "Are you going home now?"

He was about to say no. Then it occurred. This could be a great opportunity to find out more about Fiona. He could even find out something about Caitlin. So he walked into the trap. Before he could reply, she spoke for them both. "Good. Let's walk. I spent my dinner money so I can't catch the trolley. You don't mind, do you? I walk back lots of times."

Mack had planned to catch the No. 8 trolley bus. Before he could reply she had bid farewell to her crowd of twittering friends with, "See ya at school tomorrow."

Next thing he knew he was walking up the road with this frightening vixen keeping pace for pace with him. There was precious little chance to say anything as Grace picked up the conversation. It was more a monologue and less of a conversation, leaving Mack feeling out-manoeuvred. Grace Halloran was nothing like the girls he knew at Eddie Campion. In fact, she was nothing – but nothing – like he had imagined. Seeing her following her sisters to the communion rail he had suspected she was the lively one. The word precocious now jumped into his thoughts. Bashful and demure she was not.

"How old are you, Grace?"

"Almost thirteen. Why?"

31

"Almost? When's your birthday?"

"Next February. Effy's birthday is in December. She'll be fifteen, same as you."

"Do you always chat up boys like this?"

She blushed. The paleness of her skin turned an attractive rosy shade, highlighting the freckles. Then, smiling up at him, she said, "I've always been a bit of a chatterbox. My sisters think I'm a nuisance. I must admit I drive them crazy most of the time. My sister Effy is the only one who doesn't seem to mind."

"Effy?" Mack queried, puzzled. He thought he knew the names of all the sisters.

"Yes. Effy." She stopped walking, bringing Mack to a full stop almost in midstride. "Oh. Of course! Fiona is Effy. Effy is Fiona."

"Effy is Fiona?" he asked mesmerised and surprised. "Is Effy what you call her?"

"We all do. Except for my Da. Do you know he named us all in alphabetic order, A to G? Can you imagine anyone doing that? Mum wasn't at all happy but she went along with it. According to Aileen, our oldest, it was because of Fiona's middle name. It's Elizabeth, and Effy is a shortened version. Bridget says it was because 'F' was the first letter of her name so it ended up as ef-ee. Dad's never gone along with it. She's still always Fiona to him and Effy to the rest of us and all her school friends, too."

"I see," replied Mack, bemused by the torrent of information from her lips. "Effy… that's nice."

"We think so."

Her satchel looked far too heavy for her. Halfway home Mack paused as they arrived at the Express Dairy depot. Taking pity on her, he offered to carry it. This pleased Grace; the relief was obvious in her face as she hefted it to him. Shouldering it he had to admit it was some considerable weight.

"Who do you like in the Hit Parade?" Grace turned the conversation away from her sister.

"At the moment, it's The Supremes with *Baby Love*. I'm a big fan of Motown."

"Yes, it's pretty good." Pausing for a moment, she continued, "What's Motown?"

"Motown Records. Records recorded in Detroit in the USA. They don't release them here as Motown Records. Instead they're on different record labels such as Stateside or Fontana or Oriole."

"Oh, I see." Not that she appeared to, as she carried on talking about the Rolling Stones and The Kinks. Mack found it astonishing that she liked The Kink's latest chart hit, *All of the Day and All of the Night*. Not the kind of record or groups he imagined girls her age raved over. He would have bet on PJ Proby, Herman's Hermits, the Four Pennies or similar. Not Grace Halloran. The Stones were "fab" in her book, even though she found Mick Jagger ugly-looking with his rubber lips.

By the time they arrived at Grace's house Mack knew a good deal about her. Though he hadn't learned much about Fiona, or "Effy". He was desperate to know more about Grace's sister, although he'd tried not to make it too obvious. As it was he hadn't found out much at all except that her sisters called her Effy. On the subject of Effy, his petite companion of the moment remained evasive.

"Well, this is where we live. Whites Terrace. But you already know where we live, don't you, James?"

Mack passed her satchel back to her. "I do. And by the way, only my parents call me James. Nobody else does. I'm Mack to all my friends. You can call me Mack."

"As in plastic mac?" She giggled.

"Cheeky madam! No. As in M-a-c-k."

"Listen, Mack." Grace became serious. "My father is dead strict about boys. In fact, talk about boys is not allowed in our house in front of our parents. So don't let on you know me. Don't start speaking after church. Don't wink at Effy again unless you want to land her in trouble."

She surprised him with her words. All he could say was, "Okay."

"Do you promise?"

"Yes. Okay. I promise. I won't do anything of the kind. Satisfied?"

What followed stunned him. It came like the proverbial bolt out of the blue. "Are you busy Saturday morning, say about ten o'clock?"

"Why?" he asked, imagining the worst. Was she about to ask him to be her boyfriend?

"Carlisle Road Library, do you go there?"

"Sometimes. Why?" The panicky thought galloped through his head. A twelve-year-old girlfriend was out of the question.

"I'm going to be there... with Effy. Do you want to meet her?" She sounded nervous, almost breathless. For the first time there was a crack in the little red head's confidence.

"Ten o'clock?"

"Ten o'clock-ish," she confirmed. "If we're not there then we can try again the following Saturday. We never know where we will be or where we have to go, so just in case, eh?"

"Got it," he replied, his heart pounding like a jackhammer. "Is this a set-up? It's not some kind of practical joke you're playing on me?"

"It's a set-up alright, but I'm not joking. I've seen you going into Wood's after school. You never seem to be away from the shop. So I knew I could get to speak to you sometime," Grace replied, a mischievous grin lighting up her face as if she were delighted at mission accomplished. "You're about to make my sister Effy happy. She's wanted to meet you for absolute ages. In fact, ever since you came to our church. She fancies you like mad. Now I've found out what you're like, it's safe to say I can approve her choice. You're okay, Mack. You're a regular young gent. My sister is lovely and loving, special to my sisters and me. So you'd better be extra nice to her. You'll like her lots. She's going to like you too. See ya Saturday, okay?"

How grown-up she sounded for a twelve-year-old! Then she was gone, disappearing along the street before he could say any more. Inflamed by unexpected passion, his body and mind were on fire.

Feverish, almost quivering with excitement, he could not recollect how he reached home. It was an emotional haze. Fiona Halloran fancied him. Okay, so it was actually Effy. He would have to get used to Effy. Still, it was a pretty sounding name. He kept repeating Effy to himself time and time again. Filled with intense emotion, he was almost beside himself. This had turned into one extraordinary day. Mack played The Supremes' *Baby Love* over and over on automatic replay. Saturday could not come soon enough.

CHAPTER 5

Tell Him – Billie Davis (Decca F.11572 – 1963)

Tuesday 13 October 1964

Grace watched Effy's face turned paler than her usual complexion and then colour.

"Grace, how could you?" was all Effy could say, her voice scarcely above a whisper.

Grace's giddy laughter on seeing Effy's frightened face turned raucous. Watching her sister pull the bedcovers to below her chin made her laugh even more. The bedroom was cold and they could see each other's breath. Grace, wrapped up in a dressing gown, seemed immune to the cold. Sitting on the edge of Effy's bed she had sprung the start of her tale with, "Guess what? I spoke to your dishy dreamboat on the way back from town. And guess who came up in the conversation?"

Effy's expression had gone from relaxed to palpable shock in a flash.

"You should know your little sister better by now, Effy dearest. As Ma always says, I'm a proper little madam and one day my mouth will land me in trouble. I may have done that." She giggled, brushing her coppery mane and scrutinising her sister's shocked expression.

"So?" Effy's eyes were wide open.

"What do you mean, so?" Grace emphasised the "so", teasing her sister to the limits of suspense.

"You know exactly what I mean. What did he say?"

Grace wondered how much longer she could toy with her sister, prolonging the agony of suspense before telling her all. It was cruel keeping her in suspense but it was in an affectionate way. She loved Effy best of all her sisters because of their closeness in age. Sharing the tiny bedroom with Effy her whole life also meant they shared their hopes and dreams. Although Grace didn't realise it, Effy was in a profound state of emotional turmoil. James MacKinnon had been her idea of a dream boyfriend ever since she first saw him in church.

"We talked about lots. He's nice." She paused with the brush midway through her hair and then continued. "Actually he's nice, really nice.

35

He's a regular young gent. Even carried my satchel all the way from the Express Dairy depot all the way home. I reckon you'll like him."

Effy's heart was beating so hard it was racing to explode. It made her sick as adrenaline rushed through her slim body.

"He said he'd like to meet you. Okay? And before you ask me any more, it's going to be this Saturday at Carlisle Road Library at ten o'clock."

"What? This Saturday?"

"That's what I said. Why?" Grace looked at her sister. "Have you changed your mind about him? Got another dreamboat you haven't bored me about? Got something else planned?"

"No. You know I haven't. Nothing at all." Effy responded with uncharacteristic meekness. "Except… how could you be so forward? I hope he hasn't got a bad impression of us?"

Grace sniggered. "What you mean, sis, is has he got a bad impression of me, don't you? Well, it doesn't matter to me. Anyway it's time somebody did something. I thought that somebody should be me. After the wink I knew he must like you. Let's face it, Effy. If it were up to you two you'd never meet up. When's the poor lad going to get a chance to talk to you? You know as well as I do what would happen if Da saw you two talking to each other after church. In fact, never mind talking! Looking!"

"But all the same," Effy began, only to find Grace cutting her off with unusual sharpness.

"You know it's true. You do. No more excuses. I did it for you. Are you glad I did it?"

"Yes," replied Effy, staggered by her sister's boldness.

"Good. I'd hate to have gone to all the trouble for nothing. Now say 'thank you, Grace, for getting me a date to meet the boy of my dreams'."

"Thank you, Grace."

"No. 'Thank you, Grace, for getting me a date to meet the boy of my dreams'."

Effy sat up in bed. Snatching her pillow, she brought it crashing down on Grace's head as she repeated it word for word.

Grace burst out laughing and grabbed the pillow, with a brief tugging match ensuing.

Ellen stormed into the room looking annoyed and banging the door as she did so. "Will you two stop making all that damned noise! Me and Deidre can't concentrate. I've got a test tomorrow and she's got to finish her physics homework. God, Grace! You laugh loud enough to stir Lucifer in hell!"

Grace went silent, still grinning.

Effy piped up as Ellen turned to storm out again. "And Ellen... it's Deidre and I, not me and Deidre."

"Oh, shut up Effy and go to sleep." The door slammed as she left.

"Could they have overheard what we've been talking about?" asked Effy worriedly.

"What? Through these stone walls? Not a chance. She would have said something. You know what's she's like. As for Doc Deidre, she's so wrapped up in her A Levels she scarce has time to be civil. Now, let me tell you all about how I got you a date with your dream boat."

"It's not a date."

"It kind of is."

"It's not a date," Effy repeated. "I'm only going to meet him."

"Okay. It's not a date, Effy Halloran. Not yet. But I bet you'll end up going on a date with him."

CHAPTER 6

Goin' Out Of My Head – Little Anthony & The Imperials
(United Artists UP-1073 – 1964)

Tuesday 13 October 1964

Mack enjoyed a sleepless night after his walk and talk with Grace Halloran. He could scarce contain the elation knowing that Fiona liked him. There was a moment at the breakfast table when he almost blurted out what had happened. Then he thought better of it as his mum would no doubt disapprove. It wasn't a good idea. There was no one he could confide in, either, without the secret leaking like a holed bucket. Most of his classmates were blabbermouths. They couldn't keep a secret if their lives were dependent on it. He knew for a fact there were distant cousins of the Halloran girls in school. Remembering what Grace had said, he thought it was wiser not to mention it to anyone. Anyway, whose business was it beside Effy's and his own? The chivalrous choice could only be silence.

The next few days he spent for the most part in silent worrying. Worrying a great deal. Wondering if Effy would like him when they finally met each other. How would it alter things if she found out what had happened between Caitlin and Adam? How would this affect his relationship with Effy? Wisely, he judged that if he and Adam were anything to go by, Effy would be different from Caitlin. What would she be like? What should he wear? What would they talk about? It was torturing his brain. What did he know about talking to girls? Supposing he was tongue-tied? Supposing she was tongue-tied? How did you behave on a first date? Then it dawned on him. Time to follow the advice he had heard in lessons from his teachers. They all said much the same thing.

In its simplest form it boiled down to *if in doubt find out. Look it up.* Except there were no books on the subject – but there were girls. He would have to seek advice from a girl in a roundabout manner without giving the game away. No doubt she would suspect. He would pretend it was something for creative writing homework. That was exactly what he did.

During lunch hour Mack made the brave but difficult decision. He strolled over to Mary Peterson who was in his form group, astonishing his male classmates. He was overheard beginning with the rather too obvious phrase, "Can I have a word with you…?"

When the bell went to end the lunch hour Mack returned, grinning and smiling. Mary Peterson was smiling too, and shaking her head.

"I knew it!" joshed John. "You asked Mary Peterson out, didn't you?"

"Nope. Sorry to disappoint you. She's a nice girl but not my type. I needed some info," Mack replied.

"Bollocks and cobblers!" laughed Mark. "Don't take the Mickey Mouse out of us! Do you think we were born yesterday?"

"Well, now you mention it …" Mack received a playful thump on his arm as a response.

Later, in the afternoon, the nosiness started. As soon as the teacher stepped out of the geography lesson, the silence was broken. Mark demanded in a loud voice, "Oi, Peterson! Is it true Mack asked you out this dinner time?"

Mary was a quiet dark-haired soft-spoken girl. As a rule she never responded to taunts. Today she surprised the class.

"That's between Mack and myself," she purred with a knowing smile. "What if he did? Are you jealous? I bet you're jealous, aren't you, Mark? Why don't you ask him?"

"Me? Jealous? No. Not me." Turning to Mack, Mark repeated the question. "Well, is it right, Mack? C'mon, spill. Everyone's keen to know. Are you or aren't you?"

Mack smiled at Mary Peterson, doing his best to return a similar knowing look. Then he responded. "That, as the young lady said, is for us to know and you lot to guess." Both he and Mary burst out laughing together.

"I bet he did ask her out," butted in Dave Bean.

Mr Kenner returned seconds later to instantaneous silent studious activity.

Mack was to prove forever grateful for his *tête a tête* with Mary Peterson. She might have been a quiet girl but she harboured secrets of her own. Mack had based his choice for advice on carefully considered information. He kept his ears and eyes open, letting nothing pass. Mary Peterson was going steady with Kevin Riley who had left the previous year. They had been together in a discreet relationship for more than a year. He had quite often seen them together as Mary lived near to him. Mack respected her secret and had told her so before their little conversation began. What she told him about boy-girl talk left him surprised. The advice was A1 and comprehensive in its detail. Better than he could have imagined. Some of it was so obvious, he wondered why it had never occurred to him. Mary made it all sound so simple and straightforward. Though was it as simple as she had made out? He would soon find out.

The week seemed endless. Listening to Radio Luxemburg while doing his homework didn't help. Even with a thirty-foot-long wire antenna, the reception was still poor.

Mack had inherited the Ekco Valve Radio from his parents. They had bought it in 1958 replacing it with the radiogram and television set over time. The set had a brown Bakelite case with beige meshed grill. Complete with new valves, his dad had passed it on to him. Tonight it was Jack Jackson's Jukebox show playing all the Decca releases. By the time it got to Stuart Grundy's Request Show the reception had got so bad it was too much of a distraction. The distraction was not confined to the radio. Even after he turned it off the distraction was still there. The ever-present prospect of meeting Effy preoccupied his thoughts almost non-stop. To such an extent his sleep had become restless. Worse still, he was no longer seeing the sisters as sexual objects. They had become persons, not objects of sexual fantasy. What continued to preoccupy him was his brother's relationship with her sister. What effect might it have on them? No matter, he reasoned. Grace had spoken in glowing words about her sister. As different as he was from Adam, so Effy had to be as different from Caitlin. She was a person in her own right, not a copy of Caitlin. It would be about the two of them. Mack rationalised that his brother and Caitlin were their own affair, not his and Effy's.

The italic fountain pen he used was running out of ink. The nib needed replacing. His lack of concentration almost resulted in knocking over a whole bottle of black Quink ink. His mother already had issues with all the ink stains she kept finding on his shirt and cuffs. Plagued with thoughts about the prospective meeting, he finished his history homework. Not his finest effort, he reflected as he turned the lid tight shut on the Quink bottle. If he had spilled the ink it would have made a hell of a mess on the carpet.

His parents had gone for fitted carpets throughout the house except for the bathroom. Most of the families he knew couldn't afford such luxury. His father had let slip how much the Axminster carpeting cost. It had been a *jaw dropping heart stopping* sum.

His parents were watching TV. If he went down and watched some television with them it might help to take his thoughts away from Effy. He tidied up, packing his satchel for the morning. Then, to make matters worse,

40

he found himself singing the words to The Kinks' *All of the Day and All of the Night*.

The glowing crackling coal fire had heated up the room to tropical temperatures – so much so that his dad had fallen into a soporific state watching the television. His mum was busy knitting something for one of the local mum's newborn. A copy of the TV times rested on her lap, the front cover featuring Coronation Street star Pat Phoenix. Jane MacKinnon no longer appeared agitated about Adam's disappearance.

"Anything good on the box?" Mack asked.

In unison his parents uttered the same words he heard every evening. "Have you finished your homework?"

Sighing, he answered. "You know I have. I don't know why you keep asking me the same thing every night. What have you been watching?"

"Emergency Ward 10, James." His mother paused in her knitting. "Do you know the masked intruder turned out to be a practical hoaxer?"

Mack never watched soap operas. Humouring his mother he replied with mild disinterest, "Oh, yes. Who was it?"

It might have been wiser to say nothing. Instead he got the version in full as his father made for the kitchen. As he disappeared through the door his mother broke off from recounting the tale. In a loud voice she called after him, "Put the kettle on."

Mack groaned. He knew exactly what the reply was going to be. He had heard it for years and yet his parents never tired of the same exchange.

"It doesn't suit me, dear." His father called back from the kitchen.

41

CHAPTER 7

Be My Baby – The Ronettes (London Records HLU 9793 – 1963)

Friday 14 October 1964

As Saturday drew closer Mack began to fret. What was he going to wear? Friday after school he went for a haircut. He wanted to look smart for the morning. The barber gave him the cut he wanted. It was a square neck, hair length half-inch all over with Mod-style razor side cut parting. When it came to clothes Mack had been in the habit of throwing anything on that came to hand. Now he was concerned to look well turned out. First impressions needed to be good. Groaning at the selection of out-of-school clothing he could see nothing suitable. In the end, he settled on wearing a pair of dark blue lightweight summer trousers. A pale blue shirt, a navy tie and a red pullover completed the picture. The trousers weren't suitable for mid-October wear but they would have to do. Reflecting on his choice, he thought he did look somewhat primary two-tone. Superman would have delighted in his choice. But it would have to do. It was all a bit Old Mother Hubbard. His wardrobe was bare. There was nothing smarter. He would have to ask for some new gear. He also noticed in the wardrobe mirror that he needed some cosmetic attention.

It was the smell of the Brylcreem Mack found off-putting. It permeated Adam's room, making him nauseous. Unlike many of the lads he knew they lived in a big house. So he'd never had to share a bedroom with Adam. Which was just as well, because Adam's footwear and niffy noxious feet made the air in his room toxic. His horrendous acne further added to his list of serious sibling offences. *Crumplestiltskin* was Mack's favourite nickname for his acne-bedevilled brother. The nickname had guaranteed fraternal enmity. Adam was still missing. So Mack rifled his drawers for the Clearasil he knew his brother kept somewhere. There were a few blackheads around his nose in need of treating.

Friday night was bath night so it was no problem until his father banged on the door. "Are you still alive or have you drowned? Hurry up, I need to use the toilet."

Mack was in super-cleansing mode. He had taken more than an hour to scrub himself to perfectio

"Oh, Grace. What am I going to wear tomorrow?" Effy stared into their shared wardrobe.

"Nothing of mine, sis. You won't fit into anything. Besides, I've got nothing trendy. It's embarrassing. They still treat me like a little girl."

"Look at what I've got." Effy groaned in despair. "Ellen's leftovers and even some of Aileen's old stuff from when she was my age."

"Poor you. What about some of your old stuff I have to wear when you were my age?" muttered Grace.

Turning to her sister, Effy gave her a hug. "One day it will all be different. We won't be wearing hand-me-downs. As soon I'm fifteen I'm getting a Saturday job. Then I'm going to buy what I want to wear. I'll buy you some things too, promise."

"I've had a sudden thought." Grace pulled back from the hug. "I have the solution to all our problems. It's our own fault. We could sort this lack of trendy gear ourselves. Mum taught us how to use her sewing machine. Remember when we used to make those little dolls' dresses from those patterns? We should do sewing, shouldn't we?"

"What, make dolls' dresses again?" giggled Effy.

Grace gave her a despairing look before realising her sister was joking. "Well, kind of… not so much dolls' dresses as dolly-girl dresses."

"You're right, you know. That could be the answer to our wardrobe problems," Effy agreed, as it all became clear. "We could get hold of some patterns and make our own. Even recut some of the old clothes."

"Jean Sienkiewicz, a friend in my class, she helps her older sisters make dresses. And her sister is one of those Mods. So it's going to be trendy gear she's wearing. I can ask her if we could borrow some of her sister's patterns to adapt for us."

"Jean? Not the Eugenia you used to play with in Infants and Junior school?"

"The one and only. She's great. Good at languages, too. Helps me with my French homework when I need it. We call her Jean. It's easier than saying Yuuugenia."

"I saw her sister recently," Effy recollected. "She used to go round with Caitlin at school and left after her O Levels. She was wearing some patterned stockings, wasn't she? And this gorgeous shift dress looking like a top and skirt?"

"I was with you at the time, don't you remember, Effy?" Grace's eyes became small slits as she tried to remember what she had seen. "Patterned black-and-white in some kind of check, wasn't it?"

"Sawtooth, not check," Effy corrected.

"Oh, yeah. You're right. Like a repeated saw blade. So it was." Grace paused. "And didn't she look like a model out of a magazine?"

"Grace, your idea is marvellous. It's exactly what we should do. Start making our own skirts and dresses. How hard can it be?"

"Exactly, how hard can it be?" echoed Grace.

"But," groaned Effy, "what am I going to wear to meet him? Even my underwear is gross."

"Effy! He's not going to be seeing you in your bra and knickers." There was genuine shock in Grace's voice.

"Of course he's not." Effy blushed. "What I meant was these hand-me-down bras don't fit. Ellen's are well-worn and too big. My breasts flop about in them. As for Deidre's hand-me-down bras, they crush me and they're agony to wear. They're far too small and unfeminine."

"Might fit me then," laughed Grace. "I'm still a bit flat-chested."

"Here, you can have them." Effy opened her drawer and threw them to Grace.

"You're not kidding. Ugh, they're not nice to look at and faded. But," sighed Grace, "we beggars can't be choosers. This is what happens when there are seven sisters. I reckon if we had a brother he'd have wear girls' hand-me-downs, too. Thank goodness we don't have to wear Mum's hand-me-downs." Grace sniggered. "Imagine having to wear them faded pink drawers! And those horrible greying corsets!"

Snickering, the girls pulled faces at the idea. Effy swept her long hair back behind one ear and took out another bra from the drawer. "This is too baggy."

There was genuine despair in her voice. Holding up the faded object that was more shades of grey than white she sighed. "I'm going to look as if I've got crumpled tits. Should I even bother to wear one? It's not as if I'm well-endowed."

"I wouldn't do that. That would be too daring, shameless, even… titillating." Her sister couldn't stop laughing at her own joke, leaving Effy shaking her head at its lameness. "You might have to confess your bra-less sin to the Canon. Why don't you try padding it out? Stuff some tissues or something inside. Tell you what, put it on and let's see what we can do to make it fit better."

The next half hour alternated between bouts of studious seriousness and side-splitting laughter. They filled the over-large cups with ankle socks and anything else they could find. Bridget entered the bedroom wondering what was causing the hysterical laughter. Her mouth dropped at the sight of Effy who had put on a pullover over her bra-filled experiment. "God almighty! Will you look at yourself, Effy? What's happened to your breasts? I thought mine were big, but yours! Have they ballooned overnight?"

"It's time Ma forked out for a couple of decent bras for Effy. Ellen's hand-me-downs are too big. We've tried to fill them out with socks and things. This is what we've ended up with," chortled Grace.

"I thought I was big-bosomed. But you, Effy, would make Jayne Mansfield look under-endowed. You'd get some serious catcalls even at your age."

"It's the only half decent bra I've got and it's way too big."

Effy pulled the sweater over her head and Bridget gasped. "Did our mother pass this bra onto you from Ellen?"

"Yes, I needed one as I was beginning to show," Effy replied, sounding contrite. She began pulling the assorted items of stuffing from the bra cups. "Mum gave me this old one of Ellen's and some of Deidre's but none of them fit. Deidre's old ones are too tight and uncomfortable."

"It's disgraceful!" Bridget announced, sounding angry at what she had seen. It was scary seeing her when she became outraged. "Disgraceful. More than that, it's shameful beyond words. It's not even Ellen's old bra! Well, yes it is, but Ellen inherited it from me! Now *you're* expected to wear the thing! Right! I'm going to have this out. It's time for some serious words with our mother about this shameful carry-on."

The last time Bridget had been angry all the sisters had scuttled into their rooms. "You can both come to town with me on Saturday. I'll get you sorted out for some new things more appropriate in size." She began opening the drawers where they kept their underwear. As she rummaged through them, pulling them out and inspecting them, her anger increased. "God, these are a disgrace. Not even fit for a nun to wear, let alone young girls. Fit for nothing other than cleaning rags. You shouldn't have to wear worn-out under-things these days.

"Can we go in the afternoon, Bridget? Only we've got to do some…"began Grace.

"Homework first and get it out of the way," continued Effy, covering up the planned visit to the library.

"Yes," added Grace. "Effy and I have to do some research for our homework and so we need to get started early."

"Okay. Saturday afternoon it is. We'll visit Marks & Spencer's and see if they have something suitable. And if Ma gives me the tale that the housekeeping money won't stretch, I'll give Da the hard words."

Bridget would, too. She always spoke her mind, unlike Aileen who avoided confrontations at all costs. Bridget had no such qualms about confronting their father. In many respects their older sister was a second mother to them.

"Come here." She put her arms around their shoulders. "You deserve better. It's not as if you don't look after your things but this hand-me-down business has to stop. There are no more little girls in the house. Only young women."

Grace blushed.

"Seems you've begun your periods, Grace. A bit early but I suppose we've all been different in our turns."

Giving them a last squeeze she went towards the door and then turned with tearful eyes. "Love you two. Be good. Some of us have to be," she added, setting a mystery in motion.

"Our Bridget's so lovely," said Effy.

"Yes, she is. We should get this bra framed as the ultimate in hand-me-downs." Grace was busy pretending to frame it on the wall. "It would look good about here."

"You do realise it's either this or one of Deidre's tiny tit squeezers." Effy turned her mind to Saturday morning again.

"Jayne Mansfield." Giggling, Grace mimed a huge pair of bosoms with her arms. "Huge in front, tiny behind. You looked so weird."

"Did anyone ever tell you have a sad sense of humour?"

"Yes. You have, and so have lots of others besides you, but I don't care. Sometimes it's better to try and see the funny side of things. Guess it hurts less when you do."

CHAPTER 8

Little Bitty Pretty One – Clyde McPhatter (Mercury 71987 – 1962)

Saturday 17 October 1964

"You look smart this morning, James. Meeting a girl today by any chance?" joked his father as they sat eating breakfast.

For a moment Mack thought his father might be serious. Then he realised he was only passing a comment. The best strategy was to play his father at his own game.

"Yes, Dad. Exactly what I've got planned today," he countered in his best sarcastic tone. Evasiveness was the order of the day.

"So what have you got planned?"

"I'm going to the library this morning. Got to find out some things for school," he replied, sounding out the smooth white lie. "Then I thought I'd go round town looking for some 45s in the second-hand shops."

"You and your pop music. What do you see in it?"

Mack thought it wiser to avoid a long conversation over his musical tastes, so he left his father's comment hanging.

"The car needs a wash and polish. Fancy earning 7/6d to add to your savings?"

Mack fancied this extraordinary generous offer. It was two bob more than his usual 5/6d, which was pretty good. "When do you want me to do it?"

"What about later this morning when you've returned from the library?"

"Yes. Will do," he replied. Then he thought it might be a good opportunity to mention the possibility of getting a Saturday job. "Dad, I want to get a Saturday job, even if it's mornings only."

"Funny you should mention it. It so happens I may know someone who could do with a young man on Saturday mornings. Leave it with me. We'll have a chat about it next week when I've had a chance to speak with the owner."

"Doing what, Dad?" questioned Mack, surprised and intrigued all at once.

"You'll have to wait and see. Can't build your hopes up if there's no job going. Leave it with me."

"What are you two doing today?" Ellen enquired distractedly, showing no genuine interest as they ate breakfast.

"Oh, nothing interesting," Effy replied. "I'm going to the library with Grace to get some information for some homework we have to do."

"Information? What information? Since when did the good teachers of St. Jo's expect their pupils to go looking up information? Who set you these tasks?" Deidre demanded, with a hint of suspicious interest. "Nobody ever asked me to go and do some research. Not even now for A Levels."

On the outside Effy remained calm but on the inside her heart faltered. In the space of a few words what had been a straight answer was turning into a third-degree interrogation.

"Anyway," Deidre continued unperturbed, "ask me and I may be able to help you. If not we've got that set of encyclopaedias in the front room you could use."

Effy wondered if the speed of thought rivalled the speed of light. Grace, half asleep as she munched her sugar-puffs, looked up in a panic. It was down to Effy to come back with an answer. The problem was, Deidre was the brains of the family. Her general knowledge was almost as encyclopaedic as the encyclopaedias she had mentioned. But even Deidre had her weak spots. Effy knew exactly how to strike back with the right answer to throw her off the scent.

"I have to make a list of ten famous painters from the Renaissance to the present. Naming their best-known works. I also have to choose one of those paintings and give a brief explanation why I chose it." Effy gave Deidre and Ellen her best smug look; the latter had her mouth wide open. Neither of them took Art so she knew she was on safe ground.

Effy's answer transfixed Grace. Even for Effy, this was a genius fib under serious pressure.

"Lucky you!" was the only comment from Ellen, to which Deidre added, "Glad I never took Art."

"We'd better get ready to go, Grace." Effy made it sound so casual, although she'd almost reached a state of mental meltdown. Grace dashed out of the kitchen to avoid providing an ad lib answer.

"Must be keen," Ellen commented. "I've never seen her move so fast."

48

They heard the front door open. Mrs Halloran was returning from doing some early morning shopping, and Bridget had accompanied her as usual. "Is everyone up?" she enquired, sounding tired.

"I heard Aileen moving about but Caitlin's hasn't stirred yet," replied Deidre.

"Lazy trollop," Bridget muttered. "Stays out all hours, goodness knows where, then lounges in bed."

"Now, now, Bridget. That's no way to talk about your sister..." were the last words Effy heard as she left the kitchen. Seeing the bathroom empty she rushed in to brush her teeth before anyone else claimed its use.

"Open up! Quick! I need a wee!" Grace banged on the door. Still brushing her teeth, Effy let her in. Grace dashed for the toilet and sat herself down.

"Effy, you were brill throwing them off the scent. Have you noticed how Deidre gets to be more and more like Sherlock Holmes every day? She's always wanting to know everyone's business!"

"We'd better get a move on," Effy urged, breathless with excitement.

"Calm down, girl. It's only ten past nine. From our house to the library only takes ten minutes at best. How much longer do you need to get ready? Besides, you look as if you're ready now." Grace flushed the toilet and adjusted her skirt, hip-bumping her sister away from the mirror. "Move over so I can wash my hands."

Effy checked her teeth in the mirror, standing on tiptoes behind Grace.

"Any whiter sis and you'll blind him with your pearly whites," Grace joked. "And it'll all be thanks to Pepsodent who make you wonder where the yellow went!"

"Ha ha, funny."

Back in the bedroom Effy began putting on nylon stockings.

"Where did you get the stockings?" Grace gasped, watching Effy attaching the suspender fastenings to the stocking tops. "Are those the 20 denier Marks & Sparks ones belonging to Aileen?"

"Don't ask and I won't tell no lies," came the reply. "She'll never miss them anyway. She has so many unopened pairs in her drawer, it's staggering."

Effy stood up to check her legs. "What do you think?"

"God, I hope she doesn't find out. And yes, they do look nice. In fact, that colour stocking looks good on you. What's it called?

49

"Bronze."

You're lucky that Aileen is the same height and size as you. Wrinkled stockings wouldn't be a good look."

"Will he like me in this outfit?"

Effy was wearing a pale green pullover that complemented her matching dark green A-line knee-length skirt. A hint of pale green eye shadow borrowed from Ellen's makeup bag enhanced her natural prettiness. Otherwise she thought it wiser not to wear any lipstick. It might attract suspicion as she went out.

"If he doesn't think you're stunning and gorgeous he's blind. By the way, it's unpleasant and cold out there and it might rain. Better wear something on your head."

"It'll have to be the Tam O'Shanter and duffle coat. I'll borrow Bridget's umbrella in case it rains. Are you ready?"

"Almost," said Grace. "We have to look convincing so let's not forget pens and notebooks, eh?"

"Good thinking, sis!"

CHAPTER 9

Our Day Will Come – Ruby & The Romantics
(London American 45-HL-R.9679 – 1963)

Saturday 17 October 1964

Mack let out a huge sigh. Checking his wristwatch for the umpteenth time he saw it was finally time to go. The weather looked most unpromising. He donned what had been his brother's dark blue trench coat. Adam had worn it twice but once he'd leathered up in Rocker garb it was never worn again. One day his mum had decided it shouldn't go to waste, so she'd handed it over to Mack without ceremony. The coat was a bit short in the arms and tight in the shoulders, but otherwise it was serviceable.

"Must be trying to attract the library assistant, eh, James?"

Mack gave his father the best quizzical look he could muster. "Dad, library assistants are as old as you and Mum. Even the youngest one has to be in her twenties. That's well ancient."

"Do I smell my Old Spice on you, young man?"

Now Mack was certain his father was pulling his leg. The last thing he was going to do was use aftershave. "No. Why would I wear aftershave when I'm not even shaving that often?"

On reflection, he should have.

Mack decided to escape any further exchanges. It was nine thirty-five and far too early. At best it would only take fifteen minutes if he dawdled. Judging the time and distance, he walked down to the crossroads where Carlisle Road met Toller Lane. The alternative was to take the back streets by cutting across Church St. to Bavaria Place. Then he could take the main road to the Marlboro cinema and the library. The most important thing was to avoid schoolmates who lived nearby.

If he got there a little early it wouldn't matter. He could use the time looking for books to borrow or do a spot of reading. After all, what was a library's purpose if not to read? Should he bump into a girl... well, these things happened. At which point his thoughts began to unsettle him.

Supposing she didn't come at all? Was it an elaborate hoax? Was Grace Halloran playing a joke on him? Recalling his walk home with Grace reassured him that she wouldn't do that. She had been too friendly and open.

51

No. It couldn't be a practical joke – but the troublesome thought wouldn't go away.

The dreaded supposing began again.

"Suppose he's not there, Grace? Suppose he thought you were playing a prank on him?"

"Oh, ye of little faith, he'll be there. Don't worry, Effy. He's not going to pass up a chance to meet you."

"And you would know this how? You know as much about boys as I do. What we both know about them would fit on the back of a 6d postage stamp."

"But at least I've spoken to a boy. One James MacKinnon who prefers Mack to James. It took us half an hour to walk up from town. I even fibbed that I'd spent my bus fare so he would walk up with me."

"I'm sorry. I should be thanking you for setting this up. My little sister is a Cupid."

"Cupid was a boy, according to my Classics teacher. What are you implying?" Grace gave her sister's coat sleeve a sharp playful tug.

"You know what I mean," she replied, displaying how nervous she was. The doubting was there. Was it such a good idea to meet him?

Should she turn back? .

Should he turn back?

This was proving mind-bending and nerve-racking. Mack began to ponder whether he should carry on to the library or turn back while he still had the opportunity. He arrived at the library still indecisive. The building announced its 1910 Edwardian origins above the entrance. Then it hit him. Which part of the library would they be in? The Junior side on the right? Or the main Adult part on the left?

"In which side are we supposed to meet?" asked Effy. "Adult or Junior?"

Grace stopped in her tracks. "Oops!"

"Oops?" Effy reiterated. "What do you mean, oops?"

"Sorry, Effy. I slipped up. I said we'd meet there ten o'clock-ish. I never thought to say in which section. But I don't see it's going to matter, somehow."

"Why?"

"Because that's him there by the entrance."

It was too late to turn back now. Effy was trembling as they approached Mack, who had his back to them. Presumably he also had no idea which side of the library to enter. At this point Grace went ahead to tap him on his left shoulder. She ducked to his right as he turned in surprise to see Effy walking towards him.

"Good morning, Mack," Grace greeted him. "Let me do the formal introductions. Meet my sister Fiona, whom you should call Effy. Effy, let me introduce you to James, whom you should call Mack, spelled as M-a-c-k." Then, pausing for the two to come face to face, about an arm's reach from one another, Grace added, "Now we've observed the formalities I will be in the Junior section. An hour should be long enough for you two to become acquainted."

Both Mack and Effy were speechless.

"I thought you'd be staying with us?" Effy gave her sister a pleading look.

"As Tonto would say to the Lone Ranger: Kemosabe, you are on your own 'cos three would be a crowd. Meet you both back here in an hour. It's a good stretch of the legs to Lister Park." Grace gave her a heavy hint. "See you when you get back. And the both of you remember. No patty fingers if you please. The proprieties at all times."

Leaving those words in their ears, she raced up the stairs into the library. The two of them stared after her, looking uncomfortable. Effy was unsure what to do or say next.

"Hi, it's a pleasure to meet you." Mack thought it better to put an end to the silence first. "Shall we take her advice about the park? I hope it's not going to start raining. "

"Yes, we can do," she replied, concealing her discomfort at Grace abandoning her. It was typical of Grace to embarrass her, and to quote that line from the John Wayne movie they had watched on television. It had become her catch phrase for weeks afterwards. Then Effy spotted her sister at the library window. Grace gave her the thumbs-up sign with both hands before disappearing inside. How typical!

Mack began his charm offensive as advised by Mary Peterson.

"You look so pretty in that outfit." Compliments on a girl's appearance always went down well, Mary had told him. Yet it had to be within bounds, according to her. Going over the top with compliments might come over as creepy.

Effy's eyes drew him to her.

"Why, thank you, Mack." The compliment took her by surprise. "It's so nice of you to say so."

53

"Well, I can only be truthful." And indeed he was telling the truth. Now, seeing her close up, he was smitten to his youthful core. Effy was so amazing, so pretty. The colour of her eyes struck him immediately. They were the most beautiful shade of sparkling emerald and they gazed up at him with such intensity. She looked away, betraying more than a hint of shy nervousness. Mack surprised himself with a rather poetic though strange thought. *I could drown in those eyes.*

Effy reminded him of an elfin princess, one he had seen in a book illustration years ago. Her features were elfin: pale, delicate, and framed by glossy strawberry blonde hair. Her full perfect lips left him wondering if he would ever kiss them. He experienced a sudden powerful rush of emotion, imagining holding her in his arms – the way John Wayne held Maureen O'Hara in *The Quiet Man* during the storm scene. Then the no patty fingers comment made unexpected sense.

"Did your sister just quote a line from a John Wayne movie?"

"Yes. She heard it in a film we saw one Sunday afternoon. Worse still, she kept repeating it for absolute ages. And it was always with the worst *Oirsh* accent you ever did hear. It rubbed everyone up the wrong way. Especially if she saw my Da putting his arm round my Ma."

"She has a sense of humour, for certain sure. I take it she must be the family joker?"

"Yes. She qualifies for that role. So? Shall we set off to the park and risk getting caught in the rain?" Effy asked, trying not to sound too nervous. Glancing around, she hoped they wouldn't be seen.

"Yes, if you don't mind risking it. That would be nice." Mack wished he hadn't used the word "nice". His English teacher had cautioned them about not using it due to its lack of meaning.

After his first few words Effy felt reassured and drawn to him. There was something about James MacKinnon that confirmed her attraction to him. She wasn't sure what it was but she felt it all the same. He was so much taller than she'd thought. He stood a full head above her, and was slim with light brown neatly cut hair: smarter in his appearance than she recollected from seeing him at church. His hazel eyes made her feel as if she was his sole abiding interest to the exclusion of all else. She would have to overcome her shyness somehow. Effy had never been in the exclusive company of a boy before today. There were a few male cousins who came visiting on occasion but they were older and more distant. This was so different. So overwhelming, so disturbing, to finally be alone with him after all the daydreaming.

"I've never had many opportunities to talk with a boy before," she began, still nervous. "What with so many sisters, and then going to a girls' school as well. I suppose you get to speak to girls all the time at Edmund Campion?"

Mack wasn't quite sure how to respond to that. Then he remembered another piece of advice. He should be open and honest, and avoid bragging. Girls didn't go for boys who bragged about themselves. Nor ones who told lies. Effy was too special, he sensed. So he would try to be honest and avoid bragging by not pretending to be something he was not.

"Not as much as you would imagine. Yes, we are in mixed class groups but most of the girls don't often speak to the boys and the other way around. There are a few girls I speak to and it's generally about trivial things to do with what's happening in class. To be honest, I find girls a mystery."

"So you find us mysterious?" she offered, smiling as they strolled in the direction of the park.

Mack found her smile entrancing. She seemed to glow when she smiled.

"I do, but it's hardly surprising," he continued, unable to stop looking at her. "The only women I know are my mum and Aunt Ellen. And, well, they're my mum and my aunt so it's not helpful in understanding girls. I only know boys or men. There's my brother Adam, my cousin Tom, my Uncle Phil and my dad. My friends at school are all boys. So, to be honest, I don't have a great deal to go on about girls. Yes, I confess I do find you're mysterious."

"Do you mean me or all girls?"

"Both."

"Gosh, you sound so… grown-up about things. And you say your aunt's called Ellen? I have a sister called Ellen, did you know that?"

"Yes, I knew."

"How did you know?"

"My mum knows your mum from the Mothers' Union. She told me about you and your sisters and that's how I know all your names. Well, actually, it was more she told my dad and I happened to overhear what she had to say. It was usually when she was doing her regular reporting back about Mothers Union doings. I don't find Mothers Union chat interesting, to be honest. My dad pretends to switch off as soon as she starts but he doesn't.

He's actually good at listening, waiting until we finish before saying anything."

"It's not like my Da when he goes on about Opus Dei meetings. I know my sisters all switch off and disappear out of the way. My Ma goes, 'Yes dear, no dear', and so on. I don't think she listens. Isn't it a coincidence that your aunt and my sister should have the same name?"

"I suppose so." At this point Mack found himself saying, "To be honest, I used to listen to every word my mum had to say when she talked about you and your sisters."

"Why?" Effy sounded and looked surprised.

"I wanted to find out something about you. Remember, all I knew was what I saw in church on Sundays."

"And did you find out much?" she quizzed him.

"Nothing much apart from your names and ages. That was about it. I didn't even know you were called Effy. I didn't dare ask many questions because Mum would have lectured me on being nosey. Or being too young to have an interest in girls."

Mack didn't add that his dad would have teased him without end over his interest in the girls.

Effy thought it best at present not to mention how long she had had a crush on Mack. That admission might come later – if they had a later. But instinct told her there would definitely be a later.

They reached the park as it began to drizzle. As it threatened to turn into something heavier, Effy put up the umbrella and they took cover under it. Deciding it might be better to avoid getting soaked they made for Cartwright Hall. They went via the Prince of Wales Gate at the top end of the park. Once inside the hall, Mack learned how much Effy loved art. She enjoyed visiting the gallery often to view the paintings. Talking in whispers they found themselves conversing with natural ease. It was as if they had known each other for ages instead of less than an hour. It was all so normal. Before they realised it the minutes had ticked away and the hour was almost up. The rain had ceased when they emerged from the hall. They hurried back taking shortcuts, yet still arrived fifteen minutes late.

"Do you want to meet me again?" Mack asked breathlessly, mouth dry, as they reached the library.

"I'd love to," she answered, looking up at him. Then, to his utter surprise and also to hers, she gave him a little kiss on the cheek. It was so spontaneous that it never occurred to her how daring her behaviour had been. She couldn't believe herself. She had kissed him.

"So can I assume that's a definite yes?" Mack was thrilled at the brush of her lips on his cheek. It was… wondrous.

"Yes. That's a definite yes." She glanced away, feeling coy.

"When and where can we meet again?"

Grace, having seen the little kiss, chose to appear, calling out, "What was that I said about no patty fingers? Effy! How could you?"

Mack took Effy's hand in a spontaneous response. It was so soft to the touch, so small and dainty compared to his.

"Do you have a telephone in your house?" he asked.

"We do but none of us can use it. Only Bridget and Aileen can make calls. Anyway, you couldn't 'phone and ask to speak to me. I'd soon be in trouble."

"Do you ever go into town after school?"

"Sometimes. Rarely," Effy answered.

"I have an idea," Grace butted in. "Why don't you let me organise it, Effy?"

They agreed that Grace would act as a go-between. She would meet Mack outside Wood's on Friday after school. If they were prevented from meeting on Saturday morning, they agreed to a postal drop in church. This was an alternative should Grace not meet him outside the record shop. As Mack sat in the same pew in church on Sundays they would leave a message inside the missal. This would contain arrangements for another time and place.

"Good idea, Grace. So your little sister is more than a pretty face?"

Grace blushed bright red. "Less of the little, if you don't mind, but I quite like the pretty face bit."

"I know it's all like James Bond," he joked, "but it might be a good idea for the time being."

So they agreed. They would meet at the library again at the same time unless a change of plan forced them to make other arrangements.

Mack realised he had held Effy's hand all the while they had been planning, and she had made no effort to let go. Then her hand, with reluctant slowness, slipped from his.

"I've enjoyed this morning." A glowing smile confirmed her feelings. Gazing into his eyes she left Mack with the distinct impression she was unwilling to go.

"So have I. A lot." He wanted to add, "I can't wait until we meet next time." But something told him that might be going somewhat over the top.

CHAPTER 10

The Shoop Shoop Song (It's In His Kiss) – Betty Everett
(Stateside 280 – 1964)

Saturday 17 October 1964

"God, Effy. You actually stood there and planted a great big smacker on his face!"

"Don't exaggerate, Grace. It was a little peck on the cheek. To be honest I don't know what made me do it. I sort of did on the spur of the moment. It seemed such a normal thing to do." Turning to her sister, she said," I hope he doesn't think I'm a loose woman... girl... Oh! You know what I mean."

"The word you want is slapper. At least that's what Bridget calls those kinds of girls."

"Oh, God! I hope he doesn't think I'm a... slapper."

"No chance," Grace answered in her most emphatic voice. "The way he looks at you... well, it's like you're the best thing since the invention of the wheel."

"Don't exaggerate."

Grace affected a ridiculous French accent. "I'm not, 'ow you say, exaggerating. You 'ave zee Bridget Bardot touch where 'e ees concerned."

"Do you know, you can be so daft at times, Grace."

"Ah know." She continued with the ridiculous French accent, pushing her face right up to Effy's. "Zis young man ees, 'ow you say, 'ead over 'eels in lurve wiz you."

Pushing her away, Effy shook her head in mock exasperation. "Grace, stop it! It's embarrassing! How could he? He doesn't know me."

If anything she found it frightening and exciting at the same time. It was all proving so deep, so intense. Yet, try as she might, she couldn't stop herself. She kept recollecting each precious minute they had spent together. Every recollected moment made her want to explode with sheer joy.

Grace was proving to be at her most annoying. Her attempts at a French accent sounded more and more like the TV cartoon character Pepe Le Pew.

"You know, Cherie, 'e is zee locksmith of lurve.

"Who's the locksmith of love?" asked Bridget, entering their room.

"Take no notice. Grace has got a screw loose again. She's pretending she's that cartoon skunk character Pepe Le Pew!" Effy glared at Grace.

"Why doesn't it surprise me? Time you became a little less childish Grace and a bit more grown-up. Okay, ladies." Bridget unravelled a tape measure. "Bust, waist and hips. Who's getting measured first?"

Twenty minutes later the three sisters left home. In their raincoats, with umbrellas at the ready, they were on the trolley to do some shopping. Bridget was as good as her word. They were going to get new underwear as promised. Bridget was the one paying for the purchases, not their parents.

CHAPTER 11

First Taste of Love – Ben E. King (London American HLK 9258B – 1964)

Saturday 17 October 1964

Of course it would have to rain. There was no point in trying to wash the car in these conditions. Bang had gone the possibility to earn a little extra. It would have taken his mind off Effy, too, if he had been able to wash and wax the car. As it was he was in his bedroom listening to his collection of 45s. This was going to have to stop, he thought. She was turning his mind to mush. All he was doing was daydreaming about her all the time.

He wasn't exactly helping himself, either. He had played Ben E. King's *Yes* about two dozen times. Then, flipping the 45 over, he had played the 'B' side *Ecstasy* about the same number of times. His parents had gone shopping. Otherwise so many repeated plays would have attracted attention. He wished Tom could have come over as he did quite often at weekends. Then he would have been able to share this morning's event with him. Instead he was going to have to bottle it all up.

There was no one he could trust among his school friends. If he mentioned it everyone in the 4th Form would know by midday. The school grapevine would ensure it was common knowledge by the end of the day. He was not even sure he dared tell Tom how he was feeling. It was so personal. Mack was in turmoil, wishing he could have spent more time with Effy but knowing he could not. His only consolation was the thought of seeing her again next weekend. The week ahead already seemed like an eternity. Then the thought crossed his mind that he had fallen in love with her. Love was proving painful and exhilarating at the same time.

As for his brother, there was no sign of him. He seemed to have disappeared so completely, it was as though space aliens had abducted him. There was no trace of *Crumplestiltskin*. Mack knew his father had been doing the rounds, trying to find out where Adam had gone. Although his parents said nothing they were distraught at Adam's absence. Mack had gleaned he was turning up at work but where he went after work no one knew or would tell.

CHAPTER 12

Comin' Home Baby – Mel Tormé (London American 45-HLK 9643 – 1962)

Wednesday 21 October 1964

After Mack finished the evening meal he had shaken his mum by helping to wash and dry. This was an unexpected novelty. Jane MacKinnon was the kitchen slave with the men in her family never lifting a finger.

"Are you alright?' she asked her son, giving him an odd look.

"What do you mean, Mum?"

"Never mind. Forget it, James. Thank you for being so helpful. I've noticed you've made a real effort to keep your room shipshape this last week, even making your bed." She touched his forehead with the palm of her hand for a few seconds. "No. No fever. Must be some other reason. Is it a girl?"

"Only practising for when I join the Royal Marine Commandos. I'll have to stow all my kit shipshape." The deadpan expression countered her comment with success. Mack also succeeded in winding her up at the same time as covering up how he felt about Effy.

"James!" she exclaimed, a mortified look on her face at the idea. "You're not serious?"

Jane MacKinnon had been a Wren when she had met Mack's father. Both had served in the Royal Navy during the closing war years. They had received their discharge papers late in 1946. That's where they met but they refused to recount exactly how. His father had served on a Motor Torpedo Boat as a Royal Navy sub-lieutenant.

"Not the Royal Marines, James. Dear God, no. Roughest and most unpleasant men I ever met. Tell me you're joking?"

"It's a leg pull, Mum. I hear the bells tinkling!" He saw his mother's shaken face going from annoyed to relieved to laughing in the space of seconds.

"James MacKinnon, one day your jokes will be death of me." She gave him an affectionate kiss on his forehead and a hug. For the first time in a couple of years he did not protest or make horrible grunts.

"Oh, James, I want you to grow up to be a good and decent man like your father."

"Oh, I don't know, Mum. I was considering joining the Kray Gang in London after what I read in the newspaper. Demanding money with menaces looks a good way to get rich."

"Get away with you. You know the old saying. 'Fooled once'... you're not going to shame me twice!" She tapped him on the shoulder with a gentle reprimand and a smile.

As he made his way to the staircase he heard the lock turn in the door. Adam entered, looking as if nothing had happened. Even though they had serious differences Mack felt relieved to see him.

"Prodigal's back then?" Mack's question was more a statement of fact as they looked at one another.

"For now," Adam replied, a faint smile forming on his face.

"Glad you're back. Not that I missed you. Only joking." Pointing to the kitchen, Mack added, "Mum's in there as usual, Queen of all she surveys."

On that note he went up to his room. The time was right for getting the Dansette ready for action. He'd been dying to do this ever since the night when Adam had stormed out with Caitlin Halloran. Half an hour later he heard his brother stomping up the stairs. Mack gave him thirty seconds after he heard Adam's bedroom door close.

The quietness in the house was shattered. Jerry Lee Lewis's *Great Balls of Fire* blasted out at full volume. It must have taken less than five seconds for Adam to come racing into Mack's room, only to stop dead in his tracks. Mack had dropped his trousers and was mooning him as he stormed in.

Instead of losing his temper Adam seemed to see the funny side of it. Applauding with a slow handclap he grinned. "Yeah, taking the piss, I see. God, yer arse is white, you fuckin' little twat."

"So's yours from what I saw," Mack fired back, pulling up his trousers. "But without the pimples you've got from sitting on that Triumph."

"Pimples? What pimples? Pimples on my backside?"

"If I were you I'd get them checked out. If you can't see them for yourself I should get Caitlin Halloran to have a good look for you."

"Hey! Less of that!" Adam paused before springing his surprise on Mack. "She may be your future sister-in-law. Show a bit of respect."

Hearing this shook Mack. The difference for once was he did not believe Adam was joking. "Are you being serious?"

63

Adam snapped his fingers in the air. "Could be my man, could be, but not yet. Got a few things to sort out first."

"Have you spoken to Mum about this?"

Adam nodded.

"To Dad?"

Adam nodded again. "They both know. It was part of the negotiated peace settlement after what happened. You look surprised, little brother? We're keen on each other. Is that so weird?"

Mack never thought he would find himself saying this. "I suppose not, no. So congratulations are in order, are they?"

"Not yet, but soon. Loads depend on her dad. You know what he's like. Could be a bit tricky."

"Yeah, real tricky." Mack agreed – and more than a little. He was not only thinking about their reactions to Adam. Far more important was how would it affect his relationship with Effy?

"So, Mr Bookworm, what have you been up to while I've been away?"

"Nothing much. Same old same old," lied Mack.

Truth was Adam had been a real bully. Mack's life had been miserable when he was younger. Adam had enjoyed asserting power over Mack with a kind of sadistic pleasure, but he rarely bothered him these days. Mack was now as tall as his brother and still growing. The situation had changed. After a fist-trading scuffle a few months ago Adam had come off worse. Mack had inflicted some heavy-duty facial bruising. Lucky punches according to his brother – but the days of bullying were over. When it came to niggling each other Mack usually won the verbal contests. Adam couldn't match the smart sarcastic patter of his younger brother.

For years Adam had been the golden boy. Adam was the one who had gotten all the attention. At least so it appeared through Mack's eyes. Both parents had doted on Adam. He was the star from whom they expected great things. Mack was the unplanned accident who should never have happened, according to Adam. Whenever he needed a put-down he tormented his younger sibling with the tireless thought. Even if it had been true, the MacKinnons would never have admitted such a thing,

But Adam the golden boy turned out to be more 9 karat gold-plated than solid gold. When he passed the Eleven+ for St. Bede's Grammar his parents' pride and delight knew no bounds. They had held him up as a shining example to emulate. Mack could still remember the hoo-ha accompanying it. The new school uniform and satchel paraded before the whole family. All the carry-on had been the reason why he'd felt a failure and had failed. All the constant blah about his so successful brother must have made him feel second-rate at the time – especially after he didn't pass the grammar school entrance test. Failing the Eleven+ was a relegation to life's lowest ladder rung. Then wonder boy Adam began to struggle at school.

Deteriorating school reports with deteriorating behaviour each successive year revealed a baser metal. The gold-plated shine wore away, revealing the reality. The parental disappointment was hard to conceal.

Mack, having nothing to prove, began to do well as his brother's star wavered and then plummeted. Now he'd settled in at his new-built Secondary Modern, his teachers recognised a late developer. James MacKinnon was not going to be one of life's failures. Where Adam failed to cope with grammar school rigours, his brother did otherwise. Mack's situation was such that the teachers expected to enter him for a few GCEs. This was unheard of at the Secondary Modern. Meanwhile, Adam had left grammar school at fifteen. He sought out an apprenticeship with one of the local garages as a motor vehicle mechanic.

There had been many massive rows at the time. To say there was parental disappointment with their eldest was a proverbial understatement.

Robert MacKinnon was the manager at one of the big banks in the city. He had wanted to see one of his sons get to university, or at least follow him into the banking profession. He had not been a happy man when dealing with his rebellious son. In his opinion Adam was heading for a lower-class job and lower-class life with all it entailed. One's class was still a matter of some importance to his parents and to the world at large. Not only was it a sign of outward respectability in the local community, it was all about the standing of the family in the local Catholic community. Their personal standing was not affected. They couldn't say the same of Adam. Now Adam was planning to marry at his age! Okay. So he was almost nineteen but it was still way too young for marriage! What on earth was he thinking?

65

CHAPTER 13

All Grown Up – The Crystals (London HL-U 9909 – 1964)

Thursday 22 October 1964 – Evening

Eerie. It was eerie in the extreme. Adam's exceptional politeness was extraordinary if not downright abnormal. There was none of his usual surly banter. It was bizarre seeing him in corduroy trousers and a cardigan with an open-neck shirt, and in polite conversation with his parents: a jaw dropper. Only the lack of a pipe and slippers failed to complete the transformation. The denims and leather jacket were gone. His mum and dad were behaving as if nothing had happened in the recent past. They sat in the living room watching television and exchanging civilised pleasantries. It was like an episode of The Twilight Zone. Something was definitely not right. Something was going on and Mack was not privy to it.

"Ah, James. I need to have a word with you. The Saturday morning job you were after… do you still want it?"

"What's the job? Not working in the butcher's shop down the road,?"

Adam smirked. His dad grinned. "No. How would you like to work at Benny's Scooters?"

"Doing what?" Mack's interest was focused in an instant.

"Mr Jenkins, or Benny as I know him, is the owner and a client at my bank. I also know him from watching City play at Valley Parade. He and his son Michael sell and service scooters. Saturday mornings are hectic right until they close at one thirty in the afternoon. Because they are busy servicing scooters they need someone behind the counter. They need to get on without constant interruption. You would be responsible for selling spare parts: items like spark plugs, speedo cables, exhausts, tyres and accessories. Also keeping an eye on the small showroom. You wouldn't sell the scooters themselves. How does that sound?"

"Like a dream job," Mack replied.

"It'll be like working in a ladies' hairdressers." Adam smirked even more.

"What do you mean? It's nothing like a ladies' hairdressers," protested Mack.

"Them scooters are over-grown hairdryers for guys who enjoy the feel of the wind in their vaginas," jeered Adam.

That was more like his brother of old, reality breaking into the Twilight Zone eeriness.

"You can stop that vulgarity, young man! It's not acceptable in this house!" his father reprimanded him.

"Sorry, Dad. Sorry, Mum. I apologise. I couldn't resist it."

"Adam, please don't say any more," begged their mum. To Mack's amazement Adam clammed up without further comment. It was too peculiar for words.

"When could I start?"

"Why, this Saturday of course. Eight o'clock sharp so you can learn what you've got to do."

"Oh, right." Mack tried to sound pleased but inside he groaned. He would have to miss seeing Effy. It could not be worse and better all at the same time. "Will he be expecting me to turn up?"

"Yes. Bernard is going to expect you on time. Your mum will make sure you're up in time. So be prompt. I'm sure Bernard will have overalls that will fit. Pleased?"

"Yes. How much is he going to pay me?"

"You're going to be paying him," Adam cracked out. "For the privilege of working there."

"He mentioned a pound. If it goes well he'll raise it to twenty-five shillings. Not bad for five hours' work."

"Blow me sideways," Adam gasped in surprise. "That's good money for the amount of time he's going to be working."

"Then it's settled," his father continued. "Now we're expecting someone to call round. So could I ask you to go out of the way when they arrive?"

"Why? Who's coming round?" Mack asked.

As if on cue he heard the doorbell ring. He made as if to answer it but found his father on his feet with a firm arm stopping him. Adam went instead. "Please do as I ask, James."

Leaving the room Mack realised why his father being so insistent. Effy's sister Caitlin entered the hallway. Adam was being the gentleman, helping her with her coat. She gave Mack a small tight smile before entering the lion's cage as the lounge door closed.

Keeping his bedroom door ajar he tried to hear what they were saying. It proved pointless because there were no raised voices. Whatever the conversation was all about, it was taking place in a civilised fashion.

Mack's thoughts turned to his big problem. How was he going to resolve it? Desperation was filling him already at the thought of not seeing Effy. Also Adam and Caitlin could yet cause his budding relationship with Effy to suffer. Once whatever was going on became known, old man Halloran would blow his lid. The MacKinnon name would be good as mud.

Mack's mood was apocalyptic. Everything was hurtling towards some kind of disastrous personal doom. He hoped Grace would be outside Wood's tomorrow after school. Getting a message to Effy was his overriding priority. Too many coincidences were littering his life. Some of these coincidences boded well while others augured dark unpleasant possibilities. October 1964 was proving to be a hell of a month.

It must have gone ten o'clock before he heard Caitlin leave, escorted by Adam. Mack heard him return fifteen minutes later. Once his brother came out of the bathroom and went into his room, Mack went round. Tapping on the door in a quiet voice he said, "It's me."

Adam came to the door. "What do you want?"

Mack pushed past him into the room and flopped down on the bed. "Spill. What's going on?"

"It's none of your business, it doesn't concern you," Adam replied, but without any of his usual spitefulness. "Anyway, why do you want to know?"

"I may be your kid brother and we may not always get on but it doesn't mean I don't care," Mack answered in a low voice. "When all said and done we're family. Nothing's going to change that."

"Got to say, it's a genuine surprise to hear you say that. I've got to admit I've been a twat to you more times than I care to remember. And we're as different as two brothers could be but, yeah, we're always going to be family, come what may."

Adam sat down on the bed beside Mack. "Okay, sunshine. Here's the SP. Caitlin and me, well we've got engaged and we want to get married soon. That's why she came round so we could talk to Mum and Dad."

"And...?" Mack let it hang.

"And not much. They were good but you know, not too happy about it. Got the usual spiel about being too young even if you're turning nineteen soon. She's not pregnant, is she? What are Caitlin's parents going to say,

68

blah, blah. Law says you can't marry without parents' consent until you're twenty one. How would you manage to live? That pretty much covers it."

"What did they think of Caitlin?"

"Well, after what they caught us up to I'm not sure. You know what they can be like. They never want to offend anyone. Especially," added Adam, nudging Mack with his elbow, "if that someone is a future daughter–in-law."

"So you must like her a lot to want to get married?"

"'Course I do, you berk. Why would I want to ball and chain myself otherwise? She's been good to me, making me look and think about the future. Let's face it, I can't always be a teenage rebel without a cause. Got to grow up sometime. Guess getting married would make me do that. Anyhow I'm getting to the age when we're expected to settle down, only a bit sooner."

"Wow! You got it real bad!" Mack let out a low whistle. All this unexpected openness was leaving him almost speechless.

"Guess I do," Adam sighed.

"So what next?"

"Dunno. Do a Gretna Green if things don't work out."

"Oh, come on! Eloping? Are trying to kid me?" Mack let out a low laugh.

"Yeah, sure I am." But something in the way Adam said it suggested that it was no joke.

"Well, whatever happens, I hope it's going to work out for you and Caitlin." Mack meant what he said.

The teasing at school had continued. That was until someone let the cat out of the bag about Mary Peterson and himself. She was finally seen with her boyfriend Kevin. Mack acquired some short-term sympathy as a jilted lover. This lasted until both confirmed there had never been anything going on between them.

Friday dragged. The weekly short Mass before lunchtime seemed endless. The afternoon seemed determined to defy the laws of physics. The hours felt twice as long. Fretting and distracted, Mack couldn't wait for school to end to catch the bus. Would Grace be there? He had written a short letter to Effy after his chat with Adam. He hoped this final fifth version made sense.

Dear Effy,

I hope you manage to get this letter before tomorrow morning. I don't want to miss seeing you but I can't make it to the library. Please don't misunderstand. I do want to see you tomorrow. I've got a part-time job at Benny's Scooters round the corner from the Express Dairy. I can't turn it down. I'm going to be working there until 1.30 p.m. Is there any chance of seeing you later in the afternoon? Or meeting up sometime this Sunday afternoon other than as strangers at church?

Mack

He had toyed with Dearest Effy. Even contemplating signing it with "all my love". In the end he thought that might come across too strong. Sealing it in an envelope, he prayed Effy would understand that he wasn't putting her off.

Relieved at getting to Woods in good time, he didn't see Grace waiting. The shop assistant greeted him as soon as he entered. A regular at the shop, Mack was the lad with a weird taste in American records.

"Anything new in this week, Simon?"

"Got this you might like. It came with some deletions so I put it to one side. I thought it might be your cup of tea." Simon rifled through a box and produced the blue cover of a Stateside 45. "One of those pop singers you like. Marvin Gaye. It's called *You're a Wonderful One.*"

"How much?"

"Don't you want to hear it first?" Simon sounded surprised.

Mack looked behind him and out of the window. No sign of Grace.

"All right. I'm meeting someone outside anytime now. It's my friend's sister."

"Tell you what, if she turns up bring her in and have a listen together. We're open for another twenty minutes."

Mack nodded and went outside to wait. There was no sign of her. Right, he thought to himself. I'll give her five minutes and then I'll have to go up to the church. As the time was about to expire he saw Grace turn the corner, accompanied by another schoolgirl. They trudged up the street towards him. For a fleeting moment Mack hoped it would be Effy with Grace. It wasn't. He felt disappointed.

"Hi. This is Jean." Grace introduced the girl. "She's meeting her mum at the Co-op. Jean's going to be giving me and Effy advanced dressmaking lessons."

70

"Pleased to meet you." Mack gave the gangly, mousy-haired girl a warm smile.

"You too." Turning to Grace Jean said, "I see what you mean. Yummy indeed. I'll see you Saturday afternoon, okay?"

"Okay. About three o'clock."

Jean carried on trudging up the hill towards Sunwin House.

"What did she mean by 'yummy' indeed?" asked Mack, although he was certain he already knew.

Grace reddened but did not respond.

"Look, there's a problem," he began. "Come into Wood's and I'll tell you all about it."

While they listened to Marvin Gaye in the booth Mack explained the situation and gave Grace the letter to pass on to Effy. They spoke over the music, planning where and when he could meet her again. Grace agreed to put Effy's reply in the missal after confession on Saturday afternoon. Leaving the listening booth, they went over to the counter.

"How much?" Mack asked Simon.

"It's from the deletions box, so 2/6d."

As Mack paid him Grace commented, "Wow! Loaded or what, if you can afford half-a-crown for a record."

"I've been doing a morning paper round since I was eleven. I also get 5/6d pocket money if I wash my dad's car."

"Isn't she a bit young to be your girlfriend?" Simon asked, handing over the record in a brown paper bag with the Wood's design.

Before he could refute the relationship Grace slipped her arm between his. Resting her head against his shoulder she announced with cheeky aplomb, "I like older men and he likes young girls. He's so yummy."

"I hope your brother doesn't find out, young lady, or this young man and your brother are unlikely to be friends for long," advised the shop assistant.

"I don't have any brothers!" Grace feigned shock and horror as Mack attempted to pull her towards the door. Refusing to let go of his coat sleeve she exclaimed, "James MacKinnon! How could you two-time me with my sister?"

Once outside she let go laughing aloud for all she was worth. Mack was angry and uncomfortable.

"Grace! What on earth were you playing at? They'll think I'm a two-timing cradle snatcher."

71

Grace sobered in an instant and became serious at the tone of his voice. "I'm sorry if I embarrassed you, Mack. Sometimes I do silly things for a laugh. I'm not sure why. I thought it would be funny to see the look on his face. I'm sorry. I made both of us look foolish. I made me look stupid."

She sounded genuinely upset as she realised what she had done. Mack was sorry in seconds, too, for being so sharp with her.

"Don't take it too much to heart. It was only a joke," he conceded, trying to be conciliatory so as not to hurt her feelings further. She wasn't even thirteen yet. For all her scatty silliness he was starting to be fond of Effy's sister.

"One day I'll grow up. But until then I guess I'll say and do stupid things." She perked up. "One day we'll all be grown-up and have to be different, I suppose."

"No, we won't. You're a fun person. You care about your sister a great deal. How many girls would have done what you've done for your sister? Without you I would never have met her. I wish I had a caring little sister like you, too."

"Who knows?" Some of the cheerfulness returned to her. "One fine day you might."

They took the trolley bus, first checking out if anyone might recognise them. The top deck was empty so there was no problem and they discussed in whispers how Mack and Effy could meet again. Mack passed on the letter and watched it disappear into Grace's school satchel.

CHAPTER 14

Money (That's What I Want) – Barrett Strong (London HLU 9088 – 1960)

Saturday 24 October 1964

Benny's Scooters consisted of a small showroom with a dozen or so Lambretta scooters for sale. The scooters stood arranged on a slant leaving an aisle for customers to reach a flip-top counter. Behind the counter was a short corridor leading to the workshop. Immediately to the left was a large room containing spare parts as well as all kinds of accessories. This was the central hub where the workshop and shop met.

Mack arrived ten minutes early to ensure he was punctual. Bernard Jenkins, as Mack soon found out, was Benny to everyone. Including Mack.

"Don't call me Mr Jenkins again," he declared roughly after ten minutes. "Benny's my name and you can call me Benny from now on. Everyone knows me as Benny and everyone calls me Benny, except him. Sometimes he calls me Dad. At other times he calls me rude names."

"And I do, 'cos he deserves it some of the time," confirmed the young man.

Pointing to his son, Benny said, "I change his name every two minutes. Sometimes he's called Dozy, sometimes Muggins, sometimes whatever comes to mind. Now and again I call him Mick when he's not Dozy. Call him Mick."

"Take no notice of him," chuckled Mick, who had long hair like one of the Rolling Stones. Mack guessed he was about twenty. "He calls me far worse. Do you know he tried to make me wear a hairnet in the repair shop? Claimed it was for safety reasons so I didn't get my hair trapped when working with equipment. When I put it on for a laugh he called me Ena Sharples after that woman on the TV in Coronation Street. You need to watch out for my Dad. He's a regular piss-taker. Enjoys extracting the urine. So what do we call you? James? Jim?"

"Everyone calls me Mack. Only my Mum and Dad call me James."

"Mack it is then," the two men agreed.

"What do you know about scooters, Mack?" asked Benny.

Mack confessed he knew next to nothing. He received a high-powered lesson in thirty minutes. First of all they introduced him to different

73

models available. Then they outlined all the main parts that went into the scooters. After that Benny showed him the spares and accessories room. Every inch of shelving had spares. Every part had its labelled place. Mack marvelled at the organised thoroughness.

"This," said Benny, opening a huge book, "is the parts catalogue. You can find everything here priced up. If customers aren't sure which model they own ask them what year it was first registered. At the back, you'll find exploded plans of the different models. Check against these with Noddy over there to make sure it's the right part for the right model. Electricals are the toughest. The Italians insist on six volt electrics but they'd be be better off with twelve."

"Accessories?" Benny paused to draw breath. "All the carry racks, back rests, crash bars to fit the right model are at the front along with the pricing. Notice how high up we put the silencers and the racks. They're display items only. We have a right bunch of thieving gits come round sometimes. You'll soon get to know the shifty bunch. Their leader is a bastard called Mal Osborn. Thinks he's the local hard man. Looks like a big bad bear. If they waltz in you'll know who they are straightaway. They'll try to distract you when your back's turned. If there's more than three of them in the showroom use the desk buzzer. One of us will come through. Notice how the till is out of reach? One time we had one of those smarmy little toe-rags try to steal money from it. Mick caught him in the act and kicked him out. That was well funny. Booted him right up his jacksy as he tried to get out."

By the time the shop opened Mack was panicking. His head was reeling from all the information he had to remember at such short notice. To add to it he had to record each sale and issue a receipt, taking the right amount and giving the correct change. HP payments were not his remit. That was for Benny and Mick to do, at least for the time being. He heard Benny say he might have to do it at some later date. Mack realised this was going to be much tougher than he had imagined. The positive was that he didn't have time to daydream about Effy.

The weather was bad until about eleven o'clock. Rain and wind lashed the showroom windows. Then the wintry sun came out. The day brightened and the rain stopped. Customers who came in tended to be older adult riders. They seemed to know exactly what they needed so it proved easy. As the morning progressed Mack found himself coping with taking payments. His confidence grew as he found parts and rubber-stamped sales receipts. Soon it felt as if he had been doing it for ages. He even helped one

74

customer to work out which part he needed using one of the workshop parts manuals.

It was a steady first morning – which was as well because other weekends would be hectic. Benny and Mick came in from time to time for spare parts. Otherwise they were busy servicing customers' machines. Mack only saw them when customers called to pick up their scooters.

There was only one opportunity for a tea break at 10.30 otherwise it was all go. Tea-making was an added job he acquired that morning. Before he realised it 1.30 had loomed. With the last of the repairs done, the garage doors swung shut for the weekend. Mack took off his overalls and hung them up with the others.

"You did a grand job today with all the stuff you had to learn. Got some homework for you." Benny handed him a pile of brochures and a couple of recent copies of scooter magazines. "Read up about all the models. See what they say about these new models in the magazines. I'll test you next Saturday at eight o'clock."

"You did good," said Mick. "See you next Saturday."

Benny handed him a grubby pound note. "Well earned, young man."

Mack experienced a combination of relief and delight. Benny must have thought he had worked well enough to keep him on. Seeing those gleaming new scooters for sale focused his mind. He determined he was going to own one. When he reached sixteen he would get his provisional driving licence. Then he would buy a Lambretta with the money his granddad had left him. If his brother could set the precedent by buying a motorbike he would buy a scooter. Seeing the prices he realised he had more than enough in his savings account already.

As Mack turned the corner he forgot all about scooters. Effy was waiting for him. Seeing her made his heart pound with excitement. As they walked towards each other Mack could not contain himself. What should he do? Take her hand? Give her a kiss on the cheek? All these questions ran through his mind with such rapidity there was no time to decide. Before he could decide she was standing by him.

After reading his letter Effy had made a bold decision. Her fifteenth birthday was a couple of weeks away. If this was the start of something special then she would be daring. She would leave him in no doubt about her feelings. Effy was always the quiet one at home and school. The one who never said the proverbial boo to a goose. The one who never caused an upset. The mouse in the house had finally had enough.

Her crush on Mack had begun four years earlier. Maybe it was still only a crush. Maybe it would never come to anything more. Whatever happened at least she was going to do everything to make it work and last. This time there was no spontaneity, only a deliberately planned spirited act.

Placing a hand on his shoulder, she raised her heels off the ground to reach his cheek. She gave him a lingering kiss before asking, "Did it go alright today?"

Before he could respond, bewildered by the kiss, she'd slipped her hand into his. Now he was glad he had cleaned his hands with Swarfega to get the grease and grime off.

"Er, yes it went well." Mack found himself almost stuttering. "I'm going to enjoy working here on Saturdays."

"I'm pleased it went well." She gave his hand a gentle reassuring squeeze. "I thought I'd come and see how you had got on."

The kiss and the touch of her hand caused an unfortunate reaction. The embarrassing reaction was an erection so hard that he prayed it would not show.

"I'm so glad to see you again," he said, worrying about the stiffness in his trousers. "I didn't want to miss meeting you."

Effy hid her disappointment that he had not returned her kiss on the cheek. Then, almost as an afterthought, Mack took a deep breath. She had been brave enough to kiss him so he had to do the same and not behave like a wimp. Leaning over, he returned the kiss – much to her delight. The smile she gave him in response spoke more than words.

God, I'm so lucky, they both thought as only teenagers could.

"How have you managed to get away to come here to meet me?"

"I told them I was going for a walk to get some fresh air."

"And they believed you?"

"Why shouldn't they believe me? It's true, after all. I've walked down. I'll be walking back." Her teasing smile beguiled him. "If I happen to meet a certain young man on my walk that's something else. Not that my parents will be expecting me to do anything of the sort."

"Why not?" Mack left the question hanging for a response.

"I'm the quiet one, like my sister Aileen. The one who never argues. The one who's always the goody two shoes like Deidre. I'm not a natural rebel like Caitlin or Grace. I do everything to avoid causing upset, unlike Ellen. I don't stand up for others like my sister Bridget. I've decided my life's too controlled. I don't want to it to be any longer."

Mack beamed. "Effy, we sound so much alike. It's having to conform when you don't want to but you know you have to so you don't rock the boat."

"Are you expected home soon?" she asked.

"Are you?" He returned the question.

"I can't stay out too long. I should imagine another quarter of an hour. Why?" Effy replied.

"I was hoping it might be longer." His disappointment revealed itself.

"I know I shouldn't do this," she began, with a worried look in her entrancing green eyes. "Because girls of good character are not supposed to be so forward. Have you anything planned for this evening?"

"No. Nothing. Why?"

"There's something happening at home this evening. My Da wants us out of the house, so..."

"So...?" He urged her on as she paused.

"Ellen, Grace and myself are going to cinema together this evening. The thing is Ellen is going to do a disappearing act. She doesn't want to go as she has other plans. So she's leaving Grace and myself to go on our own. We suspect Ellen has a boyfriend but she's keeping quiet about him. Grace is going to pretend she's unwell before we set off to the cinema. Once we've set off Ellen will have to let me go on my own. Otherwise she won't be able to meet this boy. She won't dare to say she left me on my own. That would only lead to questions about where she was whilst I was on my own. You could go with me to the cinema so I wouldn't be on my own."

"That's brilliant. Of course I'd love to go with you. I'd love nothing better." Mack marvelled at the subterfuge involved. "So which female James Bond came up with this dodge? Grace?"

Effy blushed.

"I did." She hesitated. "I thought it would be the perfect opportunity for us to meet up and be together."

"Well, it's sheer genius." Mack bubbled with excitement. "We can have a proper first date."

"I suppose we could. Does that mean you want me to be your girlfriend?"

"Do I? Indeed I do." Stepping back a pace, taking a little bow, Mack continued with a show of mock formality, "Miss Effy Halloran, would you do me the great pleasure of letting me be your boyfriend?"

Returning a curtsey, Effy replied in kind, fluttering her eyelids. "Why, Mr James MacKinnon, this is so unexpected. Yes, I would love to be your girlfriend."

"What time should we meet and which cinema are we going to?"

There was no choice. It had to be the Elite Cinema near to their homes. Going there on a Saturday night concerned them both. Being so local people who knew their parents might see them. That was a real risk. The Gaumont and the Odeon in the city centre were both showing Certificate 'A' films. Could they pass for sixteen? Effy was not sure. It would be risky and they might end up being barred from entering. That would be humiliating. There was the further problem. The films all ended at different times. The sisters had agreed to meet when the film ended at the Elite. Going to the city centre cinemas meant that Effy would struggle to meet Ellen on time. Mack and Effy would not be able to leave together afterward, since Ellen would be waiting outside for her. There was no other option. It had to be the Elite Cinema.

CHAPTER 15

Saturday Night at the Movies – The Drifters (ATLANTIC 4012 – 1964)

Saturday 24 October 1964

For over two decades the Elite Cinema had had a rival in the Coliseum. The latter shut its doors for the final time in the Fifties. Separated by Fairbank Road the two buildings fronted the junction with Toller Lane. How the two had coexisted in such proximity was a mystery. Now only the Elite soldiered on showing movies. The hangar-like Coliseum was reduced to a carpet showroom. A large arched bright-lit welcoming window surmounted the Elite's two-door entrance. Like a harbour lighthouse it invited a handful of cinema-goers that dark evening.

To be on time Mack arrived early. The last thing he wanted was for Effy to be waiting for him outside. That would not be the done thing. As he stood across from the cinema the cold biting wind penetrated his trench coat. The weather was dismal. To his horror he watched Effy approaching with her sister Ellen. This was not quite going to plan.

The two had stopped at the cinema entrance and were exchanging words. Then, to his relief, Ellen crossed the road to the bus stop. This was awkward. If he crossed the road too soon two and two could end up making four. He watched Effy go inside. Crossing the road Mack took a gamble. Her sister might assume it was coincidence he was going to the cinema. Entering, he saw Effy in the corner of the foyer. He smiled as she walked over to him. Buying two back row tickets he heard her say, "We're supposed to be going Dutch."

"No, I'll pay."

"Mack." She began to protest. "You can't…"

"Call me old-fashioned." He took the two tickets from the cashier.

"You shouldn't have done that. I had the money to pay for a ticket."

"I know you did. Now you can keep it for another time. Tonight is on me. Shall we?" He offered his hand as they entered. Guided by the usherette's torchlight they found themselves in an almost empty back row. The cinema was less than a quarter full with the first feature about to start.

Holding hands for the first ten minutes or so they sat watching the film. Inexperienced and out of his depth, knowing what do but not when to

79

do it, left Mack worried. The books he had read about sex and some of his cousin's men's only magazines made it look and sound easy. First-time reality was another thing. Should he be daring and put his arm around her? It was not as if they had known each other long.

Effy wondered what he would do if she leaned over and rested her head on his shoulder? This was what the girls did in romance comics. Should she behave in the same way? Would he think of her as too forward? They were in the back row of the cinema in the far corner, with no one else nearby. No one would see them.

The Drifters' recent hit *Saturday Night at the Movies* was playing in Mack's head. Should he do as the song suggested? Should he pluck up the courage and try? After all, what was the worst that could happen? Effy might not want him to do it. Then he would have to hold her hand the rest of the evening. At least she would know he liked her enough to put his arm around her shoulder. Releasing her hand, he put his right arm around her shoulder. Effy, making it seem the most normal thing in the world, cradled her head into him. No protest, no drama. They were in one another's embrace. A fragrant feminine scent emanated from her. An intoxicating perfume that made him aware how beautiful this girl was, how much she trusted him. It was overwhelming. He looked down into her face. Effy gave him a long lingering dreamy look, inviting him to make the next move.

Okay, she thought. This is it. Please let's kiss. I've wanted to do this for what has felt like forever. Without realizing it she closed her eyes, surrendering her lips to him.

This was it: thrilling as nothing had ever been before. Mack was, like the Ben E. King song, transported into ecstasy as their lips met.

It was happening. It was overpowering. The sensations experienced as they kissed flooded their bodies. Her arm reached round to his left shoulder and the passion each felt was intense. Once it began it lasted to the interval. They said nothing because words were no longer needed. Mack was experiencing an unfamiliar intimate closeness. It was a thrilling experience, elating yet scary. Effy was experiencing the same. She felt as if she could lose total control of herself. They continued locked in one another's embrace until the interval. When the lights dimmed again, they resumed their kissing. Now it was gentler, more relaxed but no less intense. In complete innocence and without guile Effy's hand ended up resting near the top of Mack's thigh. Aroused as Mack was her touch proved almost too much. He did not know how he restrained himself from ejaculating.

All too soon the last of the end credits rolled. There was the usual rush for the exits. Avoiding the dreaded drum roll introducing the national anthem was not unusual. The patriotic fervour of the war years was fading. Fewer and fewer of the post-war generation felt the need to be upstanding at the end of the evening. Mack and Effy waited until the anthem finished. This was not from patriotism but to avoid anyone seeing and recognizing them.

Still inside the cinema Effy turned to Mack. Putting both arms around his neck she pressed herself against him. Mack could not help feeling terrible, knowing she had felt his bulge. But Effy didn't pull away as he thought she might. Instead she pressed her breasts deeper into his chest. Was his erection not quite as obvious as he thought it was? He was wrong. When she finally pulled back Effy blushed and went, "Oh."

"I'm sorry." He mumbled a lame apology shot through with awkwardness at his humiliating hardness.

"I'm not," she replied. Reading his embarrassment, she pressed her body against his for one last kiss. "I've read it's supposed to be normal in young men. It was… unexpected, that's all."

She let go of him. "We'd better go out alone as we planned. We don't want Ellen suspecting, do we? I'll see you outside Benny's at one thirty next Saturday."

"It's a date," he replied. "In case Ellen's late I'll wait by the bus stop across the road. It won't be safe on your own so I'll make sure you're okay. If she does see me I'll pretend… well, we were here but not together."

Mack loitered for a minute in the foyer. He pretended to study the film posters before he ventured out into the cold night. It was hard to walk past Effy pretending they didn't know each other. Crossing the road to the bus stop he waited but there was no sign of Ellen. The minutes dragged by with Effy looking more and more cold and uncomfortable. Ten minutes passed and Mack decided enough was enough. He re-crossed the road.

"What's happened to your sister?" There was real concern in his voice.

"I've no idea," came her worried reply. "She said she'd be here as soon as the film was over."

They continued to chat and then Mack suggested he should walk Effy home. But Effy was insistent she should wait. Ellen was by then twenty minutes late. Finally appearing, looking flustered, she gave Mack a piercing look as she approached.

Effy pre-empted her. "Where on earth have you been? It's late and we're going to be in serious trouble. If it hadn't been for James here I would have been stood on my own and it's freezing cold."

Mack's tone was reprimanding. "I was waiting at the bus stop and saw your sister on her own. It's not safe for a girl to be on her own at this time of night. It's not responsible to have her waiting like this. I came over to make sure she was alright."

"Don't I know you from somewhere?" Ellen, taken aback by his reprimand, eyed him with suspicion.

"As in I've gone to St. Pat's Sunday Masses week in week out for years," he replied, knowing full well she recognised him. "It's lucky I was at the pictures tonight."

The answer appeared to satisfy her. "Come on, Effy. Let's go. And thank you for waiting with my sister."

He watched them walk away down the road at a brisk pace.

As they approached home they saw Mr and Mrs Monaghan walking away. Effy never gave it a second thought, assuming they had attended the meeting this evening. But Ellen seemed to panic as she dashed past the couple, while Effy wondered what was going on. She noticed the Monaghans giving her sister the dirtiest of dirty looks. Then it occurred to her that the Monaghans were not usually visitors to their home.

As Effy entered and closed the front door their father confronted them. "Step into the front room, the two of you."

Effy's heart sank. Ellen was pale with fright. This was not going to be pleasant. For a brief moment she panicked and then thought her father could not know about Mack.

"And how was the pictures tonight, Ellen?" he demanded in his sonorous heavily accented Irish voice.

Effy noticed her sister was trembling.

"It was alright," Ellen replied, her voice betraying her nervous agitation, turning towards Effy for support. "Wasn't it, Effy?"

"It was a comedy," Effy replied, remembering some of the dialogue while she'd been entwined in Mack's embrace. "Quite funny for an American comedy."

"Was it now?" His tone was changing. Effy knew from past experience this was going to be unpleasant. The Monaghans' visit this late had something to do with this inquisition.

"And, Ellen? Tell me, did you both find it was quite funny?" The interrogation continued. "And did the two of you enjoy the film?"

Effy knew there no more dancing around the truth. The jig was up.

Ellen knew it was pointless continuing the charade. Her father had her trapped, the anger spilling out in his voice. He knew everything already.

"You have some neck on you, Ellen Halloran, telling your fibs. Trying to make a fool of your Da, were you? Do you know what the Monaghans came round to tell me a few minutes ago?"

Ellen remained stoic and silent as the explosion followed.

"You let your sister go to the cinema on her own so you could carry out your deception. Why? So you could canoodle and allow some boy to fondle you on a street corner in full view of every passerby. What does it say in the catechism? Let me remind you."

It came word for word as written. "Does the Sixth Commandment forbid whatever is contrary to holy purity? *The Sixth Commandment forbids whatever is contrary to holy purity in looks, words, or action.*"

He kept thumping the sofa armrest and repeating, "Looks, words or action", not once but over and over again in demented fashion. Effy became incensed as those words raised unpleasant memories. Memories that she had kept under control all her young life.

"No good Catholic girl should behave in such a sinful manner. Ellen, you have behaved like some hussy. Like some common street *hoor* to the shaming of this household." Then, turning on Effy, he continued with his tirade. "And you, young lady, instead of returning home, let yourself be a party to these squalid going's-on. Since when does a young girl go to the pictures on her own unaccompanied?"

"I'm almost fifteen. The film was suitable for someone of my age. I wanted to see it. Ellen said she didn't want to go so I decided for myself. And anyway," added Effy, rising to her sister's defence with unprecedented defiance, "Ellen's sixteen. If she wants to have a boyfriend then why shouldn't she? She's reached the age of consent. I'm fed up with hearing you telling us we're all sinners and impure."

It may have been wiser to say nothing. Effy could stand it no longer. Being the mouse in the house was over. She was not going to take any more brow-beating bullying. Whatever Ellen was guilty of could not be any worse than her own behaviour in the cinema. Her father had lectured her and her sisters about sin and sinfulness ever since she could remember; the damned catechism had made her resentful and this resentment had been building for some time. Tonight it was at snapping point. Defiance was ready to manifest itself. Effy had tolerated puritanical Catholicism long enough. Young as she was, the constant harrying of her sisters and herself had reached its limit.

Sean Halloran went off on one at his daughter's rebellious response. He shouted, he blustered; he threatened them with priests and nuns. His anger belonged to someone possessed, completely out of control. She had never seen him so enraged. It was unreal. Ellen was reduced to uncontrollable floods of tears. When her father paused, red-faced and out of breath, Effy was not done. She resumed the offensive before he could continue.

"My sister is not a hussy and not a whore. I'm ashamed to hear you, my own father, calling my sister such a horrible thing. This is not a convent. We are not nuns, nor ever will be. We don't deserve such ill treatment. I am sick of you telling me I'm sinful and I must not do this or do that. If my eternal soul is in danger of never-ending damnation then it will be you to blame for that happening."

Those words stunned him.

"How dare you!" he exclaimed, outraged. "I'm your father. I deserve respect. How dare you say something like that to me?"

"You earn respect." By now Effy was quivering with rage. "You're not worthy of it when it's undeserved."

"Let me quote you from the catechism. It appears you have forgotten the teaching of the Holy Mother church."

Effy cut him off before he drew another breath. "No need to quote it to me! I know it chapter and verse!" she responded with real anger that matched his. "Honour thy parents etc. Duty bound etc. You forget. You made us learn it by heart."

"Seems you learned the words but not the meaning behind them," he thundered.

"So now I'm stupid as well as a sinner?"

"Fiona Halloran, if you were a boy I would thrash you for your sinful words."

"I'm sure you would. For the love of Jesus, meek and mild, who said suffer little children to come to me? Suffer a beating? That's so Christian of you."

"You had better say no more, young lady."

"Or you'll send me to a boarding school run by nuns? The threat we've all had to put up with from when we were little?"

"Don't think I won't do it!" The cutting sharpness was clear in his voice. "The way you've behaved tonight, it's what you may be in need of for the sinful tongue in your head."

"You can't even keep me clothed." Effy vented the last of her anger. "Bridget had to buy underwear for Grace and myself. Why? Because you either wouldn't or couldn't pay."

"That's enough, Effy." She heard Bridget's voice behind her.

Effy stopped. Her father was speechless. Those words seem to hit him hard.

"May Jesus preserve me," he responded with feeling, "from this monstrous regiment of daughters God has saddled me with. First I hear of Caitlin's doings, then you two. As for you, Fiona, I can't believe how disrespectful you've been and how you've spoken to me and of your faith. I never thought to hear the like from you, so quiet, so well-behaved, and yet so seething with resentment. Get off to your rooms the pair of you. Consider yourselves grounded for as long as you live in my house. You're not to go anywhere at any time out of school hours without my consent."

Deidre sat in bed ashen-faced saying nothing as Effy comforted a sobbing Ellen. She had been party to hearing everything that had gone on and more besides. Deidre had never had the courage to articulate her feelings. Tonight Effy had proved the strongest of her sisters, braving their father's fury. She had said what they all felt but dared not voice.

"It's so unfair," Ellen kept repeating over and over between sobs. "I'm not a bad person. I'm not a hussy. I'm not a whore. All this because I was kissing a boy." Effy had her arm round her, giving her little reassuring squeezes.

"You two were the breaking point tonight – the last straw, so to speak," Deidre interjected.

"What do you mean? What breaking point?" Effy wanted to know.

Deidre was in two minds about continuing. In a low voice she decided to tell them what had been happening whilst they were out. They listened in disbelief as Deidre recounted the evening's happenings in a hushed tone.

CHAPTER 16

Black Night – Arthur Alexander (London HL-D 9899 – 1964)

Saturday 24 / Sunday 25 October 1964

Mack's genitals hurt. It had been the hardest, longest-lasting, most painful erection of his life. They had kissed for the better part of two hours and he thought he could still feel her lips on his. Of course it was absurd and he knew it. His thoughts were in overdrive. Mack was ecstatic, replaying the evening's events as he arrived home. Closing the front door he heard voices downstairs and upstairs. Adam and his father were talking in earnest, their voices serious. Upstairs, from his bedroom, he could hear his mother conversing with another female. Poking his head round the kitchen door he asked, "What's going on?"

Adam and his father ceased talking. "Come in, son. I've got some news. Caitlin Halloran is coming to stay with us for a while."

Mack couldn't believe what he'd heard. His father's matter-of-fact announcement of her arrival in the house stunned him.

"Why?"

"Let's say she's had a serious disagreement with her parents this evening."

"Where's she going to sleep?"

"Ah." His father screwed up his face. "Therein we have a problem. I'm sorry, James. You're going to have to bunk down with Adam while she stays with us or else sleep on the sofa in the front room."

"Dad!" he exclaimed. "You're joking!"

"Well, there's nowhere else. We haven't sorted out the attic bedroom. We need to move the clutter out and redecorate it."

"Sorry about that, sunshine," Adam added, sounding regretful. "It's all a bit unexpected."

"She's your girlfriend. Why can't she have your bedroom? What's wrong with you sleeping on the sofa instead?" Mack protested but he saw it was going to be useless.

"Adam has to go to work early. He needs a good night's sleep."

"I have to go to school. I need my sleep too. Or doesn't that count? Anyway, it's Sunday morning tomorrow."

The words had only managed to escape from his lips when his mother appeared.

"Poor dear. It's unbelievable. She's so upset. Fancy her father behaving in such a Victorian fashion in this day and age. How could he say those words to one of his own?"

"Why? What's supposed to have happened?" Mack tried to elicit some information.

"Never you mind, James." His mother delivered her words in a business-like fashion, accompanied by that wordless look not to ask further questions. "How was the film?"

"It was okay." Even as he replied the implications of what was happening right now began to strike. He sensed there were going to be serious implications for his relationship with Effy. "If you think I'm sleeping with his ponging feet polluting my nose you're mistaken!"

Sleeping on the sofa did not keep him awake for hours. Nor was it the thought of Caitlin in his bed. Mack had not seen her yet. She had remained in his room without coming down. No, it was the memory of Effy on the back row of the cinema mingling with the mystery surrounding Adam and Caitlin. Events were threatening to jeopardise everything for him and Effy.

Breakfast was pretty much silent with few words exchanged. For once Mack was enjoying an allowed early Sunday breakfast with Adam. Mack could tell Caitlin had been crying during the night. Her eyes were red, and puffy, dark shadows under them confirmed her misery. Her pale complexion was paler still. Mack was seeing another side of his brother too. Adam appeared changed, too, comforting her with tender touches. It was disconcerting.

Only his parents were going to Communion and so were fasting as usual. Adam, he learned, was going to make a first appearance at church in ages. He was taking Caitlin to St. William's rather than to St. Patrick's. That was also a bit of a shock given Adam's conduct in the past couple of years. Meanwhile Mack could not wait to see Effy.

Mack arrived in good time but chose not to take his usual place. Instead he sat behind his parents. When the Hallorans arrived, it was even more extraordinary. The sisters were not taking their customary places in the pews. It was clear to Mack something was not right. Not right at all. Effy looked straight through him as if he was a complete stranger. Usually her face had a tranquil expression. Not this morning. She looked annoyed, if not downright angry. Ellen looked terrible: pale, puffy-eyed and upset. Grace's glance spoke a clear message of trouble in the household. The shrug Grace gave him implied she did not know why. Effy bundled Ellen into the row across the aisle next to his. Grace went in next to Ellen while Effy sat down closest in the aisle seat immediately across from him. She and her sisters had never taken a seat so far down from the altar, and so near to him. Even Deidre had moved away from her parents seating herself two rows in front of the three youngest and two rows behind Aileen and Bridget who were sitting next to their parents.

"*In nomine Patris et Filii et Spiritu Sancti*," intoned the priest. Signalling the start of the Mass, the congregation responded. "Amen."

Mack glanced sideways, his heart beating with trepidation, hoping for a sign. Effy turned towards him with the same smile she always gave him. Placing her left hand to her lips she blew a tiny kiss across the aisle. As they were near the back of the church it was unlikely anyone would have seen. He returned the smile and blew a tiny kiss back. It would be the only kind of kiss they would exchange for a long while. When it came to walking down the aisle to communion the threesome remained seated. Deidre began to stand and then changed her mind, remaining seated. Only their parents and the two older sisters went to the communion rail to receive the sacred wafer.

Something was definitely not right. There was rebellion in the sisters' ranks. The only thing Mack found cheering was how he and Effy exchanged smiling glances across the aisle. Whatever else was going on, it had nothing to do with them. He noted her parents' expression as they returned from the communion rail. Their stony-faced father gave his four rebellious daughters a cursory glance. Mack saw him lower his eyes away from his daughters before retaking his place. Effy's mother's expression could not hide her serious upset. If Mack could fathom this so could the congregation's gossiping whited sepulchres.

His mother had warned him never to disclose any family matters if asked. There were those who prayed on their knees who also preyed on their fellow churchgoers.

"*Ite missa,*" the Priest intoned in Latin, signalling the end of the Mass.

The congregation responded. "*Deo gratias.*"

Mack found the Latin response amusing, always understanding it as "thank God it's over". Glancing at Effy he saw her reluctance to leave immediately. Rising to leave, he caught her swift communicating glance. A slight dip of the head suggested he should sit back down, which he did. They were waiting for her parents to go out first. Then, and only then, did Effy stand. Allowing Grace and Ellen to leave first she moved to one side so they could go in front. This appeared to be the signal for Mack to get up and leave. It was. He didn't know why but the reason became clear. Hidden by her two sisters in front, Effy managed to slip an envelope into his hand.

Once outside there was none of the usual family unity. The sisters divided into younger and older. Deidre appeared reluctant to choose sides. Mack had to pretend he was a relative stranger. This did not apply to his parents. They had corralled the Hallorans to one side and were in hushed, earnest conversation. All he could manage to overhear were the same constant words repeated by Mr Halloran. "No. No. No. Never."

Whatever they were talking about, it was not going too well. Meantime, Mack kept glancing in Effy's direction. Neither she nor Grace responded, although Ellen gave him a brief polite but wan smile. She was not the confident girl he usually saw on Sunday mornings.

"It's all the fault of your good-for-nothing son. He's to blame." Mr Halloran was raising his voice. Mack's attention tuned back towards the parents. The conversation appeared to have reached an impasse.

"We should meet in private to discuss this further, Mr Halloran." His father was using his bank manager voice reserved for talking business affairs. Realising their conversation was being overheard they spoke in hushed voices once more. Mack became fed up with waiting. Beginning to walk towards the parked Cortina, he collided with Bridget Halloran. It was no accidental collision.

"It's James, isn't it?" she asked, knowing full well who he was.

"Yes?"

"I'm Caitlin's sister, Bridget."

"Yes?"

Ensuring she had her back to her parents, Bridget spoke in a low husky voice. "I have to beg a favour of you."

"Yes?" Mack became aware how silly his questioning "yes" was beginning to sound. "How can I help you?"

"Please ask my sister Caitlin to either call in to where I work as soon as she can or to 'phone me at work. It is important I speak with her." She stressed the "*is*".

"I take it she knows where you work?"

"She does. I wouldn't ask you, but it's vital. I cannot stress enough that I must speak to her as soon as possible."

"If you don't mind me asking," Mack retorted, bemused, "how do you know she's at my house?"

"She's my sister. Where else could she go?" Then, almost giving him heart failure, she continued. "I've watched Effy giving you the eye. My guess is you'll be as sweet on her as she is on you."

Mack looked her in the face to brazen it out with a "no" but there was a knowing glint in her eye. What did she know? Effy would not have said anything. Grace? Grace may have let something slip.

"Not everything is as secret as you might think, James MacKinnon. You imagine nobody else notices. Think again and be more circumspect. One thing more. It appears you are going to be an uncle. Caitlin's pregnant."

Mack's jaw dropped. "You're joking. No. No, it can't be true. Caitlin expecting a baby?"

Her expression was serious. "Yes, a baby. That's exactly what she's expecting. It's not a joking matter. It can and it is happening. One unmarried sister in the family way is one too many. It's causing havoc in my family and no doubt in yours. So if you and Effy are up to no good, take this as a warning. I don't want Effy ending up the same way."

"If?" He queried in surprise.

"If there were anything going on between the two of you." The emphasis fell on the word "if". Mentally Mack blew a sigh of relief. She was suspicious but she didn't know the real truth. Yet.

"So can I count on you to pass on my message?"

He nodded. With that she re-joined her elder sister Aileen as the Hallorans left. Led by Effy the four rebellious daughters trailed behind, leaving a calculated distance.

Mack waited until he was in the car with his parents before speaking. "So, when were you going tell me I'm about to become an uncle?"

90

CHAPTER 17

I Don't Want to Go On Without You – The Drifters
(Atlantic 45 2237 – 1964)

Sunday 25 October 1964

Later in the day he found time to open the letter. Deprived of his room, he had nowhere to go until after Sunday dinner. No opportunity presented itself to talk to Caitlin. He would have to make the opportunity somehow. Mack locked himself in the bathroom and opened the pink Basildon Bond envelope. The letter and its content were so feminine, so Effy.

It began, "Dearest Mack". Five sides long, Effy's handwriting was the neatest and most precisely flowing he had ever seen. Her personality shone through the words. Re-reading the letter for the umpteenth time left him dismayed. It was a sorry tale. While he and Effy were at the cinema, Caitlin had told her parents she was pregnant.

This had turned instantly into a terrible nightmarish showdown. Sean Halloran disowned his daughter, raging against her. Making her pack her things, he had told her to leave and never return. This after she'd refused to go to Ireland to give birth to the child and have it adopted. Left with no choice, Caitlin had taken what belongings she could in a small suitcase and had gone. Having nowhere to go, she had arrived at the MacKinnons' home to see Adam. The rest Mack knew. Then, as if that were not bad enough, the Monaghans had seen Ellen as they were out walking.

She had been seen in a telephone box with some boy. They had seen him "canoodling and fondling" her according to Mr Monaghan. He had felt impelled as a good Catholic to report this sinful activity straightaway. It turned out that Monaghan was a fellow "Opus Dei" crony of her father's. Effy saw his action with much less charity. He had acted as a nasty, nosy, interfering self-righteous spiteful creep. Monaghan had no right interfering in their lives. As a consequence Ellen was in serious trouble with her father. She was in his bad books for aiding an abetting Ellen by going to the cinema alone.

Effy had defended her sister, arguing with her father. It had not gone down well. The letter did not specify why she'd argued or what the disagreement was about but Mack guessed. The upshot of it all was the four

91

youngest daughters now found themselves grounded. Even though Deidre and Grace had done nothing wrong they were guilty all the same. Effy begged Mack to be patient. She hoped the grounding would not be for too long and that it would all blow over soon. She would do all she could to see him again. It took some courage, Mack thought, for her to add that she was missing him already. Effy had signed the letter, "with all my love, Effy xxxxxxx". Seven x's told him what he most needed to know.

It sickened him, knowing what had taken place. His sole consolation was that Ellen was the one who'd been found in a compromised situation, not Effy. How much worse would it have been if it had been Effy instead? Mack's dismay turned into a troubled sadness. The thought of not seeing Effy for an indefinite period made him miserable. It was the nearest he'd come to crying since he was ten.

Later, knowing Caitlin was in his room alone, he went up. He had genuine reasons for this, like needing clothes for the morning and his school things. He took this opportunity to pass on Bridget's message. Caitlin thanked him for his kindness in getting her sister's words to her. They chatted and Mack began to realise how lucky Adam was having Caitlin. She was a warm, lovely person, much like her younger sister. Even so, Mack still could not fathom what she saw in Adam. If Caitlin was to become his sister-in-law it would be fine by him.

INTERLUDE

1965 soundtrack

My Girl – The Temptations
It's Growing – The Temptations
I Can't Explain – The Who
Strong Love – Spencer Davis Group
All Over The World – Francoise Hardy
I'll Stay By You – Kenny Lynch
I Can't Help Myself (Sugar Pie Honey Bunch) – The 4 Tops
Like We Used To Be – Georgie Fame
It's The Same Old Song – The 4 Tops
A Lover's Concerto – The Toys
Something – Georgie Fame
1-2-3 – Len Barry
Whatcha Gonna Do About It – The Small Faces
It's My Life – The Animals
My Generation – The Who

CHAPTER 18

Love Letters – Ketty Lester (London American 45-HLN9527 – 1962)

November 1965

Servicing one of the Lambrettas in Benny's workshop, Mack reflected on the past year. So much had happened. He had learned all there was to know about Italian scooters. Mick had taught him how to disassemble an engine to its component parts. He had also taught him to reassemble it all in perfect working order.

Mack had obtained his provisional driving licence on his sixteenth birthday. He had gone down to get it on the day from the offices in Hallings by St. George's Hall. No sooner was the tiny red booklet in his hands than the application for the driving test went in the post.

With help from the Jenkins, he had rebuilt a GT200 from two insurance write-offs. Taking the sound frame from one and the engine from the other he had assembled a whole new scooter. The greatest expense had come with the bodywork and side panels. The most time-consuming part had been at the beginning. Mick insisted on using powder-coating paint for an outstanding finish.

Re-sprayed tangerine and black the scooter stood out from the new ones in showroom. The quality of the paintwork was incredible, bettering the Innocenti factory original. The crash bars, rear view mirrors and front and rear racks had undergone re-chroming. Stripped, galvanised and dipped, the new chrome layer could now withstand British weathering. The cheap original Italian chrome finishes rusted after exposure to the British climate. There had been a few extra touches. The skimming of the cylinder head to increase compression was one such modification. Mick, who was always experimenting, fitted a modified carburettor and silencer. The scooter was much faster than standard GTs. The Jenkins saw this as advertising the possibilities of limited-edition custom specials. A great deal of time and effort had gone into the build. Mack did not have to pay them for their labour. They had given it free. Enquiries had soon begun from prospective buyers looking for a custom special.

The Jenkins had taken a genuine liking to him. Mack was conscientious. He was a quick learner, hard-working and efficient, and was

94

someone who shared their sense of humour. The three enjoyed having a laugh. It was a pleasure working for them. Hearing them fire off witticisms at each other was fun.

Passing the roadworthiness test, the scooter was ready for his sixteenth birthday. The whole had cost him £55 less than a new standard GT200. His parents were not pleased seeing him spend some of the money left to him by his late grandfather. But neither wished to make an issue of it, so not much came of the matter.

Between Adam and Mick, Mack learned the skills for passing the two-wheeler test. Each in turn had taken him on the test routes. Both had put him through rigorous drilling in all the manoeuvres until he was faultless. Mack was not only a quick learner, he was a natural on two wheels with excellent road sense. The Highway Code proved no problem. One of his strong points was the ability to learn and memorise information. He confounded his dad by being able to answer the most obscure rules of the road. Having taken the day off from school on a Friday, he had passed his two-wheeler test on Bonfire Night afternoon. Thanks were due to Adam and Mick's preparation. Passing the test, although nerve-racking at the time, proved easy. Mack took considerable pleasure in burning the 'L' plates. Attached to a Guy on a local bonfire that Friday night, they went up in flames. Within the month he had his pass slip converted to a full licence.

Adam and Caitlin had married. The Rocker rebel was all but gone. Only a week after Mack had passed his test Adam had passed his car test in a friend's van. Within the space of two weeks he had swapped his Triumph for a five-year-old Ford Anglia at his place of work. The leather jacket had been retired to the back of a wardrobe, along with jeans and riding boots.

A mortgage from a building society was unaffordable and out of the question. Jane MacKinnon had wanted them to stay but they wanted a place of their own. Adam and Caitlin had moved into a small rented two-bedroom terrace in Girlington. The MacKinnons had bought them a bed, wardrobe, settee, table, and chairs along with bedding. Even then Mack's mother kept buying baby clothes, nappies and so on behind his father's back – or so she thought. His father knew all about it but preferred not to notice the extra expenditure. Caitlin had given up work as the time for the birth had drawn close. The help given from the MacKinnons contrasted with the lack of it from Caitlin's parents. Bridget had bought a second-hand Silver Cross pram out of her savings and some baby clothes.

Old Man Halloran had disowned Caitlin. In the unlikely event that she had stayed he would have packed her off to Ireland. There she would have gone into a Mother and Child Magdalene Asylum. When the infant was born they would have put it up for adoption. The child would have disappeared into anonymity, most likely abroad. That was never going to happen. Caitlin had no intention of allowing it and nor had Adam.

Adam had confessed to Mack that if you got a girl in the family way you had to do the decent thing. The decent thing meant marriage and taking responsibility for your actions. If you were man enough to father a child, you had to be man enough to do the right thing. It was your duty and obligation to be a parent to the child and to support the mother. In Adam's case it was not only about doing the expected decent and right thing. It had the hallmarks of genuine love. The marriage and the birth of his daughter had not only matured him, it had softened him.

Adam and Caitlin had greeted the birth of their daughter with joy. Born on the fourth of June she had weighed in at six pounds six ounces. The arrival of the little girl brought delighted happiness to Mack's parents. They had become eagerly absorbed at becoming grandparents. Caitlin pretty much dictated the baby's name. In spite of Adam's protestations Caitlin insisted Jane would be the little girl's name. The choice had been Jane or having a female variant of his father's name. Adam had baulked at the idea of Roberta when suggested. Mack's rather jokey suggestions of Robertina, Bobette and Bobbie went down even less well. At least it had Adam in stitches. Caitlin decided the little girl's middle name should be her sister's.

Caitlin and Bridget had grown up at constant loggerheads. Their relationship had changed when Bridget found out about the pregnancy. It was Bridget who'd rallied to help Caitlin. The younger girls could not help much, although they tried in their own way. Deidre had even taken time out of her studies to knit baby things, assisted by Ellen. Before little Jane was born even Effy and Grace had managed to knit booties and hats. Meanwhile Aileen, the eldest sister, had turned more and more into a Holy Joe. Introverted, in constant prayer, a rosary in her hands, she locked herself away from it all.

A month after Jane's birth Mack and Bridget became godparents at the christening. After the baptism at St William's Mack decided to stop attending church. It was hypocritical pretence when you no longer believed. More so was the pain of seeing Effy each Sunday and pretending to be strangers. It was too much. The lyrics from Dionne Warwick's *Walk on by* kept playing in his head. In her letters Effy pleaded for him to keep coming on Sundays so she could at least see him. Writing back, he could no longer stand not being able to talk to her. He feared confronting her father in his frustration and anger. It would not end well if it did, and it had come close on more than a few Sundays. Mack was not prepared to jeopardise their relationship. Effy was too precious to him.

Meanwhile Bridget kept Caitlin informed about what was happening in the Halloran household. This leaked through to him piecemeal as he stitched snippets together from Caitlin, Adam and his mum.

Adam and Caitlin married in a mid-January Scottish wedding. The MacKinnons had seen this as the best solution to a difficult situation. Mack's family had relatives in Dalbeattie. Scottish law allowed marriage under the age of twenty-one without parental consent. Since Mr Halloran was unwilling to consent to the marriage there was no other choice. Adam and Caitlin met the twenty-one-day residency rule, stopping with relatives. Mack's grandmother made the journey from Edinburgh to attend the wedding ceremony. Granny MacKinnon, a widow, lived with her younger sister in the Scottish capital.

Adam and Caitlin married in St. Peter's. This happened to be one of the oldest Catholic churches in the area. The weather was so bad that the journey in the car with his parents took longer than anticipated. Rick Verity, one of Adam's rocker mates, had ridden all the way on his Norton to be the best man. Three others rode up with him to attend. They said it was a nightmare journey. The freezing conditions were the worst they had encountered. The day itself was sunny, bright but biting cold. After the wedding there was a get together at a local hotel where they stopped overnight. In the evening they had attended a ceilidh with Mack's relatives.

Bridget was the only member of Caitlin's family to attend. She had travelled with Mack and his parents in the car. It was thanks to her that Caitlin had all the necessary documentation for the wedding to go ahead. Bridget had not bothered to consult with her parents on the matter. Mack learned a good deal on the journey to Dalbeattie. Sitting in the front with his father as a navigator he was able to listen in on the chatter between Bridget and his mum.

Bridget confided information about life in the Halloran household to his mother. It was grim and that was understating the situation. Mr Halloran failed to send Effy and Grace to a Convent school in the Dales. Then correspondence came to light of plans to send his two youngest daughters to schools in Ireland. There was outright rebellion in the household. Her mother and sisters refused to entertain his plan. Effy made it clear she would run away if he tried to send her and Grace to Ireland. They would never find her. She would disappear without a trace. Knowing his family better than they suspected, her father conceded defeat, according to Bridget. More defiant than ever Effy had become the unspoken mutinous ringleader. Saying little, her every gesture betrayed the gulf existing between father and daughter. When it came to the girls' grounding Mr Halloran was better than his word. There was no relenting with his four youngest daughters. An eagle-eyed sharpness and attention to petty detail prevented them from going anywhere. Nor were they allowed to do any activity outside the home. He even collected them from school each day in the printing shop van.

What Mack found disturbing were the looks Bridget gave him after the wedding. With reluctance he had to partner her for a couple of dances at the ceilidh. It was no coincidence when she kept making references to Fiona with Caitlin and his mother. Mack found it puzzling that she referred to Effy only as Fiona. It seemed deliberate, the way she mentioned her sister in conversation while he was about. In doing so Bridget Halloran kept watching him. It was as though she wanted him to fall into a trap to reveal his feelings for her sister. Mack refused the bait. He had been exchanging letters with Effy via Grace's school friend, Jean.

Grace had arranged with Jean to meet him outside Wood's. That was how the new go-between arrangement began. Jean's friendship with Grace allowed her to come visiting to help with dressmaking. Mack passed the letters to her as she was on her way to the Hallorans' household. He then collected Effy's letters as Jean made her way back home. It was not always possible every week. Jean could not go round every weekend. She, too, had her own family commitments. So sometimes Jean and Grace exchanged letters in school. Otherwise Jean proved a willing and able go-between. It had worked well given the circumstances.

CHAPTER 19

Back in My Arms Again – The Supremes (Tamla Motown TMG 516 1965)

November 1965

While dropping in to see Adam and Caitlin Mack's visit coincided with Bridget's. Later he figured out it was no coincidence. Bridget's greeting was extra special in its warmth. He received an endearing smile, a hug and platonic peck on the cheek. An improbable thought crossed his mind. Was Bridget taking a fancy to him? Common sense told him it was most unlikely.

"Oh, I'm so glad you've dropped in. I have something for you." It was a pink envelope.

"For me?" came his stupefied response.

"Must be," Bridget teased. "It has your name on it. See? It says 'To Mack'. That's you, isn't it?"

One glance and he knew straight away it was from Effy. "I suppose it is," he admitted.

"Of course it is." Then Caitlin added, "'Fraid your secret is out, young man. We know about your teen romance. No use denying it anymore, brother-in-law."

"She told you then?"

"Eventually she did," Bridget revealed. "To be fair I knew quite a while beforehand. I overheard Effy and Grace talking about going to meet you at the local library. That was last year. I hope you're still fond of her. Going by her collection of your billets-doux I suspect you must be. How many letters did you write? One or two every week, about forty or so?"

"So you've been reading them?" He recollected his face reddening at the time of the admission.

"No. At least not as soon as I realised who had been writing them. Mind you, Effy did try to hide them. Almost did a good job. The giveaway was Grace's school friend Jean. I had my suspicions confirmed when I saw her exchanging some of your letters with those Effy had written. Finally, you know what I'm talking about, the silver necklace with the little heart? It was so sweet of you. To be honest, I had to make Effy tell me everything.

Getting her to confess was far from easy. A sister's pressures made her come clean in the end."

"Everything?" Mack had checked, wondering how much of their evening in the cinema had come to light.

"Why? Is there more we should know?"

"No. Nothing. Nothing at all." Mack had reddened even more recollecting the evening in the cinema.

"So? There's nothing more you'd care to reveal in a confessional the next time you're in church?"

"Bridget, don't tease the lad." Caitlin had laughed, nudging her sister with an elbow. "If he goes any redder he'll bust a blood vessel. He's near beetroot shade as it is."

"Okay. I won't tease him any more. At least not for now."

"So does this mean she can go out again on her own?"

"Not exactly. I'm working on it. It's unnatural, grounding a girl her age for so long. But my Da is as stubborn as he's stupid. Effy and Grace are now allowed to visit Caitlin as long as I'm with them as their chaperone."

"Oh, I see." His response was uneasy.

"No. I don't think you do. This Saturday afternoon, should you drop by, say around three o'clock, you may find us here."

The timing could not have been worse. He and Mick had arranged to put the finishing touch to the scooter rebuild. As it turned out Mick had not minded a change of plan. Mack had appeared at Adam's an anxious five minutes earlier than intended. As prearranged he had found Effy, Grace and Bridget waiting.

"There's not enough room to swing a cat in this living room," had been Adam's only comment as he poked his head round the door. "You and Effy go for a walk while the adults sit and talk."

"Be back in an hour," Bridget cautioned.

"And no patty fingers if you please. Observe the proprieties at all times," Grace had contributed as Effy, in her eagerness to be with him, made for the door. Once in the tiny hallway she had thrown herself into his arms, giving him a breath-relieving kiss.

"Close the front door behind you when you finally decide to leave," his brother had called out after thirty seconds or so. "And when you return make sure Effy has her lipstick back on while you've wiped it off before coming in."

Laughter percolated from the living room as they left grinning at one another.

West Park was round the corner. Mack could not help noticing how much Effy's appearance had changed. Her figure was a curvier shape than he remembered, though still slender and lithe. Her outfit was like those worn by the Mod girls he saw around the city centre. Absence had indeed made his heart grow fonder. Effy's passionate kiss had filled him with overwhelming intense relief. His own feelings towards Effy remained as strong as ever. If anything, they were stronger. Although he cherished every letter she wrote, it was her physical presence he had craved.

"Did you miss me?" Effy asked. Before he had a chance for words to leave his lips she had continued. "I missed you. Really, really missed you. It's been awful not being with you or being able to talk to you. Not being in your arms, not having you kiss me. I thought I'd never see you again. I thought…"

"You thought the same as I did," he had answered as they had sat down on a park bench.

"I'm sorry that I couldn't keep our secret from Bridget. I'm sure she's a mind reader. It was… "

"Never mind. We're here together now, that's all that matters. I can't even begin to tell you how much I've missed you. All I want to do is to have you in my arms."

As if on cue they kissed again.

"So have you've been doing some dressmaking and sewing and things?" Mack asked some time later.

"Yes, both Grace and myself have done quite a bit. Jean's sister has an amazing collection of sewing patterns. We've been tailoring them to fit us." He recollected how Effy had stood up. Unbuttoning her coat she had revealed a two-tone-style knee-length shift dress. The top part was white to below her bust line and the lower half black.

"What do you think?" She had looked uncertain, awaiting his response and approval.

"You made the dress? Seriously? It's not something you bought in a shop? Honestly, it looks amazing. Actually, you look amazing in it." Mack had not been lying. She did look amazing and he did believe the dress looked shop-bought. Not that he was a fashion expert where women's clothes were concerned. But as a Mod he knew what was at the sharp end of fashionable.

101

"I've made a few more dresses including a mini dress. Like the kind Jean Shrimpton models." He had watched her lifting the hem up four inches above her knee. "But I daren't wear it at home because it's so short."

"I'm well impressed." Mack had ogled her legs. "Can't wait to see you in that."

Effy had dropped the hem, blushing, aware why he had been staring. Instead of sitting down beside him she sat across his lap. Wrapping her arms around his shoulders she had nestled her face against his. Even now, recalling it, the memory aroused him.

Mack finished servicing the scooter. Calling Mick over to check his work he started the Lambretta with a single kick. The engine tick-over was smooth, never missing a beat. The horn and lights all worked. Mick grunted. "I'll take it round the block to make sure the clutch, gears and brakes are okay."

As Mick rode off Mack dipped his hands in the Swarfega bucket. Rubbing the green grease removing gel he cleaned up. A familiar-sounding scooter pulled up outside the workshop grabbing his attention. It was Tom's bronze Vespa Douglas that his cousin managed to stall while pulling it up on its stand in one motion.

"It's bloody brass monkey out on the road. I'm fro – zen." His cousin emphasised the splitting of frozen. Banging his hands together to restore circulation, he added, "I'm sure my balls have shrunk and disappeared inside me."

"Even with the paraffin heater on in here it's pretty Arctic," Mack agreed, admiring Tom's Parka. "Is that one of the gen M51 fishtails?"

"Sure is. Smart, eh?"

"Cool. Cost much?"

A sly grin appeared on Tom's face. "Don't ask. It was a steal deal. Want one? Got a couple to spare. To you £2."

"It'll have to wait," Mack answered, washing the greasy green goo off his hands in the filth-caked washbasin.

"Skint again?"

"Not quite, but I've got to make what I have last. Not like you working lads earning the dosh and throwing it around like confetti. By the way, how's the apprenticeship going?"

"It's shite. They keep picking on me but they do with all the new lads. Dad says I've got to live with it. Talk about getting the shit end of the stick. Still, it'll be a good trade once I'm qualified as a mechanic."

Mick returned with the Lambretta.

"Good enough, Mack. Sound job. It's all as it should be." Turning to Tom he asked, "Can I help you, sir?"

"It's okay. It's my cousin Tom. He's come over to see me."

"Ah, the infamous TC! Mack's told me zip about you other than your nickname," bantered Mick.

"You must be Mick, the infamous hairnet man." Tom responded with deliberate cheek. "Cuz says you're a genius mechanic even when you wear one."

"Cuz is right," retorted Mick, who was rarely modest, punching Mack on the shoulder. "Mack's not bad either. He could be a natural if he turned his hand to it full time. I take it you've seen the GT? Did most of it himself."

"Fair's fair, Mick," Mack protested. "That's not quite true. I couldn't have done it without you and your dad. You've both spent hours helping me, especially with the paint-spraying. It was all your handiwork. A brilliant pro finish..."

"Gawd, my head's swelling with all this arse-licking. Get him out of here before my head explodes." Mick slapped Mack round the back of his head.

"It's not time yet." Mack rubbed his head.

"It's quiet. I don't imagine we're going to have a last-minute rush in the next quarter of an hour. My dad's sorting the HP paperwork for the lad buying the Cento today. I'll see to the guy coming to collect this service job."

"Are you sure?"

"Yeah, no probs."

"Honest?"

Taking a crisp £1 note from his wallet Mick handed it over, joking. "Careful! The ink's not quite dry! Now bugger off before his Vespa gives me eye-ache. Listen, TC. Get a proper scooter. I can do you a good part-ex for a Lambretta."

"Nice try, Mr Hairnet. I'll stick with the Piaggio Clan for the time being. It's a real deal Mod scooter."

Once outside, Tom unstrapped a bulky package from his rear carrier. "Call it a late birthday prezzie."

Mack opened it to reveal a genuine US Army issue M51 fishtail Parka.

"I can't take this!" he protested.

"Don't worry about it. Like I said, it was a steal deal. Don't ask and I won't tell. Well, don't stare at it, mate. Get it on. I'm not riding alongside you until you look the part. I don't care how flash your scooter looks. You have to look cool on it when you join the 'in crowd'."

Mack exchanged his coat for the Parka with the fur-trimmed hood. Tom looked satisfied as Mack found himself in the over-sized ex-US army winter weather wear. At least a size larger, it buried him even with the thick inner liner.

"It's massive."

"You need it baggy. Looks flash when the wind makes it balloon like a sail. Anyway, you're a growing lad. You'll soon fill it out. Besides you can't join the 'in crowd' looking like a nonce. It's time you made the scene so we're going out on the town tonight in Halifax. You can bunk down at ours afterwards. But first we need to check out your threads to see if you have anything passable."

It was a relief. He was not seeing Effy until Sunday afternoon. Bridget was taking her and Grace shopping today.

CHAPTER 20

The "In" Crowd – Dobie Gray (London Records HL 9953 – 1965)

Saturday 13 November 1965

Tom's chuckling was continuous interspersed with occasional grimaces as he looked through Mack's wardrobe. "Mate, these are grim. You need some new gear. These slacks will do but as for the rest!"

"It's all I've got," came the glum response.

"Has Adam left any kit behind?"

"You're kidding. He didn't have much to start with and what's left would get me membership in a Rocker gang."

Tom became pensive. "It's only a thought. What about your dad? He might have something?"

"Now you're joking. Anything of his is going to be so baggy on me I'll look ridiculous."

"Can't do any harm to have a butcher's."

So they rummaged through his father's wardrobe.

"Not good, mate, not good at all. Mind you, this ain't bad." Tom picked out a tie with diagonal bars alternating deep burgundy and navy blue. "Would go well with a blue shirt and matching cuff links."

"That was Granddad's regimental tie, my mum's dad."

"Oh, the Brigade of Guards granddad?" recalled Tom.

"Yes. Grenadier Guards."

"The one who never forgave your mum for being a Wren in the Navy?"

"Yep. The same."

"Mum once told me he wouldn't speak to your mum after she married your dad. I asked if it was because he was in the Navy but she didn't say anything to that. I reckon it must have been the reason."

"To be honest I don't know. My mum never speaks about it. It's a bit of a taboo subject. Anyway, they did make it up after I was born. Thanks to him I've got the scooter. He left me some money in his will."

"Lucky you. I've got mine on HP. Dad had to sign the papers as my guarantor if I couldn't make the payments."

"So what about this blue Peter England shirt, Tom? Will it do?"

"Has he got some decent cufflinks to match?"

"Dunno. I'll have to ask him. The shirt will fit."

"One good thing at least."

"What's that?"

"At least you took my advice and got your hair cut real short. Half an inch all over and it suits. At least from the neck up you look the part."

"Gee, thanks, but if you remember I've had my hair cut this short before you did. At least my Sunday best brogues pass muster too. I suppose from my ankles down I look the part too, do I?"

Mack ended up wearing his dad's Peter England shirt with cadged cufflinks. The regimental tie, his own blue slacks and the shirt made a good match. The slacks, ironed until they had razor-sharp creases, looked smart. Robert MacKinnon gave permission to borrow his lightweight V-neck burgundy jumper. The complete outfit would pass muster. Tom suggested he packed everything in a tiny old battered suitcase in the event it rained on the way over and back.

After due warnings from his mother to wear his crash helmet, they set off. Taking the Queensbury route they made the journey to Halifax in twenty minutes. Both tested one another round the bends leaning into them at speed. They arrived in time for the evening meal. Afterwards they went upstairs to Tom's bedroom.

"Did you see *Ready Steady Go* this week?" asked Mack.

"Sure did. What did you think of Geno Washington and the Ram Jam Band doing *Que sera sera?*"

"They were good but I still prefer The High Keyes' version. It was the Spencer Davis Group that had me going with *Gimme Some Lovin'*. Stevie Winwood's soulful vocals and keyboard were superb. He's our age and look at how successful he is already." Mack spotted a record player. "That's new. When did you get it?"

"Last week. It's a compact Fidelity HF. Got it from one of the guys at the garage who was hard up. Even bought a couple of singles. Borrowed a few too. Got to show you some of the moves 'cos we're going down the Plebs tonight."

"What, dancing?"

"Catch on quick. You're going to meet some of the crowd. Once you're in with the right crowd you can join a circle and dance."

"A circle?" Mack looked puzzled.

"Okay." Tom grinned before continuing. "Lesson time."

What followed next was the etiquette involved. The detail was extensive as Mack listened trying to take it all in.

Tom summarised it one last time. "Let me go over it one more time. Don't forget. If you're friendly with some girls you can join their circle. They'll be dancing round handbags parked in the middle of their circle. If all the girls leave then so do you. As long as there's at least one girl in the circle it's okay to carry on. It all depends if you're on the pull. If you approach some girls you fancy chatting up but you don't know them you have to ask to join in. If you're a prospect with any of them they'll give you more than one dance. Then you can start chatting up. If it goes well you might get off with one of them. You have to agree in advance about who's targeting who, if two of you are on the hunt. If you're there to help out as a wingman you dance next to the girl your mate's not after. Does that seem straightforward enough? If your mate 'cops' for her and you're left with her mate you either keep her dancing or stop and have a chat. Few girls come in pairs because no lass likes to be on her own if her mate gets off with someone. They flock in threes or fours, making life easier or harder depending on how challenging you like it. Should they pick up their handbags and split in the direction of the toilets forget about them. They're a lost cause. If that happens, you drift off to find some friendly faces. Or dance with someone else. Or hang about and listened to the music like a spare part."

Tom finished the recap. Mack made one important comment.

"I'll help you out if you're wanting to pull a bird but I'm not out on the pull. I've got Effy and I won't go behind her back with anyone else."

Tom gave him a sickly grin as if to say he was being pathetic. "What the heart doesn't know, the heart won't grieve over. Okay. Dance steps next. Have you got a copy of this one?"

It was The Marvelettes' *Too Many Fish in the Sea*. The dance steps were simple. Two slight knees bends one way and then the other. Arms bent and always in the direction of the knee action. Finger clicking or finger popping if the record played was a good one. Since there was hardly enough room in the club, moves had to be simple. The place was too crammed for anything more.

Tom cautioned Mack. "Forget all the silly dance moves you've seen shown on *Ready, Steady, Go*. No one does them except for clueless bastards."

"What time are we going down town?"

107

"No point before eight thirty. We'll meet up with some of the crowd down in George's Square and I'll introduce you to them. I reckon your Lammy is going to cause a sensation. There's some cracking scooters down on a night but they've seen nothing like your GT."

Filled with apprehension Mack could not contain himself waiting to set off. Tom, meanwhile, was preening his appearance to perfection. After a lengthy ordeal of squeezing a few blackheads out he was still far from ready. Zits eliminated, it was decision time. What should he wear? By the time 8.30 rolled round Tom was still performing fine adjustments to his attire. Finally, he unscrewed the bottom of a piggy bank that he kept inside his bedside cabinet. He took out a small plastic bag.

"Smith, Kline and French's best," he smirked, counting out a few blue pills. "What we now call blues but what the newspapers call purple hearts. At least that what they called them when they were triangular shaped. Want to try a couple?"

Mack was aghast. "No thanks. You don't take those things, do you?"

"'Course I do. Everyone does who's on the scene. Getting popped up gives you extra feel-good energy to keep going. Sure you don't want to try a couple? It's a once-only free trial offer. After this you buy your own."

"How much do they cost?"

"Depends. These cost me 6d each. It's all about supply and demand. If there's a lot circulating then they can be this cheap but when they're scarce as much as 1/6d. You can also get Bombers, Dominos and Dexys. They're all amphetamines. Bombers are all black capsules. Doctors dole them out to women wanting to slim. They kill the appetite but they also give you a major buzz. Dominos or Dommys are the black-and-white versions of Bombers. Dexys are Dexedrine tablets and the last resort for a good night out. Sure you don't want to try?"

"Positive. I'll give them a miss if you don't mind."

Mack watched his cousin shrug his shoulders at his refusal. Tom swilled down two or three with some Ben Shaw's Lemonade he kept by his bedside.

Parka on, Mack prepared to take his helmet when Tom said, "I wouldn't bother. Unless you want to get it nicked. I've got a spare flat hat you can borrow."

Tom had the workingman's flat hat unbuttoned from the peak rammed over his forehead. It resembled a German Afrika Korp field hat when unbuttoned. Mack tried his tan-coloured spare on but it was so big it went down to his nose. Buttoning it again, Mack turned the hat around so the peak was at the back.

"Now that looks cool. It could catch on." Tom looked impressed. "Trouble is it'll blow off when you're riding."

Mack took his brother's old spitfire style goggles from his helmet. Strapping them over the hat onto his eyes, he adjusted the strap. "There. Howzat?"

"An impressive look, my man. Could catch on. In fact I'll have to get some like yours and do the same. Right. Let's go to the Go Go. Don't forget, a stylish entry into the Square is a must. If the birds think you're Steve-McQueen cool and stylish, you've got prospects. Could be tonight, could be later too, 'cos style is everything. Birds go for the sharp look."

"I'm not out to impress any girls, Tom. Helping you out, I'll give it my best shot."

It was a typical November night. The cold was made worse by a breeze which was made worse by the rush of bitter cold against the face. The journey down town took five minutes. By the time they were on Commercial St. Tom was adopting a laidback seating position. Mack wondered how his cousin could ride without eye protection. His eyes had to be streaming exposed to the rushing air. Then, before he could knew it, they were signalling to make the right turn into George's Square. The place was full of teenagers, all Mods. Scooters took up all the curving pavement edge at the bottom end of the square. All except Tom's were Lambrettas. Mack estimated there had to be at least forty or fifty scooters parked, with more arriving. Finding a space three scooters along from Tom's, he dismounted and put it onto its stand.

Unlocking the toolbox below the seat Mack thumbed a two-way switch. This cut power to the ignition. It was an extra safety measure Mick had wired in to prevent someone stealing the scooter. Lambrettas were notorious for being easy to steal. The ignitions were worthless. A thin screwdriver could open the key lock. Even with a non-standard ignition fitted it was still possible to start one up. A group of Mods chatting by their scooters were immediately drawn to them. Tom was straight into the chat.

"This is Mack, my cousin from Bradford. He used to live in Halifax so he's one of us. Mack, meet..." And so the introductions began. Mack spotted three Mod girls heading towards the group.

CHAPTER 21

A Wonderful Dream – The Majors (London Records HL-P 9602 – 1962)

Saturday 13 November 1965

"I can't stand living here any longer." Ellen was in floods of tears. "I swear I'm going to run away. I'm fed up being a prisoner bossed about by him."

Effy and Deidre sighed in unison. Grace interjected. "You think that's bad. I'll be the last one left in this Alcatraz of horrors. It'll be another four years and more before I have a chance to escape."

"Stop being melodramatic, Grace," Deidre responded in a flat voice. "When you're alone after we've left and in solitary confinement make use of the time. Become an expert on birds like Burt Lancaster in the movie. Then you can be Grace the Bird Woman of White's Terrace."

"It's all right for you to joke," Grace continued over Ellen's crying as she seethed with resentment. "You'll be in Manchester from September for five years at Medical School. I bet you'll never come back once you've left."

Deidre remained silent. Grace was making an accurate diagnosis.

"I don't know if I can last out." Ellen sobbed out the words. "I want to go down to Strawberry Hill and train as a teacher. They want me to stay here and become a nurse. I'm not even interested in nursing. All Da seems to want is to pressure us into doing what he wants. Not what we want."

"If Bridget leaves I couldn't stand it," added Grace. "I overheard her telling Mum if he didn't stop behaving like he does she was moving out into a flat. That would be dreadful leaving us to his mercies."

"He's put me off religion for life, especially this past year. What with prayer hour every evening, followed by the rosary, he's lost it. If this is what it means to be a Catholic I want no part of it." Effy made her stance clear with icy detachment. "I refuse to join in any longer."

"He lost the plot a long time ago, even before Caitlin's pregnancy. I can't believe Aileen has decided she wants to become a nun! A nun!" Ellen repeated it as though it were too surreal. "They've brainwashed her. That's what they've done."

"She locks herself away in her room and prays all the time. It's not healthy, it's not normal," added Deidre.

110

"Why would anyone want to lock herself up in a convent praying all day and all night? It makes me shudder," contributed Grace.

"No, it's not healthy," Effy agreed. She was half listening, half daydreaming, wondering what Mack was doing at that moment. Was she in his thoughts? She wished she could cuddle up to him. They had so few opportunities to be together. Every moment she had with him was precious. Effy only had to imagine being with Mack to feel intimate sensations stir. Sometimes when daydreaming she could recall the taste of his lips on hers.

Only last night drowsing in bed she had fantasised about him. Her thoughts had strayed into a haze of wondering what it would be like having sex with him. In this dreamy languorous state she reached a pleasurable release. Her soft moans had woken Grace.

"Are you all right, Effy?" Grace had asked, more asleep than awake.

"Go back to sleep. I was having a dream. A wonderful dream," she had replied.

CHAPTER 22

Come On Over to My Place – The Drifters (Atlantic AT4023 – 1965)

Saturday 13 / Sunday 14 November 1965

"Who's this, TC?" asked the tallest girl wearing a three-quarter-length dark green leather coat.

"This is Mack, my cousin from Bradford. Mack, this is Angie."

Mack acknowledged her and the two friends with a nod of the head. She was stunning, jet-black hair styled in an asymmetrical bob, contrasted with a fair complexion. Dark brown sparkling eyes checked him out with a curious intensity.

"Is that like…" She paused for a moment before adding with a flashing smile, "As in plastic mac?"

"If I had a penny for every time I've heard that I'd own a Mini Cooper by now," He answered, surprised at his confident comeback.

"So what's it short for?"

"MacKinnon. It's Scottish."

"Oh, so you're Scotch?"

She was trying to be humorous at his expense.

"Scotch? No. That's whisky. I'm part Scottish. My Dad's a Scot, my Mum's English. I was born here in Halifax."

Tom introduced Angie's two friends as Linda and Carol. It was obvious where Tom's intentions lay. The brunette with the big breasts trying to explode through her brown suede coat was the target. Linda turned out to be the girlfriend of one of the lads he had met called Steve. The girl called Angie walked over to his scooter, admiring it, keeping eye contact with him as she did.

"So, you've passed your test? No 'L' plates, I see?" Angie's hand slid with a provocative touch along the length of the leather saddle.

"Yes."

"Bet this cost a pretty penny to buy?"

"He built it himself," Tom announced, proud of Mack's achievement.

This appeared to surprise her. "Wow. Clever boy. I am impressed. How about taking me for a quick spin round town?"

"Maybe later," Mack replied, taken aback by how forward she was.

"Go on." Tom egged him on. "We'll wait for you two. When you get back we'll go down the Plebs."

Mack did not want to appear unsociable. Nor did he want to spoil Tom's chances with Carol. Donning his hat, RAF goggles and gloves, he restarted the Lambretta with a single kick. Angie climbed onto the pillion, having wrapped a silk scarf over her hair. He dropped the GT200 off its stand, backing it out from among the other scooters. Clutch released, he accelerated with blistering speed to the roundabout at the top.

Mack had fitted a pillion backrest. Instead of leaning back against it Angie wrapped her arms around the lowest part of his waist. Any lower and her hand would be playing with his manhood. He took the road towards King Cross. By the time he was passing People's Park he knew her hand placement was deliberate. She proceeded to tighten her grip on his waist. Through his parka he felt her breasts pushing deep into his back. Returning to George's Square he manoeuvred into a vacant parking spot. In a deliberate move she grasped each of his thighs near the top, sinking her fingers between them. This was as close to touching his manhood as was possible without doing so. He had extended his feet to the ground preparing to bring the scooter to a stop when it happened. The startling shock of her grip made him wobble the Lambretta to an erratic stop.

"We must do it again sometime," she said, climbing off the scooter with a bewitching smile aimed at him. Removing her headscarf she walked away with Carol. Still smiling, she gave him a long, knowing backward look. Once the girls were out of hearing, the comments began.

"Bloody hell! Did I see her grope you?" Tom exclaimed in an awestruck voice.

"Looks like she's bee-lined for you tonight, mate," prompted one of the lads he thought was called Alan.

"Talk about a man-eater. If he plays his cards right tonight she'll drop her knickers for him." Mack recalled this was Geoff. The comment had more than a hint of envy. "Lots of us have tried to cop off with her, but she's a fussy bugger. She's picky, make no mistake. When she does, it's farmer time – as in sowing your wild oats."

"Seems like you could have cracked it there, my son," added Alan.

"Give her one from me if you do," leered Vic with unconcealed lasciviousness. "Tom will do her mate Carol tonight."

"He'll be lucky. Carol keeps her legs crossed," Alan informed Vic. "I tried and got as far as her stocking top before she stopped me. She's like a clam. Keeps it shut tight."

"Well, I'll have to give it my best shot to prise the clam open," Tom responded with a mysterious smile.

"Assuming he gets off with her," Mack contributed.

"Oh, TC will." Other similar comments peppered the air. A lewd rendition of Junior Walker's *Shoot Your Shot* followed as they walked to the Upper George Yard.

"Better make sure you shoot your shot in the right hole," advised one of the lads whose name he could not recall. "Don't forget it's the one at the front, not at the back."

The Plebeians Jazz Club was the heart and soul of the local scene. Located in the cellar of a semi-derelict Victorian warehouse. It was the top venue. Entry to the club was down some steps illuminated by a red light. The Soul Sisters' *Good Time Tonight* was playing as they arrived. It was a record Mack already owned so it was looking and sounding good already. He received his red inked pass out stamp on the hand as he paid. Taking his parka off he followed the others to the tiny cloakroom down on the left. As The Soul Sisters ended Smokey Robinson's high tenor voice began to blast out with *Going to a Go Go*.

The main dance area was already packed. The only illumination came from the tiny stage at the end. Half a dozen girls were dancing there, living the dream of being Go Go dancers. It took a few moments for his eyes to adjust to the darkness. The pack of lads began to disperse around the edges. Mack stuck close to Tom as they worked their way along the back, passing the mesh grill concealing the DJ. There was a small alcove beyond it with seated couples kissing and cuddling. From their vantage point they could make out most of those dancing. Angie and her mates, along with Steve, were in a circle. Tom nudged him, indicating with a nod they should join them.

Mack made a quick decision, slipping between Linda and Carol. Tom was between Carol and Angie. By doing this he thought he could avoid direct contact with Angie. He was here for the music and the dancing, not to find himself a girl. Effy was the only one he wanted.

The dance tempo slowed as The Impressions' *It's Alright* came on. What Mack did not expect was Steve and Linda dropping out on the next record. They disappeared into a seat made vacant and look set for a long-haul snogging session. As the circle closed up he found himself next to Angie. This was not going to plan. What was worse, he could see Carol proving receptive to Tom's advances. They seemed in no immediate hurry to leave the circle. Mack wondered what excuse he could use to leave them but no excuse came to mind. They managed a whole half-hour of dancing before breaking away without warning. Mack, now dancing with Angie, wondered how to extricate himself from the situation. The earlier phrase "man-eater" sprang to mind as she danced closer to him. Then the DJ dropped the tempo completely, spinning The Drifters' *I've Got Sand in My Shoes*.

Any thought of an exit strategy came too slowly. Before he could react she closed the gap, putting her arms on his shoulders for a slow dance. There was no choice but to put his hands on her hips. It would have been wrong to refuse to dance, especially as she had made the move seem so natural. His hands touched her hips for a few seconds and then her arms went from his shoulders to entwining around his neck. She made no attempt to kiss him. Instead her body against his was explicit in what she had planned. Her hypnotic eyes gazed into his, striving to take control of him. There was a faint smile at the corner of her mouth that he was finding irresistible.

She was wearing a discreet yet intoxicating perfume. This was nothing like the floral kind his mother sometimes wore. Nor was it like the light, soft, feminine fragrance favoured by Effy. It was impossible to ignore Angie. The spicy, musk scent emanating from her was enticing. She was closer than close. If he had tried to slip a ten-shilling note between them it would have failed. Her breasts pressed into his chest. She performed a slow sensuous grind against his manhood with an inevitable result.

This girl knew exactly what she was doing and so did he, inexperienced as he was. She was seducing him. The worse part was that it was proving hard to resist Angie. Pulling her head back, she teased him with those tempting dark brown eyes. His erection stiffened as she pressed her hips even closer against him. She was doing it with deliberate intent, massaging him in an erotic way using her abdomen. Mack could not believe a girl could carry on in this way. The record came to an end and the next went up-tempo. To his relief she pulled away from him although he sensed she was reluctant to do so. He recognised the record in an instant. It was Wilson Pickett's *Don't Fight It (You Got To Feel It)*. The lyrics were not lost on him as the "Wicked" Pickett rasped out the words. Mack had not fought it while she had felt it.

When the record was about to finish Angie suggested they should have a break, taking him by the hand before she led them through the throng of dancing bodies to the refreshment area, which was a relief. She shielded his trouser-bulging erection as they pushed through the crowded dancers. Mack bought her a Coke. Conversation was impossible over the music. Angie suggested they should go outside to cool off. It was steamy inside the club and it sounded like a good idea.

"So tell me all about yourself, Mr Mack," she began the conversation as they sat down on the step outside the club.

"Nothing much to tell." Mack thought it wiser not to tell her he was still at school. Now he looked at her, she looked a little older than he had first thought.

"Where do you work?"

"In a scooter garage," Mack replied, trying to sound casual. It was true insofar as it went. Being prudent with the truth was a good idea. "What do you do?"

"Guess."

"Still at school?"

"No. You must be joking!"

"Some kind of office work?"

"I work in a chemist's as an apothecary assistant."

"Have you been there long?"

"About two years. Since I left school."

So she had to be seventeen, or older. Mack suspected she might not take kindly to being a cradle snatcher if she found out how old he was.

"So do you like working there?"

"It's okay for now. As part of the job I have to go to Bradford Tech to do the dispensing assistants' course."

They chatted about the things they liked. Mack began to relax. It didn't seem as if she wanted to snog him. Even so he was sure she was she was intent on being more than friendly.

"Can we go back inside?" she said after a while. "I'm getting cold out here. You might be stuck with me this evening."

Their pass out stamps received a cursory glance on re-entering the overheated cellar. As they reached the bottom of the stairs she took his hand once again, pulling him onto the crowded dance floor. For the next hour they danced and time appeared to stop. For Mack the music was amazing. When Willie Mitchell's *That Drivin' Beat* blasted out of the speakers the place

116

erupted. It was everything he listened to at home and more he had never heard before. The music was awesome. The thought crossed his mind that nothing was going to happen. Angie was being a tease or as Tom liked to say, "a prick tease".

Angie spotted a spare vacated spot along the side and dragged him over to it. Next thing Mack knew he found himself seated with Angie on his lap, her back to him, looking out on the dancers. To keep herself balanced she got him to put his arms round her waist and then leaned back into him. Try as he might, he could not control his manhood. The erection was back. Tom and Carol appeared from nowhere. The girls exchanged words into one another's ears.

"Listen, Mack. I'm taking Carol back home on the scooter for a bit of you know what," Tom whispered in his ear. "So I'll see you at our place later, alright?"

"Alright."

"By the way, Angie's missed the last bus so can you take her home on your scooter? Good man. Doesn't appear the man-eater's hungry tonight." It was an obvious dig.

"I suppose you're off to taste clam, then?"

"You betcha. See ya at the Ponderosa, Hoss."

With that they disappeared through the crowd before Mack could respond to the insult. The club was beginning to empty with fewer dancers left.

Angie swivelled round on his lap and placed her hand on his left shoulder. "You don't mind taking me back home, do you?"

"No, why? Are you wanting to go?"

"Not yet. Let's dance." She stood up. They continued dancing until Fat's Domino's *It Keeps Raining* played. This, she told him, was one of the two records played to end an evening in the club. When the lights came on he could see the black polythene sheeting covered the ceiling. Sweated condensation starting to drip from them. They collected their coats and left the club.

CHAPTER 23

The Wrong Girl – The Showmen (London American HLP 9571 – 1962)

Sunday 14 November 1965 – After midnight

There were still a few scooters parked in George's Square as they rode out of the town centre. Following Angie's directions they came to Saville Park. Taking a side road, Mack remembered it was close to his childhood home a few streets away. Angie lived in a large terrace house along Manor Drive. The cold night air was bitter, hovering above freezing. She insisted on luring him in with the promise of a coffee even though it was the early hours of the morning.

The fire was still burning behind the safety guard as he sat down on the settee. Tasteful modern G Plan furniture filled the warm living room. Emerging from the kitchen Angie brought two mugs of coffee on a tray.

"Won't your parents mind me being in their house this late at night?" he asked, somewhat concerned about her parents finding him alone with her. The last thing he needed or wanted was a confrontation with an angry parent.

"Don't worry." Angie put a hot mug of coffee in his hands. "My dad works nights and doesn't come in until eight in the morning. He's working the weekend shift so we're alright. Anyway, he wouldn't mind you here in the living room though he might if he caught you in my bedroom."

"What about your mum?"

"Her?" Angie gave a quiet restrained laugh and sat down next to him. "She's out for the count. She's on Valium during the day and sleeping pills at night. If a bomb went off she'd sleep through it. Nothing's going to disturb her. My sister Gillian is a nurse and is away on a family planning course. We're as good as on our own."

"I see." He sipped the coffee, wondering what was coming next.

"I've got you all to myself so don't worry." There she was teasing him again with those brown flashing eyes devouring him. Mack thought he was being stripped naked mentally by her. The crazy thought came to him that it was guys who did this to girls, not girls to guys.

"I've got a…" he began, wanting to explain about Effy.

"Girlfriend? That's all right. I had worked that out. Most blokes can't wait to come on to me. You seemed too petrified to do so. I knew you were

118

not a homo." She giggled, reminding him of the bulge in his pants. "And you're not exactly bashful. I figured there had to be a girl in your life."

"Right."

"Doesn't mean I don't want to make out with you."

"Right."

The desire in her eyes became clear. "I need you to understand I don't want a steady boyfriend. I'm not interested. I don't want to settle down. Not for a long time. I want to have some fun."

"So what are you saying?"

Angie shook her head bemused. "What I'm saying is… I want to borrow you from your girlfriend for an hour or two this morning. Then she can have you back."

Taking the coffee mug from his hand she placed it on the coffee table. Straddling his lap, she pinned him under her knees. He watched her dress ride up, exposing her stocking tops. Placing a hand on each side of his face, she gave him a long intense tender kiss. Mack's mind was in turmoil as his whole body stiffened. He did not want to go behind Effy's back. Effy meant everything to him.

"Relax." Her warm breath in his ear excited him as she nibbled his ear lobe. "Enjoy it."

He should have stopped Angie. Instead here he was succumbing to her advances. It was all happening so fast. In his inexperience he did not know how to handle it. Not that he had had much of a chance to do otherwise. It was wrong. It was so wrong. He was betraying Effy but aroused by Angie he could not stop.

"Remember, Mack," she whispered in his ear, her hand feeling the bulge in his trousers. "It's a one-off situation. I want to have my wicked way with you. I don't want you falling in love with me or any such nonsense."

"Why with me?" he almost stuttered, trying to get the words out.

Angie's answer took him aback.

"What?" She began pulling the zip down on his trouser fly, pausing to nibble his ear lobe again. "It's not only you fellas who get urges? Let me tell you, we women get urges too. Right now I want you so much it hurts. I doubt you would believe how much. I can't seem to help myself. The moment I caught sight of you tonight I knew it had to be you. I had to have you. Call it animal instinct or lust or whatever you like but that's how I felt."

119

She had him exactly where she wanted. By the balls. Her hand had worked its way down into his underpants. "I need what you have inside these inside me."

"Aren't you scared of getting pregnant?"

She gave him a mysterious smile. "Stop worrying." The next thing he knew they were going up to her bedroom, with his hand in hers. Once in her room he watched her pull out a small container from a cupboard drawer. She took out an object resembling a rubber-shaped dome.

"What's that?" he asked. By now he was doing everything in his power to stay calm.

"It's a diaphragm. I put it inside myself and it acts as a barrier stopping your man goo making a bambino. I'm going to the bathroom to fit it. I won't be long. Get out of your clothes and into bed," she ordered.

"Are you sure about this?" Mack could not believe what was happening. It was unreal.

"No. I was having you on." She looked back at him, pausing for effect. "God, you're so naïve. Yes. I'm sure, really sure. Now be a dear. Slip into bed and warm it up for me. And I want you in it stark naked so be quick."

As she left it came to Mack that he was about to lose his virginity. This was the Holy Grail all young men his age dreamed about. Stripping down to his Y-fronts he slipped under the quilt between the sheets of the single bed. As he waited for her to return he looked round the room. There was no mistaking this room for anything but a true boudoir. With stuffed toys and dolls on a chair in one corner it couldn't be otherwise. There was a small white dressing table with a mirror and lots of small items laid on the surface. The room was a little larger than his own and done out in a pink and white patterned wallpaper. Angie was gone about five minutes before returning, having removed her dress. Wearing a lilac full slip trimmed with purple lace, swaying her hips, she sat down on the side of the bed. Teasing him she began to undo her stockings from the suspender belt. He was betraying Effy but aroused by Angie he couldn't stop. Undoing the suspender belt she dropped it on the floor. Taking the slip off revealed a matching lilac bra and lacy briefs.

"Help me with this hook, will you."

Mack found himself undoing her bra. Angie hid it under her pillow saying, "I hate putting them on first thing in the morning when it's cold."

Mack could not take his eyes off her breasts. They were not large but firm and his first close-up sight of naked female breasts since infancy. Angie smiled, pleased to see him ogling her naked breasts. "You can feel them in a moment when I get under the sheets." She displayed no shyness whatsoever delighting in his appreciative glances.

Still wearing her briefs Angie cuddled up to him in the bed. "I'll let you take them down when you're ready. But let's not rush it. Try to make it last. Don't worry about going in. I'm not a virgin but I'm certain you are." Before he could answer she had placed a finger on his lips to silence his denial.

He put a free hand to her breasts, feeling the delicate softness of her skin. Gliding over his body her feather-light caresses explored him with gentle slowness. Then her lips gave him tiny kisses, moving down his chest and stopping short of his underpants.

"I thought I told you to take them off." Pulling back the bed covers, he watched Angie remove them and drop them beside the bed. "You won't be needing these for a while."

Under the covers once more, Angie's hand moved to his thigh. The next thing he knew she was stroking his testicles and moving along the shaft of his penis. It was all he could do to prevent himself from ejaculating.

Taking his free hand from her breasts, she guided it down inside her briefs. The pubic hairs were soft to the touch as his hand slid down to her opening. She was sticky wet, warm and willing, murmuring faint almost inaudible words in response to his touch.

"Kiss my breasts," she whispered. Mack complied, finding it arousing. As he did so his finger slipped into her. This was unlike any descriptions about sex he had read in books and Tom's stash of men's magazines. Withdrawing his finger he began a tactile probing of the opening. His fingers encountered a curious fleshy button. Massaging it with gentle firmness he wondered what it was. Angie's reaction was instantaneous and electrifying.

"Oh, God!" Angie cried out. "Don't stop, don't stop! Keep doing it! You've hit my sweet spot!"

She was writhing under his touch. Without warning she touched his hand, stopping the motion. Her body convulsed. Her opening sprayed a fine wetness into his palm, taking him by surprise.

"Take them off!" she commanded, urgency in her voice. "Quick before I come. I want you inside me right now."

121

It was easier said than done but he somehow he managed to get the briefs off. Parting her legs he spread them straddling her as she guided him inside. The sensation of entering was intense and exhilarating. His heart rate hit a crescendo as he penetrated as far as he could. The sensation as her vaginal wall contracted round his erection was extraordinary. Three pushes matched by three swift contractions from Angie's and he emptied into her. Angie's fingernails dug into him, one hand gripping his back and the other his buttock. He heard her moan and hoped he had not hurt her.

So this was sex. It was brilliant, it was incredible, it was everything and more than he had ever imagined. He had lost his virginity at sixteen to an amazing looking girl. He withdrew from her as his erection faded. Both were breathing hard from the exertion.

"I didn't hurt you, did I?" he asked.

"Well," she began, "I've never come so fast and so hard before. It was a real ten out of ten fuck. You definitely hit my sweet spot. Boy, were you good. And no. You didn't hurt me. I was enjoying it too much."

The use of the "f" word was startling. Girls swore?

She reached for a couple of Kleenex on her bedside cabinet. "Better clean yourself up. I don't want my mum finding your starch stains on my bed sheets."

She disappeared into the bathroom down the corridor. He heard the tap running. Angie returned a few minutes later to find her briefs and slip them back on. Clambering back into bed she cuddled up beside him. "You'll have to go in an hour or so."

Afterwards felt awkward but in a good way. Mack asked, "Have you had sex lots of times before?"

"No. No, I haven't. Some of the lads down the Square think I have but I haven't. Ninety nine per cent of them I'd never let near me. You are a one-off exception. I'm not a slut even if I'm behaving like one tonight."

"Don't say that. I don't think you're a slut."

Almost as though she hadn't heard him she continued, "It's not right. Fellas can be Jack the Lad and sow their wild oats while we girls get a bad reputation for doing the same. They seem to forget. Every time they have sex before marriage it's happening with some girl who has feelings."

As an afterthought she added, "A lot of girls are going to get wet dreaming about you when they're in their beds."

Hearing the female side of it was a major revelation. It had never occurred to Mack to see sex from a girl's perspective. Many things in his recent life began to make a great deal more sense, especially about Adam and Caitlin and not forgetting his relationship with Effy. Angie told him all about her past experiences.

Her first sexual encounter had happened before she had left school, with a boyfriend. He was five years older and she was underage. When her much older sister found out, she got her the diaphragm, fearing Angie would get pregnant. The romance had broken up when he left her not long after for a woman his own age. Since then, sex had only happened twice with one other bloke and now with him. Angie told him she enjoyed having sex but was going to be careful with whom and when in the future. She had no intention of getting a venereal disease or getting pregnant. Nor did she want to be stuck in a relationship like her mum and dad until she was sure she had met the right person. Getting married just because she'd had sex with somebody was stupid. When she found somebody who would love her and treat her right, then she would settle down. They talked for quite a while. Angie even asked him to tell her all about Effy.

That was unreal, almost surreal, talking about Effy after what they had done together. Strange as it seemed he didn't feel as guilty as he knew he should. Angie said Effy sounded a sweet girl who needed him in her life given what had been happening to her. This was crazy coming from a girl with whom he had just had sex. A while later, she had began to fondle him again. Before long they managed to have sex a second time. Soon after they finished Angie rose, slipping on a dressing gown. It was time for him to get dressed. It was time to go, though he felt reluctant to do so. He would have liked to stay longer. Dressed, she ushered him downstairs. As he fastened up the parka she took hold of both his arms.

"When you see Effy don't say a word about this to her. It wouldn't be worth it. Trust me. It would wreck the good thing you have together. She's too young to handle an upset like this. I'm guessing too nice because you're such a lovely fella. I know what it did to me finding out. Please don't let it happen to her. Tonight never happened. Are we clear?" she reiterated. "You'll see me lots of times again down at the club. We can dance and we can chat and we can be friends. Good friends, I would hope. I'd like that. But that's it. Don't avoid me. Don't ignore me because you have some kind of guilt trip. Promise? I'll always remember tonight, as I'm sure you will. I'm glad I was the one you lost your virginity to. Truth is, I'm actually closer to being eighteen and you must be sixteen. There's a difference in our ages. And if you turn up with Effy one Saturday night don't be afraid to introduce us. We'll pretend nothing ever happened because this is our secret and it will stay our secret."

"I understand. I don't believe I would ever ignore you. It will remain our secret. Promise." He pretended to pull a zip across his lip.

"Don't ever forget, feelings are something you have," she said, "not something you are. That's what tonight was all about."

"Do you know Angie, you're... amazing. I bought this Ketty Lester record called *Some Things Are Better Left Unsaid*. It's your advice in a song."

"Lend it to me sometime." She gave him one last kiss and then pushed him out in the frosty cold early morning.

There was no silencing the scooter as he pulled into the back yard. Tom had left the back door open. Mack tried to get up the stairs without making a noise but failed. Every step creaked, sounding loud enough in the dark to wake the whole of Halifax. As he neared the top of the stairs he saw his uncle standing on the landing, "It's not a burglar, is it?" He heard his aunt's concerned voice.

"No. It's another alley cat returning after a night on the tiles."

"Sorry," Mack apologised in a whisper. "I didn't want to disturb anyone."

Entering Tom's room he found his cousin sitting up in his bed with the light on. The sleeping bag was on the floor ready for him. He began stripping off again. "Can't you sleep?" he whispered.

"No," replied Tom in a whisper. "I'm still high. Got to wait for the blues to wear off so I can come down. Come over here. Got something for you." Mack sat down on the edge of Tom's bed.

"What?"

Tom stuck the first three fingers of his right hand under Mack's nostrils. They had a salty pungent aroma. Not unpleasant, but with an odd familiarity, recognizable from his own recent experience.

"God, is that what I think it is?"

"The clam got prised." Tom grinned. The triumph was evident. "You've now had a sniff and whiff of Carol's poontang."

"You're disgusting."

CHAPTER 24

Some Things Are Better Left Unsaid – Ketty Lester
(RCA Victor 1394 – 1964)

Sunday 14 November 1965 – Later in the day

When she did not see Mack sitting in church Effy became upset. Had he been involved in an accident on his scooter? Seeing his parents seated in their usual place she realised that could not have happened. Mack had restarted attending Mass again after their reunion. Seeing him even if only for a brief while in church meant everything and Mack understood it. She loved him even more for doing this knowing how he felt about religion and her father.

The thought of him injured in hospital was too awful to think about but seemed unlikely. Was he unwell? If he was she would not see him at Caitlin's in the afternoon. The thought was distressing. Grace could see how Mack's absence had upset her sister.

On returning home, Effy found it hard not to mope. She tried to avoid brooding by busying herself. Attempting to revise for her mocks proved impossible. Struggling to concentrate on irregular French verbs, her thoughts kept returning to Mack. Time passed with unbearable slowness. Clock-watching only made it harder. Then the terrible supposing began to run through her head. Supposing he had become tired of her. Supposing he no longer wanted her for his girlfriend? Supposing he had found another girlfriend?

When the time came to set off Bridget found Effy in her coat pacing up and down raring to go. Bridget exchanged amused glances with Grace but neither dared to say anything. The walk to Caitlin's became a race walking competition. Her sisters tried asking Effy to slow up. In the end Bridget and Grace let her race ahead.

It was ten to three when Effy turned the corner of the street where Caitlin lived. There was no scooter outside her sister's house. The anguish was beyond words, a pain in her heart. Bursting into the tiny living room she found Caitlin by herself. There was no sign of Adam and worse still there was no Mack. The disappointment showed. Caitlin knew straightaway why Effy was verging on tears.

"Mack's not here. That's not like him. I do hope nothing's happened to him?" The words echoed her concerned despondency.

"Not yet. He may be late, Effy. Stop fretting."

"Where's Adam?"

"Upstairs trying to get Jane to sleep."

Effy slumped down onto the settee in silence. The supposing began all over again. It only ended when Bridget and Grace finally appeared. That was when she noticed the three sisters exchanging glances with each other.

"I'm being silly, aren't I?" Effy sighed. "There'll be a good reason why he wasn't at Mass today."

"More than likely," was the collective response.

Adam came downstairs, noticing the strain right away. "What's going on?"

One glance at Effy told him everything. "Now then, Eff, there's nowt matter with him. He went over to Halifax with Tom yesterday afternoon on the scooter. They were going out together last night. Aunty Ellen must have made him stay for Sunday dinner. Don't worry, lass, he'll roll in before long like a bad penny."

"You shouldn't say that about your own brother. He's a good lad," Caitlin chided him.

Effy supposed Adam was right.

Mack had overslept. The Sunday roast turned out to be breakfast. Tom was the worse for wear, experiencing the dreaded come-down effect of the amphetamines wearing off. Neither had slept much as Tom could not stop talking: another side effect of the pills. A thorough strip wash brought Mack round. Real or imaginary, he thought he could detect Angie's scent on his body. He was behaving like a criminal concealing the evidence. If he ended up kissing Effy she might notice. Although he kept reliving having sex with Angie it already seemed unreal. There was only one course of action he could take. To pretend his encounter with Angie had never taken place, that it was a figment of his imagination. There was no way he could hurt Effy. The more he thought about his behaviour, the more he realised that feeling guilty wasn't going to help. When it came down to it he still loved her more than anything. Yes, that word love was there again. She meant everything to him. He had done the unthinkable by betraying her trust in him and he would have to live with it. Angie was right in cautioning him to say nothing. Logic told him he would only be admitting his guilt for his own sake, not for her sake.

126

Mack looked at his watch and made his excuses to his aunt and uncle for leaving in a hurry. Thanking them for having him he made a dash to get back to Bradford. Tom had already arranged for him to stop over the following Saturday. On his way out he reminded Mack that next weekend it would be an all-nighter.

By the time he reached Adam's house Mack was forty minutes late and cursing. There had been a heavy downpour. The parka had a degree of water resistance but was not up to torrential downpours. A lack of sleep together with the drenching from the rain had left him looking terrible. Before he could say anything to Effy or her sisters his brother spoke first.

"You look like a drowned rat. Take that soddened parka off out there. We don't want water all over the living room floor."

"Pass it over to me, Mack," said Caitlin, showing more kindness and patience. "Let's see if we can get it drying out in front of the fire. What's the rest of your clothing like?"

"Dry-ish except for the trousers."

"Stop joking. Look at the state of them. You'd better take them off. Adam, get a pair of your old jeans for Mack to wear while I try to dry these in front of the fire."

"Come on, sunshine. Let's do what the boss says. Be quiet when you go up. I've only just managed to get the baby off to sleep. Don't want her waking up."

"So you put baby to bye bye's? You do surprise me. Dad would never have done it."

"I'm not my dad. She's my child. Why shouldn't I do it? There's nothing sissy about a father putting his child to bed."

"No." Mack found himself agreeing. "I suppose you're right. We don't have to be like the older generation, do we?"

When Mack came down Caitlin told Effy to go into the kitchen to make him a hot drink. Mack joined her. Once alone in the kitchen Effy gave him a quick hug and kiss and then set about making him a mug of Bovril at his insistence.

"Effy, I'm sorry I'm late. We were up most of the night. To be honest neither Tom nor myself got many zeds."

"I'm glad you're safe." The relief on Effy's face was tangible. "I was so worried that something bad might have happened to you."

Mack took her into his arms, hugging her to him while they waited for the kettle to boil. "I'm so sorry for making you worried."

"What were you doing, to stay up so late?" Effy asked. At that moment, looking into those innocent emerald eyes, he knew how much she cared about him. Mack also realised how much Effy meant to him. Sticking as close to the truth as he could he would omit everything that happened with Angie. Mack told her all about the club, the fantastic music, the dancing and the atmosphere. Rather than pretend not to have spoken to any girls he mentioned Angie and her friends. Effy listened as they drank their coffees.

"Were they pretty?" came the inevitable question within seconds.

"Yes, especially Angie." He paused, taking great care over what slipped off his tongue next. "But she's almost eighteen and not as pretty or attractive as you."

It was true that Angie was older. Angie was, well… stunning and attractive, yet so different in every way from Effy.

Mack added, "She's almost the same age as Caitlin." This stopped short of telling the lie that Angie could not fancy him given her age. That would have been untrue. It had not been love but sheer lust on her part and, on reflection, his too. Effy seemed to accept the age difference. She could not imagine someone Caitlin's age taking much notice of Mack, as good-looking as he was.

"Somehow," he continued, "we have to find a way for you to come with me. You'd love it. It's an amazing spot. We could have a great time dancing the night away."

Effy sighed. "Oh, I wish I could, I do. I'm so fed up with life at home. I'm so miserable and so are my sisters. Sometimes I begin to wonder about Ellen's sanity. She's desperate to break free from the home that's become a prison. To make matters worse, my father's insisting she becomes a nurse and stays here. Ellen's heart is set on becoming a primary school teacher. As far as she's concerned she wants to get as far away as possible from home. She wants to go and train down South in Twickenham. Only Deidre knows she's got a get out of jail card because they want her to become a doctor. So it's all right for her to go to Manchester as a medical student. As for Aileen, well, she's always been a bit of a Holy Joe. Now she's decided to become a novitiate nun. If it wasn't for Bridget I don't know what would happen to Grace and myself. To make matters worse Bridget's threatening to leave home and get her own flat. I couldn't stand that. She's the only one who won't put with up my father's nonsense. Otherwise our lives would be horrendous. The trouble is she can't do anything more than that. Her life can't be brilliant. She's never had a boyfriend. At least not as far as I'm aware because she's never mentioned one. That's not right either."

Mack did not know how to respond to this intense flood of information. Her family life contrasted with his family life and his cousin Tom's family life – and for that matter his school friends' lives too. It was unbelievable to the point of cruel absurdity. The only thing he could do was to be reassuring and give her tender hugs. Effy was not done. Sobbing as she spoke, the turmoil kept pouring out of her.

"Neither Ellen nor Deidre know about us. One day Ellen is going to find out. How will she react knowing I've kept us a secret all this time? At least knowing I have you has helped make life bearable. Ellen never had a chance to get back in touch with the boy she was seeing when it all blew up. Imagine how it would have been for us not seeing each other without Grace and Jean? Bridget thought it better not to say anything and keep it quiet under the circumstances. Can you imagine how Ellen's going to feel?"

"It might be best to tell her before she finds out. I can understand why none of you have said anything about us. But it might be better to come clean before it's out into the open." Mack response was calm and measured.

"Oh, I'm not sure about that…" Effy commenced but trailed off.

"The longer you keep the secret the worse it will appear. Ellen will think you didn't trust her to keep it secret. Besides, I could do a Grace and get in touch with her boyfriend and let him know the score."

"It's too late for that now. He was in the Upper Sixth at Bradford Grammar and went off to Cardiff Uni last summer. There's no chance of them getting together again."

"Well, I suppose we could try to find her a fella."

"Oh, and exactly how would they go out on dates?"

"One of my teachers keeps telling us that there are no problems. There are only solutions we haven't found yet."

"Okay. Find a way to solve our problem," Effy entreated. "I would love to go out with you to Halifax and stay out most of the night. I can't imagine how you can solve our problem."

Mack gave her a crafty smile. "I have a germ of an idea but it all depends on Adam, Caitlin and Bridget to make it work."

"Go on…"

"Effy, I'll need to have a chat with them to sound it out. Until then, you'll have to be patient. Remember. To every problem, there is always a solution."

"Jimmy Mack," Effy said, looking him in the eyes, "I do hope you have one."

"What did you call me?"

"Jimmy Mack. I'm sorry I wanted to use your name and it came out like that."

"It's a cool-sounding name. I don't mind it."

CHAPTER 25

Everything's Gonna Be Alright – Willie Mitchell
(London HLU 10004 – 1965)

Tuesday 16 November 1965

"Do you realise what you're asking us to do?" Caitlin queried.

"Even if we agree to go along with your idea, Effy's still too young. She's only fifteen," added Bridget.

Mack played his next card with tactful coolness. "She's sixteen in two weeks' time."

"That's still a bit young," Bridget countered.

Mack resisted the temptation to mention she would soon reach the legal age of consent and all it implied. Effy would then be old enough to elope and marry in Scotland. That would not be politic after what happened to Caitlin and his brother. Somehow he had to convince them of his idea. This involved bringing something more to the discussion.

"And what about Ellen? Effy tells me she doesn't even know about us. How's she going to take finding out about us and how we've been meeting in secret this past year? Deidre doesn't even know, does she? I bet neither of them will be too pleased you've been keeping them in the dark. Effy already feels guilty about deceiving them. Isn't it time they knew? Isn't it time they all had some freedom too? Now's the time seeing as your dad's begun to slacken his supervision. He's no longer even bothering to pick them up from school."

"That's easier said than done," Bridget responded. "Ellen's not like Effy. She's prone to emotional outbursts. If she had known about you two she might have let it slip by now. I don't think she would mean to do it. The problem is she's susceptible to saying things without realizing. As for Deidre, I don't believe she's bothered about boys."

"Why? Has she ever told you? Or is she less of a bookworm than you think? You can't tell me Caitlin and Effy are the only girls in the household who like boys."

"Less of the boy," Adam butted in. "Mack has a point. From what I've seen Ellen's frustrated she's denied male company. As for Deidre, well, she may be a bookworm but it doesn't mean she never daydreams about young men. If I was a betting man I wouldn't take the odds."

The time had come for Angie's words to find a voice in this conversation. "Guys are not the only ones who have urges. Girls do as well. It's normal and don't kid me you don't."

"That's what worries us about you two," Caitlin responded.

Mack was up to the challenge. At some point he knew they would raise the spectre of Effy getting pregnant. "I'm not going to get her pregnant. I would never do that to her because we're both too young. I've too much respect for Effy. Besides, you and Caitlin are warning enough where that's concerned."

Going on the offensive was working. If they had reservations about his conduct then they were disappearing.

"Seems to me," Adam intervened, "he's learned from our mistakes. Let's face it, if anything is going to put them off it's seeing what happened to Caitlin and myself. Especially since the baby was born. Nothing like nasty terry-towelling nappies to put a bloke off. Not forgetting being short of money all the time."

Mack wrinkled his nose, remembering Caitlin changing a nappy – although watching Effy do a nappy change without getting squeamish proved thought-provoking. Still, it was the kind of things girls needed to know for the future.

"Look," Mack continued with his gambit. "Let Ellen pretend to do some 'babysitting', sharing it with Deidre. Then let them go out somewhere like the cinema on a Saturday or Friday night. Effy and I could do the same every other weekend night. I promise I'd bring her back before the scooter turned into a pumpkin."

Observing the sisters' responses he could see his proposition was under genuine consideration. He needed to add a little more. "Ellen would think twice before being loose-lipped. Especially if she knew she would wreck her chances of going out by saying the wrong thing. Anyway, we don't need to tell her everything straightaway. I'm sure Effy and I can pretend we haven't known each other long, at least for a while. We could broach the truth later."

"So are you contemplating going into sales as a career after leaving school?" Bridget turned to Adam and Caitlin, joking. "I bet he could sell London Bridge to some unsuspecting tourist given half the chance."

They continued to discuss the matter for another half hour. It was getting late in the evening. Bridget had to get back home and needed to catch a bus. It was inclement, cold and drizzling. Adam offered to drive her home but Mack suggested taking her down on the scooter. Bridget kindly declined his offer but agreed to a lift in the car. Mack needed to get home since he was facing a mock exam the following afternoon. Last-minute cramming confronted him. Worn down by the arguments Bridget left the decision to Adam and Caitlin. If they agreed to the plan she would go along with it. Yet Bridget knew she would have to be the one who made the proposition to her sisters. Mack was confident they would go for it. Then there would have to be an admission about Effy and himself. This he could and would handle.

Adam came round the following evening to collect a few things he claimed to have left behind. His actual purpose was to have a word with Mack. "God, you're some salesman, sunshine," he greeted his brother, who was busy in his room revising.

"Hi, what's up?" mumbled Mack, his concentration disrupted.

Endgame.

"Bridget agrees to go along with the idea."

Check.

"Seems she's had a bellyful of dealing with her dad. But it's not without pre-conditions from the three of us. You have to agree to them or no deal. We'll want your word on them, and Effy's, too."

Checkmate.

"First, no going out until you have done your mocks. I don't want you blowing your chances of passing exams like I was stupid enough to do."

Game over.

"Done."

"Next. No staying out all night. We want her back in the house by midnight and definitely no later than one in the morning. Got it?"

"Got it."

"And the obvious! I don't want my young sister-in-law preggers. Clear? It's for your own good too. Capiche?"

"Clear."

"You get her a skid lid and something warm and waterproof to wear. You also take care when she's on that hairdryer of yours."

"Okay."

"I mean it. No showing off or doing stupid things to impress her."

"Like you did with Caitlin."

"I'm not kidding, Mack. I'm serious. If anything happened to her or to you we would have to live with it for the rest of our lives."

"All right, I get it. No worries. No taking risks. Anything else?"

"Yes, now you mention it."

Mack groaned. "What else?"

"Our mum and dad don't need to know about this, got it?"

"Fine. Done and done."

"Good. On Friday we'll work out the mechanics using a diary."

It was beginning to get annoying.

"Oh, and one more thing."

"Go on."

"You and your little love bird better get your story straight for her sisters. Don't forget to warn little Grace about it, either."

"Wilco and out."

"Don't give me that Biggles bull-shite either. So what do you have to say to your big brother?"

"Dunno, what do I have to say to my big brother?"

Adam skimmed the top of his head as though giving him a pretend slap. "Thanks would be nice."

Mack thanked him. As an afterthought he asked, "I'm curious about Bridget. How come she doesn't have a fella at her age? Has Caitlin ever told you why?"

"All I can tell you is she has and she hasn't. Caitlin won't spill the in's and out's of it so I've given up asking. Seems there is a bloke in her office. That's all I know. I suspect she's scared to tell her parents about it. It's strange. My money's on a married guy but that's my wild guess. What I do know is she's said she won't leave until Grace has finished school, though I wouldn't bank on it. Sean Halloran's becoming more of a fruitcake with each passing week."

"Well, I suppose we'll find out sometime. Anyway, I'm glad things are turning out alright for you and Caitlin. Mum and Dad stood up to the crease to help you two out. It can't have been easy for them or for you."

"Oh, they had good reasons for helping us out."

Mack gave Adam a quizzical look. "What do you mean by that?"

"You're a bright lad."

"Yeah, I like to think so. What's it got to do with anything?"

"Good at sums?"

"Not bad."

"Enjoy a bit of history?"

"I do actually. Where are you going with this?"

Adam gave him a peculiar look. "When you've got a moment or two sneak into their bedroom. Bottom of the wardrobe, Mum's side, you'll find family documents and things. Take out their marriage certificate and do your Sherlock Holmes on it."

"Why?"

"I reckon you'll work it out. Take a look at the date when Mum got discharged from the Wrens. Her Navy discharge papers are there along with our birth certificates."

"Is there some great mystery about this?"

"Check it out. Mum and Dad aren't quite as respectable or prim and proper as they'd like you and everyone else to believe."

"Oh, yeah?"

"Oh yeah. A most definite yeah! Old Chinese proverb, Confucius says, many nails to build one crib but only one screw to fill it." With that pearl of wisdom he was gone from the room, leaving Mack puzzled and mystified.

CHAPTER 26

Mohair Sam – Charlie Rich (Phillips BF 1432 – 1965)

Thursday 25 November 1965

Mack was unwell on the Monday morning. During the night he developed a high temperature. This culminated in feverish sweats and a sandpaper-sore throat. In the morning he awoke leaden and lacking his usual get up and go. Every atom of energy had drained from his body. His mother dosed him with Aspro. Staying in bed he tried to do some revision but was too ill to do much. Mack was almost never unwell. Missing school was something he had not done for years. His recent day off for taking the two-wheeler test had been the exception. Getting soaked on the scooter was the cause of his being unwell according to his mother. Mack doubted her diagnosis, suspecting a virus instead. Then on Wednesday, perking up, he had an unexpected visitor.

Dave Bean had decided to take a sickie. They had been in the same registration group until the end of Fourth Form until Dave left school. Rather than stay on in the Fifth the lure of a plumber's apprenticeship proved too strong.

Dave had changed in that short while becoming a Mod too. In his smart black leather coat and wearing a three-piece suit he looked the business.

"Took the day off on a sickie. Thought I'd come visiting as I was passing and saw your scooter was outside. Thought you had to be in. What you got? 'Flu?"

"No. More like a heavy cold or a virus I picked up. How's plumbing working out for you?"

"It's bloody filthy work. Especially when you have to take out old toilets and pipes. Bends caked and clogged full of shit are a bit nasty. Drains aren't too clever either. Not the cleanest work, but you know what they say? Where there's muck there's money. Nothing truer. It's a good earner even as an apprentice so I can't grumble. Gaffer's a bit of a bugger at times, but he's okay. I like your scooter. Man, it's a work of art. Word doing the round is you built it yourself. That true?"

"I had help," Mack replied, not feeling much like talking about it. "What you been up to?"

For the next hour Dave enlightened him about his doings on the Bradford Mod scene. Mack learned top Bradford Mods or Faces went to a club in Manchester called The Twisted Wheel. Dave had been a few times and was now going most weekends with the real Bradford 'in' crowd. The Continental in his opinion was for the local "Tickets" or "Numbers". Dave defined these as Saturday night Mods, not the gen article. The gen article went to Manchester, usually to the Wheel or sometimes to The Oasis or The Jigsaw. Tickets and Numbers went to the Continental and envied the style of the "Aces" and "Faces". The real deal oozed style and class at all times in the way they dressed, walked and talked. Paying attention to the smallest details in all things was key to avoid being a "Ticket" or "Number".

Removing his leather coat Dave showed off his suit to Mack. It was a classic dark blue pinstripe. The jacket, fitted at the waist, had a three-button fastening with slanting pockets and two 10" vents. The top pocket contained a crème-coloured silk hanky. Under the jacket, he wore a matching waistcoat.

Dave had bought a roll of cloth from a local mill shop and then had it made up by a Jewish tailor on Green Lane. He was having another one made up. It would be ready in a fortnight. You didn't have to go to Burton's or John Collier's. With a bespoke tailor you got an original hand-stitched suit to your individual specs. It could cost less than buying from High Street chain-stores if you sourced your own cloth from a mill shop.

Dave entertained him further with tales of his recent pill-taking. This confirmed that most Mods were taking them at the weekends. His priceless gem of a tale was about a gate-crashed party. He had sneaked into the home of a top Face in Allerton.

Having managed to get a girl into one of the bedrooms he believed he was about to score. Crawling under a pile of coats he had hitched her skirt up and pulled her knickers down. Trousers round his ankles he had been on the verge of jumping her bones. The Face whose party it was had yanked him off her, throwing him out with his trousers round his ankles. It had been a downright embarrassing interruption. Dave couldn't stop laughing recounting the incident.

Dave's visit cheered Mack up no end. By the following morning he was back in school. By Saturday, he was working at Benny's as usual. It was to prove an eventful morning.

CHAPTER 27

Stupidity – Solomon Burke (London American HLK 9763 – 1963)

Saturday 28 November 1965

Saturday mornings at Benny's Scooters were busy and trouble-free. An occasional customer might dispute the cost of a repair with Benny but that was all. No one attempted to steal items although Mack had learned how to spot ones who might. They had a tendency to lose their nerve when Mack made it clear he was onto them. Today the small showroom was busier than usual. Serving a regular customer he saw Mal Osborn and three of his mates entering the showroom. Their far-too-casual manner alerted him at once. Shifty looks eying up the merchandise set sirens off in his head.

Mack had seen Osborn in the shop before. On that occasion Benny had come in from the workshop to get something and had stopped to watch his every move. Not long afterwards Benny banned Osborn and his gang from the premises. They had attempted to steal some kit. Benny and Mick were in the workshop completing a repair. Although both Benny and Mick had warned him to ring the buzzer if anything was going on, today he would not have time. Giving every appearance of buying something, Osborn was covering two of his mates. They were tying to be surreptitious in attempting to help themselves to a fly screen. Mack spotted them as they were about to free it.

"Excuse me a moment, will you, sir." Mack addressed the customer he was serving as he came out from behind the counter. In a voice that rang through the showroom he warned them. "Put it back, please."

As he strode towards them they froze midway in the act of thieving.

Osborn stopped Mack with a palm thrust to his chest. Threatening Mack he attempted to intimidate him. "You don't want to do that, pal. You should go back to the counter before you get hurt."

He was as tall as Mack, weighed at least a couple of stone more and was at least a year older. According to rumour Osborn was the *numero uno* thug around town. In street parlance, the bear-like bricklayer's mate was more like a German Tiger tank. Mack never paused to consider the potential consequences. Grabbing Osborn's fingers from his chest in one swift move he bent them as far back as he could. Almost in simultaneous motion, using his left hand, he locked Osborn's arm at the elbow. With a twisting motion, he forced Osborn's finger to point upwards at right angles to him. Swift pressure from Mack's foot behind the knees brought him to the ground. The split-second timing and speed took his opponent by shocked surprise. Disabled Osborn yelped in agony from the pain. There was nothing he could do as Mack stood on the back of his knee, keeping his arm and wrist joints locked in an excruciating painful hold. Someone was ringing the buzzer furiously but Mack was too preoccupied to take notice. One of the thieves he didn't recognise by name pulled a flick knife from nowhere. A huge ring spanner, hurtling at what seemed like a bullet, hit the knife hand with tremendous force. The impact caused him to scream in agony and drop the weapon. Seeing what was happening, the other thief scarpered, followed by his accomplice.

"Don't even think about picking it up," he heard Mick's voice bellow. "If I hit you with this one you'll be coming round in hospital with your jaw wired. All right, Mack, let him go before you break his wrist or arm. Not that I'm right bothered but it would mean having the coppers round."

"Get off me, you fucker!" Osborn kept repeating in frustrated anger. Mack applied pressure once more as a reminder of the pain he could inflict. Releasing his grip he let Osborn go. If Osborn tried anything Mack intended to plant a kneecap in his gut.

"I'll fuckin' get you for this, you bastard. I'll rip yer 'ead off and stick it up yer arsehole."

"You reckon? It might be me doing it to you instead," came the stone-cold reply. As an afterthought Mack added, "Next time I will."

Mick rushed down the aisle, pushing past him and clutching the biggest wrench Mack had ever seen. Looking like a man possessed, he chased Osborn and his mate out of the door. The customer he had been serving, a middle-aged man, had had the presence of mind to bang the buzzer on the counter. Mack hadn't heard it in the fracas but was glad when he found what had happened. If Mick Jenkins had not come to his rescue, dealing with a flick knife could have been deadly.

"You want to be careful, young man," the customer said, looking relieved. "That's as nasty a bunch as I've ever seen. I reckon one on one you could have given the big bloke a real hiding. But with his mate pulling a knife on you, well, it could have turned out bad."

When Mack reflected on those words he knew the man was right. One thing was for sure: this was not going to be over until it was over. The

Osborns of this world always came back for more. It was then that the adrenaline shooting through him left him trembling like an aftershock.

Mick stormed back in. "Never seen them move so damn quick. Bloody bastards. Fancy pulling a bleeding knife, that's what you'd expect from a wannabe doing it the coward's way. I swear I'd a brained him with this wrench if he'd gone to pick it up. You okay, Mack?"

"I'm fine, and thanks. It was going to turn ugly if you hadn't arrived. Still, I'd have warned his mate to back off or I'd break Osborn's arm. He wouldn't have done anything because I would have. I'd have left in no doubt about doing it, too."

"Break his arm?" Mick sounded astonished. The customer looked incredulous. "You're bull-shitting me."

"No, it would have been dead simple. I could have snapped his arm like a twig."

"You should have hit the buzzer instead of taking them on. They haven't been round for while. They must have figured you'd be easy and bottle out of a confrontation. What the hell were you doing to him? You had him yelling in well-deserved pain."

"It's a kind of wrist lock they use in Japan."

"What? Like Jiu Jitsu?"

"Yeah, something like."

Mack explained he had seen it in a book on self-defence borrowed from the library. Practising with Tom, he had learned a few of the moves including that one. He had never expected to use any of them. Now he found it amazing how effective this move had been.

Mick and the stunned customer regaled Benny on how Mack had dealt with Osborn. Much to his embarrassment, he had to demonstrate the move on Mick in slow motion.

"A clever move, I must admit. And you learned it from a book, you say?" Benny was thoughtful at the same time. "The trouble is, it's a one trick pony. He'll never fall for that again. And I'll be honest. They're a bunch of villains. He'll come looking for you, mark my word."

"Well," replied Mack, sounding complacent, "I'll worry about that when it happens."

"Dad, we should introduce him to Leonard. What do you think?" suggested Mick.

Father and son exchanged glances. "Not a bad idea, son. Leonard's the man when it comes to street brawling."

140

"Who's Leonard?" Mack asked.

"His nickname's 'Thirty-seconds' because his fights lasted less than thirty seconds," Mick explained.

"You'd like him, Mack. He'd like you. He's a born and bred Scot too, like your dad's side of the family. Married a local lass and settled here in Yorkshire. Lives a stone's throw from your house. He's a widower now. Served in the Argyll and Sutherland Highlanders in Korea back in the early Fifties."

"So why should I meet him?"

Mick chortled. "Leonard worked as a part-time bouncer in some of the dance halls when he came out of the army. He was a pro when it came to beating up troublemaking Teddy Boys. On one occasion he took on five of them at once. It was his longest scrap. It took him a whole two minutes to deck 'em all. Man, he's legendary. A quiet chap, slow spoken, not big and brawny like you'd expect a bouncer to be but well 'ard."

"I'll pop round and see him," said Benny, and he did.

Benny's description of Leonard Macintyre was unerring in its accuracy. Mack guessed he was at least ten years older than his father. Softly spoken, his Highland accent differed from his dad's Edinburgh accent. His terrace house was modest. The living room still had echoes of a woman's touch, even though his wife had died five years earlier. Photographs of her were everywhere. They did not appear to have had any children.

"Benny's told me how you dealt with Osborn. He said it was impressive. Show me exactly what you did to him in slow motion on me."

So Mack obliged, taking him through the moves one step at a time.

"And you say you learned this from a book? Impressive to say you mastered it from photos. The Koreans have a system of fighting using the same kind of methods. Full of locks, twists and pressures against the joints of the body. I remember seeing a demonstration a long time ago. It takes a great deal of training and practice to become accomplished."

Leonard went on to describe what he had seen in the Second World War and the Korean conflict. Then, after a while, having offered Mack a mug of tea, he got down to business.

"Do you go looking for fights, young fella?"

"No. Why would I?" Mack answered. "But I won't let anyone walk over me because they think they can."

141

"Good answer. What I wanted to hear you say. Benny gave you a good character reference. Coming from Benny, high praise indeed. He's also told me about the chap you put down. Clowns like him seldom learn their lesson the first time. His type always comes back for more. When he comes back let's make sure it's the last time."

Mack spent quite a few evenings after school sparring in Leonard Macintyre's back yard. Learning his street fighting techniques left Mack full of admiration for the man. The five techniques he mastered were simplicity aimed at ending a fight as soon it began.

At their last session Mr Macintyre told him, "Remember what you've learned. Fists are for fools. There are better things you can do with your hands and other parts of your body in a fight. Don't forget. What hurts the most is the blow you don't see coming. That applies both ways. Self-control is the important thing in any brawl. Know what you're going to do, stay focused, never lose concentration. If you ever have to sort him out come back and let me know how you did."

CHAPTER 28

Sweet Talkin' Guy – The Chiffons (Stateside SS 512 – 1966)

February 1966 – Revelations

What would Deidre and Ellen say when they found out Jimmy Mack was her boyfriend? Effy experienced a deep sense of guilt knowing she had to confess her deception. How would they react to her admission? Would they feel she could not trust them? Would they ever trust her again when all became known?

Neither Ellen nor Deidre understood why Effy was tagging along with them to Caitlin's. It was not her turn to go visiting. Bridget explained it away by saying now the mocks were over she could join them. Grace was not going so it made visiting easier. As they had left Grace had signalled crossed fingers to Effy wishing her good luck. Grace would have loved to go along under more normal circumstances. She liked to see the baby and play with her. Today was not going to be normal. Under the circumstances it would be better if she stayed away. Effy was a bundle of nerves and it showed. They trudged through the dirty slush that earlier in the week had been pristine snow.

"Effy, whatever's the matter?" Deidre showed concern. "Are you not feeling well?"

"She does look a bit... I dunno..." said Ellen, observing Effy, "a bit funny? What's the matter, sis?"

"Nothing, I'll get over it in a little while one way or another."

"What do you mean by one way or another?" persisted Ellen.

"Leave her be, Ellen. No doubt she's worrying about something and nothing. You know what's she like." Bridget pretended to be dismissive but could not help feeling a little anxious herself. This was not going to be an easy afternoon.

Effy's nervousness made her feel ill. Deidre and Ellen were solicitous and becoming over-concerned. This only made her feel worse, wondering how they might feel towards her shortly. Deidre even offered to walk her back home but she was steadfast in refusing. By the time they reached Caitlin's house Effy was trembling. How would they take the revelation about Mack and herself? Had she been awful keeping it secret all this time?

143

How would Mack explain it away to them? On and on the thoughts ran through her mind. At least Bridget and Caitlin would be present. Unzipping their boots, removing their coats, they came into the living room. Caitlin was sitting in an armchair by a blazing fire breast-feeding the baby. Adjusting her clothing, she greeted them as they entered one by one, with Effy last.

The settee seated two. Bridget made sure Deidre and Ellen squeezed in beside her. Caitlin took one look at Effy and told her to come over and sit on the armrest by her. There were voices coming from the kitchen. Effy immediately recognised Mack and Adam talking. She couldn't make out what they were saying. Whatever it was they sounded cheerful and in good humour. Hearing Mack's voice was enough to cheer her, too. They did not have long to wait for the two brothers to come into the cramped living room.

"I take it you all know my brother, James?" announced Adam, adding, "Although one of you knows him much better than the rest."

"Will you make everyone a cup of tea or coffee, Adam?" Caitlin asked, making it clear what was about to take place. Deidre was about to volunteer when Bridget intervened. Pushing her back down into the settee she went instead. Mack went over to Effy. Taking her hand in his, he kissed her on the lips. Then he sat down on a free chair, making Effy sit sideways on his lap. Effy blushed but was proud of how he seemed to take command of the situation. Even Caitlin, used to Mack and Effy together, raised eyebrows at how he was broaching the subject. It was daring and theatrical.

The expressions on Ellen and Deidre's faces were priceless. Effy smiled with relief, almost feeling more at ease.

"Effy and I did not mean to have secrets from you. We decided it would be best if we came clean about ourselves. We've been seeing each other. That is, insofar as the situation in your family has allowed us. We've been going out for walks on Saturday and Sunday afternoons for a while."

Deidre interrupted him, speaking to Effy. "Good for you, Effy. No wonder you looked a little nervous coming here. That explains everything. Now I come to think of it I thought there was something strange going on every Sunday at Mass. I thought I was imagining it at the time how you kept glancing at him. Now it makes sense."

Deidre's comment came as a surprise; she had more to say which proved astonishing. Renown for her reticence, Deidre sprang to life.

"You must have got to know each other here when visiting Caitlin. Oh, how sweet! I'm delighted for you! Well, James, she's a lovely girl but I suppose you'll know that already."

"She is," Mack confirmed.

"Wait a minute," Ellen joined in, recovering from the surprise revelation. "You were with Effy at the Elite that night, weren't you?"

"Yes, I was. You're right. You were late coming to meet her. We had to wait for you to turn up so you could walk home together."

"Of course." Ellen gave him a suspicious look.

Mack was prepared. "That was the night Caitlin came to stay at my parents' house after your father told her to leave. Mind you, I didn't know that at the time. It came as a bit of a shock. I had to sleep on the sofa for ages afterwards."

"I see," said Ellen, accepting Mack's version. "So when Caitlin married Adam and Effy came visiting with Grace she already knew who you were. Oh, it all makes perfect sense now. You'd better treat my sister right, James, if she's your girlfriend."

"Oh, he does and I'm sure he will. He's a perfect young gent," Effy added.

"No wonder you wanted to have a night out with each other," said Deidre. "It's so logical. Effy must have told you lots about us being prisoners at Colditz Halloran in the war against Opus Dei."

"Something like that." Mack found himself bemused by Deidre's descriptive response.

"So, if we pretend to babysit for Caitlin we can manage to get out and have a bit of fun? Go to the pictures, meet up with our friends and such?" Ellen brightened.

"It'll have to be every other week," explained Bridget, bringing in a tray of hot drinks. "You'll have to pretend, mind you."

"Won't you want to go out with Adam?" asked Deidre.

"Goodness no! We can't afford to go out. Adam's not earning enough. If it wasn't for his parents helping us we couldn't manage. His mum buys quite a few of our groceries for us, not to mention the baby's clothes. They even bought us this second-hand TV set. Adam has to coast the car down hills to save on petrol."

The revelation shocked Mack. He had no idea how difficult they must be finding it.

Caitlin continued. "I'm so grateful to Bridget, too. She's been a real tower of strength."

145

The conversation turned to the logistics of going out and how it would work. At some point in the conversation Deidre made a staggering announcement.

"Look," she began. "If Ellen and Effy come and pretend babysit every Saturday night it will keep matters much simpler."

"But won't you want to go out?" Effy protested, surprised.

"Surely you'll want a night out with your friends?" queried Bridget.

"I have my A Levels coming up. I need to ensure I achieve the grades to get into Manchester. That means some serious revision. They may have offered me a place but I still have to get the grades. No grades of the right kind, no place. I've no intention of missing out. It's my guaranteed get out of jail card. Once I'm at Medical School, I'll have time to enjoy myself and make up for what I've missed. Besides, becoming a doctor is something I want to do with my life. When I'm there the social life is bound to be good. Who knows, I may even find me a good-looking young man like Effy."

Mack coloured hearing this. Effy put her arms round his neck, pressing her head next to his.

"Are you sure about that, Deidre?" Bridget's reaction was surprise.

"What? Finding a good young looking fella like Effy? Why not?"

"No, you silly biddy. About letting Ellen and Effy have every Saturday night off?"

"Oh, I see! Yes," confirmed Deidre. "Logic dictates yes." She pushed her glasses back up the bridge of her nose. She was right. Once in Manchester as a student she would be free to lead her own life.

"If I went out they would suspect something was going on. The household pope of Church Halloran will see me doing what I should be doing. I'll be revising, which is what I need to do. He'll need convincing I'm doing it. You two go and have the fun you deserve and have missed out on. He's deprived me of having time to enjoy myself, but at this stage it doesn't matter. Passing exams with the right grades does. It will be the kind of quiet revenge I'll enjoy, knowing he's not getting his own way. I'll be thinking of you happy and free of him for a few hours. That will be satisfaction in itself. His holiness Halloran has done enough damage to his daughters to scar us for life."

The sisters found hearing Deidre's bitterness towards their father astounding. Reserved, studious, ready to give way, Deidre had exposed her darker feelings. This openness on her part was refreshing, confirming she shared her younger sisters' feelings.

146

"By the way, it's not James. He doesn't like James," Effy explained, trying to lighten the conversation. "Only his mum and dad call him James. Call him Mack. All his friends do."

"Not as in plastic..." Ellen began, only to find herself stopped before the word came out.

"No!" Mack and Effy chorused aloud.

CHAPTER 29

Going to a Go Go – Smokey Robinson & The Miracles
(Tamla Motown TMG 547 1965)

Saturday 19 March 1966

The journey from Bradford to Halifax on Mack's scooter was exhilarating. At least it was a cold dry evening and not raining. Tucked in behind Mack, Effy sheltered from the freezing air rushing past. Even so, she was shivering when they finally arrived at his Aunt and Uncle's house.

"This is Effy." Mack introduced her once they were inside.

"So pleased to meet you at long last. My son Tom has been telling me all about you two. Take your coat off, dear. Mack knows where they go. Oh, and put those helmets somewhere safe so we don't trip over them. Sit down here by the fire and warm yourself through. You must be cold from the ride over."

Effy, buried in the parka Mack had bought for her, took it off. Even though it was the smallest available, it was still two sizes too large.

"Aunty Ellen, will it be all right for Effy to get changed here?" Mack asked. "She's brought her going-out stuff with her."

"You've brought a dress with you?"

"Yes, it's in the vanity case my sister lent me."

"Shall we check to see if it needs ironing?"

The dress did not look creased but Mack's aunt decided to give it the once over. Meanwhile, Mack found himself banished to the backyard to lend a hand. Tom and his uncle were busy doing a minor repair on the Vespa. Effy was soon made to feel at home. Mack's aunt loved the dress. Learning that Effy had made it left her impressed with the two-tone shift design. One side was a fetching mint green and the other black. It looked as if it had come straight out of the fashion pages of a magazine. Long-sleeved, it was otherwise plain without frills.

Mack and Tom came in.

"Hi, Eff," Tom greeted her. "You going dressed like that?"

Effy was wearing a pair of tan jean-style trousers with a roll-neck sweater to keep warm on the scooter.

"No, I'm wearing the dress your mum's insisting on ironing for me."

148

"She's one talented young lady," Tom's mum added. "She made it all by herself. Do you know it looks like it could have come straight off a Richard Shop rack?"

"What are you going to be wearing, James?"

"Go on. Show Mum."

Mack took off the parka to reveal his dark blue suit.

"Goodness me, that is smart!"

"It's a mohair and wool blend," added Tom. "Tell Mum how you got it made up. Go on."

Mack explained it was part Christmas present and part paid for by money earned at Benny's. Dave Bean had told him about a mill shop in Great Horton where he had gone and bought a roll of cloth himself. Then he had it made up at a local one-man tailor's in Green Lane, the same one Dave used. His dad had paid for the suit to be handmade. It worked out cheaper than buying from Burton's and he'd specified exactly how he wanted it.

Tom was keen to point out the finer points of Mack's new suit. Fitted at the waist, jacket longer than usual, three-buttoned, with twin 12" vents. The slanted pockets included a third small ticket pocket on the right.

Effy had found him a piece of silk and made it into silk hanky to fit in the breast top pocket. Trousers were straight parallels without turn-ups. According to Tom the five buttons on each cuff as well as the narrow hand-stitched lapels revealed true Mod style.

His aunt gave him the impressed once over, saying, "You look even smarter than my brother in his stiff collar and bank manager best. As for you, what have you done with my son? You sound like some poncey writer for a fashion magazine, not my Tom."

Mack spluttered, suppressing laughter. Seeing Tom's speechless reaction to his mother's little joke was comical.

"Is your scooter fixed yet? What's your father doing?" Ellen Catford continued.

"Dad's tidying up. He'll be in soon," Tom responded. Reaching the door, he paused to give a dramatic pretend flick of his hair. "Do you know? My mum can be such a hussy."

Ellen Catford ignored her son's theatrics. "Better get yourself ready if you're going out with James and Effy."

Mack listened to the conversation between his aunt and Effy while Tom was upstairs. Effy explained she had started a Saturday job as a part-time sales assistant at Dorothy Perkins. During her lunch break she would

149

check out the clothes they were selling for her age group. She and Grace then drew their own modified sewing patterns for dresses. It was real female talk. They discussed dressmaking intricacies such as stitching. What made him feel good was how his aunt and Effy were hitting it off after less than an hour.

"Do you know something, Effy? I often wish I had a daughter. It's all men in our families. If it wasn't for James's mum I don't expect there would be another female relative within fifty miles. And they all have sons too."

"Is this Effy?" Mack's uncle interrupted, entering the room. "It must be. Tom warned me Mack's pretty secret was coming."

"Pleased to meet you, Mr Catford," Effy responded. "Mack's told me so much about you and Mrs Catford."

"Has he now?" his uncle responded, giving Mack a wink. "All good, I hope."

"Yes, definitely."

"Well, Mack. So this is the young lady we've to pretend to your mum and dad we know nothing about, eh? She's bonny. I can see the family resemblance with her sister Caitlin. What do you reckon, Ellen?"

"Yes, she has a look of her sister. Mack says all seven of you girls look a great deal alike. Is it true?"

"I suppose we do. Grace is a little different. She's freckled. Her hair is a much deeper copper colour. I imagine most people would recognise us as sisters."

"You should go and get ready, dear. Use my bedroom and excuse the mess. There's a dressing-table mirror and a full-length wardrobe mirror. Mack will show you where it is and then he can come back down. I don't want him peeking in while you get changed."

"As if I would," Mack replied, knowing his aunt was joshing him.

Effy didn't take long to change. It was not warm so she slipped into her dress, put her Jaeger-style cardigan on, and reapplied her makeup. The Catfords' home was like her own. It didn't have central heating but it did have an indoor bathroom and toilet. Travel clothes now packed in the case, she returned to the warmth of the living room with its blazing coal fire. Mack was chatting with his aunt and uncle as she entered. Her reappearance caused an immediate stir. The hemline was four inches above the knee.

"I thought it might be a little short when I ironed it. I didn't like to say anything, dear." Ellen Catford paused. "But I must admit it does look eye-catching on you. You have the legs to carry it off."

150

"Is that one of those new fangled mini skirts I've read about in the papers?" her husband asked, looking up from his copy of the Halifax Courier.

"Don't be silly! Can't you see it's a dress she's wearing?" his wife retorted.

"It's not too short, is it?" Effy looked at Mack for reassurance.

"No, it's not," said Mack. "You look great."

Tom came down a second or two later before further comments were passed on her hemline. Sporting a new blue and dark purple broad stripe boating blazer, he looked sharp. Tom's appearance invited immediate comment. Phil Catford lampooned his son's sartorial splendour. His gruff rendition of *Dedicated Follower of Fashion* had them grinning. Tom took it well, even singing along with some of the lyrics.

As they buttoned up parkas and wrapped scarves around their necks Ellen Catford said, "Effy, you need to come back and get changed before returning to Bradford. The last thing you need is to get your death of cold going back on the scooter."

"Aunt Ellen, it might be well late. I have to get her back by midnight to Caitlin's. Otherwise Cinderella's grounded by her sister."

"Mack, you make sure you bring her back here first, do you hear me? It's one thing to go down to town dressed like this. It's another to ride all the way over to Bradford in the middle of night when it's freezing cold. In fact, Effy, leave your case here. We'll be in bed when you get back. I'll leave the fire backed up. You can change back into your pullover and trousers downstairs before he takes you home."

"Should I?" Effy asked Mack, who shrugged his shoulders.

"I suppose my aunt's right. It won't be at all warm on the way back."

151

CHAPTER 30

At the Club – The Drifters (Atlantic AT 4019 – 1965)

Saturday 19 March 1966

Mack's reputation among the Halifax Mods had grown. Among the scooters packing George's Square every weekend, his GT200 stood out. The Lambretta's unique paintwork made it the envy of other scooter owners. His wardrobe had expanded with a careful selection of casual clothes. Fred Perry polo shirts with Levi's sta prest trousers gave him the smart sharp look. Now the suit was going to enhance his rep further. His mature assured poise affected the kind of Mod cool many tried but could not emulate. Since becoming a regular Mack attracted attention and not only among the males. Tonight local girls long fixated with him would suffer dismay. Only Angie Thornton was a constant reminder of his infidelity. Otherwise no one had come between him and Effy,

No sooner had Mack and Tom parked the scooters on the curve in George's Square than others they knew ambled over to chat. Effy's first time in the town, plunging into the unknown, filled her with apprehension. Dismounting, she pulled down the scarf masking her face. Removing the helmet her long strawberry blonde hair tumbled onto her shoulders. The young men chatting to Mack stared in disbelief. As Effy was given to natural shyness, the sudden attention proved overpowering. Immediately seeking refuge she took Mack's hand, standing as close to him as possible.

Mack introduced the circle of young men by name. Effy struggled to remember who was who. It was disconcerting and unexpected to find herself the focus of so much attention. After a few minutes some of the group moved away. Tom whispered something in Mack's ear, laughing as he did so.

"What?" she asked.

"Seems you caused quite a bit of a reaction," Mack whispered into her ear.

"Why? Is it this parka I'm wearing or something?"

Mack looked at her in wonderment and planted a gentle kiss on her mouth. "Or something."

"Or something what? Tell me?" she begged.

"It's you. They're blown away. They think you're gorgeous."

152

"Me? Gorgeous? Are you teasing me, Jimmy Mack?"

"No. I would never tease you about that."

"You two lovey doveys ought to get a hotel room." The mushy romantic overload was too much for Tom, judging by the pitying look he gave them.

"Aren't you meeting Carol?" Mack asked.

"She's so last week. We've broken up."

"You don't seem upset about it." It was surprising news to Effy. Not that she had ever met the girl.

"It's no big deal, Effy." Tom shrugged. "It's like the Marvelettes record. There's plenty more fish in the sea."

"I take it you got fed up of clam?" Mack grinned, knowing it was an in-joke between them.

"Some of us get bored with the same old dish. You know me, Mack. Always tempted with side dishes. You know what they say; variety is the spice of life. My taste buds craved a new taste." Tom licked his lips, making his cousin chuckle at the lewd inference.

"Touché," Mack acknowledged the coded reference to Effy and himself.

"What's all this about clam?" Effy asked, revealing her naiveté.

"You don't want to know," the two cousins replied in perfect synchronicity.

As the three of them began to walk towards the Plebs they bumped into Angie. Accompanied by her friend Linda she was coming from the direction of the Vic Lounge. Linda spoke first on spotting them. "Why, looky looky, who do we have here? It's Halifax's answer to the dynamic duo! TC and Mack!"

"How ya doing, ladies? Going down the club?" Tom answered back.

Effy sensed the taller, stunning dark-haired girl was studying her with a strange intensity. Mack, noticing what was happening, took the initiative. "Angie, this is Effy, my girlfriend from Bradford. The one I told you about."

Angie walked up to Effy, speaking to Mack yet still looking her over with that same intensity. "Mack never told us you were so pretty. God! You could be a model or film star. Hi, I'm Angie Thornton, a friend of these two. We thought you were a figment of their imaginations, didn't we, Linda? I thought they were spinning us a line but it seems they weren't."

"She's a bit of a looker," Tom admitted.

153

Mack had dreaded this meeting, knowing it would be unavoidable. Angie turned to him with an enigmatic smile. "All those girls who've been angling to get off with you. They never stood a chance, did they? I can understand why, having met Effy finally."

Effy found this inexplicable and unsettling. She recollected what Mack had told her about Angie. He had downplayed her attractiveness. She was not only attractive. She was stunning. Even in her leather coat Angie's slim body showed off her curves. Effy experienced a strange fleeting feeling of insecurity: a feeling she dismissed as fanciful. Yet strolling to the Upper George Yard, listening to their chatter, she thought that it did seem they were only friends. Mack was mentally breathing sighs of relief. Angie Thornton had been as good as her word so far. He dreaded Effy ever finding out what had happened between them. It was an unforgivable transgression whose revelation he could not begin to contemplate.

Sam & Dave's *You Don't Know Like I Know* was playing as they pushed their way onto the dance floor. There could not have been a worse choice of record as Mack danced, listening to the lyrics. He knew exactly what that woman had done to him. This was not lost on Angie. Smiling the whole way through the song, she never once glanced in his direction. For Mack it was scary and disturbing having Effy and Angie so close to one another. Effy was too immersed in dancing to the music to be aware of anything, which he found a relief.

For Effy it was all such a new exciting experience. Mack had taught her the dance moves, which she had picked up without difficulty. Betty Everett's *Getting Mighty Crowded* came on next. Whatever the thoughts running in his and Angie's minds, they were not in hers. Lost in the music and dancing she had succumbed almost trance-like to this new joyful experience. To make it all the more excruciating, on came Solomon Burke's *Need Somebody to Love*. The dancers joined in the chorus, pointing at people they knew. Mack had to admit Angie was discreet in playing down the *I Need You* chorus while still smiling. He knew exactly why she was still smiling. It could not get any worse but it did. The DJ's next spin turned out to be Barbara George's *I Know*. As the trumpet break in the record came on Angie's face lit up, and she joined in the lyrics about not needing her any more. The capper came with Mack's favourite song by The Detroit Spinners. It was as if the sequence of songs was deliberate and intended to remind him of his infidelity with Angie. *I'll Always Love You* had the line about never being out of his mind.

All this was lost on the most important person in his life. Effy was enjoying herself so much that the happiness shone through in her smiles. Things could not be better. When The Soul Sisters' *Good Time Tonight* played she became euphoric. Here she was with the boy of her dreams, dancing to this brilliant music he loved so much. Being here with him was a joy-filled and exuberant experience.

After a while Angie leaned over to Linda, saying something in her ear, and Linda did the same to Effy. Mack noticed her nodded assent. Then Angie did the same to Mack. "We girls are going to powder our noses. Hope you don't mind. I'm going to take Effy away from you for a few minutes so we can get to know one another."

Mack experienced a sinking feeling in his stomach. Was Angie going to do the unthinkable? Angie took in his expression in a split second, disappointed at his reaction. Delivering a hissed reprimand in his ear, she made her annoyance clear. "For God's sake, I'm not going to say anything. I couldn't be so heartless. Get a grip on yourself."

Leaving those admonishing words in his ears, she signalled the girls to leave.

Mack and Tom walked off to the side to wait for them to return.

"Where's Linda's Steve tonight?" Mack asked.

"He's off on a pill run to Manchester. Should be back soon unless he's been unlucky enough to get busted by the Feds."

"Got your eye on anyone tonight?"

"Not decided yet. Picked one or two I quite fancy. Can't decide which one to try. Got to see if I can catch their eyes. If they glance twice at you in a minute or two you have a chance. It's all in the eyes, old bean. Looks like Angie's making Effy her new friend."

"That's got me worried." Mack confessed. "I wonder what they're talking about?"

"It'll be the usual girl stuff, makeup and clothes. It's not like they're going to bad-mouth you. Man, you're a top bloke to them. At least it's what Angie's always saying. She's single-handedly made your rep. You're on your way to becoming a Face. With a girl like Effy on your arm you've more pulling power with the chicks than a magnet to iron filings. It's a shame, which is okay by me."

"A shame? How's that?"

"More of them for me. If you don't want to sample what's out there I'll do it for you, no probs."

"Somehow, knowing you, you probably will."

The girls seemed to be gone quite a while. Mack became more and more agitated and impatient for Effy's return. Tom got bored waiting and finally headed off towards a trio of girls dancing near the DJ room.

Returning at last, Angie and Linda exchanged a few words with Effy before starting dancing. Effy made her way over to Mack as The Supremes' *I Hear a Symphony* began to play. Glowing, she placed her arms around his neck, moving her swaying hips against his to the music. He had never seen her happier. Glancing over her shoulders, Mack caught Angie smiling at him. That was even more disconcerting. Mack could not help wondering what they had been saying to each other. The tempo of the music slowed, allowing Mack and Effy to dance in each other's arms. It was Joe Tex singing *A Sweet Woman Like You*. The lyrics fitted Mack's emotional state of the moment as he held Effy in his arms. The song was exactly what he needed to hear. The guilty feeling drained away as he lost himself in the embrace.

CHAPTER 31

How Sweet It Is (To Be Loved By You) – Marvin Gaye
(Stateside SS 360 – 1964)

Sunday 20 March 1966

It was past nine when Caitlin woke her up. Mack had managed to get her home a minute or two after midnight. His aunt's advice to get changed before travelling back had proved sensible. The journey had been bitterly cold, with a late frost whitening roofs. Reluctant as she was to leave Mack at the door with one last kiss, she had been glad to get inside.

Her sister was waiting like an anxious parent. Adam had already gone to bed. Ellen had been back for two hours, having gone to the cinema with friends from the Sixth Form. Effy had to share the tiny bed with her. That must have proved an ordeal for Ellen. As cold as ice, Effy stole her sister's warmth. Even with an extra hot water bottle it took her some time to warm through and stop shivering.

How long it took her to descend into dreamland she had no idea. She could not stop reliving the night out at The Plebs. It had been as good if not better as Mack had said it would be. The atmosphere in the club and the dancing – it was unlike anything she had experienced before. Now she appreciated why Mack loved soul music with such a passion. They had even spent half an hour entwined and kissing – doing the same as other couples around the edges of the dance area. For the first time in her life she had experienced the freedom to be herself.

Effy never revealed to Mack what had passed between her and Angie. When curiosity got the better of him he had tried to find out. She had dismissed it as girl talk, which was the truth. She didn't reveal what Angie had said in private because it made her feel insecure. Knowing that so many of the local girls were after him was worrying. But Angie had reassured her: so far, Mack had resisted all their charms. The downside was that even Mack could succumb to temptation. He was a bloke, after all, and blokes gave into temptation and straying. Angie seemed so grown-up, so worldly wise. Effy accepted what she had to say. It was the added further advice she offered which made her blush, even at the thought.

Recalling Angie's words made her wonder why she had been so open. They had only met that evening but Angie spoke to her as if they had been friends forever. It was as if she knew so much about her already. Effy found it odd, though rather heart-warming. Beyond her sisters she had no real female friends, not even at school where she was the quiet introvert. She had always relied on her sisters. Angie had been at pains to stress she was a good friend to both TC and Mack, emphasising that friendship was as far as it went. They were too young for her but were a good laugh, and fun to be around. Although Angie seemed so mature and grown-up Effy couldn't help wondering if she was that much older. Mack had told her Angie was closer to eighteen but she didn't come over as eighteen.

One thing Effy promised herself. She was going to do whatever it took to make Mack know how much she cared for him. No other girl was going to get a look in. She would do whatever it took to keep him.

Ellen and Caitlin wanted to know all about what she and Mack had been up to in Halifax. Sparing nothing except the kissing and cuddling, Effy gave them a detailed account. She described how packed George's Square was with young people. Told them about the countless scooters parked in the square. How Mack's scooter attracted attention because of its appearance and speed. Her account was graphic and detailed. She described the club, the music and the dancing. Told them all about the clothes the Mod girls were wearing. Recounted it all.

"I'm envious," Ellen responded after she finished. "I wish I could go over. Sounds fun being a Mod. Would you let me go with Mack next week instead of you?"

For a brief moment Effy thought her sister was being serious. Then she realised she was joking. Was she imagining it or was Ellen envious?

"Did you like Mack's aunt and uncle?" Caitlin asked.

"They're such lovely people. His aunt even insisted on ironing my dress again although it was hardly creased. She even made Mack bring me back to get changed into something warmer before returning. I may have shocked his Uncle Phil with how short the hemline was on my dress."

"Could you could shorten one of my skirts? Pretty please?" Ellen implored her sister.

"How short?"

"About the same length as your dress."

"Which skirt?"

"One of Aileen's old skirts. You could put your magic touch to it and make it a bit more special."

"If Effy took the hem up so much you could never wear it in the house," interposed Caitlin. "Da would have a fit if he saw you in it. I've got some time on my hands. Why don't I shorten it for you instead? Effy has her O Levels coming up so she'll need to revise and cut down on the dressmaking for a while."

"Caitlin, can I bring some dresses I've made and leave them here, please?" Effy asked. "Then I can decide what to wear when I go out with Mack without arousing suspicion?"

"Yes, can we, Caitlin?" Ellen joined in. "Can I leave some here too? It will look less suspicious like Effy said if we can get changed here."

Caitlin's resigned sigh passed over them. After a moment or so she agreed with a nod. There was hardly any room in her wardrobe but she could hardly turn them down. While the baby was still young she could sleep in the bedroom with Adam and herself. They would not be able to keep doing it. At some point in the not too distant future little Jane would have to be in the spare room. They could always try to exchange their second-hand settee for a bed settee downstairs.

Adam came into the room. "Okay, ladies, time to go to church. Let's squeeze you into the car and get off down to St. William's."

Mack had stopped going to church yet again, to his parents' disappointment. It wasn't unexpected. There had been family discussions but in the end they had not made an issue of it with him. They reasoned he would let his conscience decide whether to remain within the church or not. From talking with Effy he learned that she had the same views on religion as he did. She still went through the pretence more for Caitlin's sake than for her father's.

Her sister had remained a Catholic, albeit now attending a different parish. Though Caitlin continued to go to church she no longer went to Confession or Holy Communion. Neither did her younger sisters. Even Bridget had stopped going. Only Aileen continued to observe the sacraments. Effy had told Mack how her father tried to bully Grace now because she was refusing to go to weekly Confession and Communion. The youngster was steadfast in her stand. The new Protestants of the Halloran household banded together. Withdrawing from taking part in evening prayers they had made their line in the sand. Even Bridget had succumbed in the end and joined the

159

rebellion. This had followed after a tremendously fiery exchange with her father. The endless recitations of the rosary were now reduced to Aileen and her parents.

Mack could not begin to imagine the atmosphere in the household. Effy and Ellen's vivid account seemed so unreal as to be beyond envisaging. He wondered if they were exaggerating. But according to Bridget and Caitlin, they weren't.

That morning, whilst his parents went to Mass, Mack remembered. Adam had said something about checking his parents' wedding certificate. It had gone from his thoughts until today. This Sunday morning provided the ideal opportunity. So he decided to do as Adam had suggested.

Half an hour later he left their bedroom. His parents' motives for helping Caitlin and his brother were clear, as was the reason that his grandfather had behaved in the way he had with his mother. Nor did it have anything to do with his mother's enlistment in the Royal Navy.

It did not take a mathematical genius to work out. Adam had been born six and half months after his parents married. Mack's initial reaction was shock. From the dates it was obvious they had sex before marriage. Adam was not the only one capable of getting a girl pregnant before marriage. His own father had done the same with his mother. The dates on the marriage and birth certificate told no lie. Neither did his mother's discharge papers from the WRNS. She could not have been much older than Caitlin when it happened. She must have been about twenty or so when she got pregnant with Adam. No wonder they had been so sympathetic to his and Caitlin's plight. No wonder his grandfather had refused to have anything to do with his daughter. Knowing what he knew, Mack did not know whether to thank Adam for the truth or get ticked off with him. The thought of his parents having done something so unlike them did not sit well. His dad was always using the biblical quote about the truth setting you free. The truth was not what it appeared when they had kept it hidden. Shame must have played a part in it. Then he had studied the photo of his parents in their naval uniforms. They looked so young and so happy together. Mack had a new understanding. It was the realisation they had not always been his mother and father. There had been a time when it had only been the two of them. They had fallen in love with one another as he had with Effy and Adam had with Caitlin. The more he thought about his parents the more Mack understood how much they loved one another.

Remembering his childhood years he recalled the constant attention they gave each other. The little hugs and squeezes. The affectionate kisses. Mack recollected his mum sitting down on his father's lap and nestling up to him. It was exactly what Effy did when they were together. It made them less like parents and more like young people who had grown into adults. It was peculiar to see them in that light but it made complete sense now as never before.

CHAPTER 32

Summertime – Billy Stewart (Chess 8092 – 1965)

Thursday 7 July 1966

Leaving school proved less traumatic than Mack expected. There was nothing more he could do now the exams were over except wait for the results. He had only taken two O Levels and seven CSEs, which was all the school offered. Providing he got pass grades in at least two subjects he would start A Levels in September when he went to St. Bede's. The grammar school was allowing a few secondary school boys from the Moderns to enter the Sixth Form.

Benny had agreed to let him work an extra two days a week. They were making him do the equivalent of an apprenticeship scheme in his own time. This allowed him to do more and more jobs on customers' scooters. It worked well for the Jenkins's business. They got an extra pair of hands for less than the going rate while Mack got the skills and knowledge as well as an extra three pounds a week. What he learned he put to good use, helping to repair or service some of the Halifax guys' scooters on his days off. This brought him in some extra money. In a good week he could earn another two or three pounds but it was not money he could rely on.

Mack toyed with the idea of leaving school altogether to become a mechanic like his brother. Effy dissuaded him from doing it. His parents would not have wanted it either. In all fairness he knew he could do better studying for A Levels.

Meanwhile, Effy had taken seven O Levels, confident she would pass with high grades. She had made good use of her time between studying, chores and leisure time. At the start of the summer holidays she found a second part-time job. It was at C&A, filling in for shop assistants on vacation. Saturdays were still at Dorothy Perkins. Midweek evenings she busied herself sewing and dressmaking with Grace. Meanwhile Ellen had found a summer job working at a local bakery as a sales assistant. Both were keeping up the pretence of babysitting at Caitlin's.

Effy and Mack were pushing the clock boundaries back further and further. They were now coming in at two in the morning and on occasion even later. Ellen had started going to The Continental 'Hole in the Wall' with her friends. Effy's talk about the Mod scene had converted her sister.

Tom had tried to persuade Mack to go on holiday to Newquay in Cornwall. A large Halifax Mod contingent was heading there during the Wakes holidays. They would spend a week in Newquay before moving onto Torquay for the second week. But Mack had to say no, much to Tom's disappointment. Working at Benny's meant he could not take a break. It allowed Mick to have his ten days' holiday. When he returned Benny could go off with his wife on holiday for the first time in years. It needed at least two to work in the shop without closing it for a fortnight. The Jenkins promised to pay him twenty-five pounds for the full-time cover work. This was an offer he could not turn down. What was more important was the thought of leaving Effy for two weeks: something else he didn't want to do. Her mentioning in passing that young men coming into C&A were chatting her up settled it. Taking off to Cornwall and Devon might give her the impression that he did not care enough about her. It was the exact opposite of how he felt. The thought that some sweet-talker could take her away from him in his absence worried him.

Knowing the situation in the Halloran household he believed he should stay close to home. He needed to be handy in case anything happened. Quite what he would be able to do if anything happened was nebulous. At least he would not be hundreds of miles away, unaware of what was going on.

Mack need not have worried about Effy taking up with some other guy. The only young man in her life was Mack. Effy turned down all prospective admirers with polite bluntness. For those persistent ones who continued to pester her, she had the store detective ask them to leave her alone. When Effy learned Mack was not going on holiday with Tom she felt relieved. Two weeks without seeing him would have seemed an eternity. There was also the worry that being with TC could lead him into straying. Tom's reputation for notorious philandering was well-established. He saw himself as a junior version of Alfie, flitting from girl to girl and even back again when the mood suited him. As much as she liked Mack's cousin, she did not believe for one moment he was a good influence. The whole business of taking pills had become a bit of a habit with TC. Effy hoped Mack had enough common sense not to get drawn in. The Manchester Drug Squad had caught Linda's boyfriend in possession of 200 bombers. The consequences for Steve had been dire.

With Steve out of circulation the supply in Halifax was drying up. Since the passing of the Dangerous Drugs Act in 1964 the police had been keeping tabs on the Mod scene in Halifax. This was happening in many other towns and cities. Some of the Square regulars had found themselves searched on suspicion of possession. Policemen in plain clothes frequented the Vic Lounge and Upper George. Supping their pints they eavesdropped on conversations. They were even known to have come into the club.

The Plod was easy to spot. To be a Mod there had to be a degree of passion for fashion. Age as well as bad dress sense betrayed plain-clothes police. No one ever got caught. Anyone going down to an all-nighter had already dosed up with "doobs" before coming into town. It was during this drug drought that Tom persuaded Mack against his better judgment to do a pill run. As it turned out Mack's presence prevented the deal from souring in a bad way.

Tom claimed to have a contact for supplying pills in Oldham. Huge quantities of blueys were leaking out of the Smith Klein & French works in Liverpool. This was true insofar as anyone could ever know the truth when it came to drug sources. One thing was true. When it came to the supplier of amphetamines this dealer did exist.

Mack picked Tom up straight after work. They made the journey over the Pennines to Oldham. It took them two hours to find the address in an out-of-the-way rundown street. It turned out that the guy wasn't there; he was down the road in one of the local pubs. Tom had a name and not much else to go by. It was looking like a wasted journey but Tom insisted they try the pub.

The public house was of the sawdust and spit kind filled with an unsavoury looking clientele. Mack later told Tom he had frequented better public lavatories. The pub was a tobacco and ale-stenched dump. They could have used an axe to cut their way through the choking near purple haze of cigarette smoke.

In their parkas the pair stood out like proverbial sore thumbs. Tom walked over to the bar and asked if anyone knew Scooby. As it turned out, Scooby happened to be coming out of the toilets. The barman pointed him out. The kindest description Mack gave the sallow-faced Scooby was of a down-at-heel bum masquerading as a Mod. With his pinched face and scruffy attire, even calling him a Mod was a stretch.

After some verbal dancing around the subject they got to the point. Sitting in a quiet corner with Scooby and his mates, Tom negotiated a price: a pretty good price, as it happened. At 6d each wholesale with a retail of 1/-

164

he and Mack would double their investment. Having clubbed together they had £8. In the end they struck a deal for 350 drinamyl tablets because it was a quantity buy. Mack had made the decision to hold the money for safety's sake. He was not too happy with what was going down. His senses were telling him something was not right. The deal seemed too good and he suspected it was. Others had been "rolled" for less money. Some were conned by blue dyed aspirin passed off as purple hearts. This bunch were untrustworthy and up to no good.

Mac remembered the tale of one of the guys getting ripped off. Yamaha had recounted how someone rolled Acky near Piccadilly in Manchester. The two had gone over early on a Saturday evening with funds collected from friends. Acky had been foolish going to do the deal alone, leaving Yamaha waiting. The seller took off with the money before Acky had realised something was wrong. Mack had no intention of allowing the same to happen, insisting on being present with Tom. When the money and pills changed hands he planned to ensure there was no trouble.

As it turned out Scooby was a pharmaceuticals wholesaler to the local Mod population. When they came round to his house it seemed safe. Scooby had left his mates behind at the pub. Or so they thought.

The terrace house where the dealer lived turned out to be an absolute dump. Scooby's stepmother had flaked out on the settee. She was snoring her head off, surrounded by empty pale ale bottles with the TV turned up loud. At least it drowned out the sound of the myriad flies buzzing about their heads. The room hummed of wet dog and cat piss as well as the smell of stale beer and cigarettes. The furniture looked like it had fallen off the back of a rag and bone merchant's cart. Tom reckoned Harry Steptoe and his dad would have died of shame if they'd lived there, it was that appalling.

As the dealer counted out the pills in tens Mack looked on. Tom used his thumbnail to scratch the surfaces of random pills with his thumbnail. The pills were kosher blueys as manufactured by Smith Klein & French. Tom estimated there must have been at least a thousand more in the jar. Deal done, Mack handed over the money, a mixture of £1 and 10-shilling notes. Tom deposited the pills in a clear plastic bag and tied it with a knot. Exchanging pleasantries the twosome made for the scooter parked outside. Emerging from the front door Mack saw three of Scooby's mates from the pub coming at them. He knew instinctively what was going down. They were about to have the pills taken from them in an elaborate scam and get beaten up at the same time. This was not a moment to panic but to act on automatic as Lenny had taught him. Taking out the attackers first before they did it to them was vital. Few assailants expected their victims to attack.

Without waiting Mack went for the leading youth. The assailant was not expecting to find himself assaulted. Mack delivered the perfect Glasgow kiss. Carried out with speed, determined ferocity and timing, it was over in a split second. The sound of the nose-cracking seemed louder than it was. The youth fell flat on his back as Mack shoved him with considerable force to the pavement. His nose looked as if it had exploded, streaming blood onto his clothing and the ground. The youth behind his mate had stepped out of the way, avoiding him as he fell. Hesitating, he left himself open to Mack's clinical violence. It was an ill-timed decision to pause. Mack drove the flat palm of his hand upward below the jaw. Done with such force, the sickening sound of colliding teeth was audible. Following up in one single smooth motion, arms went about his opponent's neck. Twisting him round Mack kneed him in the guts. The guy threw up his stomach's beery contents as he spun away from him. Two down and the one left to go did that. Turning, he made off down the street as fast as his legs could take him. Scooby, party to the set-up, dived back into the house and slammed the door shut before Tom could get to him.

"Leave it, Tom! Let's get out of here before any more of his mates surface." The adrenaline was kicking in which was never good in a fight situation, hence the need for speed. Lenny was right. You had to strike fast before the adrenaline sapped your muscles and reactions.

Gunning the scooter Mack pushed the Lambretta hard for all it was worth. He only stopped after he had put ten miles behind him on an empty stretch of road.

"Hand them over," Mack commanded in a tone brooking no dispute.

"What you gonna do?" Tom asked, bewildered, passing him the bag full of pills.

"Watch."

"You can't be serious," said Tom as Mack took the pills from him.

"Watch me."

As they passed Halifax Royal Infirmary the police, with blue lights flashing, flagged them down. Two beefy constables emerged to subject them to checks starting with documentation.

They found nothing wrong with Mack's licence, insurance and tax disc. So they insisted on searching them. Emptied pockets revealed nothing illegal. The two cops began snooping round the vehicle. They checked the

166

toolbox, finding nothing. Lifting up the seat and looking underneath it they found nothing. Unscrewing the petrol cap they peered into the fuel tank and again found nothing.

"I see your spare's flat." One of the constables pointed out the spare wheel behind the backrest. "You need to get the spare fixed as soon as you can. Nothing worse than not being able to change a flat when you have two flat tyres."

Following this advice, the police left, disappointed at not having made a collar. Tom turned to Mack, saying in a hushed awestruck voice, "God, you're spooky. How the bloody hell did you know the Feds were going to stop us?"

"I didn't."

"You must have done. Why else did you deflate the spare wheel and stuff the pills inside it?"

"I did it in case we did get stopped. And we did get stopped, didn't we? They're always stopping anyone riding a scooter on the off chance they're hiding something. Don't you get it? Parka-wearing Mod on a scooter equals a drug-taking troublemaker."

"Do you want know something, Mack? You are one mean, scary bastard. I'm glad I'm on your side. I wouldn't want to be on the other taking you on. If you don't end up beating the crap out of someone you'll run rings round them with your Chess Master mind moves."

"After we sell these pills that's it," Mack resolved with quiet determination. "Count me out. If you want to go risking it, you do it. Don't involve me again."

Tom accepted that it was a good idea to quit. It was their first and last score. Within three weeks they had sold the lot, making a hefty profit. Tom sold them at 1/- each for the first three hundred. Mack didn't want anything to do with the selling, which was as well since he didn't know who would buy. Not a problem for his cousin, who did. The last batch of fifty Tom bought for himself, paying Mack for his extra twenty-five. They had each turned their £4 investments into tidy profits. In the end Mack had a bag full of shillings and sixpences amounting to £10.

His original plan had been to buy something for Effy. His decision not to do so was moral. The thought of buying a necklace or earrings with tainted money would remind him where it had come from. There was no way he would allow her to wear something bought with tainted money. Anything he bought her would be with money he had earned by working.

167

CHAPTER 33

Shotgun Wedding – Roy 'C' (Island Records WI 273 – 1966)

Thursday 7 July 1966

"Why do you want to know?" Caitlin raised an eyebrow at Ellen's question and gave her a suspicious look. "You've not done something you shouldn't, have you?"

"Of course not. I'm not a slapper," Ellen replied.

That was diplomatic, thought Effy, after Caitlin's pregnancy out of marriage. Caitlin remained cool to the unintentional tactless words of her younger sister.

"It's, well… precautionary, if you get my meaning," Ellen continued. "Supposing Effy was in a… let's say… uncontrollable situation with Mack…"

"Oi! What are you implying?" Effy found herself open-mouthed at the comment.

"Well, don't say it hasn't crossed your mind," Ellen continued.

"It may be one thing to think about it and something else to actually do it." Effy voiced her annoyance.

It had crossed her mind more than once recently. If Mack tried something she didn't believe she'd want him to stop, consequences or not. But she was not about to admit it in front of her sisters. Given her feelings lately she was curious like Ellen. Not so much about the mechanics of the sex act as the preventative side.

"I was only being hypothetical," Ellen continued, unabashed. "You're most likely to succumb to temptation among us."

"Thank you so much! I don't suppose the word tactful exists in your vocabulary?"

"Oh, stop being so prickly. Anyway you've admitted you think about it. I have to admit I've thought about it, even though I haven't got a steady boyfriend. Doesn't mean I want to have sex right now. And if I did, I'd want to make sure I didn't get pregnant unless I'd married."

Caitlin chuckled, which struck Effy as amusing. "If only life was so simple and straightforward, Ellen."

168

"What do you mean by that?"

"You'll know when the right man and the right moment comes along. You may not be so positive about the status of your virginity then."

"So? Are you going to tell us?"

With Jane sucking on her dummy and watching her aunties from Mummy's lap, Caitlin began.

"Are you sitting comfortably?" She took off Daphne Oxenford, the Listen with Mother BBC radio presenter, to a tee. "Then I'll begin... Let's start with men and condoms..."

If they were to avoid an unwanted pregnancy it would be a disservice not to tell them. As a married woman, with a child, she had options. As single young unmarried women her sisters' options were few. She told them about the Family Planning Association and what they offered. There was also the Brooks FPA now offering advice and help to unmarried women. Caitlin told them from her own experiences even more than they had expected to hear.

"There is no such thing as the safe time of the month when you can have sex. It's even possible to get yourself pregnant after the end of your period. So take that as a warning," Caitlin finished.

"So you're not on the birth control pill?" Ellen clarified.

"No. I'm not so sure about it. It could have unforseen side effects."

"Did you ever consider having an abortion?" Ellen asked.

"Never. I would never kill an unborn child of mine. I couldn't do that. Besides, you can't trust back-street abortionists and it's illegal. You could end up bleeding to death or infertile. Even had I wanted it would have cost at least fifty pounds. That was out of the question. Neither of us had that kind of ready money. Anyway, Adam wouldn't allow it any more than I would."

"How did Adam take the news when you knew you were pregnant?" Effy pried.

"It was a shock. Adam didn't know what to say at first. Then he said the baby was going to need a father and asked if I'd marry him. I confess this did come as a shock. I was half expecting him to run and abandon me. He did the opposite. Believe it or not, he actually apologised for getting me pregnant. Then he hugged me, said he loved me and proposed right there and then."

"Wow!" exclaimed Ellen. "You were lucky."

"Yes, lucky to have found the right man. So here we are, the three of us. I wouldn't change a thing."

169

There was a brief silence as the two younger sisters reflected on what they had heard.

After a while Effy asked, "Is it hard to insert a diaphragm?"

"Depends how squeamish you are about it. It's not for everyone and you have to use it with a special barrier cream called a spermicide."

"Spermicide? Sounds a bit like suicide."

"It is for sperm that venture in. It kills them off."

Effy remembered Angie Thornton saying her older sister worked in family planning. There might be a way she could lose her virginity without getting pregnant. Now that she was sixteen and a half she was at the legal age of consent.

"Note well, sisters. Nothing is completely foolproof," Caitlin warned. "The end result is what sitting's on my lap. By now you know how much hard work it is once they arrive. So be careful before you let anyone pull your knickers down."

Caitlin was directing the words at her. Effy did not bother to protest this time. Instead, sighing and turning to her sister, she said, "Well, Ellen, I'll have to sew extra-tight elastic into your knickers."

"Me? It's you who should be the one to do that! I haven't even got a steady fella!" Ellen retorted in shocked outrage.

"Strikes me it was you who was keen to know all about contraceptive precautions. Sounds a teeny weeny bit suspicious to me?" Effy teased.

"It helps to know these things." Ellen gave a tart almost exasperated reply. "I hope you were taking note and listening to everything Caitlin told us."

Effy gave a winsome smile. She had been taking note, glad that Ellen had broached the topic with Caitlin. As much as she loved Jimmy Mack neither of them was in a position to envisage marriage. Getting pregnant was not an option to contemplate. Sex was a different matter.

CHAPTER 34

I'll Do Anything (He Wants Me To Do) – Doris Troy
(Cameo Parkway C101 – 1966)

Saturday 9 July 1966

Mack's parents entrusted him to look after the house while they holidayed on the South Coast. They planned to revisit some of the places where they had first met. Adam would pop round to check up on him to make sure there was no partying. That was rich. It had been Adam's partying that had messed up the house and Mack made a point of it to his parents.

The MacKinnons set off around three on Saturday morning to avoid holiday traffic. Driving down to the Portsmouth area they planned to stop with friends from their Navy days. Afterwards they would spend a few days on the Dorset Coast, stopping off in Bournemouth.

Robert MacKinnon was not a happy man when they drove off. World Cup games were starting and he had mixed up the dates when organizing the trip. This did not matter a jot to Mack and Effy. They had no interest in football even if it was the World Cup.

The prospect of having the house to himself left Mack elated. Effy's face also lit up with delight when he told her. When they set off on the scooter from Adam's they never made it to Halifax. There would not have been much point. Most of the crowd had disappeared during the Wakes holidays. Nothing much would be happening apart from the World Cup.

Effy was quite surprised on entering the MacKinnons' house. It was not as large as her home, though it was anything but small. The home exuded comfortable affluence. The downstairs had plush wall-to-wall fitted carpets that even extended upstairs. Slipping off her shoes, she enjoyed the feel of the carpet pile through her stocking feet. There was nothing fuddy-duddy about the MacKinnons' tastes. The eclectic yet tasteful contemporary Danish furnishings were everywhere evident in the reception rooms. There was an Ercol sideboard in the lounge along with the largest TV set she had yet seen. Mack explained it was a Philips 23". None of this was cheap.

As he showed Effy round it was as though she had come home. The strongest, strangest, most inexplicable sensation came over her. She would

171

come to live here. It was a fanciful notion yet it persisted even as she tried dismissing it.

Mack had managed to buy a small bottle of QC cream sherry. They drank most of it together until Effy almost verged on the wrong side of tipsy. Finally calling time, she refused a refill.

"You haven't shown me your bedroom yet, why not?" Her whisper sounded innocent enough though her thoughts were far from innocent. Knowing they were going to be alone in the house she wanted to test the limits. How far could she go without going the whole way? In recent months she had let him fondle her behind when they were kissing in the darkness of the club. She had even allowed him to touch her clothed breasts inside her parka. This evening, having the house to themselves, she was in the mood to experience more. Effy knew Mack respected her, restraining himself from overt moves. Adam and Caitlin's situation had served as a strong deterrent. Effy had long ago realised they could not keep getting aroused without release.

"You do keep it neat and tidy," Effy commented on entering his room. "I don't know why but I thought it might be a bit messy."

"Unlike Adam I've always kept everything organised and shipshape. Don't get me wrong. I can get messy when doing school work."

"No posters or pictures of pretty models, no pinups? No Jean Shrimpton? Twiggy? No Pattie Boyd?"

"No. After Adam wrecked the wallpaper in his room I got banned from putting anything up. I keep your photo hidden along with the snaps Tom took on his camera so my mum and dad can't find them. They only come out when I'm in on my own."

Effy sat on his bed, bouncing on it, testing the mattress springs. Sliding her legs onto the bed she reclined with practiced elegance and teasing seductiveness. "So this is where you dream about me at night?"

"I suppose it is," he replied, nervous yet excited. Finding her on his bed in such a provocative sexy pose was beyond his wildest expectations.

"Do you know what I want to do?" Effy tried to sound as sexy as she knew how. Her teasing seemed almost relentless to Mack.

"To go back downstairs?"

"Not now. Not yet. Later."

"What do you have in mind until then?" His heart was pounding with anticipation, his mouth dry.

"How about we slip under the covers? I want to cuddle and snuggle up to you. We can't go all the way. You do understand, don't you? I don't want to end up like Caitlin. Not yet anyway."

Sliding back off the bed she stood up, turning her back to him. "Unzip me, would you? I don't want to get my dress creased. Besides, it will be more comfortable without it on under the covers."

Mack was about to ask if she meant it. Of course she did. Effy was the one making the moves. She had lured and snared him. Undoing her zip, he watched as she took her dress off to reveal a plain waist slip and matching white bra. He stared entranced as she slid with an effortless motion between the sheets. It was so unexpected. He had daydreamed of this happening countless times. Now that it was happening he wondered if he should pinch himself to see if it was real.

"Do you mind if I take my Levis off?"

"You'd better. I want to feel you not your denim rubbing up against me." Aided by the relaxing effects of the sherry her inhibitions had fallen away. She made a daring suggestion. "Why don't you peel everything off except for the underpants? Then I can let my hands wander all over your near naked body."

"Indecent haste" best described Mack discarding his clothes. Never, in all his teenage fantasies, could he have anticipated this happening. Effy was in his bed encouraging him to join her. Like Angie she challenged his masculine understanding of the feminine. It was not only him wanting her. She wanted him. They lay together, holding each other and exchanging kisses.

"If you unhook my bra it can come off."

Trying to unhook the bra with one hand Mack failed, feeling inept. Effy sat up and unclipped it, amused at his artless efforts. Her breasts were firm, small yet even, silky soft to the touch. As he felt her nipples her breast rose, responding to his attention. Not knowing how Effy might react, Mack took a chance. He kissed each nipple alternately for several moments.

Running her hand through his hair, she exulted in his attention to her breasts. Then, with a languid, soft, caressing motion, she moved her hand down his backbone. Arriving at the waistband she stopped. Her fingers slid inside, pausing for a brief instant before submerging to the wrist. With intent her hand travelled round the hipbone to his erection. He struggled to contain himself from her tactile exploration.

173

Effy cosseted his testicles with the gentlest of touches as a moan of pleasure left his lips. Her hand wrapped round the shaft and moved to the tip as she sensed his pleasured response.

"Is all this supposed to go inside me?" she whispered. "It's much bigger than I thought. I can't imagine my poor tiny opening coping when the time comes and we can finally go all the way."

As if on cue his hand went to the top of her thigh, pulling her slip up to the waist as it did so. His hand moved down to her knee and began a slow ascent, reaching her stocking-top and suspender. He slid the flat of his palm upwards between her thighs, and let it come to rest against the pubic bone. Effy trembled at this first encounter. He tried to pull her briefs down from the front but her hand stopped him.

"No." She restrained him with quiet firmness. "They stay on. You can put your hand inside them. I won't mind. But they stay on for now. If you took them off I might not be able to stop myself. We can't take the chance. I could get pregnant."

So Mack complied. He knew she was right. His hand went down the front to her opening. She stiffened with expectancy. The gusset of her briefs was wet and sticky on his hand. As he slid his fingers along her opening, her vagina released more of the sticky wetness. She moaned in response to his probing fingers. Mack remembered Angie's sweet spot and how she had exploded. Locating the same, he heard Effy gasp out aloud as he massaged it.

It was as if a switch had flicked the power on. It was akin to a pleasurable electric shock rippling through her body.

"Oh, sweet Jesus!" Effy cried out. "Oh, my goodness!"

Mack continued to apply a firm gentle pressure on the fleshy button.

Taking hold of his erect penis she instinctively performed the masturbatory motion. Unable to turn away from her, his hand now clamped tight by her thighs, he ejaculated, unable to stop himself. Effy was having her own uncontrollable orgasmic rapture, her thighs locking his hand. She was aware of his warm semen spurting on her lower abdomen. In erotic free fall nothing mattered but the moment.

As they both subsided from the intense individual experiences Effy unlocked her thighs. His penis softened as she withdrew her hand, the end still continuing to release a light after-flow.

Mack was apologetic. "I'm so sorry I couldn't stop myself."

Effy touched her abdomen where he had ejaculated feeling its stickiness. "Goodness. It's messier than I expected. Do you always… you know… release so much?"

"Pretty much," came his shameful admission. "Let me run you a bath. I'll put the immersion heater on. It will take about half an hour to heat up. We had it installed last year so we could have hot water when we wanted it."

"You don't have to, I can go and wash…"

"It's no problem. I feel so bad about this." He jumped out of bed and disappeared downstairs.

Effy enjoyed having a bath. She had to sponge the parts of the slip clean where his semen had gone. The slip soon dried in the airing cupboard. Mack even produced a dressing gown he owned but which he claimed never to wear. Drying herself off, she went back to his room and watched as he put a fresh set of sheets on the bed.

"I didn't realise you were so domesticated."

"I'm not," he answered, grinning. "I thought I'd better get them in the washing machine. I don't want my mum wondering what I'd been up to."

"Do you know how to operate one?"

"I'll figure it out. How hard can it be?"

"I'll show you before I go and make sure you do it right."

"Can I tempt you back into bed again?" He suggested cheekily.

"Go on then." Taking off the dressing gown she dived between the bed covers, wearing her bra and briefs.

"Aren't you going to take your bra off?'

Effy gave him one of those looks. Without a word she took it off disappearing under the covers.

"I hope you're not a sex maniac," she whispered as they snuggled, "at least not until we're ready to go all the way."

"With you in my bed I'm likely to be a raving sex maniac."

"How did you know where to touch me like that?"

"I read about it in a book," he lied, silencing her with a kiss.

It was after midnight before they got out of the bed. The pure pleasuring of one another in intimate ways had satisfied their cravings.

"I want to do this again," Mack whispered in her ear as he helped zip up her dress. "And again, and again."

"So why don't we? I'll pretend I'm going up to Caitlin's after work and come here. I'm sure I can manage at least twice this week. My parents

175

are letting the chaperone leash slip these days. They won't suspect. Mind you, I'll have to be back home by eight thirty so we won't have as long as tonight. How about that?"

Effy was as good as her word. She came round on the Monday, and then on the Thursday. They played house for two evenings acting like a young married couple. She even helped Mack to do the laundry, showing him how to use the twin tub. Each time they slipped between the sheets for an hour or so. Mack had to resist the temptation of trying to have full sex with Effy, which was not easy.

With each intimacy Effy considered allowing the natural course of events to happen. She had even allowed him to pull her briefs down mid-thigh for easier access. There was a part of her that hoped he would succumb and she would not resist. In the end Mack held back and Effy understood how silly her state of mind was. It was as well they had so few opportunities for intimacies.

Their brief trial honeymoon ended with the return of Mack's parents. Robert MacKinnon got to see England beat Germany 4–2. So delighted was MacKinnon senior he even broke out a bottle of twelve-year-old whisky to celebrate. His sons shared a "wee dram" or two with him. It could only have delighted him more if Scotland had won instead of the "auld enemy".

Mack took Effy to the cinema that evening rather going over to Halifax. Alfred Hitchcock's "Torn Curtain" was showing. They could be together alone in the darkness. The truth was he was finding it hard to conceal his relationship with Effy from his parents. One Sunday afternoon their secret was finally exposed. A surprise visit by the doting grandparents to Adam's was no surprise but orchestrated.

CHAPTER 35

I Spy For the FBI – Jamo Thomas (Polydor BM 56709 – 1966)

Sunday 7 August 1966

Sunny skies and soaring temperatures were perfect for zooming around on the scooter. Effy needed no persuasion in such ideal conditions when Mack suggested a trip out.

They rode over to Shibden Park in Halifax to avoid local attention. The park was an ideal place to visit on a warm, lazy, sunny Sunday afternoon. Walking hand in hand they chatted about everyday things. Today was no different from other times. Conversation was never forced, flowing with natural ease. Disagreements were rare. When they happened the twosome resolved them with lightness and humour.

To Mack his relationship with Effy seemed close and loving like that of his parents. To Effy Mack seemed mature beyond his sixteen years: loving, thoughtful and considerate. She adored the way he was a patient listener. He was the male role model she wished her own father could be. Nothing much appeared to faze him. At worst he could get annoyed, though he never appeared to dwell long on annoyances. Always calm, always cool, he kept complete control when others became rattled. She had once asked him how he could be so cool and calm. His answer made complete sense.

According to his father the MacKinnon clan motto was *"Audentes Fortuna Juvat"*. Translated from the Latin, this meant *"Fortune favours the bold"*. You could not be bold and panicky. Boldness was about staying cool under pressure so you could be decisive when it mattered. Effy admired Mack for those qualities and wished she could be more like him.

On returning to Adam's, Mack spotted his father's new car. A dark blue Ford Zephyr had recently replaced the Cortina. Riding past the house he stopped at the end of the road. Turning to Effy he suggested being careful what they said when they met his parents. It would be better if he did the talking. Both wished they could be more open about their relationship. How Mack's parents would react knowing about them was a troubling unknown. Leaving Mack to do the talking was the smart move. He could be better than a courtroom lawyer when it came to glibness. Mack avoided lying if he could. He slanted the truth employing a kind of diplomatic evasiveness. Effy had learned this from him and had even begun to do the same herself at home with disarming effect.

In cricketing terms Mack played the straight bat. Going on the defensive, he greeted his parents, saying how surprised he was to see them. He had no intention of offering any explanations for the scooter ride.

His parents had met Effy before but did not know this younger sister well. With her granddaughter in her arms, Mack's mother appraised Effy, making the teenager uncomfortable. It was a close and rather too obvious scrutiny.

"Did you enjoy going on the scooter, dear?" Mack's mother asked. "You've been gone quite a while. Did James take you far?"

"We went to Shibden Park. I've never been there before. James told me the house dated back to before Tudor times, to the early fourteen hundreds."

"Did he now?" His father joined in, giving Mack the oddest of looks. His son recognised this as one of Dad's opening gambits.

"The weather was so pleasant. I thought Fiona wouldn't want to stay in. I offered to take her somewhere she hadn't seen before." Mack made it sound convincing and casual. It was the actual truth and nothing less as it happened. They had never been there. Which was not to say they had not passed it countless times, travelling back and forth from Halifax.

"And does he take care to ride in a safe manner, Fiona?" His father was baiting a trap, no doubt expecting a different answer than he received.

"I suppose so," Effy answered. "I never felt unsafe. It was enjoyable going on the scooter." The implication was unspoken. When his father said "does he" he was implying it was not her first scooter ride.

"I always ride safely, Dad. And I certainly wouldn't want anything to happen to Caitlin's sister. Besides, you can see how much of a squash it gets in here. I thought it might be great to get out in the sunshine. The riding conditions were perfect today."

Adam had determined to have a dig at Mack and Effy's expense. "Better watch these two, dad. You never know, mum. You may end up with a new daughter-in-law."

Effy blushed, giving Adam one of those "what are you playing at" looks. Nor was she playing the shy girl. The blushing was all too genuine. The thought that one day she might marry Mack had crossed her mind too many times to recall.

"Leave it out!" Mack said, irritated by Adam's comment.

Caitlin protested. "For heaven's sake, Adam. Stop teasing them."

Ellen decided to add her two-penny worth to try to make light of it. "A scooter ride to Halifax on a Sunday afternoon and you're halfway down the aisle already, sis. Good going."

"Look, what's all the fuss about? Cut it out, will you." Glancing towards Effy, still blushing, Mack added, "It's not like we did anything wrong. Going for a walk in a park is hardly like getting engaged, is it? Or are we living in Victorian times?"

"So will you be seeing each other again?" His father had no intention of beating around the proverbial bush. He cut straight to the heart of the matter.

"I expect so. Fiona comes round quite often to see Caitlin and the baby. So do Ellen and her other sisters. I get to see her here."

His mother intervened, addressing Effy. "Fiona, why don't you come to tea next Sunday afternoon? You know where we live, don't you, dear? If not, James can fetch you on his scooter. Then we can get to know another of Caitlin's sisters better."

Mack did not like the sound of that. What was going on? The way his mum had emphasised "you know where we live" was ominous. Why would she say that to Effy? They knew something. They were up to something. "I'm sure Fiona won't want to as she likes to see Caitlin and the baby at the weekends."

"I'm sure Fiona won't mind missing an hour or so, will you, dear?" his mother continued, dismissing Mack's attempts to obviate her plan. "I insist you come, Fiona. You will come, won't you, dear?"

Effy glanced at Mack. She was not panicking but he read her expression. Her eyes told him everything in an instant.

Almost with calculated intent Robert MacKinnon added, "What an excellent suggestion, Jane. It will be pleasant indeed to have a young lady round at the house. Should make a change from those young men who keep popping in to have their scooters mended."

"Mr and Mrs Halloran may have plans and we know they can be awkward. Shouldn't Fiona check first?" Mack knew attempts to foil his parents were not going to work after noting his father's use of the word "again".

"Caitlin has already mentioned they will be out next Sunday, according to Bridget. So it won't be a problem, will it, Caitlin dear?" continued his mother, brooking no argument.

179

"I suppose not." Caitlin was flummoxed. It was obvious her mother-in-law had an agenda of her own concerning her sister.

Effy tried one last ploy to put off visiting the MacKinnons. "I don't want to put you to any trouble, Mrs MacKinnon."

"Oh, it won't be any trouble, Fiona. No trouble at all," was the triumphant checkmate response, "will it, James? Both your father and I will be looking forward to it."

They knew.

CHAPTER 36

Gonna Fix You Good (Every Time You're Bad)
Little Anthony & The Imperials
(United Artists UP 35345 – 1966)

Monday 8 August 1966

Monday midday found Mack outside C&A waiting for Effy. There had been no opportunity to talk yesterday. As soon as they met, Effy hugged him and they shared a long unrestrained kiss. They made their way to the Exchange railway station where Effy could sit and eat her lunch as they talked.

"They know. Don't they? About us?"

"They know something. But quite what, I have no idea." Mack put his arm around her.

"What will they ask?" She looked so vulnerable, it made him feel instinctively protective. "Please don't say they'll try to stop us seeing each other. I couldn't stand it if I couldn't be with you."

"They can try. I doubt they'd succeed. No, I suspect they'll most likely want to vet you. One thing I'm sure, they'll try an honesty check."

"A what?"

"I suspect someone must have seen us coming and going when you came round. A neighbour has more than likely grassed us up."

"Oh, God no! You mean when I stayed late that Saturday night?"

"Don't panic, Effy. Remember, what they know is hardly anything. What they suspect is something else. At best they may have seen you leaving at about eight o'clock midweek."

"What's the worst?"

"They saw you leaving at one in the morning."

"Oh, dear God, we could be in so much trouble. Oh, Mack! What are we going to do?"

"Stop panicking. Like I said, what do they actually know? We play the honesty card and admit everything when questioned."

Effy sat upright, almost dropping her half-eaten sandwich in alarm. "Everything? Even what we got up to in bed?"

181

"No! You must be kidding. My mum would have a litter of kittens if we did that. Tell me something, do you feel guilty about what we got up to in bed?"

"No. Not at all."

"Okay. Neither do I. In our version of the truth we have done nothing wrong. So we don't need to mention it. Anyway, what we do to each other is our affair. I doubt they'll dare to ask. This is how it's going to go down. At some point the inevitable question is going to be, did we go all the way? Well, we didn't. Hand on heart you can say nothing happened so there's no chance of getting pregnant. True?"

"True."

"So nothing happened, right?"

"Right."

"Do you imagine they're going to ask about anything else? I doubt it. They'll assume we kissed and cuddled. We can admit to that. They'd be expecting us to have done at least that much. They'd be too embarrassed to ask about anymore. In fact, I doubt they would even ask us about kissing."

"What do we tell them about how long we've been going out?"

"Let's tell them the truth. Eighteen months going on nineteen. After all, they want the truth so we'll give it to them. The best form of defence is attack. We'll go on the offensive. Now how about we go about it this way?"

By the time Effy returned to C&A she was much happier. Not only was she reassured but also amused by the stratagem Mack had outlined. Mack was right. Denial was not an option. Telling the truth, insofar as it was relevant, was best.

CHAPTER 37

Think – Chris Farlowe (Immediate IM 023 – 1966)

Sunday 14 August 1966

"Ready?"

"Ready."

"Let's go and get it over with." Mack opened the front door, ushering Effy in first.

Hearing them enter, his mother came out of the kitchen into the hallway. Mack helped Effy off with her jacket. As they had planned, Effy delivered the opening broadside. "Should I hang it up under the stairs with the rest of the coats?"

"Yes, dear. James, show Fiona..." She had no chance to finish. To her surprise, Effy was already hanging the jacket up. Removing her pinny, Jane MacKinnon returned to the kitchen and reappeared again in seconds. All three walked into the lounge, Effy leading the way and heading towards the settee as planned.

"Do sit down, Fiona. You've been here before, haven't you?"

"Yes, Mrs MacKinnon. I came here when you were on holiday."

Mack suppressed a smile. In tennis speak it was advantage Effy. His mother, he assumed, had been expecting to wheedle a confession out of them. Instead the open admission was taking her off balance. His father, who had been in the adjoining living room, joined them.

"A pleasure to see you again, Fiona. Mrs MacKinnon was worried you might take fright and not come to tea."

"Why would I take fright, Mr MacKinnon? I couldn't turn down such a kind invitation. Especially as you've both been so kind to my sister and Adam."

Mack was enjoying this. He would have liked to shout out aloud, "Ding! Round one, Effy!" but suppressed the idea. Effy was following the script to perfection.

"It seems Fiona has been here before during our week's holiday," Jane MacKinnon added, sitting down in her favourite armchair.

"I take it," Robert MacKinnon began, "you've been seeing one another before last Sunday?"

"As a matter of fact we have. We've been going steady for eighteen, almost nineteen, months. Including the time she was first grounded by her dad."

Surprise was writ large on his parents' faces.

"Who's Effy?" Robert MacKinnon looked puzzled. "Is she another one of your girlfriends?"

"No. Fiona is Effy," emphasised Mack.

"Apart from my Da, it's the name everyone else calls me at home. Only my Da calls me Fiona," Effy clarified.

"Oh!" Robert MacKinnon exclaimed. "How strange!"

Mack was not sure why his mum had not queried Fiona's name. He was sure she knew it was Effy and not Fiona. He started to wonder why.

"Well, you've kept that quiet," continued Robert MacKinnon. "I suspect I may know why you did, but carry on."

"The evening Caitlin came to stay was the same evening we went out for the first time. We went to the Elite up the road. You know the rest. We weren't sure how you'd react if you found out we had been seeing each other. We didn't want you worrying that we'd end up doing the same as Adam and Caitlin. Which, by the way, we haven't."

Taking his hand in hers for moral support, Effy joined in the conversation. "We like being together. We understand we're much too young to be doing anything foolish. Seeing what motherhood is like for Caitlin I don't want to end up in the same situation. Besides, I'd like a career first."

Mack's reading of the situation showed a degree of instant relief in his parents' demeanours. Their anxious stiffness melted into a more visible relaxed attitude.

"Don't blame Adam or Caitlin and her sisters for keeping 'schtum' about us. It was more about giving the other sisters some freedom as well as Effy. They've been like prisoners in the house, not being allowed to go anywhere with friends. Not exactly normal, keeping them penned up. We were also concerned what your reaction would be. What with everything going on in Effy's family."

Robert MacKinnon addressed his wife after what seemed a longish silence. "Well, Jane, that should take away much of the concern on your mind."

Mack's mum remained suspicious. "So what were you doing when you came up to the house during the week? Our neighbours saw you coming here twice."

184

Mack decided to say something outrageous, knowing how susceptible his mum could be. "We played at house. Seeing what it'd be like being a married couple."

"You did what?" Jane MacKinnon exclaimed, startled.

"Stop it, Mack." Effy glared at him. "I came to help him out. I showed him how to cook a simple meal. We had something to eat. I made him wash up the pots, pans, plates and cutlery building up on the draining board. He didn't have a clue about using a twin tub. James wanted to wash his clothes so you didn't have to when you returned. Nor did he know how to deal with his stained overalls from Benny's. I had to show him what to do. He had some idea about using the vac, except he didn't bother emptying the bag. It was getting clogged and couldn't suction. I had to make him take out the rubbish too."

"She also gave me a lesson in how to iron my shirts," Mack added for good measure.

Mack's father began to grin and then laugh. "I remember someone else who helped me with chores when I was a bachelor."

Jane MacKinnon gave her husband a frosty look, which transformed into a smile. It reminded her of something similar when she was a young Wren and Robert a dashing bachelor on shore leave.

"Well, what can I say, Effy? You've succeeded where his mother could not. So what did you teach him to cook?"

"I kept it simple. I showed him how to make bangers and mash. If he'd tried to fry sausages and onions on his own he would have incinerated the lot. Or worse, set the kitchen on fire."

By the time they sat down to tea it was obvious Effy was winning his parents over. In the end Mack let Effy's natural charm do all the work.

Jane MacKinnon had taken to Effy's sister Caitlin over time. She had accepted her as a decent girl caught out by circumstances not too dissimilar to her own. With Effy it was so different, even strange. There was something lovable about Caitlin's sister. Jane warmed to her as though she could be her own daughter.

In the coming weeks they would form an inexplicably close relationship. Effy would never be an unwanted rival for her son's affections. It was hard at first, accepting her son had someone else in his life. The consolation was that he had found someone she would be fond of in the months ahead. It was not because Effy Halloran was sensible, practical, bright and endearing. There was no doubting how besotted she was with

James, as he was with her. This much was so striking and obvious in the way she looked at him, hanging on his every word. What else could a mother hope for in a rival for her son's affections? She sensed there was a special bond between the two teenagers. Something seemed to say that destiny had brought them together. Her best friend was right about Effy Halloran. She was delightful.

Robert MacKinnon smiled to himself as he listened to the young pair. Lost in his own thoughts he recollected the winking incident. He never suspected his comments would one day lead to this. Destiny was strange indeed. He had joked about his son courting the young lass and lo and behold it was exactly what had happened. He was thankful he only had two sons. If there had been seven they might all have ended up marrying Halloran girls. There was no doubt about it. James was turning into a handsome young man. His girlfriend Effy was turning into a beautiful young woman. They seemed made for each other. It was a shame her father was such a religious zealot. Old Man Halloran was a fanatic, unable to see what a treasure surrounded him. One day, when it was gone, what would his religious zeal have cost him?

Like his wife Robert MacKinnon knew the practical realities of relationships. You married the woman of your dreams but you also married into her family as she did into yours. This was an inescapable fact of life. You could never untangle from this wider relationship.

Mack and Effy felt a sense of relief that his parents accepted them as a couple. It would be some time until they understood the true impact of their romance on his parents. For the moment, they considered it a victory in a battle that was never a battle. His parents had genuine concerns for the two sixteen-year-olds. At least now it was all out in the open, taking away some of the pressures. For Effy it was one less problem: one less worry to harbour in a troubled home life. In the next couple of years she would find the MacKinnons' home a refuge from her own.

CHAPTER 38

Secret Love – Billy Stewart (Chess CRS 8045 – 1966)

Sunday 14 August 1966

"How did it go?" Ellen wanted to know as she came into her younger sister's bedroom.

"Fine," Effy replied, solemn-faced and non-committal.

"Did they sweat it out of you?"

"About the two of us?"

"Stop playing games. Yes. Unless you have another boyfriend tucked away that you haven't told us about?"

"We told them everything. All about going steady for ages."

"How did they take it?"

"Before they threw me out of the front door? Or afterwards on the doorstep?"

"They never!" Ellen exclaimed, looking mortified. "How awful! And I thought they were such lovely people."

"God, she's so gullible!" Grace burst out laughing. "I'm supposed to be the baby of the family but even I wouldn't have fallen for that."

"Oh, ha ha! Do you know, Effy? You're getting more and more like your boyfriend. His warped sense of humour is like a disease because you appear to be catching it."

"I'm sorry for winding you up, sis." Effy paused. "You may be right about the sense of humour. Actually, they were so nice after we admitted going steady. His mother said I was welcome to come up at any time without needing an invite. In fact, she'd love me to come up and help her with some dressmaking sometime."

"I reckon our Effy is like one of those hypnotists." Grace began performing movements like a stage hypnotist. "Mesmerises them by going, 'look into my eyes... you are falling into a deep sleep...'"

The divulged information impressed Ellen. "You may be right, Grace. Looks like she could charm the apples off a tree. Now for the bad news: Bridget is leaving home. She's renting a flat and then she says she'll be buying her own house."

"You're kidding!" For Effy this news stunned and upset her. "Tell me you're kidding?"

"I'm not." Grace's mood became gloomy in an instant. "Bridget's been threatening it for a long time. Now she's twenty-one she'll be able to do that."

"I wish I was kidding, Eff. Sorry, it's true. She says she's going to have a word with the four of us about it."

"I wonder if she'll let me come and live with her?" Grace sounded plaintive, near to tears. "She can't abandon us, not like that."

It was true. Bridget, their guardian angel, was leaving. She broke the news to her four younger sisters. It was time to go but they were not to worry. She would be dropping in three or four times a week in the evenings to make sure nothing was amiss.

Deidre was already confident she would be gone to Manchester in September. Ellen still had a year to go before her A Levels and was less happy. Effy would be starting in the Sixth Form. If she had not performed well in her O Levels she considered not bothering taking A Levels. The difficulty was that deep down she knew her exams had gone too well. Grace saw the future in stark contrast, coming as close to tears as her personality would allow. Aileen was also leaving to enter a novitiate. The household was shrinking, though not their father's oppressive zeal.

Effy had grown more intolerant of her father, even refusing to speak to him. It appeared to be mutual. When he spoke to her his words were harsh, emotive, charged with religious zeal. Effy had become adept at retaliating, using pointed theological counters vexing him further. Mrs Halloran, who was closer to her daughter, tried to reconcile them. All too often she ended up supporting her husband, if not actually agreeing with him. Ellen, unlike Effy, kept her head below the parapets as the skirmishing became worse. All she hoped was to be able to get through her last year of the Sixth Form. If it came to it Ellen vowed to take drastic action. She would not let her father's bullying intimidation win. Grace kept to her room, siding with Effy. At least now they could visit Caitlin without Bridget's chaperoning. Providing, that was, they returned by the due hour. The babysitting scam continued to work.

CHAPTER 39

Oh How Happy – Shades of Blue (Sue WI 4022 – 1966)

Sunday 28 August 1966

The summer holidays were drawing to a close. Deidre had passed her A Levels, achieving the required 4 A's she needed to get into Manchester. Even though it was a month before she could leave for the hall of residence, she had already packed in readiness.

Effy was also delighted. She had passed all seven O Levels with 1's, much to her delight. Mack, who had only entered for two GCEs and seven CSEs, was also pleased. He had passed Math and Economics with GCE Grade 1's. The CSEs consisted of Grade 1's in English, History, Commerce and General Science. The rest were 2's and 3's. It would be enough to start a three A Levels course at the grammar school. That was not the only change.

Bridget had moved out of the family home into a small two-bedroom flat in Shipley. On their days off from their part-time jobs, both Effy and Mack had gone round to help decorate the flat. Mack had assisted his father, learning the basics of home decorating. He had even assisted Adam and his father when his brother had moved into the rented house with Caitlin.

Bridget, working during the day, returned to her new home pleased with their efforts. They had transformed the flat in three days. She had wanted to pay them but they refused to take any money. Bridget intended the flat to be temporary until she could learn to drive. Then she would look into buying her own house.

The Bank holiday weekend was looming. Some of the Halifax crowd were heading for the seaside on their scooters. A group decided to head for Bridlington on the East Coast, the others to Blackpool. Since Effy was working Saturday she and Mack decided to catch up with Tom and the others in Blackpool on Sunday. They agreed a pre-arranged time and place on the Golden Mile.

Mack collected Effy from his brother's house at six on the Sunday morning. It took over two hours to make the journey. They spent another thirty minutes driving up and down the front, looking for the others. Finally, spotting Tom, Mahmoud, Acky and the rest they pulled up to a café on the front. Mods from all over the North West had congregated in the resort. The girls who turned up had travelled by train or coach, going into B&Bs. Some of the guys had slept under the pier after going to Blackpool's Twisted Wheel club on Coronation Road. Unlike its superior Manchester half, it only stayed open until two in the morning. TC, Acky and some others had broken into the railway yard and slept inside the railway carriages. Effy found it hilarious listening to tales like these. Boys seemed to live such exciting and daring lives.

Paul had become the proud owner one of the latest SX200s. He was exchanging tips with Mack about planning to have the cylinder bored out to 225cc which meant nothing much to her. Effy listened to their conversation but the technical talk went over her head. Surrounded by a bunch of lads who were listening in, she felt out of it.

Much to Effy's relief, Angie Thornton turned up, accompanied by Linda and Carol. After the usual banter from the lads the girls got their teas and coffee. Effy joined them, leaving the males to their raucous carrying on. Angie sprang a surprise. She had not only passed her driving test, she had actually bought her own car less than a week ago. Driving to Blackpool so soon after passing her test was remarkable. According to Linda, Angie was a natural-born driver, better by far than her own dad. Angie asked Effy not to say a word to anyone and keep it secret. Otherwise everyone would want to treat her like some glorified taxi driver. It was fine to tell Mack because he was a good friend and would not let it slip.

Angie was always delighted to see Effy. Over the past months they had become firm friends. The three girls regaled her about the antics of the B&B landlady. She was like the ones portrayed in the saucy seaside postcards. Then talk was all about the evening at The Twisted Wheel. Chatted up by boys from Burnley, then by others from Blackburn, it had been flattering. Carol was the only one who had copped off with someone, a boy from Burnley. Linda, still waiting for Steve, had steered clear. Angie confessed she did not fancy any of them so she and Linda stuck together.

When Linda and Carol went over to chat with the guys Effy asked Angie if they could speak in private. Excusing themselves on the pretext of getting some fresh air the two young women went for a walk on the front.

"Your hip is about to start hurting," Angie interrupted Mack and Paul on the way out. "I'm going to prise your better half from it to get some fresh air. We won't be long."

Mack never gave it another thought, listening to tales of thievery. Paul was recounting how one of the guys had stolen food from the self-service counter. Busy at the till, the staff were unaware of his open pilfering bravado. Taking requests he passed the stolen items over to others sitting close by.

When the girls came back a quarter of an hour later Angie joked, "How's the hip? Did it miss Effy?"

Effy sat down on Mack's knee and planted a big kiss on his lips. "My hip was starting to miss him a little," she admitted.

"So was mine," Mack added, grinning.

"Time you two got a room at a B&B," Paul suggested.

Angie and Effy exchanged glances, their faces lighting up in smiles.

The rest of the afternoon, until closing time, they spent going in and out of pubs. These were the pubs with jukeboxes playing good Soul and Motown. Most of the bar staff did not bother to refuse underage Mods from consuming beers. Mack bought Effy a couple of Babychams. Instead of downing Double Diamonds like the others he stuck to Cokes.

Mack and Effy left Blackpool early so they could get home before her curfew. Although feeling stiff from the time spent on the Lambretta she had enjoyed the day. Effy intended to keep what she had planned secret from Mack.

On Bank Holiday Monday, her mother and father having gone out for the day, she came up to Mack's. They spent the afternoon listening to his extensive collection of Soul records. His parents even allowed her to go up to his room. Listening to the records, they exchanged a few kisses and cuddles. The record they both liked was such a rare find that Mack kept it secret from everyone on the scene. He had tried to find other copies of the original release on London Records but so far had found it impossible. It was Darrell Bank's *Open the Door to Your Heart*, which was now part of his 200 45 rpm singles collection. These singles never left home nor were ever loaned.

Later they had tea with his parents. There was a party over at Southowram in the evening to which they had an invite and decided to go.

Thanks to Ellen, this was possible. Her sister told her parents that Caitlin was unwell and needed Effy for an extra night to help out.

CHAPTER 40

My Boyfriend's Back – The Angels (Mercury AMT 1211 – 1963)

Monday 29 August 1966

"So what makes Soul music so good, then? Don't say it's great. Explain why it's so great."

Mack and Effy stood cornered in the crowded kitchen sipping soft drinks. It was the last day of freedom before starting the Sixth Form. They had found themselves unwittingly sucked into this unwanted conversation. It was meant to be a Mods-only party. According to someone this "smart arse" Hipperholme Grammar "nixie" had gate-crashed the do. A smug sense of superiority in the way he kept smirking had already riled a few. Having a "nixie" swaggering from room to room muttering "fucking Mods" signalled a clear intent to cause trouble.

"Do you have a soul?" Mack asked, planning some kind of clever putdown. Effy recognised what was about to take place.

"I don't believe in pseudo pretentious religious crap. There's no such thing as a soul."

"It's pointless telling you if you haven't got a soul. You need a soul to understand Soul music."

"Oh, how facile. Is that the best you can up with ss an argument?" Smartarse's sneering was palpable.

Effy tugged Mack's arm, seeing him getting more irritated with every moment of taunting derision. "Go on. Explain it to him."

Mack calmed down at her touch. She was right. Explanation was better than confrontation. He began. The detail was encyclopaedic. Soul music had its origins in the gospel church choirs of Black Americans in the USA's Deep South. Singers had translated the inherent emotion gospel music possessed into secular form. Infusing their songs with passion they created a secular version of Gospel music. Soul singers sang about falling in love, failed love, infidelity, having a good time and even protesting about civil rights. Mack gave it in full as Tom and others listened. Ray Charles, Sam Cooke, Otis Redding and Marvin Gaye received mention. So too did Motown and the Memphis sound in context to the Civil Rights movement and Martin Luther King. Soul music was not simply good time music. It was music breaking down the barriers of ingrained racism. Soul music made the young generation aware that colour didn't make people inferior. Under the skin everyone was a human being deserving of respect.

Smartarse was an educated lame brain. Responding with belittling racial jeers, he found Tom and the others laughing at him. They had been listening to Mack and making informed additions to his explanation.

"So what music do you listen to?" Mack tried politeness through gritted teeth.

"I quite like The Stones and The Beatles."

"Like The Stones' *Little Red Rooster*? First performed by Howlin' Wolf. Did you know the lyrics were by Willie Dixon? How strange! They're both black Blues men from the American Deep South. The same goes for *I'm a King Bee* performed by Slim Harpo, another Black Blues singer. *Can I Get a Witness?* Sung by Motown's Marvin Gaye, one of the best soul singers around. He's black, too. *Walking the Dog?* That's a Rufus Thomas original as recorded on the Stax label in Memphis. He's black as well. All those songs are on The Stones' *England's Newest Hit Makers* album. They're all original songs written and performed by black artists and nicked by The Stones. As for The Beatles, don't get me started. They lifted *Anna* from Arthur Alexander who recorded the original version."

Tom chipped in. "Don't forget *Money* by Barrett Strong."

"So, Mr Smart, Rolling Stones ignorant arse, here endeth the lesson. Don't even get me going on jazz. Next you'll be telling us Miles Davis and John Coltrane are white."

"Louis Armstrong's white too, isn't he?" someone mocked.

"I know he's black," Smartarse scoffed, trying to defend his injured pride. Assorted counter-jeers and laughter followed as he backed out of the kitchen.

Tom turned to Mack. "Brian was right. A first-class know-all wanker who thinks we're all uneducated oiks. Looky, looky who's turned up."

Angie Thornton's arrival elicited the usual male attention. Eventually she made her way across the room to meet up with Mack, Effy, Tom and his latest flame, a girl called Lynn.

"Hope you brought your own drink." Tom greeted her with a raised bottle of Double Diamond. "They ran out of booze a while ago."

"I don't drink and drive so it's not a problem." Then, turning to Tom's new girlfriend, she added, "If I were you I'd catch the bus home. Don't take any chances on the back of his scooter. I was daft enough to cadge a lift home with him once when he was well pissed. Never again. I thought we were going to get killed crashing into the back of a lorry."

"Don't exaggerate, lass. I'd only had three pints of Tetley's."

"Three pints more than you could handle," came Angie's quick-fire put down.

"Anyway, there was never any chance of hitting the back of that lorry. I had it all under control. Thought I'd get you frightened enough to wet your knickers."

"You mean like you shat your own Y-fronts?" Angie turned to Mack and continued. "I need to have a chat with Effy for a minute or two."

"Go ahead," Mack replied.

"In private."

"Is it more girl talk? Are you keeping secrets from me, Effy?"

"Don't be nosey, some things are not for men's ears. Don't worry. It's nothing for you to get concerned about," Effy responded, giving him a quick peck on the cheek.

Mack watched them disappear outside. When they returned ten minutes later they saw him deep in conversation with a group of guys from the Square. Angie stopped her from going straight over. "Stop with me for a while. I know you're crazy about him but sometimes you need to give him some breathing space."

"You're right. I suppose I am a bit too clingy," Effy confessed.

"Yes, you are. Let's hope neither of you ever meets someone else you like better."

Angie's words made her cold at the thought.

Smartarse approached them, trailed by a nervous-looking sidekick. Angie gave them a brief glance. Turning to Effy she uttered one word. "Gimps."

Effy didn't know what that meant but she had a good idea it wasn't flattering. In a low voice she asked, "What's a gimp?"

Angie indicated the two making their approach.

Smartarse's chat-up opening was shallow, corny and delivered with unbelievable arrogance.

"You look a lot like my next girlfriend."

"And you look like the bloke I turned down seconds from now."

Effy spluttered into uncontrollable laughter on hearing Angie's near instantaneous comeback. Smartarse failed to appreciate Angie's humour. He appreciated Effy's reaction even less, his inexplicable anger taking both girls

195

by surprise. "What's so funny, you dumb prossy tart? Think you're special, do you? Because you've got a clever-dick boyfriend?"

Effy winced from the pain as he grabbed her left arm in a vice-like grip above the elbow.

"Oi! Get your hands off her!" she heard Angie cry out as she tried to break his grip on Effy's arm. Letting go, he shoved Angie against the wall.

"Outside." Mack spat out the word, appearing as if from nowhere.

"I wouldn't," Smartarse's side-kick warned. "He plays for the County 15 under 20s squad."

"Does he now? Good for him. Outside. Now," Mack insisted.

"With pleasure."

"Mack, please don't," he heard Effy say.

"Don't worry, Effy." Tom followed them out, grinning. "Mack will be back in two shakes. Anyway we don't want blood splattered everywhere on the wallpaper and flooring. Our hostess's parents wouldn't appreciate it."

"Angie, are you okay?" Effy asked, rubbing her arm.

"I'm fine. Nothing broken. What a shit!"

Tom opened the door and called to them less than a minute later. "Mack needs you to come outside, Effy. Angie, you too, somebody has something to say to you both. Well, don't hang about, quick."

"Oh, God, I hope Mack's not hurt." Effy dashed out, followed by Angie and others who had heard the commotion.

Mack was standing over Smartarse whose nose was streaming blood onto the tarmac drive. He had Effy's assailant's arm extended up into the air, his hand pressing against the elbow joint. Smartarse's hand was bent upwards in an unnatural way at the wrist. Mack's foot was on the back of the rugby player's knee.

"You've behaved like a prize bastard. Now I'd like to hear you apologise to my girlfriend and my friend Angie."

"I'm sorry." Smartarse grunted in pain.

Mack applied more pressure to the three joints. "Properly and with sincerity please, like you mean it."

The pain on Smartarse's blood-splattered face was clear. "I apologise, honest."

"Come along, you can do better than that," Mack chided him like a schoolmaster. Applying more pressure to wrist and elbow encouraged a quicker response. "Allow me to help you out. Repeat after me, and do try making it sound genuine. I am a disgusting arrogant bully…"

Smartarse repeated the words in a guided litany.

"…who insults young ladies and uses violence against them. I am an unmitigated ill-mannered shit. If I'm caught doing this again, a bust nose will be the least of my troubles. I apologise for calling this young lady a dumb prossy tart. I apologise to the other young lady for pushing her against the wall. In future I will treat all girls and women with the due deference and the proper respect they deserve. Good boy."

"Good boy," Smartarse repeated as Mack finally let go.

"Can I suggest in the politest way I know how that you bid everyone good night? And then fuck off back under the stone from where you came?"

Bested Smartarse nodded, knowing it was time to go. Leaving with his disconsolate sidekick he said, "Good night," as Mack had requested.

There was a round of applause from the Mods. They had gathered outside watching it all in silence. There was plenty of back-slapping and comments passed on Mack's handling of the situation. "Firkin' twat deserved it," said Tom, providing a blow-by-blow commentary of the incident to those around.

Mack came straight over to Effy and took a look at her arm. "That might bruise by tomorrow. We need to get a cold compress on it. Let's see if they have something we can soak in cold water and wrap round it."

Angie leaned over and kissed him on the cheek in front of Effy. "Thank you for what you did. You're a regular Galahad, a proper knight in shining armour. Effy, you're so lucky to have Mack. Hold onto him. Don't let anyone steal him away from you."

"I won't." Her eyes sparkled as she looked into his.

CHAPTER 41

You Can't Hurry Love – The Supremes (Tamla Motown TMG 575 – 1966)

Thursday 1 September 1966

Mack's first week in the Sixth Form was neither remarkable nor welcoming. There were over two hundred students in the Sixth Form. Arriving on the Lambretta drew immediate attention to him. Parking in the area reserved for students' vehicles he noticed a few familiar faces. He remembered them from the Junior School. Not that they had been friends with him back then. They seemed surprised to see him but said nothing, though he received the odd casual acknowledgement of his presence. Other than that Mack didn't expect them to greet him as a long-lost friend from the Junior School. After five years they had their own established patterns of friendship. Most of the boys he had mixed with had gone to Edmund Campion.

The main school building was old but well-maintained. The Sixth Formers had their own purpose-built study block across from it. The first half hour was confusing as he tried to find out where to go and who to see. By the end of the morning Mack had started a three A Level course, opting for Economics, Math and History. He had to sit O Level English language in the November external. His CSE Grade 1 was not deemed good enough for possible university entrance. Since it was Language and Literature combined it might not be acceptable. It was also suggested he took an extra science. Mack opted for the Human Biology course called Anatomy, Physiology and Hygiene.

Compared to his former teachers he found the grammar school teachers a breed apart. He took to the Economics teacher and to "Sugar Ray" Robinson who taught history. He came to have a great deal of respect for the latter. The English teacher he found condescending, mocking his modern school origins. The P.E. teacher, who took the APH course, was a "real" bloke in every sense of the word. At least he treated Mack and the rest of the group in a no-nonsense manner as young men and not boys. Mack got to like and respect him over the coming year.

The workload came as a shock, though not the work itself. The work wasn't hard but coping with the quantity took some organising. There was plenty of back-up at home when it came to Economics and Pure Math and

198

Statistics. His father could help him with those should he need it, but they were no big deal. Medieval History was nothing comparable. The amount of note-taking and essay-writing was another matter. Mack found it fascinating and interesting, although the quantity of factual content he had to absorb was staggering.

Effy found it different too. Choosing her A level subjects had not been easy since she had no real idea what she wanted to do. Having been an all-rounder in the Fifth Form did not make it easier finalizing a choice. In the end, she opted for English Literature, Math and Art. Choosing these subjects gave her career route options later. This was not her main problem.

Her secret love affair was no longer secret. By the middle of the second week it was top of the Sixth Form hot gossip charts. Word had filtered down from the Upper to the Lower Sixth via the grapevine. It was all Ellen's fault for letting all and sundry know. Mack and Effy already enjoyed quasi-legendary lovers status in Grace's year. This was due to Grace's friend Jean. Grace was adamant. She refused to subscribe to the romanticised "legend" spread by Jean. She had even asked Jean to tone it down.

Effy had always been the quiet studious one among her fellow pupils. It was not a complete surprise to her classmates that she had found a boyfriend. Her growing beauty had been bound to attract someone. The only surprise was it had happened when she was only fourteen and that she had kept it secret so long. Effy found it disconcerting to be the focus of so much gossip and so many questions. There were the usual comments passed in her hearing. "It's the quiet ones you have to watch." Her refusal to talk about Mack made her love affair even more intriguing. She wished Ellen had kept quiet, leaving it secret. It was tiring being asked, "Okay, Juliet, when do we get to meet Romeo?" There were other similar comments. Her response was to follow Mack's dictum of staying cool and calm. Effy was unaware how much she had blossomed and changed over the summer. So adult in her conduct with others she could be unnerving. She failed to realise how mature, poised and intimidating she now appeared to those around her. Her cool, calm persona was a façade but it served her well.

Effy's new found prominence rested on her mysterious *demi-monde* Mod lifestyle as publicised by Ellen's gossip. She was still an ingénue, not at all as those in the Sixth Form were beginning to fictionalise. Changes had indeed happened. Hardened in emotional battles with her father she had found an inner resilience and strength. Achieving outstanding results had given her a genuine belief in her own abilities. Effy had changed alright although she was not yet aware of all these changes to herself. Changes such as these are not always self-evident.

Presenting a note excusing her from school on Thursday, Effy left mid-morning. The note was a forgery. Angie was waiting for her outside in her light green Triumph Herald.

"Did you have any trouble finding your way here?" Effy asked.

"Dead easy. No problems. Your directions were spot on," Angie replied. "The route through the city centre was tricky. I usually drive straight to Tech so I know how to get there. Finding Manningham Lane wasn't hard, but the sign-posting wasn't brilliant."

"I hope I'm not spoiling your day off. I'm so grateful for this. I don't know how else I could get sorted without your help."

"What are friends for?" Angie answered, starting the car. "And don't worry, Eff. My sister doesn't judge. She only helps you to stay safe. That's what her job's all about. Does Mack know yet?"

"God, no!" Effy exclaimed. "I'm keeping it as a surprise."

"Tell me you're not planning to make it his birthday present?" Angie asked, sounding flippant as they drove past the Locarno towards the city centre.

"Now, there's a thought," Effy answered.

A quick glance in her friend's direction confirmed that Effy was smiling to herself.

"Good grief, woman! You got it bad, and that ain't good." Angie grinned, shaking her head. Her memory of the night with Mack remained vivid. She was envious, while wishing at the same time she was not.

Effy had become one of her closest friends, much to her surprise. They had taken to one another from the first time they met, which was bizarre seeing that Angie had seduced Mack. She was genuine in her dread of Effy learning about her and Mack. That must never happen, for all their sakes.

The two young women were different in so many ways. Yet they found themselves drawn to one another. Effy admired Angie's worldly-wise approach to life. Angie wished she could be more like Effy, a little more naïve, innocent and straightforward. Of all the people she had met, Mack and Effy were the special ones she treasured as friends. There was an affinity between the three of them. Quite why this was so, she was unsure. Angie was just happy and pleased it existed for them to share.

CHAPTER 42

Baby Take Me – The Steampacket
(Performed live 1966. Recording released 1990)

Saturday 10 September 1966

It was the tenth of September. A night they would always remember. Mack and Effy finally persuaded a reluctant Adam and Caitlin to let them go to an all-nighter at The Plebs. Effy couldn't wait, excited at knowing she could stay up all night with Mack and her friends.

The Steam Packet was on the bill. Even without Rod "The Mod" Stewart, the line-up was still impressive. Long John Baldry, Brian Augur and Julie Driscoll were the band's core performers. The guys in the Square were keen to see Julie Driscoll who was something of a Mod beauty icon. Long John Baldry was the girls' handsome heart throb. Some even hoped for a chance to cop for him. For those in the know Baldry was a lost cause with females. Tom tried to explain this to Lynn, his new main squeeze. The singer batted for the other team and was open about it. Lynn, like so many of the girls, refused to believe it. How could someone so handsome and gorgeous be homosexual?

Tom turned to Mack for help. "Tell her, will you?"

"'Fraid it's true, Lynn. Anyway, what does it matter? Even if he was into women why would he have any interest in teenage girls?"

"You don't know that!" Lynn became petulant. "He might."

Effy smiled and shook her head, finding the debate about the singer's sexuality pointless. "What does it matter what he does in his private life, anyway?"

"What if he took a fancy to Mack?" Tom sniggered. "You'd soon be whistling a different tune."

"I don't see Mack being his type, not with me on his arm." Effy clutched Mack's arm as though to protect him.

"Uuuuh, I do fancy your boyfriend," Tom teased her with a limp-wristed pawing action.

"Give it a rest, Tom." Mack chuckled, slapping Tom's hand away. Then he added, with his best nasal Kenneth William's impersonation, "Stop messing about!"

The queue inched forward towards the cellar doorway steps.

"Are you two clean tonight?" Mack asked.

"We're well soiled," Lynn replied.

"She's had a couple of Dexys. I've popped three Dommys," Tom added in a conspiratorial whisper. "Enough to keep us awake. Are you two staying all night?"

"We'll see, won't we?" Mack looked at Effy. "It all depends on how tired we get."

"Anyone seen Angie?" Tom asked. "It's not like her not to come out to play."

"She's inside helping out in the cloakroom tonight," Effy informed them, realising as the words came out that she was letting something slip.

"When did she tell you that?" Mack gave her a puzzled look.

"Last time I saw her." Effy tried not to appear flustered by her unwitting slip. It was true but it had happened two days ago when Angie had picked her up. Their journey to Halifax had been secret. She did not like to deceive Mack who accepted what she said.

The Steam Packet came on late. It was worth the wait. Even without Rod Stewart the band was still brilliant. Long John Baldry was on top form as was Julie Driscoll, who not only looked good but sounded superb. One of the most bizarre moments came when they performed a song they called *Baby Take Me*. Bizarre because it was Tina Britt's *The Real Thing* using their own lyrics. Even so, the Baldry and Driscoll duet was brilliant. Baldry did an excellent version of *Baby Don't You Do It*. Brian Augur on the organ performed an incredible jazzy version of Dobie Gary's *The 'In' Crowd*. This had the packed audience going. All the regulars in the club immediately related to this live version. They were familiar with the Ramsey Lewis live version. Time flew and the set came to an end all too soon. An extended powerhouse version of Marvin Gaye's *Can I Get a Witness* brought the house down. Roars of applause demanded an encore and they got it.

Effy managed to stay awake until about five in the morning. Resting on Mack's lap her head nestled on his shoulder she dozed off. Mack did not like to wake her. So he let her drowse. For twenty minutes he enjoyed every moment of feeling her next to him. The delicate fragrant scent in her hair and the soft warmth of her skin were all the aphrodisiac he needed. She fired his soul as he held her. There was nothing he would not do for her. With Effy's arms wrapped around him, lost in sleep, Mack reflected on how her love for him was so sweet and tender. She was everything to him, beyond meaning.

Effy woke with a start. "I'm sorry, I didn't mean to fall asleep."

"Do you want to go back?" he asked.

She shook her head, sweeping her long hair behind her ear. "Not yet. Let's stay a little while longer. I want to be with you for as long as possible. It's going to be a whole week before I can see you again. Seven days are too long without seeing you."

"I keep wishing we could be together all the time."

She gave him a loving squeeze.

Tom and Angie wanted them to stay so they could hang out in the Beefeater later. Mack said it would have to be another time. They needed to get back, grab some sleep. Then they would have to complete any outstanding schoolwork for the coming week.

Caitlin was up with Jane when they returned. Like them she had been up most of the night. The little girl was teething and it did not help she was always awake by first light.

"Look who's here!" Caitlin cooed to her daughter. "It's Aunt Effy and Uncle James, the night owls. I wonder what they've been doing? Should we ask Uncle James if he's been a well-behaved young man and not done anything he shouldn't with Aunty Effy?"

"Seriously, Caitlin?" Effy responded, miffed. "I'm not going to be losing my virginity in a cellar club filled with a couple of hundred people watching a band. So Jane, little darling niece, take no notice of your mummy's suspicious dirty mind. Aunt Effy is a well-behaved young lady. For now."

"Jane's happy to hear you say so, aren't you dear?" Caitlin spoke to the little girl as part of the ongoing conversation. The little girl attempted something sounding like a reply in baby gibberish.

"But who knows, little Jane? Little girls grow up and become young women. They change their minds about being well-behaved virtuous young ladies." Effy directed her words at Caitlin.

"That's uncalled for, Effy." Caitlin thought Effy was referring to her own past.

"What makes you think I was talking about you?" Effy looked Caitlin in the eyes.

There was some kind of silent exchange going on he could not fathom. Mack was finding this turn in the conversation by Effy so unlike her.

203

"If we were going to have sex we'd pick a bit more romantic spot than The Plebs."

"Is Ellen still sleeping?" Effy asked, changing the topic.

"She's out like a light. Came back on the last bus from that 'Hole in the Wall' place. Seems some bloke down there keeps annoying her and won't take 'No' for an answer. To be honest, she looked and sounded upset. I don't know what happened but it could not have been pleasant. She wouldn't tell me."

"I'd better get off," said Mack. "I need some shut-eye and then I'd better crack on this afternoon with that history essay for Tuesday."

Effy went to the door with him, giving him one last hug and kiss, and whispering in his ear, "I'm not planning to be virtuous for much longer." Whether it was tiredness or his imagination playing tricks, Mack doubted his hearing.

Effy whispered words that reminded him of lyrics from a Temptations record. "I'm gonna make love to you that's so true, you won't believe it. So get ready. And don't be a perfect gentleman either when the time comes."

Her words on the doorstep left him stunned. As she closed the door, with a sultry wicked glint in her eyes, he wondered if his imagination was playing tricks. He almost stumbled over his own feet wondering if it was all in his mind. Had he heard her say those words? She was right. Seven days were far too long to be apart.

CHAPTER 43

The Good, the Bad, and the Ugly (Main Title Theme) – Ennio Morricone
(United Artists Soundtrack LP – 1966)

Friday 23 September 1966

The sound of two scooters arriving in Kirkgate attracted no attention. The street was full of scooters on a Friday night. Mal Osborn never saw Mack and Tom coming as he jawed with his mates and a lone girl. Tom would later describe what took place next as a "Pearl Harbour move". They found Osborn standing on the corner below the Continental. He knew nothing about the attack until kicks to the back of the knees sent him crashing to the pavement. Osborn went down under the impact of Mack's simultaneous palm strikes to the sides of his head. Delivered with tremendous ferocity the combined blows repeated in rapid succession were blistering. The pain was intense and excruciating.

Osborn was aware of his girlfriend screaming, "Stop it!"

"Oh, shit!" escaped from his mouth. What he heard next were the words of vigilante justice.

"Your boyfriend, is he? Do you know he tried to rape a girl last Saturday night? No, I bet you didn't. This fucking cunt of yours is going think twice before he forces himself on another girl."

Reaching into his parka pocket Osborn tried to get a weighted key chain. As he attempted to stand, a kick to his coccyx sent him sprawling to the ground again and he roared in agony.

"Remember me? Remember when you said what you were going to do to me? Rip my head off and stick it up my backside, eh? Guess what? I'm going see if I can stuff your dick down your neck while it's still attached to you."

Looking up he saw Mack. Nothing much frightened Mal Osborn. The sight of his steely-eyed attacker driven with calculated icy anger did. Osborn was guilty of the crime. Painful justice was coming his way.

Mack had known nothing about the incident. Effy turned up with Grace at his house having sneaked out to recount the horrific tale. They told him how this Osborn character had persisted in pestering Ellen for weeks. Twice he had tried to force his attentions upon her but she had rebuffed him.

205

Then, while going to catch a bus on a deserted Sunbridge Road, he had assaulted her. Before she could react he had grabbed her from behind by the hair. Dragged into the dark alleyway round the corner from the club they had struggled. Smothering Ellen's cries with vicious kisses he tried to silence her into submission while simultaneously groping her. With his hand up her skirt and between her legs he had growled, "You know you want it. Let's get them off." Frightened as Ellen was she had resisted. Fighting back, digging her nails in deep, she had scratched his neck. Osborn retaliated with a brutal slap to her face causing a dark weal to appear the following day. Incensed Ellen had reacted by kneeing him in the groin with considerable force. Freed from his grip she left him doubled up and yelping in pain. Running back into the bright lit street she reached the safety of others. Later, once in bed and safe at Caitlin's, she had broken down in tearful silence.

It was only on waking that Effy realised something was wrong. Her sister was distressed. Refusing to tell her anything, Ellen tried to explain away the facial bruising. Claiming she had slipped colliding against a wall did not ring true. Effy did not believe her for a second and told her so. It was a concocted excuse and they knew it was. Ellen tried to carry on as normal but by Wednesday had broken down in floods of tears in front of Effy and Grace. Then they had learned the truth.

Ellen had begged them not to say anything to anyone. She blamed herself for the incident. Somehow it was her fault for giving out the wrong signals. That was most unlikely. Ellen was too plain-speaking to be a tease. Effy suggested going to the police. Then she realised her parents would learn about their babysitting scam. Bad as that would be, their father's reaction would be even worse: so awful that she would rather not contemplate it.

Ellen feared Adam finding out in case he took the law into his own hands. This was something they could not allow to happen. If he ended up beating Osborn to a pulp it might land him in jail for assault. Then how would poor Caitlin cope alone with Jane?

Ellen's state and confession had shaken Effy and Grace. Unaware of Mack's previous dealings with Osborn they decided to ask his advice. They sneaked out of the house while their father was out. As it happened his parents were not home too when they called, which was fortunate. Robert MacKinnon was still at work; Jane MacKinnon was out last-minute shopping. Mack listened with concealed but mounting anger, trying to remain calm, despite contrary feelings. Remaining silent, he decided on the next step. In the meantime he suggested they leave it with him: at least until the weekend so he could work out how best to help Ellen.

Mack knew what he had to do. Riding over to Halifax that evening he called in at his cousin's house on a pretext. Tom listened to the tale, struggling to believe what he was hearing. They made up their minds in seconds. After disputing who should be the one to kick seven bells out of Osborn Tom finally agreed to leave it to Mack. Mack would have the privilege of taking Osborn apart. Tom would act as shotgun. Anyone trying to help Osborn would have to deal with him.

Mack grabbed Osborn by the hood of his parka and swung him round. "Bring his bird over. Let her have a good look at his neck."

Pitiless, Mack yanked the paisley cravat from Osborn's neck to reveal the deep scratch marks. Turning to the girl who had been protesting non-stop about his violence he snarled, "I suppose he told you the cat scratched him on the neck?"

"He doesn't have a cat," she replied, her voice fading. "Must have been a hell of a cat to do that."

"Yeah, about your height and build." Tom laid on the sarcasm as he wielded a length of heavy-duty chain. "I bet he treats you the same and all the other birds he knows? Or do you enjoy getting roughed up and abused?"

This struck a nerve. "You bastard! I'm not good enough for you, is that it? Chasing other skirts behind my back. Forcing them to do stuff too. So it's not only me, is it, covering up the bruises with makeup?"

Lenny had warned Mack about the blow you never saw coming. A weighted key chain with a sharp end could cause disabling damage. The blow to the top of his shoulder stung. Had his downed opponent managed to get up to his feet he would have hit Mack across the face and head. This would have caused serious injury. Luck was on his side. Osborn was not going be so lucky. Mack did not allow the surge of adrenaline to sap his fighting ability. Focussing, he took control of himself, overcoming the disabling rush.

Meanwhile two of Osborn's mates, transfixed by the speed of the attack, intervened. Tom snap-kicked one on the knee. Using the heavy-duty length of chain as a flail he discouraged the other. One of Osborn's chums tried to snatch the whirling chain only to suffer repeated hits on his arm. This encouraged him to stay out of it, along with others who had come over to see what was happening. The paralysed onlookers could only watch Osborn meet callous vigilante justice.

The burly youth was going to regret his stupidity in using the key chain as a weapon. Osborn never saw the elbow coming as Mack broke his nose. His punishment was about to become a majorly brutal and humiliating spectacle. Quite what the exact sequence of events came next was a blur.

"Thirty-seconds" Lenny had told Mack when a man was down the fight was over. Tonight that wasn't going to happen. Kicking Osborn to the ground Mack watched him rolling into the middle of Sunbridge Road. A passing car almost ran into him. As he tried to get to his feet he collided with one of his pals who had attempted to jump Mack. What ensued next may have appeared comical. Mack played football with Osborn and his pal. Alternating, he kicked each one in turn all the way down the hill from the corner of Sunwin House to Thornton Road. They had no opportunity to get to their feet. Pulling a bloodied Osborn up by the hood of his parka he pushed him against a shop door at the bottom of the road. One hand pinned Osborn at the throat. The other clutched his genitals, exerting a tremendous agonising vice like grip. Adopting a Clint Eastwood steely drawl, Mack outlined his battered opponents' future.

Osborn was to clear out of Bradford because the city wasn't big enough for the two of them. Mack recommended he should go and play elsewhere. Keighley might be a good place. If Mack learned he was frequenting anywhere in Bradford on a weekend then he'd get paid another visit. The next time they came visiting they would come with company. If word ever leaked out about another molested girl he would lose his balls for real. The final squeeze made Osborn verge on passing out. The savage thrashing to which he he'd been subjected had broken him. Never beaten in a fight with such merciless thoroughness, there was genuine fear in Osborn's eyes. He wasn't sure whether the threats were genuine or not. Of one thing he was certain. He planned never to tangle with MacKinnon again after this ruthless drubbing.

Mack walked back up the road, meeting Tom part-way.

"Sorted?" his cousin asked.

"Sorted."

"Man, I thought you were going to kill him. You damn well came close. He's going to suffer some serious hurt for days. I hope you didn't bust any of his ribs." Tom tried to make light of the assault but Mack had horrified him. The dark remorseless dispassionate way he had dealt with Osborn was frightening. His cousin had taken this would-be rapist to the brink of hospitalization. The broken nose would need medical attention.

Osborn could even have broken ribs from the vicious kicking down the road. It was GBH. Nothing less. People went to jail for acts of Grievous Bodily Harm.

"Thanks for backing me up and riding shotgun. I wouldn't have been able to handle it on my own."

"You'd only do the same for me. It was a pleasure to watch a maestro street-fighting man at work. I was hoping you'd use a line like, 'Let me introduce my self as the best-selling author of Russian Rupture. I'm Doctor Ivana Kickyourbollocksoff.' But that bit about making him swallow his own dick? That was way cool. The kind of line you might expect in a Clint Eastwood Western."

"Clint Eastwood? Now that's taking the mickey mouse!"

"Definitely not. You're not as rugged as him, true enough, but you kick ass like him. What are you going to tell Effy?"

"The less the better. I suspect she'll go barmy if she ever finds out what I've done tonight." As an afterthought Mack added, "I think I overstepped the mark tonight even if he had it coming."

"Yeah. You kind of did. It was bit too GBH. The Krays would have been impressed. The local Beak a lot less."

"I went over the top, didn't I?" Mack need not have asked. Behind the jocularity Tom's worried expression confirmed it.

"Look. Why don't I have a word with Ellen." Tom changed the subject, injecting lightness in his voice. "Effy doesn't have to know the full SP. Better still nobody should know the full SP if we're honest."

"Good idea. The less they know the better. The Krays?"

"Yeah. Agreed. The Krays would love your style." Pausing for a moment or two, Tom continued. "We could persuade Ellen to come over to Halifax? I could collect her and then bring her back. Would she be up for coming out to play with us?"

Mack looked at Tom with disbelief. "Sometimes, I can't help wondering, are you for real? What's Lynn going to say?"

"She's so last week," Tom replied, grinning. "We may as well keep these Halloran girls in the family, eh?"

Mack shook his head. "Listen, she's a year older than you. What makes you imagine she'd want to go out with you?"

Tom flashed his disarming smile. "My natural charm and winning ways. What more could a girl ask for?"

"What indeed? Forget about clam tasting. There's no chance. She's not that kind of girl."

"You reckon?"

"I'm pretty sure. And not after what's happened to her."

"Don't worry, cuz. Ellen seems like a nice lass. I'll do my best to behave around her."

"God, you're a confident bugger."

"I can't help it. It's the way I am."

Of course, Effy did find out. Ellen was to blame as usual. Secrets were anything but her forte. Effy was upset with Mack. Her upset might have been far worse had she learned the truth. Instead Tom's sketchy edited details made the fight sound tame, nothing worse than a slight scuffle. Effy's upset was more in fear that there might be serious repercussions for Mack. There were none. She did not stay mad at him for long.

Ellen brightened on hearing of Osborn's comeuppance. Tom lived up to his playboy reputation. He and Ellen had met on several brief occasions at Adam's in the past. Tom charmed Ellen into coming to Halifax on the Saturday night. Mack and Effy were heartened. They were glad she was getting over her ugly experience so fast. Mack suspected Tom must have been looking for an excuse to ask Ellen out for quite a while. That, on its own, was to prove fatal in a non-fatal way. Tom fell for Ellen.

The following year Mal Osborn ended up in a high-speed crash on his scooter. An unverified rumour spread he had castrated himself on his scooter's handlebars. The impact had thrown him forward groin first with tremendous force. A news item in the Telegraph & Argus confirmed the accident. How true the castration tale was Mack never learned but it seemed improbable. Even a bastard like Osborn did not deserve to lose his genitals. Although on reflection he did.

CHAPTER 44

When a Man Loves a Woman – Percy Sledge (Atlantic 584001 – 1966)

Saturday 1 October 1966

"What is it with the menfolk in your family?" Jane MacKinnon questioned her husband. "Now your sister's son has taken up with a Halloran girl!"

"It's nothing to do with me," protested Robert MacKinnon, feeling affronted by the personal criticism. "You have to admit they're all bonny lassies in the Halloran family. I can't fault the boys for their tastes in girls."

"Do you realise," she continued after a brief pause, "if we'd had another child and he'd been a boy he would have been the same age as their youngest?"

"What's that got to do with anything?" Robert MacKinnon gave his wife a quizzical look.

"No doubt he'd be falling for her too."

"But we haven't. We decided two would be enough."

"What are you two grinning about?" Jane MacKinnon looked at her son and nephew. "And isn't Ellen a bit old for you, Tom? Quite what your mother will have to say about you dating an older young woman, I dread to think."

"That's so funny, Mum." Mack smirked, giving Tom an elbow dig in the ribs.

"What is?"

"An older young woman."

"You know exactly what I mean. Don't get smart with me, James."

"Mum's met her," Tom countered with a broad grin. "She didn't see there was anything wrong with Ellen being older. Thought she'd be more mature and sensible as a girlfriend. She's the first one I've brought back to the house my mum's actually liked. And she wasn't even my girlfriend when we went over last weekend. Anyway, it's nothing serious, Aunt Jane. It's not like Mack and Effy."

Mack gave Tom another, harder dig in the rib.

"How long do you expect Effy and Ellen to carry on these secret shenanigans? I'm surprised their father hasn't found out what's going on."

211

"He's never ever paid a single visit to see Caitlin since she left home. Not even to see his granddaughter. He doesn't even ask the girls about her." Mack stated the obvious.

"Neighbourhoods have eyes and ears, James. It only takes one unwitting comment from someone and it will be out in the open. What then?" His mum had a point. "Don't assume pretending to babysit Saturday night will work forever."

"Your mother's right," his father added.

Tom spelled out what Mack was thinking. "What's the worst that can happen? The girls are older now. Old Man Halloran can't carry on treating them like kids, keeping them banged up like jail birds."

"Besides," Mack added, "nothing much we can do about it – at least, not until or if it happens. Que sera, sera, and all that."

"Have you thought what might happen if their father throws them both out? What then? They couldn't stay with Caitlin for more than a night or two. Adam couldn't keep them."

"Adam wouldn't have to," Mack replied. "They'd move in with Bridget in Shipley. Bridget's always said she'd take care of them. In fact I'm certain she would."

"Is her flat large enough for two teenage girls to move into? Besides, does their sister earn enough to keep them both until they go to college or university? Otherwise they would have to leave school and start work, which would be a shame. They're such bright young women."

"Effy could always bunk up here with Mack if the worse came to the worse." Tom sniggered and then let out a painful grunt as a much harder elbow hit his ribs. "Hey, cut it out, cuz, I was only jesting."

Jane MacKinnon exchanged looks with her husband. "Thank you for the suggestion, Tom. I don't think it would be appropriate."

"Well, not sharing the same room," Tom began correcting himself. "You've got Adam's old room."

"Like Mum says. It wouldn't be appropriate, even with a separate room." Mack then planted a disturbing thought for his parents. "Effy's not their daughter or their problem. Why would they? Besides, she would be my problem to sort out."

"What do you mean, James? She would be your problem?" His mother stopped knitting.

212

"If she's thrown out she'll have to leave school and start work. I'd leave too. Whatever happens to Effy also happens to me. If Bridget couldn't cope someone would have to help. We'd manage somehow; people do."

Robert MacKinnon said, "And how, pray tell, would leaving without finishing your A levels help?"

Mack's bombshell, devastating and intentional, was not only for effect .

"I suppose it would be inappropriate. We'd have to move in together and share a place. Don't suppose we would be able to afford more than a bedsit to start. We would have to live in sin for a while…"

"Stop right there, James." His father became stern. "You cannot be serious. What? Throw your whole future away? Living in sin? Good grief, son! Don't even think it!"

"It would only be temporary. We'd have to do our A Levels at Tech on a night. Might take longer but we'd do them in time."

"I can't believe I'm hearing this, James." His mother was staggered by her son's proposals. "You would, in all seriousness, consider doing that?"

"If I had to. I'm only talking about a worst-case situation for the two of us. Anyway, it's only contingency planning. If Effy and Ellen got given the doorstep by their crazy old man then Bridget would take them in. She'd take care of them for as long as it took. I suppose she'd look after Grace, too."

Tom's follow-on contribution was not helpful either. It was noted but not ignored.

"We know five guys our ages who've rented a terrace house in Brighouse. They've all either left home or got booted out. It's a do-able proposition, Uncle Rob."

"What's Bridget's flat like?" Robert MacKinnon asked, attempting to change the course of the conversation.

Tom looked at Mack and then back at his uncle and aunt. "Dunno. We're popping over this evening before going to Halifax."

"Palatial it's not," said Mack. "The word Bridget uses is bijou. It's a tad small. There are two bedrooms, sort of. The main one's decent, about the size of mine. The spare might get a single bed in it. If stick came to lift they might manage, somehow."

"Why are you going over to Bridget's? Shipley is in the opposite direction, isn't it?" his mother pointed out, still shocked over Mack's contingency planning.

"The girls haven't heard from her this week which is unusual. She hasn't been round to see them. It's not like her not to drop by. Thought we'd take them over and check to see if she's okay."

"That's kind of you," offered Robert MacKinnon. "Thoughtful indeed."

"Will it be okay to stop over tonight after I drop Ellen off?" Tom asked.

"Of course, Tom. You don't have to ask. It'll be like old times when you and James were small boys," Mack's mother answered without hesitation. "Your Uncle Robert won't mind. It's too far to be driving back and forth to Halifax. You'd better do that for as long as you and Ellen go out together."

"Appreciate it, Aunt Jane."

"We'd better get off to pick them up. Assuming Ellen's not spending an hour like last week getting her war-paint on."

"Ellen only wanted to look good for me on our first date."

"Tell me, Tom – don't you find it strange having a girlfriend with the same name as your mother?" Robert MacKinnon asked.

"I know it'll sound weird, Uncle Rob, but no. It never occurred until Mack mentioned it. Mum's always been mum to me, not Ellen. Mind, my dad finds it well funny."

"I want you two to drive safely," Jane MacKinnon cautioned them both. "I don't want either of you or those lovely girls getting hurt because you were not being careful."

"Don't you mean Tom's *older young woman*, not girl, Mum?"

"Go on with you, you know exactly what I mean. You're becoming exasperating, James MacKinnon."

"And it's ride, Mum, not drive. You drive a car and ride a scooter."

"Stop lecturing me, young man. You know what I meant."

With those words still ringing in their ears they left the house.

Effy made Ellen speed up her beauty regime after the previous Saturday's messing about. Mack took them over the shortcuts by the golf course and down Moorhead Lane to where Bridget lived. Effy's sister had the ground-floor flat in a large Victorian house off Albert Road. A light was on in the front room, with the interior obscured by net curtaining. Bridget's expression seemed to change when she answered the doorbell. Their visit had taken her by surprise. The fact she was in a dressing gown appeared strange.

"Well, aren't you going to invite us in for a few minutes? We can't stop long, anyway." Ellen pushed past Bridget, not waiting for an invitation. "We're off to Halifax. I'm going over with Mack's cousin, TC."

"We couldn't help worrying about you, Bridget," Effy began. "We thought we'd better..." Her words trailed away as she caught sight of a man on the settee in the living room.

"I've not been avoiding you, Effy. I've been ill this week and at home all the time. Sorry I couldn't come round to see you."

"You could have 'phoned to let us know," grumbled Ellen.

"I've been laid up in bed and I don't have the luxury of a telephone in the flat," Bridget replied with a hint of annoyance. "Let me introduce you to Greg. Greg is my neighbour in the flat above. He's been ever so kind to me, running errands while I've been unwell. Greg, these are my sisters, Ellen and Effy. Mack is Effy's boyfriend and this is his cousin Tom."

"Who is now my boyfriend." Ellen emphasised the "my".

"I see!" Bridget exclaimed, taken aback by that surprising snippet of information. "How and when did this happen?"

"Last weekend."

"It's a long story, Bridget. No time to tell you now. We've got to be going. We thought we'd better check to see if you were okay. Sorry to hear you've been unwell. Please to meet you... Greg," Mack interjected. "We won't disturb you two any further."

Greg, a handsome man in his late twenties, shook hands with each of them in turn. "A pleasure to meet you all. I'd better go, Bridget. We don't want to give these young folk the wrong idea about us. I'll check on you later to see if you need anything."

"I'll come over tomorrow evening to see you at Ma and Da's." Mack noted the pleading look she gave Greg as he went out. She continued, "Tell Caitlin not to worry. I'll try and get to see her midweek after work. By the way, I received a letter from Deidre yesterday. She's enjoying Manchester. Sends all her love. She writes she's going to send you each a letter next week."

As they were fastening their helmets outside, Tom spoke in a hushed voice to Mack. "I bet she was '*laid up*'. I can guess who was laying her and all."

"You're right." Mack tried not to laugh, containing his reaction to a gleeful grin at Tom's aside. "Did you notice he was in his socks? No shoes?

He hadn't even managed to button up his shirt the right way. He was across with his buttons."

"Actually, now you mention it, no I didn't, Sherlock. Is there anything you didn't notice?"

"My dear Watson, I never miss vital clues. Don't quote me but I do believe Bridget had next to nothing on under her dressing gown."

"Fuck me, Sherlock! Your powers of observation and deduction are incredible. Ever thought of a career with the Feds? You'd make a great Inspector Lockhart. There'd be no hiding place with you on the job."

"He's a superintendent in the TV series, not an inspector."

"Bloody smartarse too, like a copper."

"What are you talking about?" Ellen asked Tom.

"Bridget getting laid."

"What did you say? Are you implying something about my sister?"

"He meant getting laid up in bed."

"Anyway, she's a good Catholic girl who would never dream of sex before marriage." Ellen ignored Tom's deliberate sexual innuendo.

Tom and Mack exchanged glances, grinning.

"Well, she wouldn't." Ellen's face suggested even she was mulling over being wrong though not wanting to admit it.

Standing chatting in George's Square Effy turned to Mack. "That was embarrassing. We came at a bad moment to see my sister, didn't we?"

"You think?"

"I don't think, I'm pretty sure. Well, for a start, I don't believe she had anything on under her dressing gown. Did you notice he had no shoes on? He was in his stocking feet."

"Yes, I did notice. It was somewhat obvious, that and his shirt buttons not fastened right. I have a strong suspicion he's been getting his feet on the sofa with Bridget."

"There's more." Effy pressed on. "I'm positive he's one of the solicitors in the partnership where she works. I'm sure he's the Greg I heard her mentioning to Caitlin. The one who's supposed to be trying to get a divorce?"

"It's none of our business. Bridget's over twenty-one and can do what she likes."

"God, I hope she knows what she's doing. I'm sure I heard her telling Caitlin his wife wouldn't give him a divorce. Changing the subject, look at

216

Ellen and Tom. One date last Saturday and he's her boyfriend. How's he taking it?"

"Taking it? I don't follow."

"Being her trophy catch."

"Her trophy catch? You mean his, don't you?"

"No. Hers. It's a shame. I can't see it lasting. They're so different," sighed Effy. "TC's such a womaniser and nowhere near as grown-up and mature as you."

"I've no need to be a womaniser. I've got you. You're my sugar and spice and all things nice."

"I don't want to sound soppy and clingy, but do you still love me, Jimmy Mack?"

"More than you would believe, Effy Halloran. I can't ever imagine being without you, not ever. I do love you. I'm not ashamed to say it aloud," he whispered with humorous intent.

"You're terrible, James MacKinnon, making fun of me like that."

"I do love you." Mack shouted the words out aloud.

It was the first of October. The Jimmy Powell Band was playing at The Plebs. The club was capacity-packed as usual.

Later Tom told Effy about the conversation between Mack and his parents. Effy cried. Not from sadness, but from joy. Jimmy Mack would give up everything for her, as she would do for him. It was what a man would do when he loved a woman and what she would do for him as a woman.

CHAPTER 45

Headline News – Edwin Starr (Polydor 56717 – 1966)

Thursday 6 October 1966

Mack arrived home to find his mother carrying a suitcase down the stairs.

"What's going on, Mum? Are you going somewhere?"

"I've decided to leave your father."

"What?" he exclaimed, stunned.

"Gotcha!" She beamed, seeing the shock on his face. "This is my way of paying you back for all the times you decided to wind me up. I hope it's a salutary reminder it can work both ways, young man."

"Oh, nice one, Mum. You had me going for a moment." It was a great wind-up, he had to admit, and long overdue. "What's the suitcase for?"

"We've had a telephone call this afternoon from Great Aunt Moira. She says your granny has had a bad fall. Your father has arranged to have a few days off so we can travel up to Edinburgh to visit her. I've packed a case with some clothes for the trip."

"Is Granny MacKinnon all right? She's not seriously hurt, is she?"

"I don't know, but your father worries about them both. They're not as young as they were."

"Hang on, Mum, Moira's your age, isn't she? She's not that old."

"Cheeky young pup! Are you saying I'm old? Moira's at least a good dozen years' older than me. She's in her early fifties."

"When are you going?"

"Tonight when your father comes home. We'll have something to eat and then set off."

"Should I pack a few things too?"

"You're not going, James. Your A Levels are too important for you to miss lessons. Besides we'll be back either Sunday or Monday depending on what we find when we get there."

"It's my birthday on Saturday. You'll miss it."

"I know but there's nothing much we can do about it this time. We'll do something together when we get back. You'll most likely want to spend time with Effy, Tom and your friends at the weekend. It's not like you would be staying in anyway."

"Gee, thanks Mum, abandoning me like this."

"I'm sure you can fend for yourself while we're away for a few days. Your Aunt Ellen will be travelling up with us as well. If the worst comes to the worst then I'm sure Caitlin will make you something to eat. You could try making something yourself. But if you do, I want my kitchen spotless when I return. One more thing."

"What's that?"

"I want you to promise me you won't have a party while we're gone."

"Cross my heart and hope to die. There will definitely not be any party happening while you're away. There wasn't one in summer and there's not going to be one now." But two could have a party, he thought, as he envisaged Effy in his bed again.

His parents left shortly after seven that evening. Mack put extra effort into finishing off outstanding essays to leave the weekend free. Doing so ensured that he and Effy would have as much time as possible together. His parents were giving him the perfect birthday present: an empty house.

Luck was on his side too as the last lesson on Friday was cancelled. He could leave for home sooner and did so via Cunliffe Road and St. Joseph's College. Parking his scooter opposite the main gate, he waited for the girls' school day to end. Effy would not be expecting to see him. Sharing the good news with her as soon as he could was important. Ten minutes later the school began to empty. Mack had to smile.

The contrast between the oldest and the youngest was striking. The ladylike Sixth Formers contrasted with the ragamuffin Lower School pupils dashing out.

Grace Halloran was the first of the sisters to leave the building. Mack went unnoticed at first. It was only when Jean joined her with a group of friends that Grace became aware of his presence. Crossing over to him, making her friends stay back, she spoke as she approached. "What are you doing here?"

"Giving your friends something to gossip about. According to Ellen, yours truly and Effy are the talk of the grapevine."

"Well, if you weren't you're going to be. You need to be more careful," she warned. "You never know who's going to blab to our parents."

"I wouldn't have come down here unless it was urgent. Sooner or later it's going to come out. Nothing ever remains a secret forever. How's life treating you? It's been a while since I last spoke with you."

"As good as it can be living in our house. I swear my Da's getting worse, not better. It's not pleasant. The three of us avoid him as much as possible. Ellen's still civil with him. Effy point blank refuses to talk to him unless it's unavoidable. Ma's a nervous wreck with it all. I worry about her."

Ellen and Effy came out together, stopping wide-eyed and open-mouthed on seeing him. Rushing over, Effy looked overjoyed. Caution swept away, dropping her school bag on the Lambretta seat, she hugged and kissed him.

"For goodness sake, woman, have a little dignity and control yourself. You're in full view of everyone, including some of the teachers." Ellen looked embarrassed and turned away. "I hope none of them say anything to Ma and Da on parents' evening after seeing you in action."

"Sod them," Effy replied with uncharacteristic words. "I don't bloody well care who knows about the two of us any more. Are you going to give me a lift near to home?"

"Yes, of course. I've got some news," he whispered in her ear, his warm breath sending a tingling sensation through her body. "My parents have gone to Edinburgh. My Gran's had a fall."

"Oh, no! It's not serious, is it?" Effy showed genuine concern as she heard the news.

"No, it's not." Then he leaned over and whispered in her ear. Effy's face lit up; she could have been the envy of any femme fatale.

Returning the whisper she said, "The timing couldn't be better. I have a most special birthday present planned for you."

"What is it?"

"My virginity."

"What are you two saying to each other?" Ellen asked, miffed at her exclusion from their sweet nothings. "Do you know? You two lovebirds can be quite vomit-inducing. Come on, Grace. Let's leave them to whatever they're planning."

"I'll let Jean know I won't be walking back with her and the others. Besides, someone has to tone down the gossip mongering after this." Grace left them and walked back to her waiting friends.

"Grace," one of her friends began. "He's so cool, so gorgeous and good-looking."

"See. I told you, didn't I, I wasn't exaggerating," a delighted Jean gloated. "He's a yummy hunk."

"Your sister's copped a choice fella," chipped in another.

"Now you've all seen him can we cool it with the gossip in future, please?" Grace requested, already tired of hearing the adulation frenzy feeding her friends.

CHAPTER 46

Long After Tonight Is All Over – Jimmy Radcliffe (Stateside 374 – 1966)

Saturday 8 October 1966

"C'mon, cuz. We won't be any trouble. Look, you and Effy have the lounge. El and me will use the living room."

"Please, Mack," Ellen begged. "You and Effy won't even know we're in the house."

"We won't disturb you," Tom continued. "And you won't disturb us. We'll do our thing while you do yours. Look, you know how hard it is to get a bit of privacy."

Mack looked at Effy. Effy looked back at Mack. It wasn't quite what they had planned.

"Well, Effy?" It was tough refusing Tom and her sister.

"If Mack says it's all right, then it's all right with me. How about we go upstairs and they use the lounge?"

"Okay." Mack caved in to their request. "On one condition. If you take Ellen back to Caitlin's and come back, you don't disturb us. Doss down on the sofa in the lounge."

"So you two are planning to stop all night?" Ellen didn't seem surprised.

"That's the general idea, sis."

"Why do you think Mack told Adam and Caitlin it was another all-nighter? When we know there isn't one?" Tom clarified. "We should have realised what you two were up to. I'll tell you what, we'll crack the bottle of sherry and then…"

After the third glass of sherry Effy had relaxed. "Okay, birthday boy. Let's leave my sister to the tender mercies of TC and go up."

"Why does everyone call Tom TC?" Ellen asked, her mild QC intoxication evident.

"Because his name is Thomas Catford?" suggested Effy, bubbly from the sherry.

"Actually, no, it's not as strange as it may seem, Ellen. Go on, Tom. Tell her why." Mack got up off the sofa and joined Effy at the door.

"You know the TV cartoon series Top Cat... Officer Dibble?" These were the last words they heard as they closed the lounge door and went up to the bedroom.

Once inside Effy sat down and opened her handbag. Mack recognised the little box in an instant as she took it out. A tube of cream followed by condoms.

"Do you know how to use one of these?" she asked, passing him a Durex.

"I've got a good idea," he said, grinning. "How did you get these?"

"Angie arranged for me to see her sister at the Family Planning Clinic in Halifax."

"Angie did?"

"Yes. When she told me what her sister Gillian did, I asked her for help getting sorted. I'll tell you all about it later. I'll be a minute or two in the bathroom."

It was bizarre. The girl who had taken his virginity was helping Effy lose hers. It was too crazy to contemplate. Mack shook his head, unaware he was doing so. His seventeenth birthday was turning out weird and wonderful.

"By the way," Effy asked, "why are we whispering?" Giggling, she disappeared into the bathroom. Mack stripped to full nakedness in seconds. Switching on the small bedside table lamp, he turned off the main light and slid between the sheets. Ten minutes later Effy returned.

"I'm sorry, it took me a bit longer than I thought it would. I had to make sure I had it in the right way. Help me undress?"

Mack needed no further prompting. He unzipped her dress and watched as Effy took it off. She did so with tantalizing slowness, her hips swaying. The full length slip followed.

"How do you like me in these?" she purred. "Could I make a career as a stripper?" Her matching bra and briefs were the sexiest lacy kind bought for the occasion. Standing before him, looking self-conscious in her seductive underwear, she murmured, "Why don't you take these off? They're going to be a bit superfluous."

Unhooking the bra Mack then slid the briefs down her silky soft thighs. Stepping out of them, her voice nervous and fluttering, almost breathless, she whispered, "Are you ready?"

Once under the covers he turned to switch the bedside lamp off.

"No, don't turn it off. Not until later," Effy begged. "I want to see you as well as feel you. Besides, you'll need the light to put the condom on the right way."

"Are you sure you want to go ahead?"

"Never surer," she answered. "I want you to know something before we start."

"What?"

"Please don't laugh, please don't say I'm silly. The first time I saw you in church I fell in love with you."

"What? When I was ten years old?"

"Yes. I knew I wanted to be with you one day. Don't get me wrong. Back then I didn't know about sex but I had such a crush on you. That's never stopped. It's no longer a crush or infatuation. You are my everything. Anyway, let's not talk. Let me hold you. Let me love you. I need you, I want you now more than ever."

Tactile explorations accompanied by slow intense kissing led to the anticipated moment.

Angie had warned her the first time might be a little painful but not that bad. The best thing was to relax as much as possible. Getting entered the first time was uncomfortable but not unbearable. Using a lubricant could make it much easier. Angie had also recommended getting tipsy but not drunk to aid relaxation. The three large sherries had helped. Angie had also warned her not to expect fireworks unless she was lucky. Mack spread her legs apart, his fingers opening her in readiness, massaging her sweet spot. She restrained him, afraid of having an orgasm before he penetrated her and messing it all up.

It was not quite how Effy imagined it would be. She was not lost in the moment in some kind of ecstasy. Instead she found herself preoccupied with the mechanics of what was taking place. Her thoughts were buzzing with a combination of adrenaline-driven excitement and anxiety. All her mind could focus on was what was happening to her body.

Mack was doing his gentle forceful best to penetrate her. Trying not to make it too painful for Effy, he could not stop remembering his experience with Angie. Angie had not been a virgin so entering her, though tight, was not as constricted as Effy. Her hands gripped his hips with increasing pressure as he gained access. Then he felt himself inside her as she expanded to accommodate him. The sensation was wonderful as his penis became enveloped inside her. The exertion of coming together had made their breathing heavy and noisy. They were unaware of the sounds each had been making.

That was it. Her virginity was gone. It was not such a big deal after all, though it had hurt. Mack was where she wanted him, joined with her, locked in this intimate embrace.

"Are you okay?" he asked.

"So far so good. Don't stop, carry on."

A couple of minutes later she heard him groan as he ejaculated. Effy did not orgasm the way she had when he had turned her on before. Still, she did experience a tremendous glow of satisfaction verging on exultation. Fulfilment rippled through her body.

Mack withdrew as he found himself going from hard to slack. He was afraid the condom might slide off inside her. He hoped it hadn't torn with the exertion. That could be a disaster, spoiling it all. It came out intact. This time he had some tissues handy to clean up. Only later did they find some spots of blood on the sheets.

"How do you feel?" he asked in a whisper.

"Good," she answered, looking up at him. "I love feeling so wanton, so sinful, wicked and depraved. It's liberating. What have you done to me, James MacKinnon, you terrible man, taking advantage of a poor maiden so?"

"You are joking, aren't you?"

"Moi? Never. If that's how it feels..." She paused, kissing him. "Don't ever stop having your wicked way with me. Guess what?"

"What?"

Effy delivered an impressive if quiet impersonation of Marilyn Monroe. Singing happy birthday, she substituted Mr MacKinnon for Mr President, making him laugh.

"Long after tonight is over I will never forget it. I will always love you, always be yours no matter what," Effy murmured.

CHAPTER 47

Mr Bang Bang Man – Little Hank (London American HLU 10090 – 1966)

Sunday 9 October 1966

"Wake up!" Effy shook Mack, her voice low.

"What's the matter, Eff?"

"I can hear voices in the next-door bedroom. Are your parents back?"

"God, I hope not! Are you sure?"

"Listen."

He could hear the bed creaking. "It'll be Tom. He must have decided the sofa wasn't comfortable and Adam's old bed was better."

Then they both heard another voice.

"That's Ellen. Oh, my God! The dozy cow! I warned her about him!"

Before Mack could do anything Effy had leapt out of bed heading for the door. Only on reaching it did she realise she had nothing on. "Where's your dressing gown?"

"Whoa, but you're beautiful naked." Mack dived out of the bed for the wardrobe. "It's in here. Wait till I've got my Levis on before you do anything."

Passing her the dressing gown, he reached for his jeans. He was too slow. Effy had the dressing gown on in a flash. Before he could put his jeans on she was gone. He heard the bedroom door open as he struggled into his jeans. Then Mack lost his balance trying to put them on while attempting to follow her. He tripped over himself and fell.

Effy flung open the door to Adam's old room, the dressing gown coming loose. Ellen and Tom were in the bed together.

"You stupid moo," she shouted, angry and accusing. "I warned you what he was like. You've known him less than two minutes and you jump into bed with him. Suppose he's made you pregnant?"

Ellen looked embarrassed. Tom was verging on laughter.

In a contrite voice, looking surprisingly scared, her older sister blurted out, "Nothing happened, I kept my knickers on, Eff."

"Nice tits, Eff!" Tom stared where the dressing gown had parted without her noticing. Realizing she had exposed her breasts she covered up, cheeks blushing.

Mack came up behind Effy. "God! TC by name, TC by nature, except TC should stand for Tom Cat. You can't stop yourself, can you?"

"Cuz, nothing happened. Honest." Tom protested his innocence. "Ellen will tell you. She kept her drawers on all night."

"That looks like all she kept on." Effy eyed her sister's bra and other clothing on the floor. "Are those Tom's underpants by the bed?"

Ellen went crimson. Bed covers pulled up to her chin, in a tiny scarcely audible voice she confessed. "Yes."

"Do you want to pass them to me, Eff?" Tom indicated the underpants. "Or should I get out of bed as I am?"

"God, you're incorrigible, Tom." Mack shook his head. "Pick up your own dirty kecks after we've gone out."

"Don't start with the morality, cuz. We heard what you two were up to through the wall. God, we found it embarrassing. You were both a bit unrestrained and then some. Your bedsprings could do with oiling, too. We lost count how many times we heard you two going at it. Well, actually, I exaggerate. Three times, was it, in six hours?"

It was Effy's turn to go crimson on hearing that.

"I reckon." Tom continued a broad grin on his face. "If you'd gone for it one more time, El's virginity would have been a mere technicality."

"No, it wouldn't." Ellen appeared to thump him beneath the covers.

"Come on, Effy. Let them get dressed. Sounds like nothing serious happened."

"No damage done, Eff," Tom added almost apologetically. "El's still *virgo intacto.*"

"I swear if it was otherwise I'd neuter you myself." Effy sounded as if she meant it, too, leaving the room miffed.

"Mack, sorry mate, we'll have to put these sheets in the twin tub. Er, I had a slight spill a couple of times."

Slamming the door behind them they returned to his bedroom.

"I can't believe my sister!" Effy exclaimed, still angry, slipping back under the bed covers. "She's known him two minutes and she almost let him get his way with her. He's like a sex-mad alley cat. She's not much better. No wonder they call him TC. He's like a Tom Cat in need of a visit to the vets."

"Eff, that's harsh. He's a bloke with a great-looking girl. What do you expect? A saint? And where does it leave me after last night?"

"That's different." Effy pulled the bed covers up to her chin in a defensive motion. "We've been waiting do this for ages and at least I've taken precautions to stop me getting pregnant. Besides I love you and you love me."

"Tom's right. You do have nice breasts."

Mack cuddled up to her again.

"Oh, no. Not you too, Mack. You can't be going hard again! Don't tell me you want to do it again. I only brought three Durex with me."

They were making a mess of the bacon and eggs fry-up. "We should forget about ever trying to get jobs in the catering trade. We'd stand no chance." Mack stared disconsolately at the charred bacon.

"It'll be right for me. Slap them rashers between two pieces of bread with loads of ketchup or brown sauce and it'll do me fine."

"It's your stomach, Tom. Me, I like my bacon a little less on the cremated side."

"I need to say something, cuz. I know it's me that's got the rep for getting round the birds. This time the record needs setting straight. It wasn't my idea to use Adam's bed for a frolic. El suggested it, honest to God, swear on the bible, etcetera. I thought she was joking, especially after all the good Catholic girl crap she gave me last week. Soon as she knew you and Eff had some one-on-one time she wanted it as well. Don't kid yourself. Ellen may be a virgin but she's a randy virgin, if you get my drift. I'll tell you something for nothing. I've had to work overtime to cajole most girls for a bit of nookie. This is in strictest between thee and me, lad. Ellen couldn't wait to get her kit off and get between the linen. Okay, so she stopped short of going the whole way but it was touch and go. We came as close as it's possible in knowing each other in the biblical sense without actually doing the deed. She worked my little old man like an expert, not once but twice, hence the mess."

"Whoa, don't tell me any more, Tom. It's too graphic. I'd rather not hear how she came close to wanking you to death."

"Sorry, mate, but after we heard you two doing it all night long you can hardly blame us. Anyway, how long's this fornication been going on?"

"Would you believe it was our first time?"

"You're joshing me!" Tom was incredulous at the revelation. "And on your birthday too! Epic, man! Bloody epic!"

Effy was in the bath, enjoying the warmth of the water lapping around her. Luxuriating in a little of Jane MacKinnon's scented bath foam was a pleasure. Ellen was working on her makeup in front of the mirror.

"I'm not a slut, sis! I may have behaved like a slut last night but I'm not one. Honest. I'm not. And don't blame TC. It was my fault. I was feeling randy. He's bit of a tearaway I know but I do like him. Believe it or not, I found him attractive after we met for the first time last year. I never expected he would ask me out as he's younger than me. When he did it was thrilling. After going down to the club last week I took to him. There's something about him I find irresistible. It's not like it's love. Or at least it's not at the moment. Who knows exactly what the future holds? Anything is possible, I suppose. No, last night was more like lust at second sight."

"Lust?" queried Effy, almost rising up above the bath water in disbelief.

"I can't explain it any better. I wanted him. I mean I so wanted him. And I was passionate in wanting him to want me. Only the fear of doing a Caitlin stopped me from going the whole way. But it was pretty close. I don't even know how I stopped myself or him. God, Eff, I get so frustrated at times. It's like an itch you can't scratch."

"I'm glad you didn't do it!" The idea of Ellen almost risking pregnancy was disturbing. "You need to get some practical help about family planning. Let's chat about it later."

"I guess you must have got the contraceptive side of things sorted?"

"Oh, yes. It was a definite must. I have a confession to make. I came close once before without precautions. I realised we couldn't carry on taking chances. It's like playing Russian roulette with your body. You can't chance it hoping he shoots another blank. A couple of minutes of pleasure and before you know it, a lifetime of motherhood before we're ready for it. That's why I got myself fixed for it not to happen, at least not yet. We need to get you sorted before you scratch that itch too hard."

"Suppose you two should break up? You won't be a virgin if you end up marrying someone else. What then, Eff?"

"I can't imagine I'd want to marry anyone else. I have no regrets about last night. It's a night I'm going to treasure forever, no matter what the future holds. Being a virgin is no big deal. It's my body to share with someone I love."

Ellen stopped applying her makeup. Staring at her reflection in the mirror for a few seconds she resumed applying the makeup. "Do you know something, Eff? You're one hundred per cent right. Like you said, it's my body to share with someone I find to love. And if it doesn't last it doesn't last. But what we feel at the time for one another, that does."

"So, what about you and Tom?"

"I do like him even if he's younger than me. I'll see how we go."

"Do you know what, Ellen?" Rising from the bath Effy wrapped a towel round herself. "When he's twenty-one and you're twenty-two, what difference will a year make?"

Ellen considered her words while applying eyeliner. "I suppose you're right about that too. So, what's it like as an ex-virgin? Do you feel any different?"

Effy smiled at her sister. "No different at all. It's still me. I've not changed. It's one less thing not to have hang-ups over. From now on what we do with one another won't plague us with doubts and insecurities. Now we can get on with making love not dreading the possible consequences."

"So, you don't feel guilty, sinful or in the wrong?"

"No, no and never. *Verum Amor Vincit Omnia.*"

CHAPTER 48

Knock On Wood – Eddie Floyd (Atlantic 584041 – 1966)

Saturday 15 October 1966

"Ellen, this is my really, really good friend, Angie. Angie, this is my sister." Effy made the introductions as they met in George's Square. "Angie, promise not to laugh. She's TC's latest flame."

Angie suppressed laughter but it was clear she found it amusing. "You must think I'm being horrible. I promise I'm not."

"Am I missing something here? What's so funny?" Ellen looked both puzzled and annoyed by Angie's reaction.

The attractive dark-haired girl with lively smiling eyes scrutinised her. "Are there any more male MacKinnons or Catfords still left in the wild? Or have you Halloran girls hunted down the lot?"

"'Fraid the last of the species is now in captivity," Ellen responded with a clever comeback of her own. Both Angie and Effy found that comical.

"What's the joke, girlies?" enquired Tom as he and Mack walked up to them.

"Do you know the one about the hunter getting hunted by the hunted?" Angie teased.

"No."

"Good, it's better you didn't." This set the three girls laughing again. It was a joke better not shared.

Mack guessed immediately it was some comment to do with Tom. One glance at Effy told him he was on the right track. "We're nipping over to the Vic Lounge to find Colin Graham and Brian Warner. We'll be back in five minutes. You don't mind, do you?"

"Oh, I don't know," Effy replied. "In five minutes some handsome fellas could come along and sweep all three of us of our feet. Then where would you be?"

"What, in Halifax? Don't make me laugh. There are only two handsome fellas and they're both stood right here already." Turning to Angie Tom said jokingly, "Good luck finding a third."

231

"You think you're so funny." Angie gave him a playful punch on the arm. "If wit was shit you'd be constipated."

Walking away from them in the direction of the Vic Lounge Tom turned to Mack. "Do you know this joke about the hunter?"

"It's lame and I've forgotten the ending," Mack lied, trying to be tactful. "It's not worth repeating and you wouldn't find it funny."

Effy took Angie to one side, asking in a quiet confidential voice, "Would your sister be able to help Ellen like she helped me? I'm concerned what might happen to her with TC. He's all charm and she's no resistance."

"If Ellen's planning on being his steady the sooner she's sorted the better. He's on permanent heat, according to the girls I know he's been with. Let me have a word with her now. Did my sister give you enough rubbers, by the way? If she did, then give Ellen a couple until I can sort out an appointment for her. By the way, have you done it yet?"

"Yes, and thanks for all the good advice. It worked like a charm."

"I suppose congratulations are in order. Welcome to the wonderful world of womanhood. Things will never be the same again. Okay, we'll stall the boys and go for a coffee in the Beefeater so I can have a talk to her. We'll tell them we'll meet up a bit later."

Ellen looked unhappy at not being part of the conversation, knowing they were taking about her. As they returned, Angie touched her on the shoulder. "Ellen, we need to talk."

"I can't help wondering what their confab is all about. Any idea?" Tom asked Mack. They were reclining on their scooter seats against the pillion backrests.

"You know what girls are like when it comes to twittering. They flock together like birds of a feather."

"Oh, Jimmy Mack! That's so funneeee!" Tom mimicked Effy.

"How are things going between you and Ellen?"

"It's early days but she is a bit special. Put it this way, I won't be ditching Ellen in a hurry. She's more likely to ditch me before I do her."

"Blow me down. My hearing aid's faulty. I'm sure I imagined you saying you wouldn't ditch her."

"I'm surprised she's taken up with me. Girls like Ellen are usually way out of my league. They always go for older guys, not someone younger.

Besides, I'm not clever like her. Compared to me she's grown-up and sensible."

"What? Ellen? You have got to be kidding."

"Compared to me, yes, she is. It's what I like about her. She's got her feet planted on the ground and she knows what she wants to do in life. Pity she's got an asshole for a dad."

"Don't do yourself down, Tom. Blokes are not supposed to be as mature as girls at the same age. It's your bad luck, that's all."

"Bad luck? What bad luck?" Tom raised himself to a seated position.

"To have found yourself an older young woman."

"Now your Ma was funny when she came out with that."

"You should serenade her with that Bobby Darin song when you're together."

"Which one? *Dream Lover* or *Multiplication?*"

"Neither. *If I Were a Carpenter.*"

"I've said it before. You're a regular piss artist, MacKinnon."

"Could be. I bet you five bob you wouldn't dare serenade her with the words?"

"Not even for a fiver, sunshine. Bet you wouldn't dare sing it to Effy?"

"Make it ten and you're on."

"No thanks. I'll keep my money. It's the kind of stupid thing you would do to win a bet."

"What's the stupid kind of thing Mack would do for ten bob?" It was Ellen's voice behind them. All three girls had sneaked up behind them to listen in on their bantering.

"Mack bet me he'd serenade Effy with the words of *If I Were a Carpenter* for ten bob."

"You were smart not to take the bet. I wouldn't have been happy to see you lose your money," said Ellen.

"Well, he wouldn't dare anyway," Tom goaded Mack. "He'd be too chicken to do it anyway."

"Why wouldn't he? He would for me. I wouldn't mind," declared Effy, indignant at Mack's unwillingness to do it for her.

"Go on. I dare you, Mr Super Cool. Serenade my sister," Ellen pressed. "She told you she wouldn't mind."

"This I've got to hear," Angie joined in. "They've dared you. Are you a man or a mouse?"

233

"More like a chicken." Tom began to cluck, making chicken noises.

"I don't know all the words so I couldn't anyway."

"Come off it," scoffed Angie. "Everyone's heard the opening lines. Serenade her with the carpenter bit then."

"I know you're not the best singer in the world," Effy implored him with a smile. "Prove them wrong for me, please."

"No chance, no way." Mack was decisive in his firm insistence. "Not in front of this lot. I'll never hear the end of it."

"Please! For me!" Effy pleaded with a slight irresistible simper.

"One of these days, Tom, I'm gonna drop you right in it for this. And I won't forget. And as for you, Ellen Halloran, don't even get me started."

Mack stood up. Glancing round to make sure nobody else was in listening range he sang to a smiling Effy. It was only four short lines but the last one about having his baby made him go bright red.

"Bravo. Sing her some more." Angie delivered a brief clap. "Seeing and hearing is believing."

"See? I told you I did the smart thing not taking his bet." Tom was jubilant. "I know what he's like."

"Go on, Effy. Now give him your answer seeing as you egged him on to sing it for you," Ellen insisted.

Effy blushed, performing the same slight curtsey she had when she first agreed to be his girlfriend. "Of course, I would be most honoured."

"I reckon that was a proposal, don't you, Tom? Angie?" Ellen sounded serious but gave Tom a sly wink.

"Yes, and she accepted him. We all heard him propose and we heard Effy accept," Tom confirmed.

"Can I be a bridesmaid?" Angie joined in, speaking to Effy. "I've always wanted to be a bridesmaid."

"Oh, cut it out, will you! It was only a joke," Mack protested.

"So!" Effy tried to look offended, joining in the teasing. "You've proposed to me, Jimmy Mack, and now you're refusing to honour your proposal. There is such a thing as breach of promise in this country. And in front of witnesses too."

Angie linked arms with Effy. "If he doesn't take you to Fattorini's on Monday to buy you a diamond engagement ring, the judge will hear from me."

Ellen linked Effy's other arm. "And you'd better be careful because a shotgun wedding is the last thing my little sister wants."

234

"Knowing her dad he'd blows his nuts off with a shotgun if he found out!" Tom pretended to fire a shotgun at Mack's crotch.

Acky pulled up next to Mack's scooter on his Vespa Douglas, which was identical to Tom's. "What's going on?"

"Mack's proposed to Effy." Angie gave him a wink to let him in on the joke.

"Can I come to the wedding? When is it? I like a good wedding."

"Take no notice. They're all taking the piss."

The club was busier than usual with many unfamiliar non-regular faces. *Boogaloo Party* by The Flamingos was playing as they pushed into the middle of the dance floor. The next half hour saw the atmosphere build, with each record. Willie Mitchell's *Everything's Gonna Be Alright* blazed out of the speaker system as the place heaved with dancrs.

Land of a Thousand Dances greeted the arrival of a three-man camera team. Mack only became aware of them when a bright light shone into Effy's and Tom's faces from behind. Turning his head he found himself blinded by a spotlight for the cameraman. A third had a pole with a furry covered mic attached hovering above the camera. This explained all the new faces descending on The Plebs. They must have heard the jazz club was going to be featuring on TV. The sound of James Brown's *Outta Sight* slowed the dance tempo and the film crew disappeared. When *Sweet Talkin' Guy* came on Ellen gave Effy and Angie a look and then dragged Tom off into a corner. Effy began giggling.

"Okay, what's the joke?" Mack asked over the sound of the music.

"The prey has become the hunter."

When The Temptations' *The Way You Do the Things You Do* came on, Mack mimed the words at Effy. She blushed, having to keep glancing away during the song as the lyrics hit home. The following weekend would be the last carefree one. Herbie Goins and the Hightimers were headlining the all-nighter. Even at 8/6d for a ticket there was eager anticipation to see the singer and band. They agreed it had been a good night out. The last record Mack and Effy heard was The High Keys' cover of *Que Sera Sera* as they left.

CHAPTER 49

Number One In Your Heart – Herbie Goins & The Hightimers
(Parlophone R 5478 B – 1966)

Saturday 29 October 1966

The doors opened at eleven as advertised. The queue to get in to The Plebs had stretched out from the Upper George Yard into Cheapside. Rather than hang around the town centre until the club opened Angie had invited them round to her home. Mack, Effy, Tom, Ellen, Linda and her new boyfriend, as well as a couple of her own friends, made up the group. Everyone had been sworn to secrecy at Angie request. She did not need "gate-crashers" looking for a party.

Her parents had gone out for the evening by the time they had all arrived. The evening was adult and civilised as they chatted and listened to records.

Tom and Ellen knew in advance that the bedrooms were off-limits. They did not seem to mind, even though their ardour showing no signs of cooling. Later they spent most of the all-nighter clinging like limpets to one another. Angie's comment about passionate mouth-to-mouth resuscitation had everyone in stitches. When Mack asked Angie why she had not got herself a bloke yet, she had answered, "I still haven't found who I'm looking for."

During the evening Effy asked after Mack's mother. Thinking nothing of it he mentioned his mum had been sick most mornings during the past week. He never gave it another thought but he noticed the girls exchanging strange looks. He told them that his mother had said it was a tummy upset. Ellen was on the verge of saying something when she caught her sister's eyes flashing a warning look.

The band was great. Goins' performance was amazing and soulful. The album would prove to be disappointing by comparison with the live event. The songs performed were a mixture of covers of known soul tunes like *Pucker up Buttercup* with the odd new tune. They also performed a jazzy style cover of *Thirty Six, Twenty Two, Thirty Six. Outside of Heaven* was well-received. *Coming Home to You* was superb, the horns' precision astounding and worthy of the Mar-Keys. The group received ear-splitting applause for *Cruisin'* and *Number One in Your Heart*. For Mack and Effy *Number One in Your Heart* was special. The climax came with *Turn on Your Love Light.*

About four in the morning the DJ reminded them of the jazz club's origins. Jimmy Smith's *Walk on The Wild Side* received an airing. Cozy Coles' *Big Noise from Winnetka Pt. 1* followed, climaxing with Dave Brubeck's *Take Five*. Then it was back to Soul with a bang. The Four Tops signalled dance action again, going back to back with *It's the Same Old Song* and *Reach Out I'll Be There*. Junior Walker's *(I'm a) Road Runner* kept the action fired up. When Willie Mitchell's *Secret Home* played it called time on the foursome to head back to Bradford. It had been a great night out but daybreak was about to bring everything crashing down to the ground.

CHAPTER 50

Que Sera, Sera (Whatever Will Be, Will Be) – The High Keys
(London HLK 9768 – 1963)

Sunday 30 October 1966

As the scooters pulled up outside of Adam and Caitlin's home, the light in the living room came on. The sight of Adam half asleep, looking upset and unhappy, greeted them.

"All four of you had better come in."

It sounded ominous and it was. Caitlin, who had been asleep in the armchair, woke up as they entered. Like Adam she looked terrible. She had been crying. That was plain.

Mack's first thought was of little Jane. Had something happened to their daughter? Then it dawned. The playing around was over.

"The shit hit the fan tonight with a full lorry load. Mr Halloran himself deemed it worthy enough to call in person tonight. It's been anything but pleasant. We even got a visit from the police, thanks to him. I can't even begin to imagine what he told them. Your father," Adam now addressed Effy and Ellen, "went mental. He ignored Caitlin as if she never existed. Had a go at me for aiding and abetting you two to carry on with these two. I'll spare you the details of what he said. It was disturbing and unpleasant in the extreme."

Mack's heart sank on hearing this. The inevitable had always been there at the back of his mind. Sooner or later they had known it would come to light. Now they had to confront the consequences. He glanced at Effy and Ellen prepared for the worst. He was in for a shock. Expecting floods of tears was not how they reacted to the news. He was about to see Effy in a new, almost frightening way as she took command of the situation. Ellen, who he thought would weep and wail, remained cool and composed. There was an unfamiliar steeliness in her demeanour too. It was unlike anything he and Tom had seen in Ellen before.

Effy began steely-voiced, face impassive. "First of all, I'm so sorry you have had to put up with what's happened tonight. Neither Ellen nor I wanted you subjected to the stupid old goat's madness. He may have fathered us, but he's not been much of a father. More like some misogynistic patriarch

238

treating us like inferiors. Both Ellen and I have been preparing for a while. We knew it would happen sometime. If he wants to have a confrontation, by God I'm going to give him one he'll never forget. And when he's had my ten guineas' worth we're taking our things and leaving. If we never see him again it'll not be too soon."

The look in Effy's eyes was scary. Neither Mack nor Tom could believe this was the sweet, gentle, forgiving Effy they knew. She was icy, yet incensed at the same time, her fury calculated yet restrained. This was her dark side that Mack had never experienced. In the next minute she became a stranger. The reaction to Effy was not confined to Mack and Tom alone. Even Caitlin and Adam found themselves taken aback.

"You can't be serious," Caitlin gasped, staggered by what she heard.

"Don't worry. We've talked it over and over, planning what we would do next. We know we can't stop here and we won't. It would be impossible and unfair on the three of you. You have enough of a struggle as it is. As a temporary measure we'll have to stop with Bridget long enough to get jobs and find a place of our own."

"But you can't drop your A Levels like this," protested Caitlin.

"Watch us!" exclaimed Ellen, the depth of her anger clear. "I'm not putting up with a living hell a moment longer. Nor is Effy. We've talked it through often enough. Our exams will have to go on hold. Later when we're working we'll look into retaking them at Tech in the evenings."

"Don't be silly, don't do this." Caitlin was desperate, trying to dissuade them. "You have to try to put up with it a little longer and get your qualifications. You two are so bright. Don't ruin it for yourselves."

"It's over." Effy stated abruptly.

It was clear they were not listening, their minds made up.

Ellen spoke again. "We have a favour to ask of Adam for this morning. We'd like him to drop us at the house so we can pack our things in the car while they're at church. We've been expecting this to happen so we've been preparing. Some of the things are ready to go already. So if you can bring our things here, we'll walk back after we've told him a few home truths."

"Make no mistake, Caitlin," Effy continued. "He's going to wish he'd never fathered us after I'm done with him. We're not his chattels fit only for indoctrination and imprisonment. We're not tainted with the sin of Eve. What kind of moron would say our guilt is inherent and we are to blame for the loss of paradise? He knows what he can do with his misogyny. Stuff his religion and stuff his poisonous, idiotic theology. He may not have wanted seven daughters but that's what his God gave him. And by that God of his he's going to rue the day he made our lives a misery."

"When all's said and done he is still our father," beseeched Caitlin. "We have to have some charity and forgiveness or we become as misguided as him."

"Don't bother to defend him," snapped Ellen. "He reckons I'm a whore and Effy's a heretic fit for burning at the stake. Since you left home you don't know the half of what we've had to listen to and live with."

"Well, now he'll have a fornicator and a heretic to deal with." Effy flared, losing the composure she had so carefully controlled. "And I want him to live with that knowledge of me."

It was a blatant revelation. The silence was resounding.

Adam finally broke the silence. "Looks like you're crossing the Rubicon, Effy, and burning the bridge behind you. Are you sure that's wise?"

Mack's heart sank with Effy's revelation. Now it was out in the open. He was not so much surprised by Effy as he was hearing his brother's classical allusion. Mentioning the Rubicon seemed peculiar and most un-Adam-like.

Caitlin's expression ranged from shock to disappointment to upset at Effy's outburst.

"And you? You couldn't keep it in your Y-fronts, could you?" Adam accused Mack.

"Don't blame Mack. Don't just assume he seduced me. It takes two to tango. If anything I'm as much to blame if not more so. I wanted him as much as he wanted me. That's what happens when you love someone," Effy informed Adam with emphatic bluntness. "And you're a fine one to lecture us, given what happened to you and Caitlin."

Adam raised his hands in the air in silent response, withdrawing from further comment.

"Oh, Effy!" Caitlin began to sound despondent. "What if you're pregnant?"

"Well, it won't be for lack of precautions," Effy replied, realising the impact of her revelation on both Caitlin and Adam.

"Eff, don't say any more," interrupted Ellen, quiet-voiced and pleading. "Caitlin and Adam have been wonderful. You've said it yourself. They are not to blame for our Da. They've only ever looked after our best interests. Don't forget what you've told me. Adam and Caitlin have helped

240

us to enjoy the happiest times we could ever have wished to have. Imagine if you and Mack had been unable to get together? Imagine what it would have been like for me? I would never have met Tom. Nor had some of the best experiences yet in my life. Where would we be without them?"

Ellen's words made Effy stop. There were tears in her eyes. Turning to Mack, she buried her head in his chest. He held her close to him, stroking her hair.

The room was silent as everyone took in what she had said.

Ellen continued. "We're out of options. If burning bridges is all that's left to do, that's what we have to do. The wreckage he's wreaked should finally confront him. He should remain in no doubt about it."

"What about Grace? Are you going to leave her behind?" Mack asked, absorbing every word of Ellen's.

"What else can we do? I hate the thought of leaving her alone in the house. Effy and myself are old enough to leave home and go. Grace isn't. We couldn't take her with us, at least not yet. Besides, there's not enough room at Bridget's flat. It'll be bad enough the two of us descending on her out of the blue."

"There are other complications you're not yet aware of to do with Bridget," revealed Caitlin. "She has problems of her own which you won't know about."

"You mean what's his name, Mr Smooth? Do you remember what he's called?" Tom asked Mack, displaying his usual lack of diplomatic tact.

"Greg."

"Yeah, Greg. We sussed him out as soon as we saw him round at Bridget's flat. No doubt he's giving her some guff about how happy they'll be when he's finally got a divorce."

"Shut up, Tom! You don't know the whole story." Ellen was sharp with him. "Neither do we. We'll have to work round it."

"I'm too tired," yawned Effy. "We know what we have to do. So will you help us to get our things in a few hours? Otherwise, Mack and Tom will have to shift what they can as best they can on their scooters."

Caitlin looked at Adam and then gave him a brief nod of assent. She was unable to argue further against the sisters' proposed course of action.

"Okay, you two. On your own heads it is. I'll help you cross the Rubicon."

"We'll come too and lend a hand," volunteered Mack.

241

"No," Effy replied, sounding more like the girl he knew and loved. "We don't want you two involved – at least, not yet. It's a family affair. As much as I love you, as much as you want to help, I want you to stay clear. Come over this afternoon. We'll see where we are by then."

CHAPTER 51

That's Enough – Roscoe Robinson (PYE International 7N.25385 – 1966)

Sunday 30 October 1966 – Later

Mack had set his alarm to wake up by 9.30. Tom, not pilled up for once, had clambered into the sleeping bag on the floor and gone to sleep immediately. His final words to Mack were to wake him at the same time. Tom was as concerned as Mack about the girls.

The alarm seemed to go off almost as soon as he'd fallen asleep. Even with the best of intentions it took him more than another forty minutes to come round. By the time he'd washed his face, and tapped Tom with his toe to rouse him, his parents had returned from Mass. Pulling on a jumper as he went down the stairs, he met his father coming up presumably to wake him.

"Glad you're up, James. We've had a less than pleasant encounter with Mr Halloran outside church this morning. Seems he's not too happy about you and Tom as well as Effy and Ellen. Actually, let me give you the gist of his words in the rather colourful vernacular he used with me. If he caught you two anywhere near his two daughters he'd cut your balls off and feed them to the local dogs."

Tom, listening in from the top of the landing, leaned over the banister rail. "Morning, Uncle Rob, Halloran and whose army? No chance, Mack'd stuff him and kick him into touch in under a minute. For a supposed God-fearing bloke he doesn't sound too peace-loving."

"Which, James, also brings me to the disturbing tale I've heard from Mr Jenkins. He heard how one evening you beat up a couple of youths within an inch of their lives in Bradford. Is it true?"

"They had it coming, Dad."

"So it was you?"

"One of them had it coming. He tried to rape Ellen one Saturday night," Tom explained as he came downstairs.

"So it was you. I could not believe a son of mine would have taken part in such a brawl. Seems I don't know my son as well as I thought."

"Like Tom said, he had it coming. It was before Tom and Ellen became an item. Effy and Grace found out and told me about it. Ellen was

243

distraught over what happened to her. Don't blame Effy for telling me. She didn't know what I had planned for the guy once I knew who it was."

"Bernard told me this chap was a piece of work you had previous dealings with in the shop. Was he the same one?"

"He was. The same."

"I can't say I'm pleased hearing about your brawling. If it's true what he tried to do then Ellen should have gone to the police to report him."

"Yeah, right, Dad. First of all, it would have blown the girls' chances of getting out of Stalag Halloran. I wouldn't have been able to see Effy. Second, the police never believe girls and women who complain a bloke has raped them. They always take the bloke's side. Besides, he didn't actually succeed in raping her. She managed to kick him in the nuts and get away with nothing more than bruising on her face where he hit her."

"So what about the other chap?"

"Him?" jeered Tom. "He thought he'd lend his mate a helping hand. It was two against one, while I was keeping others from wading in. They were fair odds for Mack. He whupped their backsides real fine. It was epic bordering on legendary, Uncle Rob."

"Was it now?"

"Sure was, and if El had been my girlfriend then I'd have done the same as Mack. He would have backed me up same as I did for him. You have to stand by your girlfriend's family.And if anyone tried it on El now I'd do the exact same."

"Leaving the brawling to one side for the moment. Let's have the pair of you in the living room. Your mum and I need to talk with you about the Halloran situation and other things."

The next hour proved to be remarkable in many ways. Mack told his parents about what the two sisters had decided to do. He was keen to stress the difficulties that leaving for Bridget's would cause. It was not only about giving up school but the three of them living in the same tiny flat. His parents, saying nothing, recalled his recent threat to leave home and said nothing. Mack had refused to give them an undertaking not to do anything foolish.

When his parents pressed Mack on the matter he refused to answer. Tom joined in saying all four could move into a rented house. Tom's timely suggestion was not implausible. Tom could bear the initial costs until Mack and the girls got work. Jobs were easy to come by so this was a threat Mack's parents treated as serious. It was like pouring petrol on a smouldering fire.

Plausibility was the name of the game. At the end of the round-table talks Robert MacKinnon made a suggestion. The girls, accompanied by Adam and Caitlin, should come for a Sunday meal. Tom would go to Adam's to invite them. Meanwhile, Mack and his father would drive to Shipley to talk to Bridget. Before they set off on their respective journeys Jane MacKinnon dropped a bombshell.

"There's something that your father and I have to tell you, James. There's no easy way to go about this, but actually we're excited and happy. Well, at least now we are. It was a huge shock for both of us when we first found out." Jane MacKinnon's usual composure faded. As she gazed at her son, her nervous breathlessness struck him as strange. This was unlike the confident woman he knew as his mother. Finally she uttered the words, "I'm expecting."

"What are you expecting?" Mack asked puzzled failing to grasp what his mother was trying to tell him.

"God, you're a right dumbo!" chortled Tom. "Your mum's expecting a baby, you Noddy. Congrats, Aunty Jane! What do you hope it's going to be? Better not be another boy, eh? There's still Grace Halloran left on the shelf."

Icy looks greeted Sean Halloran. The sisters had waited for his return, sitting in the living room. They afforded him no opportunity to start his verbal assault. They stood up together to confront him. For once, instead of Effy taking the lead, Ellen as the elder of the two announced in a singularly chilling voice, "We're only here long enough to tell you we're leaving home. For good, if it isn't clear enough for you."

Effy added, "We've packed our things and they're gone. So are we in a moment or two. Consider this our adieu, Father dear. We are leaving before you throw us out."

"It's what they call a pre-emptive strike these days," continued Ellen. "So it should stop you having to tell us to get out and never darken your doorstep again."

"You can't up sticks and leave like this," he spluttered, taken off-guard by their twin verbal attacks. "You have school in the morning. You have A Levels you need to be studying for. You have nowhere to go, and no money."

The girls held up Post Office savings books in simultaneous defiance.

"We have enough saved between us to find a place on our own and get full-time jobs," Ellen declared. "In fact both Effy and I can get full-time jobs at either C&A or Dorothy Perkins tomorrow. We can be working full-time from Tuesday morning."

Their mother collapsed in an armchair, distraught and shaking. She understood the chilling seriousness in her daughters' voices. "They mean it, Sean. They're not joking."

"Then I'll be calling their bluff. Go and..."

"Let me guess, Daddy dear – and never darken your door again?" Effy anticipated his words. "Okay, let's go, sis. Any more words are a waste of breath. Let's see what excuse he comes up with explaining our leaving home and school. That should prove interesting."

Grace, mesmerised by her sisters' performance, threw her arms round Effy. "Take me with you. Please take me with you. Don't leave me here with him on my own or I swear I'll do something horrible to myself."

"I can't, Grace, you know I can't. You're not of legal age to leave home and we can't take you. But as soon as you're sixteen we'll come for you."

The explosive tirade was unlike anything the sisters had experienced before. Halloran's language reached unprecedented levels of raging abuse. It became a tantrum to end all tantrums. Their mother, having broken down in tears, begged her husband to stop without avail. Grace, now in floods of tears too, clung to Effy like a barnacle to a rock in a storm. Effy and Ellen exchanged looks, maintaining stony expressions and silence. They let the torrential tirade wash over them. His words no longer had any power to cower them.

"Flesh of my flesh? No that cannot be possible, you are no daughters of mine. You are nothing but sinful *hoors* of Babylon. Whoring yourself around this city and God knows where else. So bent on destroying the good name of this family with your harlotry. You have no shame, filled with sin like all womankind who are the sinful issue of Eve. Womankind bears more guilt than man. It was a woman seduced by Satan who distracted her husband from his obedience to God. This is why women are below men and must forever carry that ignominy and shame within themselves. As the great scholar Tertullian wrote, *'Woman is a temple built over a sewer, the gateway to the Devil. Woman, you are the devil's doorway'*."

"Appears to me, Father dearest, you must share in the guilt. You've worshipped at least seven times in that temple built over a sewer. Seems to me you must have enjoyed the pleasure of entering the devil's doorway." Effy's sarcastic response was priceless. Ellen's stony expression cracked with unbridled laughter.

Her witty riposte left him floundering, staggered by the sheer audacity of the words. Effy was not done yet. "You should have taken note of Matthew 19:12 and become a Eunuch. You could have saved yourself a great deal of trouble. One day you'll wake up to your loss. As my boyfriend said to me, you had a treasure about you and you couldn't see it nor care for it."

"You've become lost to me, Fiona. The heretical thinking at work in the Holy Mother Church has poisoned you. Your blasphemous words and thoughts wound me."

"Take this as read. I do not believe in your deity. I can neither relate to it nor worship it."

"Are you telling me you're an atheist, girl? You don't believe in God?"

"No, I don't believe in your distorted vision of God. Now it's time Ellen and I left. We've taken enough abuse and insults for too long. You cannot make us fear any longer nor will we be cowed by your words. I wish I could love you as my father but you're a poor excuse for one, even worse as a man. You're nothing more than a bullying thug treating the women in this house as one step above animals. Mack's only seventeen and he's more of a man than you'll ever be."

"It's bad enough I have one daughter saddled with that Scottish trash. To have another daughter fall in with that disreputable family beggars belief."

"He's English. Not Scottish. He was born and raised in Yorkshire. At least he's not a misguided religious zealot from the peat bogs of Ireland. As for insulting you, you might like to meditate a little more on how you've treated us. We can't understand how Ma has put up with you for all these years. None of us have ever understood. It can't be love. It must be fear. Blind fear of you and what you stand for."

"Go! Go before I strike you. Go and be a *hoor* with that so-called man of yours who is so much better than your father."

"Whores do it for money. You need to get your definition straight. I am not a whore. I would never sell my body to any man. But I would give it

247

to a man I loved without a second thought. And I know he's better than you. I know he is."

"Effy, please don't say anything more," Ellen interrupted, fearing what her sister might say next. "Something's are better left unsaid. Let's leave."

"Go on with you! Don't bother to crawl back here. There'll not be a place for you here without true heartfelt contrition and repentance."

"In your dreams," Ellen answered. "If I never come back it'll be too soon."

Effy's response was cutting and brutal. "As they say in America. Don't call us we'll call you. Never."

"For heaven's sake girls, you don't mean to abandon your own home like this?" pleaded their mother. "Please don't leave like this with such hard-heartedness and bitterness. Your father is a good man who doesn't always show the love he feels for you."

"He's now demonstrated what passes for love in his mind," replied Ellen. "And you, Ma, would be better leaving him. Why do you persist in sticking by this misogynistic excuse for a human being? You're nothing more than a misused and abused chattel."

"Give me a minute, I'll get my things. I'm coming with you," cried Grace. "If you're going, I'm coming too."

As she tried to dash upstairs her father seized her and threw her onto the settee. Such a violent act had never happened in the Halloran home before. "You'll be going nowhere, Grace Halloran. I'll at least save your soul from their godless ways."

"Wait till I report you to social workers about the violence we've seen." Effy's voice seethed with rage. "We've seen your parental violence and we'll swear blind you've been mistreating her."

"Get out. Get out," he screamed. "No social worker will believe harlots and trollops. I disown you both."

"To late to disown us," Ellen responded, enraged. "We disowned you a long time ago."

Then they were gone, leaving Grace and their mother clutching each other and sobbing.

CHAPTER 52

Meeting Over Yonder – The Impressions (HMV POP 1446 – 1965)

Sunday 30 October 1966 – Late afternoon

Bridget was alone in her flat when they arrived. Fear appeared in her face when she opened the door to them. Her first thought was of Caitlin and the baby. But Robert MacKinnon put her at ease immediately. Caitlin was fine, and so was the little girl. They were here on an altogether different matter.

Once seated, Mack's father explained why they had come. Bridget sighed as she listened. Effy and Ellen's charade was over with the inevitable consequences and repercussions. Bridget had hoped it might have remained secret for a while longer. The girls would have to stay with her. Robert MacKinnon could tell at a glance that the flat would not be suitable for all three sisters and he asked Bridget how she would cope with her two teenage sisters. She shrugged. Somehow she would cope. There was no choice. How? She still had to figure that out. Knowing her father, she dreaded to hear what might have transpired. There was little likelihood of either father or daughters backing down.

Bridget's concern was for her sisters' futures. They were intelligent young women. Ellen wanted to become a teacher. Effy was bright enough to get to university. Somehow, she would have to try to make it happen for the sake of their futures.

Ever practical in fiscal matters, Robert MacKinnon asked how she would cope. At first, Bridget was reluctant to reveal her finances. It was only after he asked Mack to return to the car that she disclosed her situation. Having to sit in the car annoyed Mack. But on reflection he could understand why Bridget might not want him to know about her earnings. It was all a bit tricky. No doubt his father was looking at all viable options for Bridget and her sisters. They were much longer than he expected as he waited in the car.

Almost an hour later they emerged together. Robert MacKinnon explained that Bridget was going to join them at home. They would have a family discussion on the best way forward for Effy and Ellen. If the girls had indeed left, then they would need to be present.

It was a full house on their return. Adam, Caitlin and the baby were already there. Caitlin was helping Jane MacKinnon in the kitchen. Effy and Ellen were also there, looking exhausted but unbowed. Effy was playing with her niece on the living-room floor. Tom was sitting on the settee next to Ellen, with his arm around her while she rested her head on his shoulder, eyes closed. Mack took off his parka. Hanging it up, he joined Effy.

"How was it?"

"Awful. Ellen was a star. We burned the bridges so we can't ever go back now. Oh, well, *que sera sera*."

"Dad spent an hour with Bridget. They must have talked about how she's going to cope with you and Ellen living in that tiny flat."

"Really?"

"Yes. Really."

"Effy, Mr MacKinnon has left the lounge free for me to speak with you and Ellen. Come and tell me everything that's happened," Bridget invited.

Effy leaned over and kissed Mack. "Got to leave you for a little while. Look after our niece. I'm sure you can handle it."

Looking after his niece was harder than he expected. The little girl began to cry as soon as Effy had gone. Adam came to his brother's rescue.

"Don't worry about it. She's not used to you. Spends all her time with women so you can't expect her to take to you as she does with them. There's a limit to even your charms."

The sisters stayed closeted for a long time. Caitlin had left the kitchen to join them. By the time Effy and Ellen emerged from the sisters' conclave they looked drained of all energy. Nor did they appear in much of a mood to talk. Mack and Tom had chatted in private upstairs. Both agreed not to ask the girls anything further until the dust had settled. Tom even admitted it must have been traumatic for the pair. "Least said, soonest mended," he suggested; it seemed the best policy.

Cooking for nine was a huge task, but Jane MacKinnon managed with help from her daughter-in-law. Seating nine was not quite practicable. Eight could get round the extended dining-room table. Caitlin ate and fed the little girl in the living room, seated in an armchair. Meanwhile, Robert and Jane MacKinnon made all their visitors welcome. Avoiding the matter on everyone's minds, they cheered everyone up with anecdotes. Neither Mack nor Adam appreciated these since the stories were about them when they were young. Tom was having a good laugh at their expense when Jane

250

MacKinnon recounted one his mother had told her. Then it was Mack and Adam's turn to laugh at his expense. The sisters enjoyed hearing these anecdotes that brought a few laughs and cheered all present.

After the meal Mack and Tom did the washing up and drying, supervised by Adam. Adam avoided clean-up duty by dealing with his baby daughter. Together the four sisters and his parents closeted themselves in the lounge.

It was nearing eight o'clock. Tom was going to have to return to Halifax. Work awaited him in the morning. Reluctant to go, he wanted to know the outcome of all the talking, especially about Ellen.

To Mack it was amazing how his cousin had become so taken with Ellen in such a short time. They were such a strange pairing. Neither was exactly renowned for their tact. Both spoke their minds. A spade was a spade. Tom was down to earth. No academic, but when it came to mechanics or engineering he had a lot of skill and talent. Ellen was clever, bookish with a sense of purpose. She could be up in the clouds flying around like a lost balloon. When grounded she fostered encouragement in others. No wonder she wanted to be a teacher. At least that was Effy's assessment of her sister. Yes, they were a strange pairing. But somehow a pairing that worked, beyond the obvious chemistry they shared.

Tom was about to go, having agreed to 'phone Mack the following morning. He wanted to find out what they had decided and how this would affect him and Ellen. No sooner had he started to don his parka than they all began to come out of the lounge. Ellen came straight over to him. "I'm going to live with Bridget. I have to stay on and do my A Levels. Will you still want to go out with me?"

"Doll, I'll be over next Saturday to pick you up."

"Make that Friday evening. I can't wait until Saturday." She gave him a crushing hug and a kiss. Mack half expected her to make some snotty comment to Tom about not calling her "doll". But much to his surprise, she didn't appear to mind, giving him another kiss.

"Mack, your mum and dad want to have a word with you. If I were you, I'd expect the worst."

This didn't sound promising. He went into the lounge ready for a confrontation. Passing a grinning Caitlin and a tired but cheerful Bridget, he wondered what Ellen had meant.

"Sit down, son. We have something important to say to you."

Mack sat next to Effy who had the faintest of happy smiles.

251

"After a lengthy discussion we've agreed. Effy will stay with us," explained Jane MacKinnon. "She will have Adam's old room for the rest of this school year. But I want it understood by the pair of you. It will be on the strictest understanding that there is no sexual misconduct under this roof. Your father will fit a lock on the door. Effy will keep it locked at night should you get any ideas about going in there, young man. You will observe the proprieties at all times. Is that understood?"

Mack nodded his assent.

"If either of you disobey this rule Effy will have to go to Bridget's. Is that clear? While Effy is in our care you will treat her like a sister, even if she is your girlfriend. Have I made myself understood? When Ellen goes to Teacher Training College, then Effy can move in with her sister for her final year in the Sixth if she wants."

It was astonishing and unexpected news, which took Mack totally by surprise. It was too good to be true. It was good and bad news wrapped up together.

"One more thing," his mother added. "You can be responsible for taking Effy to school every morning. You can collect her in the evening on your scooter. I'm sure it's one concession you won't mind making.

"Effy is going to get her things and bring them back here tonight with Adam. Your father will take Bridget and Ellen to Adam's to get her things before driving them to Shipley. Caitlin has promised not to tell her parents where they are should they come calling. Bridget has agreed to do the same. Though from what Effy and Ellen have told us, it seems unlikely he will come looking for them. He sounds such a heartless and forbidding man."

Effy's first night in the MacKinnon household was so weird yet so wonderful. She had spent occasional hours with the MacKinnons, but now here she was, living with them. It was spooky when she remembered the uncanny feeling of someday coming to live in this house. The someday had come to pass. She was going to be living here. The thought of Mack next door was heart-warming but also upsetting. He was so close, yet this closeness might as well have been on the other side of the planet.

For Mack it was no different. She was within reach yet unreachable. It was more than he could stand. He spent the rest of the night in a semi-sleepless torment, wanting to feel Effy's lithe presence beside him. It was torture of the worst kind. Mack had given his word. Keeping his word might not prove possible with temptation so near. Now he understood why Ellen had said to expect the worst.

CHAPTER 53

Woman's Got Soul – The Impressions (HMV POP 1429 – 1965)

Monday 31 October 1966 – All Saints' Day

"I didn't see Grace in school today. I asked her friend Jean if she could pop round tonight to check Grace was all right. I don't know if Bridget will be able to go tonight. She usually drops in Sundays, Tuesdays and Thursdays to see if everything is okay."

"What are you afraid of?" Mack asked Effy as they sat across the dining table from one another. "Grace wouldn't do anything silly, would she?"

"I don't know. I miss her already. We've shared a room since she was six months old. It's so strange not seeing and talking to her."

"She's a lovely kid." Mack tried to console Effy. "I like her. She can be funny at times. Don't worry too much. Either she'll be in school tomorrow when the dust has settled at home or Jean will have some news for you and Ellen. I don't suppose Ellen will have said much to you about moving in with Bridget?"

"Not much apart from Bridget complaining she wriggles about in bed too much. They're going to get a single bed to go in the tiny bedroom. Greg came round late last night after your father dropped them off. He said he would help out."

Mack sniggered.

"What's so funny?"

"He'll want Ellen out of Bridget's bed quick sticks."

Effy planted a gentle tap on his shin. "Oi. Watch it! That's my big sister you're talking about!" The grin on her face revealed she shared the implied thought.

"What are you studying tonight?" Mack peered across the table.

"English Lit. I have to make some notes on Chapter Three of Jane Austen's *Emma*. Then I've got some equations to solve for tomorrow. After that I'll be carrying on reading another one of her novels. What about you?"

"I have Economics notes to read up and organise for an essay. How economists classify economic resources as factors of production."

"Sounds dreary and boring." Effy rolled her eyes. "I'm glad I'm not studying it."

"I have to confess Economics is dry. I can understand it. It's not hard but it can get tedious. It's not a subject I'd want to study at university if I ever go."

"Is that all for tonight?" asked Effy, surprised. "They don't give you much to do for homework at Bede's."

"Like you, I've got some reading to do for history. I've got to read up about the Albigensian Heresy and Crusade. I swear, the more I read about religion the more I wish I was an atheist, not an agnostic."

"I don't know what to believe anymore. I'm like you. It seems to me as a female I'm not as important or as valued as a man. That's what I love most about you and your family. You've always treated me like an equal, the same way your dad treats your mum."

"I'm glad to hear you say that, Effy." Mack's mother had overheard her as she came in to check on them. "I wouldn't care to see James treating any of our sex any other way. Robert has always treated me as his equal. We may be a traditional couple with me staying at home rather than working. I could have carried on working after James was born. Instead I chose to be a housewife. I believed it was more important to help raise my children and wish I had done so after Adam was born. It wasn't easy when we first started out on married life. Which is not to say you can't have a career and also raise a family. It was my choice alone. Robert agreed with my decision. I admire your sister Deidre. She's so brave for choosing to enter such a male-dominated profession as Medicine. She won't find that easy being a woman."

"Times are changing, things will improve," Mack responded. "But you only have to look at Effy's father to realise there's still a long way to go."

"He forgot the most important teaching." Jane MacKinnon sat down besides Effy. "God created humanity, male and female, to reflect the divine nature. For Robert and I this has always implied full equality. When it comes to understanding the two sexes both must have full equality. As women we have the responsibility of bearing children. It is our biological role and it's inescapable. Our bodies are different and meant to be so. Our minds work in different ways too, governed by what God intended for us as women. What must always be unacceptable is that we are less because of what we are."

"Moving off the subject, I have a question I need to ask you, Mum."

"What is it, James?"

254

"When you were deciding who should come to live with us, why did you choose Effy? After all, Ellen may have been a better choice. Less of a temptation and distraction, so to speak."

"I suppose we could always do a swap if you don't want Effy and would prefer her sister."

"Don't twist my words. I'm happy she's here. I want to satisfy my curiosity about your reasons, that's all."

"I would have thought you might have worked it out for yourself," Jane MacKinnon answered. "After all the trouble to keep your romance going, keeping you apart may not have been the wisest move. This way we can keep you together while stopping any foolishness."

"What foolishness, Mrs MacKinnon?" Effy asked.

"Yes, Mum. What foolishness?" Mack knew exactly what she was going to say.

"Why, leaving home to get dead-end jobs and 'live in sin' as you put it, James. What else?" She paused, glancing at them both, and then continued. "That's exactly what you planned, isn't it?"

Effy nodded.

"Mack would have joined you in a heartbeat. I could no more let it happen to him than I could to you, my dear. You're both intelligent young people who would waste your lives if you did such a foolish thing. Besides..." Jane MacKinnon put her arm around Effy in a motherly fashion. "As I've got to know Effy I've taken to her. I'm sure Ellen's lovely too but Effy is the right one to be with us. She's like the daughter I wish I could have had."

"You may still," commented Mack. "The new addition could well be a girl. You can't assume it'll be another boy."

"Let's keep our fingers crossed, shall we? Now it's time I left you to get on with your work."

"So, before you go, Mum... It's a bit formal for Effy to carry on calling you Mrs MacKinnon, isn't it? Since I'm supposed to treat her as a sister, shouldn't she call you Mum?" Mack suggested, tongue-in-cheek.

"He's right. It's too formal calling me Mrs MacKinnon all the time. Please call me Jane. After all, that's my name. I'd prefer that too. If you should ever marry my son I wouldn't mind you calling me Mum. But out of deference to your own mother, Jane would be best for the present."

"Does that mean I can call you Jane, too?" Mack probed, knowing full well what the answer would be.

"No, it does not! For goodness sake! I am your mother and you will refer to me as mum or mother until my dying day. Gracious me! What a silly thing to ask! As if I would let you!"

Effy caught the twinkle in her eye as Jane MacKinnon spoke.

"So, what should she call dad?"

"I'll ask him," his mother replied.

"She can call me dad if she wants to." Robert MacKinnon's voice sounded from the kitchen; clearly he had followed the conversation. "Or 'Rob' will do. I'll leave it with you, Effy. Whichever you find most comfortable. And no, James, it's still dad, before you ask."

CHAPTER 54

Nowhere To Run, Nowhere To Hide – Martha & The Vandellas
(Tamla Motown TMG 502 – 1965)

All Souls' Day – Tuesday 31 October 1966

"Thanks for abandoning me, Eff. There wasn't anything I wouldn't have done for you but you couldn't even take me with you. You left me behind like you didn't care."

Grace's angry reproach hurt Effy. She felt her sisters had deserted her. The upset caused tears to well up in Effy's eyes. "We couldn't do anything else, sis. We had no choice. I… we… didn't want to leave you behind."

"He's gone off his rocker, he's completely barmy. Comes home in vile moods and takes it out on Ma and me. Won't even allow Bridget back in the house, either. Refuses to speak to her. Says she's undermined his authority with us. He thinks you and Ellen are stopping with Caitlin. I take it you're not. Are you both at Bridget's?"

Unwilling to lie yet unwilling to tell the truth, Effy was in a quandary.

"Fiona Halloran, Grace Halloran, you're late for your next lessons. Go to them, please." A teacher's voice interrupted their exchange on the corridor.

"Meet me outside after school, Grace. We can talk about it then."

"And say what?"

Dashing to her class Effy was the last to arrive behind the teacher.

"What do we make of Emma Woodhouse's attitude towards the Martin family…?"

Effy, trying to stop her tears, attempted to remain involved in the lesson. Leaving her sister behind all alone with no one but her parents saddened Effy. Grace was right. They had abandoned her, although knowing she would be without their support. She and Ellen had only thought about themselves. No. It was untrue. Anger and desperation had compelled their departure. What else could they have done? Grace, so silly, so amusing, so cheerful – how, oh how, could they have abandoned her? Grace was quite right to have used that word. Abandoned. They had abandoned her. Tears

257

were rolling down Effy's cheeks. As she tried to wipe them away with her hanky it was obvious to those in the group that she was distressed.

"Boyfriend trouble, Fiona?" enquired the teacher.

"No, Miss. Family problems."

"Would you like to leave the class for a few minutes?"

"No, Miss. I'll be fine."

"Are you sure, Fiona?"

"Yes, Miss." Effy tried to put a brave smile on her face as she realised everyone in the class was staring at her. Somehow, she was able to keep control of herself during the rest of the morning. Later she caught up with Ellen during the lunch period and burst into floods of tears in front of her sister. Ellen was also upset but remained calm. She understood how special the relationship was between Effy and Grace. They were the two youngest and had always stuck together as they grew up. Grace looked up to Effy like no one else in the family. The two had a singular bond. To see the bond tried was painful.

"We'll have to see what we can do about getting her out of the house. I'll talk to Bridget tonight. Meanwhile, let's try and cheer her up after school. Do you think Mack can come up with something? He's usually resourceful at finding solutions. By the way how are you settling in with the MacKinnons?"

"Oh, they're great, so kind and so caring. What a family should be. Mack's mother wants me to call her Jane. His father said I could either call him Dad or Rob. I call him Rob but he seems more like a dad to me already."

"Well, Eff, seems you have your feet well under the table, girl. How's lover boy coping with you so near yet so far away?"

"He's a bit frustrated and he's not the only one."

"I'll bet he is. Mind you, I would be in the same situation if I was next door to Tom."

"It's frustrating but I've given them my word. I can't go back on it. We'll have to cope somehow. We'll find opportunities wherever and whenever they turn up, I'm sure."

"Have they fitted the lock on your bedroom door yet?"

"Not yet, but I suspect his dad will get round to it pretty soon. Trouble is, every night I get into bed, I can't stop thinking about what you and Tom got up to in it. It's uncomfortable, not to mention weird."

"Oh, don't be such a baby! It's not like you're sleeping on the same sheets, is it? Besides, we did nothing compared to what you two did. Get over it. Mind you, I suppose if I had to sleep in Mack's bed, where you'd lost your virginity, I'd find it weird as well. Do his parents suspect?"

"I don't know. I hope not. Not unless you or Tom let something slip. If they do know they've not given any sign."

"Us? No chance. It's one piece of information we won't divulge. We have sworn ourselves to secrecy about it. Especially when we were in the house ourselves at the time and up to no good. Seeing how you blabbed all in front of Caitlin and Adam they're most likely to be the source. Caitlin's as thick as thieves with his mum. Still, I can't imagine Caitlin would tell her. That would be so unlike her. She's the only one among us who's been good at keeping secrets."

"Oh, God. If Caitlin let anything slip I won't know where I'd put myself. "

"Most unlikely. I'm certain Adam wouldn't. I'm sure they wouldn't. You and Mack are like Sandra Dee and Troy Donoghue in *A Summer Place*. Seeing you two in action together has been like watching a movie. In fact someone should make a movie called *A Summer Place 1966* starring Mack and Effy."

"And I suppose you find it amusing?"

"No, not at all. Romantic, yes. Dramatic, yes. Entertaining, yes. Making me feel envious? I can say a definite big yes indeed. You two may have found what others search their whole lives hoping to find, yet never do. Amusing? No. Never."

"Anyway, I'm not as pretty as Sandra Dee," sighed Effy.

"No. You're not. Compared to her you're beautiful. I've watched guys of all ages drooling over you every time we've been out in public. I know I'm pretty but you're stunning and you don't even realise it. You could be a film star or a model or both. That's no lie. As for Mack, he could be Sean Connery's replacement as a James Bond in years to come."

"Give over! As if!"

"You haven't a clue, have you?" Ellen went on. "The girls in your year and mine are in total envy of your looks. Your flawless complexion, rarely seen with a spot or blackhead, is enough to drive them spare. Your hair is a gorgeous colour and shines like it has no business to do. Well, you do take a lot of care and time on your looks but make no mistake. You have a figure most girls envy and dream about. It's as near perfect as it could be. Well, our figures are one of the things you and I have in common. It looks like Grace will be fortunate, too, the way she's filling out."

259

"Okay, enough is enough. Back to Grace – what do you suggest we say to her?"

Grace was sullen when they met. No matter how Effy and Ellen tried to cheer her up nothing worked. They were in her "bad books" and they knew it.

When Mack finally arrived to pick up Effy he realised all was far from well. It was obvious. Effy was tearful. Ellen looked glum. As for Grace, her face was a tale in itself. There did not seem any obvious answers how to solve Grace's problem. She was far too young to leave home. With O Levels looming in a year's time it only made matters worse. If she left home and went to Bridget's the police might get called in along with social workers. Mack imagined Effy's position could end up under scrutiny. The more he thought about it the less likely it seemed. Ellen would experience no problem because of her age and living with Bridget. Then again, Old Man Halloran, having washed his hands of Effy and Ellen, might not bother with them. They were as dead to him as he was to them. Grace was another matter. She was the youngest, and the most exploitable.

The Halloran family reputation at the church had to be in tatters by now. Grace was the only daughter still attending Sunday Masses. Aileen was at some convent or other. Bridget and Caitlin attended other parishes, concealing the disintegration of the family. Deidre was in Manchester. Effy and Ellen's disappearances were altogether on another plane. They no longer attended their own church, or any other. This could not have gone unnoticed with the locals. Mack's thoughts turned to Grace once more.

Even if she ran away from home there was nowhere for her to go. There was nowhere to run, nowhere to hide. At best running away could only be a temporary act of rebellion.

Grace cheered up as he approached. Taking her to one side, he spoke to her in a subdued voice, bringing a smile to her face. She gave him a hug and a peck on the cheek. There was a further, lengthier exchange between them, with Grace doing all the talking. Returning to her sisters she seemed more like her old self. When Effy asked her what Mack had said, Grace replied she was not to worry. Where there was a problem there would always be a solution. They had to be patient. Her sullen behaviour had appeared to change in an instant after speaking with Mack.

When Effy asked Mack later what had passed between them, he replied, "Nothing of any importance."

Grace apologised for her brattish behaviour. Ellen commented later, "It was all a bit Jekyll and Hyde with Mack acting like an antidote."

Mack thought it wiser not to enlighten Effy about what had passed between them. Not that he had much choice. He hated not being open with Effy about his exchange with Grace.

"Now, Sir Galahad. I don't propose to wait for you to come up with a plan to rescue this fair maiden. I have a plan of sorts to rescue myself. You'll know when it happens. The important thing is that my sisters shouldn't worry when it takes place. Mack, I want you to promise me you'll reassure my sisters I will be okay. It's important they know nothing and don't panic. I will be quite safe, I can definitely promise you. That's all you have to know for the time being. Promise me? I need to have that promise from you. It's time for you to repay me for introducing you to Effy."

"How can I promise if I don't know what you have planned?"

"It's better you don't."

"I hope it's nothing stupid, Grace? I wouldn't want anything to happen to Effy's favourite sister. You're a bit special to me too."

"No, it's not stupid; it's lovely knowing I'm special to you too. I've grown up since we first met. Or are you so obsessed with Effy you haven't noticed how I've changed lately? I'm not the same silly little girl who introduced you to my sister anymore."

There was no arguing with that. Grace had blossomed into an attractive teenage girl on the verge of womanhood. With reluctance Mack had given her his promise to say nothing about whatever she was planning.

CHAPTER 55

My Guy – Mary Wells & My Girl – The Temptations
(Stateside SS228–1964) – (Stateside SS378–1964)

Saturday 12 November

"It's a fantastic offer, Angie. Mack and I truly appreciate it," replied Effy. "But now I'm living at Mack's we need to play it safe until I'm seventeen in a few weeks."

"We'd love to come with you to see Ben E. King at the Twisted Wheel," added Mack. "But now Effy's moved in with us we'll have to get my mum used to the idea of us going to all-nighters. It's not like it was when Effy stopped at Caitlin's." Mack and Effy's shared disappointment at having to miss such an opportunity was obvious. They had both wanted to go to the Twisted Wheel for some time. Now they'd been offered a lift in Angie's car and they had to turn it down.

"I know it won't be the same as Eff and Mack coming but TC and I appreciate you taking us instead," said Ellen.

"It would have been a bit of a squeeze, all six of us in the Herald. At least you'll have Linda to hold your hand while you powder your noses together." Tom's lewd implication was clear to everyone.

"Oi, watch it, TC! Or you won't be going. I'll take El with me and you can stop here on your own." It was obvious Angie was also disappointed that Mack and Effy could not come.

"Okay, you two. When you can go I'll see if I can borrow my uncle's Bedford van so all of us can go over. How's that?"

"Sounds good to me," Mack responded. "It's such a shame we can't go over tonight."

"Anyway, his dad is giving Mack driving lessons. You never know, we may get lucky. He might let him borrow his car when he passes his test," Effy added, clinging to Mack's arm.

"Or I could beat him to it and pass first. Then I'll buy a motor too and you can all come with me and El."

"You only managed to pass your two-wheeler test last month and you plan to do your driving test sometime soon? How many attempts did it take? Three, or was it four?" teased Angie. "I had more lifts with you taking

262

L plates off than I care to remember."

"I'll have you know," Tom responded, "I passed last August before I'd even met El."

"For the fourth time."

"But I passed."

"It's a wonder they let you pass. If I were you, El, I would be saying your prayers every time you ride pillion with him!" retorted Angie. "If he passes his test for a car in the next ten years it will be a miracle. I've seen sheep with better road sense."

"At least I won't be distracting the guy doing the testing like you did," he came back, as quick as a flash. "Ah! You didn't think I knew, did you? I heard Linda telling the tale."

Angie blushed bright red.

"You know what she did, eh? Wore a skirt so short the guy could see her knickers when she sat down."

"He shouldn't have been looking!"

"Low-cut top, too, with a bit of a plunge! Semi see-through, wasn't it, with a matching half-cup bra and a touch of the peek-a-boo to egg him on? Linda gave me the full SP. I bet there was steam coming out of his ears seeing you in an outfit like that!"

"Well, at least he passed me first time!"

"I bet his glasses misted up so he couldn't see what you were doing driving round."

"He wasn't wearing glasses."

"If I'd been him I'd have failed you and made you do it again! I bet he'd have loved another eyeful of you in that outfit."

"Has anybody ever told you you're a few clowns short of a circus?"

"No, but is it true that cannibals don't eat clowns because they taste funny?"

"If we come across a cannibal he'll have no trouble munching on you, that's for sure."

"Will you two give over," El said, rocking with laughter. Mack and Effy tried to keep straight faces at the ongoing exchange but they had also begun to laugh.

Angie turned to Ellen. "I don't know how I put up with him, El! I'm surprised you do, to be honest."

"It's my natural charm," Tom grinned, putting his arm round Angie. "It's irresistible. You and me, we should become a top double act like

263

Morecambe and Wise or Mike and Bernie Winters. I can see our names up in neon lights. Catford & Thornton, or Thornton & Catford, topping the bill at the London Palladium! I can be the funny one, you can be the straight one!"

"Keep talking, someday you might say something halfway intelligent and funny! Okay, El. Once he gets his paws off you can give him a good slapping for molesting me. Are we going to set off?"

"We'll meet up with you next weekend, Angie," Effy said to her as they made to go to the car. "Look at it this way – it'll give you an opportunity to get to know El a bit better."

"Do you have any time off on Thursday? I could meet up with you for a coffee. I can drive over and meet you in the afternoon."

"Ring me Monday at Mack's and I'll see if we can meet up."

"Okay. Will do."

With that they left, leaving Mack and Effy alone. "I wish we could have gone with them. Did I hear you say you were going to meet up with Angie in the week?"

"You don't mind, do you? I like Angie as a friend. We don't get to spend much time together and do girl things like window shop. It's lovely to have a girl friend that's not a sister. Don't get me wrong – as much as I love my sisters, it's great to know someone who's not family."

"No, of course I don't mind."

"Okay, let's go see this Frog band." Effy took his hand, ready to make a move.

"They're called Wynder K. Frog, not the Frog Band. I wish we could be alone again tonight like before."

"So do I." She turned to him, her eyes bright and shining. "But it wouldn't exactly be the best night."

"Why not?"

She whispered in his ear. "Wrong time of the month. We're going to have to find somewhere soon to be alone. I want to have you so bad I can't stand it at nights knowing you're only next door. It's so cruel."

"You're so right. My parents might not notice if I slipped sleeping pills in their supper-time cup of tea. What do you think?"

"Speaking of which, there's a parents' evening coming up. Legally, as I'm no longer at home but in *loco parentis* with your mum and Dad, should they be the ones to go?"

"Are you being serious?" He stared at Effy incredulously, noticing her grinning as they walked towards the club.

264

"Well, they are responsible for me. According to your mum and dad, when they agreed to have me live in their home, I would be in *loco parentis*, under their care. It's something to do with English law now they're looking after me. Bridget told them and she should know, according to her friend in the flat above."

"That should be fun!" Mack exclaimed with glee. "Promise you'll let me be there when you show them the letter to make an appointment. I can't wait to see their faces! If I've got to treat you like a sister, then they have to treat you like a daughter. Should be good for a laugh!"

"Hey, you! They already treat me like a daughter!"

"They're going to wonder what's going on when Bridget turns up for Ellen." Mack was finding the whole thing amusing. "I should go with them in my capacity as your older brother."

"You would, too, but your mum and dad won't let you."

The band was better than Mack and Effy anticipated. They were an instrumental band with not much by way of vocals. Most of what they played were cover versions like *Mercy, Incense* and *Don't Fight It (Feel It)*. Their version of *Sunshine Superman* sounded brilliant. Highlights came with their cover of the Spencer Davis hit *Somebody Help Me*. An amazing version of Frankie Vaughan's *Green Door* received tremendous applause. Those were the standouts of an electrifying night.

Mack got the DJ to play The Temptations' *My Girl* back-to-back with Mary Wells' *My Guy*. As a recognised face, on the rare instances he asked for a record it got played.

CHAPTER 56

A Lil Lovin' Sometime – Alexander Patton (Capitol CL 15461 – 1966)

Sunday 13 November 1966

Mack played the record he had found in Vallances. It was the only copy he had been able to find. He had tried to order another copy but without success.

"It's brilliant." Effy was genuine in her excitement, having heard the Alexander Patton single. Mack had made her fall in love with soul music. "If they played it at the Plebs it would pack the floor."

"You'd better go and show my mum the parents' evening letter." Mack slid the record into a special protective card sleeve.

"Will you come down with me?" pleaded Effy, looking apprehensive.

"You can be a real scaredy cat at times." Mack grinned. "You're amazing. You have a ballsy apocalyptic nuke-out with your dad, yet you're timid over a small thing like a parents' evening. Right, let's go and see mum."

"Not your dad?"

"Well, him if you like. I don't suppose it will matter."

"We'll give it to your mum." Effy made the decisive choice.

"What's this *'we'* bit, Kemosabe?" Mack teased. "It's your parents' evening letter."

For a brief moment Effy was that young nervous girl he had first met. He reassured her. "It's going to be alright. For heaven's sake, don't worry. I'll be by your side when you hand it over."

The look on her face was priceless.

Jane MacKinnon read the letter and looked straight at Effy. "That won't be a problem, dear. Rob can drive me down and I'll go and see your teachers. So, in two weeks' time – Tuesday evening it is. Will you make appointment times as early as possible after six o'clock, Effy? You might like to come along to show me where to find your teachers."

"Can I go too? Seeing as I'm Effy's unofficial 'brother'?" It was a bit of a cheek and he knew it. Even as he spoke a wide grin formed on his face.

"Trying to be clever again, James! Stop it!" His mother gave him one of those half serious, half joking looks. "Besides 'brothers' don't kiss their 'sisters' like I saw you doing earlier."

Effy went scarlet, her eyes studying the kitchen lino.

"I don't mind you exchanging kisses and embraces," said Jane MacKinnon with a smile. "It would be unnatural for you not to but do try to keep it in bounds. You may find it hard to believe but I was as young as you, Effy, so I know what it can be like. As for Rob – well, like most Navy men, he was a bit of an octopus trying to get his tentacles round me."

"Mum, that's disgusting." Mack pretended to be horrified. "That image of you and Dad is going to scar me for the rest of my life!"

"You should remember this, James. When you look at your father and me as we are now, the same fate awaits you both. We oldies serve as a constant reminder of your future selves. You won't always be young, handsome and beautiful. Time will take its toll on you both."

"Thanks for the cheerful thought, Mum."

"You look amazing for your age, Jane," was Effy's counter to Mack's comment. "I do hope I look as good as you when I'm the same age."

"Thank you, dear! It's a shame my son can't say the same. I'm fortunate his father doesn't appear to see the flaws caused by the passing years! And if he does at least he's kind, pretending not to see them."

"So what's your tip for staying young and beautiful, Mum?"

"Don't smoke and don't drink. It's that simple. Smoking is such a disgusting habit. I made your father stop when I first met him. Do you know he was smoking a whole packet of Capstan full strength every day. It was like kissing an ashtray. I told him if he didn't stop I wouldn't let him kiss me. I also made him shave off his beard by using the same threat. It was like I was kissing a broom. He insisted on trying to look like the sailor on a Player's cigarette packet. He looked twice as handsome once he'd shaved."

"It worked too." His father entered, having overheard part of the conversation. "Smoking was and is a rather nasty habit. You two youngsters shouldn't start. It's addictive and the smell clings to your clothes – ruins your sense of smell and taste. As for the beard... it was great for straining soup and beer."

"You know it was unhygienic. And it smelled like a secondary ashtray as well as scratching my face," Jane MacKinnon muttered tartly.

"Take it for granted, Dad. Neither of us will smoke, will we, Effy?"

"No chance." Effy shuddered. "No one in our family ever has either. Even when you don't smoke, if you go where others do, your clothes end up smelling something awful."

"Most of us don't smoke. Tom doesn't, Angie doesn't, and Linda and Steve don't. Come to think of it, most of Acky's crowd doesn't smoke. Only Carol and Linda smoke out of the girls. As for the beard, I don't think so. They look gross. I prefer the clean-cut look. I intend to always look smart and sharp, not like some beatnik."

"Oh, that's a shame!" Effy began. But Mack cut her off before she could say any more.

"No chance. Not now, not ever. Don't bother fluttering your eyelids either, trying to persuade me to grow one. It's never happening."

"We've got a parents' evening next week," Jane said to her husband, changing the topic while suppressing laughter at her son's outburst. "You'll have to drive me down to St. Joseph's."

"What, the girls' grammar school? Why?"

"It's Effy's parents' evening. We'll have to see her teachers and get a report on her progress."

"Oh, I suppose we will now you mention it. *Loco parentis* and all that. We can't expect Róisín to be going under the circumstances. I'll have to ring Bridget at work and let her know. The teachers will find it strange seeing you instead of her mother."

"We have to drop in on Adam and Caitlin this evening. I thought I'd take them this meat pie I cooked this afternoon. With Caitlin unwell I don't suppose she's been able to do much, lying in bed. She won't have felt like cooking. As for Adam's cooking skills, they're worse than yours, Rob."

"Oh, don't I get a dishonourable mention in dispatches?" asked Mack.

"At least you'll have a go which is more than Adam or your father will. Without womenfolk they'd starve to death in days. With you it might take a fortnight."

"Cheers, Mum! I feel a whole lot better for your vote of confidence in my cooking. Your comedy skills are definitely coming along!"

"I wasn't being funny. I was only telling you the truth." Jane turned to her husband. "We should go now if you don't mind. We'll only be gone about thirty or forty minutes. Effy, you can babysit Mack and make sure he doesn't burn the house down while we're gone."

"Mum, are you taking night classes in stand-up comedy? 'Cos if you are you could do with a better scriptwriter for your gags."

"I'll bear that in mind," Jane MacKinnon replied as she put her coat on. "Next time I meet Bob Monkhouse."

Effy stood by the lounge window watching the MacKinnons drive off. As soon as the Zephyr had disappeared, she shot past Mack, grabbing him by the hand. "Come on then! We don't have much time, handsome. Your room now! Don't bother getting undressed. I'll be two minutes."

"I thought you were on your period?"

"I was. Yesterday. It's stopped. It's our lucky break. Or should I say, you're in luck and I'm good for a... you know what."

It was longer than two minutes – closer to five. Coming into his room from the bathroom Effy handed him a Durex and put her briefs on his bedside cabinet.

"Like they say in the movies: light, camera, action." Effy climbed onto his bedcovers, hitching her skirt up to her waist. "What's the matter? Aren't you in the mood?"

"I'm always in the mood – only surprised at how keen you are."

Jumping off the bed, she tugged at his Levi cords. They came off with his underpants in one swift motion before he'd even undone the zip on his fly. "Hurry up, slow coach. We need to be quick so don't dawdle."

Five minutes later, her breathing returning to normal, she turned to Mack. "God, did I need that!"

"We both did. Was it okay?"

Effy gave him a long kiss, removing the condom from his now flaccid penis. "It's safe to say my itch has been well and truly scratched and satisfied. You'd better let me dispose of this. Knowing you, you'd leave the evidence under your bed for your mum to find. You have to be a little more discrete like I am."

"Satisfy my curiosity, will you? How do you dispose of them?"

"Your mum kindly supplies me with special disposable sanitary towel bags. I seal them in those."

An hour later his parents returned home.

Mack was reading about the Concordat of Worms.

"Busy, I see," observed his father. "Is it interesting, what you're reading?"

"Yes." Mack turned a page. "I quite like History. Much more interesting than Economics."

"What's Effy doing?" asked his Mum, noting her absence.

"What she usually does on Sunday evenings. Taking a bath."

"She doesn't usually have a bath this early in the evening." Jane MacKinnon looked puzzled.

"She's tired after last night. Says she wants an early night to catch up on her beauty sleep."

"At least she's sensible. You could do with going to bed earlier too, young man. You're as bad as your father, stopping up to watch the dot disappear on the television screen. It wouldn't hurt you to get to bed earlier."

"I've given her my dressing gown to use. I know it's a bit big for her but she didn't remember to pack hers when she jumped ship. You don't mind, do you? I never wear it anyway."

"You'll have to get the girl one, Jane," said his Father. "Can't have the lass walking around in her nightie."

Mack wondered what difference it would make, since he'd seen her in the altogether. It was enough imagining her in a baby doll nightie to make him start hardening. It was a shame she didn't have one.

"I wonder if she's washing her hair, too?" his Mother thought aloud. "She might want to use my hairdryer."

CHAPTER 57

Emergency 999 – Alan Bown Set (PYE Records 7N 17192 – 1966)

Monday 14 November 1966

Effy could not understand why Grace's form teacher wanted to see her. All was soon clear. There had been a telephone call from her irate father who wanted to know if Grace was in school. Did Effy know where her sister was? Her reply astonished the teacher. Effy informed her she did not know since she was no longer living at home. Of course, one question had to lead to the inexorable next. If Effy was not living at home, where was she living? Her first instinct was to tell the teacher to mind her own business. Possessed by a devilish impulse, Effy decided to push the bounds of respectability. Her calculated response was aimed for maximum shock value.

"Why?" Effy replied with a wide-eyed innocence, sounding as if chocolate could not melt in her mouth. "Don't you know? I'm living at my boyfriend's house at present."

The teacher's reaction was interesting. So it was true. Mack was right. People became open-mouthed when they heard something they could not quite believe.

"I see." The teacher was struggling, wondering what to say next as she smoothed the sides of her skirt with both hands. "Do your parents know where you are?"

"No." This was going to be enjoyable. Effy maintained the sweetest and most innocent demeanour she could muster. "My father doesn't care a jot about my sister or myself. He was so self-righteous and Victorian when he threw us out. He told us never to darken his doorstep again. Said I was a Babylonian harlot and an atheist."

The teacher looked aghast while Effy kept a straight face. "Are you telling me the truth? You're not making this up?"

"Why would I lie about such a thing, Miss?"

"You say you are living in your boyfriend's house?"

"Yes, Miss. That is what I said."

"And how old is your boyfriend?"

It was irresistible. Effy was having too much fun toying with Grace's form teacher. Now there would be gossip in the staffroom.

"Why? What has his age got to do with my sister? Anyway, she's not at his house if that's what you want to know. She may have gone to my older sister's in Shipley. You can ask my sister Ellen to see if Grace has gone there. Ellen is in the Upper Sixth. You do remember her, don't you? Ellen Halloran? She used to be in your registration group when she was in the Fourth Form." Then, pretending to have an afterthought, Effy added, "She may be at my married sister's in Girlington."

During the whole conversation it never occurred to Effy that Grace was missing. There was nowhere else for Grace to go other than Caitlin's or Bridget's.

"So, you have no idea where Grace could be?"

"None at all, Miss. Can I go back to my lesson now?" Effy asked, laying on the sweet innocence with the aplomb of an actress.

"Yes, of course you can, Fiona."

"Thank you, Miss." By the time she reached her class she was in stitches about having taken the rise out of Grace's form teacher.

Ellen met Effy during the lunch break. "Having you been taking the piss out of Grace's form teacher, Eff?"

"What do you mean?" Effy pretended to be puzzled but she expected what came next.

"Don't come it with me, sis. She was asking me all sorts of questions and not only about Grace having gone missing."

"Grace won't be missing. She'll have gone to Caitlin's if she hasn't gone to stop with you and Bridget."

"I hope you're right about Grace." Ellen paused. "Her form teacher asked me if it was true we'd got kicked out by our Da."

"What did you tell her?"

"I said it was more a case of leaving before he actually threw us out. Then she asked me if he'd called you a baby harlot."

"A Babylonian harlot, not a baby harlot."

"Yeah, that was it, a Babylonian harlot. I said yes. And then she asked me how old your boyfriend was and if you were living with him."

"What did you tell her? Please say you didn't tell her I was living with him and his parents."

"God, no! I said nothing. Told her it was none of her concern." Then the proverbial penny dropped. "Oh, my God! Eff! You've never let the biddy think you'd shacked up with him? You never? Seriously?"

"I said I was living with him in his house, which is true. I am. She never asked me about it being his parents' house. I let her draw the wrong conclusions on her own."

Ellen gasped and then hooted with laughter. "This goody-two-shoes girl's gone bad. It's all Mack's fault. I blame him. He's making you as bad as he is with these word games he plays. Tom warned me about his verbal game playing. Tom reckons Mack should become a politician. He'd be good at evading the truth behind half-truths."

Immediately following afternoon registration, Effy found herself grilled by her own form tutor. That proved less entertaining.

According to their father she and her sister were runaways. At this point Effy blew an already too overloaded fuse. The form tutor was quite shaken by the angry ferocity of her responses. This was not the Fiona Halloran the teacher thought she knew. Effy reasoned if her father stooped to lies she would retaliate with her own skewed version of the truth. They were the ones thrown out on the street. Her father, she explained, had assaulted Grace as they left. Ellen and she had witnessed this. That might warrant an investigation by social workers, and even the police?

As for herself, she had never experienced feeling so angry. Her father thought she was old enough never to darken his doorstep. If that was so, then she was old enough to decide where she could live and with whom. At this point she clarified, in an icy yet angry manner, how she came to be living with the MacKinnons. Her older sisters had decided she should live with her sister Caitlin's in-laws. All the school needed to know she was in *loco parentis* with the MacKinnons. If the college had any problems with that they could consult her sisters as well as the MacKinnons. Her form tutor had to offer a mumbled apology for any misunderstandings.

It was only when she returned home that Effy learned Grace had indeed run away. Grace, it turned out, was neither at Caitlin's nor at Bridget's. Grace was definitely missing. Effy was beside herself.

So this was what Grace had planned. Mack wracked his brains. Where could she have gone? If she was not with one of her sisters then was she at one of her friends' places? It was possible but unlikely. He doubted she would be with Jean. There was only one possibility. It seemed unlikely but the more he thought it through, the more likely it seemed. One thing was going to be unavoidable. He had to keep his now impossible promise to Grace. Telling the sisters not to worry. But telling them not to worry was never going to work. By implication he would get the blame for what Grace had done. How was he going to convince them he knew nothing of her plan? Worse, how would he explain this to Effy when she was already verging on hysterical panic? Revealing what he knew would make Effy blame him for concealing the truth. There was nothing for it. He would have to be as straight as he could with her. Better to bite the bullet and absorb the fallout if it stopped the hysteria and tears. Effy was blaming herself for having deserted her sister, for not having done more. As soon as he said anything he knew he would get the blame and be in the wrong. He cursed Grace, hoping he was right in guessing where she had gone.

"Sit down. Calm down," he began. "I've got something to tell you."

"What? What can you possibly say at a time like this when she's missing? God knows what's happened to her."

"Grace asked me to tell you she would be okay if this happened. You and your sisters are not to worry."

"What?"

It did not go well. Mack tried to explain what Grace had said to him. No matter how much he stressed he did not know what Grace had planned, it did not seem to make any difference. Effy had never been angry with him. But now her anger was all too real. Hurtful words flowed in a torrent from her lips. She even hit him in the chest. For her size she packed a hit that almost sent him sprawling. She accused him of being evasive, of lying, of covering up, of not trusting her. Jane came in when she heard the verbal onslaught. She struggled to comprehend Effy's bitter outpourings. At the sight of Jane MacKinnon Effy subsided into sobs.

"Come here, Effy. Come to me, dear. And you, James MacKinnon," said his mother, sounding accusing and somewhat harsh, "had better tell me everything from the beginning."

Jane MacKinnon put a comforting motherly arm round Effy making her sit down on the settee;.

"Right." Mack, aggrieved, hurt and upset by Effy's hurtful words began. "Here's the truth, the whole truth and nothing but the truth. Nothing's hidden. It's as straight as it comes."

His account of what had transpired between him and Grace was clarity itself. No, he did not know what Grace had planned. Yes, he had suspected but never believed she would do a runner. No, he should not have promised her anything. He should have known better but that was with hindsight. About Grace's whereabouts he had no idea. He had his suspicions and reckoned he knew where she might be. More than anything he wanted

274

Effy to forgive him for not telling her what had passed between Grace and himself.

"Go and fetch a hanky for Effy from the top drawer of my dressing table," his mother commanded. "Then when Effy's wiped her tears you can tell us where you think Grace may have gone."

On his return with the hanky he waited while Effy wiped away the tears. Effy appeared to have calmed down but he was still in the doghouse. It was as well there was no kennel in the backyard or he would be in it for sure. He was certain there had been some exchange between his mum and Effy while he was upstairs. He wished he knew what.

"Now, James. Where do you suspect Grace is? The sooner we know, the sooner we can do something about it."

"There's only one place where she can be hiding out. Grace must be dossing down in Manchester in Deidre's room in the hall of residence. Let's face it, it's the most likely and logical place. There's nowhere else for her to run and hide."

"I sppose she could be there." Effy replied in a flat emotionless voice.

"If you have Deidre's address I can ride over to see if she's there – if necessary, get her and bring her back," Mack offered.

"That won't be necessary. We will see if the operator can get us a telephone number and try to contact Deidre first. Until we are sure she's there it would be pointless going over. Besides, it will be much quicker in the car, not to mention warmer and drier. Effy, do you know the address?"

She nodded.

"James, get the pad and pencil by the telephone and bring it here."

Mack did as asked, aware that more words were being exchanged out of his hearing. On returning he watched Effy write the details down, while ignoring him completely.

When his mum left the room Mack tried to sit next to her. Effy moved away and sat in the armchair, making it clear she didn't want him near her.

"Effy, please," he begged. "I'm so sorry. I really am. Don't hate me for what's happened. I never meant to hurt you. Can't you forgive me?"

Effy remained silent and stubborn, refusing even to glance at him.

"I'm the one who loves you. Please don't treat me this way. Look me in the eyes and you'll know how sorry I am. If I'd known how much hurt this would cause, I would never have promised Grace to keep quiet."

It was hopeless. "Okay. Be like that. There's nothing more than I can say. If this is all it takes for us to fall apart there can't be much of a future for us."

He left the room, hoping Effy would say something, but she remained silent. Closing the door behind him he saw his mother standing in the hallway holding the telephone to her ear. Motioning him to come to her, she said, "I've got a number for the hall of residence. We're fortunate that Effy remembered the name of the hall and the address. I've asked one of the students to see if they can locate Deidre."

"Jolly good, Mum. I'm going upstairs. Effy won't even speak to me. She's never going to forgive me for what's happened. After all we've gone through together and it ends like this."

"Don't be silly, James. She's upset. Especially after all the things she said to you earlier. She doesn't know what to say to you yet. Leave her be. She'll come round, mark my word. You've still got an awful lot to learn about how women behave."

His mother's words left him unimpressed. Never in all the time he had known Effy had she behaved like this. Disconsolate, he turned and climbed the stairs. He heard his mother say, "Deidre Halloran? It's Jane MacKinnon. I'm glad I managed to get hold of you. Now, no shenanigans please, no beating about the bush. Is Grace with you? Her mother and sister are beside themselves. I've had your mother here most of the afternoon. She is? James guessed right..."

Mack went upstairs. He had been right. At least they had found her. Then it struck him. Had his mother said Mrs Halloran had been here the whole afternoon? Well, it didn't matter anymore. After this fiasco, no doubt Effy would be moving out. Their relationship would be over. He wanted to cry, hurt at the thought of their break-up. Staying upstairs the rest of the evening he tried to work but he was so miserable that he got into bed and went to sleep.

CHAPTER 58

In The Midnight Hour – Wilson Pickett (Atlantic AT4036 – 1965)

Tuesday 15 November 1966

It must have been midnight or later when Mack found his bedcovers pulled back. Was he dreaming or was this Effy climbing into his bed? He reached for the bedside lamp and switched it on. It was Grace, yet not Grace as he knew her. This was a seductive Grace, naked and passionate, straddling him. In an instant he was awake, sitting up in bed in the dark, shocked to the core by what had proved to be a dream.

As he fell back onto the bed in his semi-waking state, the future appeared bleak. Even his mind was torturing him as he tried to sleep. The night seemed endless as he tried to succumb to sleep, still obsessing about Effy. Nothing worked as he tried to clear her from his mind. A gradual drowsiness overtook him once more. Now, as he drifted in a half waking half sleeping nowhere land, he imagined his bedroom door creaking. Rolling over, he buried his head in the pillow.

Someone was slipping in beside him; he felt the coverlet being pulled back. Was he dreaming again? If he was it was too real. Breasts pressed against his back, warm breath caressing his neck. A small hand came from behind to rest on his chest. Whispered words flowed in his ears.

"Ssssh, it's only me. I'm sorry, so sorry. I can't believe I could have said all those horrid things to you. I love you more than anything. I couldn't bear it if you didn't love me anymore. Please forgive me. I wasn't thinking straight, worrying about Grace."

Turning to face her he knew he was not dreaming. The distinct scent of her hair and softness of her body seemed real enough.

"I thought I was going to lose you," he whispered. "It was the worst feeling ever."

Her lips met his in a brief kiss; her soft hands wrapped around him in a tender embrace. "Hold me for a little while. I'll have to slip back to my room. I couldn't wait until the morning to speak to you. I love you so much I can't believe how awful I was. You are my everything."

Mack could not remember how long they lay together. The next thing he knew the alarm clock was ringing. He was alone in his bed, wondering if it had been another dream. Had she come into his bed last night?

Effy and his mum were in the kitchen having breakfast when he came down.

"You two are going to be late if you don't get a move on," said his mum. "I've got some porridge on the go. You'll need something warm inside you today. There's a sharp frost outside."

Effy gave him a huge smile. So it was not his imagination.

"What's happening about Grace?" he asked.

"Your father's going to collect her from Manchester this evening. He's going to bring her back here. I will have to go with him under the circumstances. Effy will tell you more. I dare say as you missed her mum's visit last night you'll want to know more. Mrs Halloran is planning to leave her husband. Until she does she's asked for Grace to stay with us."

"What about Effy? How does this change things for her?"

Jane MacKinnon looked at Effy and then at Mack before answering. "Nothing changes for Effy. She can stay with us for as long as she wishes. This is her home for as long as she wants it to be. Even her mother agrees it would be best under the circumstances."

It was the part about *even her mother agrees* that left Mack thinking. As he was to learn, Effy's arrival in their home was never unplanned. Nor had it been unknown to Mrs Halloran. The truth behind all of it was turning out like an onion unpeeled layer by layer by layer to reveal yet another truth. If truth corresponded to reality someone had acted to prevent them knowing it. Were there other events of which he and Effy knew nothing? There was a link between his mother and Effy's mother that he had never suspected. It was central to this ever more revealing version of the truth. It had to be the maternal Mafia of the Mothers' Union. Did Effy know about this? Or had she, like him, also been in a state of ignorance?

Once outside the house, as they donned helmets Mack had to ask the question. Did Effy know anything about their mothers' involvement? Effy shook her head, puzzled. She was as clueless as he was. Both agreed they needed to know what was going on between their respective mothers. Effy had to admit it was strange. If the mothers were in on it, then Bridget and Caitlin had to be as well. By implication it might also include his father too. Effy's reaction to the news her mother was planning on leaving her father surprised him. It was as though it was not unexpected. As he kick-started the

Lambretta into life Effy pulled her scarf down from her mouth. "It's no surprise. It was inevitable. You don't wreck an entire family and expect the mother to stay. Love and loyalty can only take so much."

Traffic on the ring road was heavy. Mack took a few backstreet routes to get near to Lister Park. Crossing the main road to get down to St. Joseph's was always tricky. By now the gossipers had accepted Effy's arrival at the college on the back of the Lambretta. Removing the helmet and parka she was in the required Sixth Form uniform before entering. Leaning into him for a kiss she said in that sweet sexy voice, "I need to make it up to you for being so awful. If your mum goes with your dad to get Grace we'll have the house to ourselves while they're gone. You do know what I'm saying?"

"Oh, I don't know, Eff... I've got a pile of homework to do tonight." He was joking and expected her expression to be one of amazement.

"Really? You expect me to believe that?" Effy's beguiling smile showed she was aware he was joking. "I give you ten minutes after they leave before you relieve me of my underwear. And with that thought preying on your mind for the rest of today I'll leave you for now."

On his way up the hill to Manningham Lane he passed Ellen walking down the hill at a fast pace. He waved to her as he roared past, the scooter's silencer emitting metallic rasping notes. A trail of blue two-stroke exhaust smoke billowed into the cold morning air.

Effy was right. Imagining relieving her of her underwear interfered with his concentration all day. In every lesson, including his free study period, his mind was on her body. Instead of the economic means of production it was the thought of caressing her breasts. In the Math session he could only think of pulling her briefs down. The plaguing thoughts made him go stiff a few too many times and not without embarrassment. *Before you relieve me of my underwear.* Effy knew what to say and how to say it to work him up.

Ellen caught up with Effy at lunchtime, unaware of the latest about Grace. The news perked her up but also made her angry; she said she would give Grace a serious piece of her mind. Ellen was not inclined to blame Mack for Grace's runaway escapade. In her opinion it was all Grace's fault. Like her sister Ellen found herself intrigued by the collusion of the mothers. No doubt in due course all the secrets would come to light. The news of their mother finally leaving their father was no great surprise. Ellen snorted. "About time. But I won't hold my breath. I'll believe it when I see it."

279

CHAPTER 59

Rescue Me – Fontella Bass (Chess International AR 45.188 – 1965)

Tuesday 15 November 1966 – Later

Minutes after his parents set off for Manchester Mack had relieved Effy of her underwear. Sex was passionate, frantic, intense and explosive. He had ensured she climaxed. In the afterglow of the act, as they lay side by side, Effy recounted what Angie had told to her.

"You won't believe what Angie's great-grandmother once said to her. The best way to keep a man happy is to keep his belly full and his balls empty. They celebrated sixty-two years of married life. What do you think of that?"

"Think of what – the advice or sixty-two years of married life?"

Effy chuckled as she snuggled up to him. "The advice, for heaven's sake."

"Pardon me for sounding shocked. Her great-grandma said that? How old was Angie when she heard that gem of wisdom?"

"She was twelve."

"Twelve! What made her tell you that?" Mack was curious.

"Curiosity killed the cat." Effy pinched his nose. "I imagine knowing I was going the whole way with you. Anyway, seems like sound advice to me."

"I won't argue with you about her advice. I can't believe you talked about sex and intimate private stuff in that way with Angie."

"Why not? Why shouldn't we talk? Just because we're women, why shouldn't we be open and frank about sex with each other? You men talk about it all the time. Why should we be any different? At least we don't make it sound smutty and disgusting."

"I've not mentioned anything about us doing it to anybody. It's too personal." Mack imagined Effy describing what they did to one another to Angie.

"Neither have I," Effy reassured him. "What we do to each other and how is private and our affair. It's not like we talk about those intimate details, for heaven's sake. How could you think I'd do such a thing?"

"Sorry. You had me beginning to wonder."

They heard the front doorbell ring. Leaping off the bed they made frantic grabs at items of their scattered clothing.

"I'll go and see who it is. You'd better go and get dressed while I go down." Mack pulled his trousers on and reached for his jumper.

Effy had scooped up her clothes and was heading for the door. Pausing, she said, "Give me that used Durex. Quick. I'll get rid of it like I did with all the others. Good grief! I see I'll have to empty your balls more often!"

"Now's not the time for joking, Eff. Quick and don't stand in front of the window stark naked whatever you do."

"Who said I was joking?" were her parting words as she giggled, dangling the full Durex in the air before disappearing. Mack headed downstairs. Silly thoughts ran through his mind. There had been no chance to wash his hands. His and Effy's body fluids were all over them. Then he realised. Although he had managed to get his trousers and a pullover on he had forgotten his underpants and socks.

When he opened the door the sight of Effy's mother made him freeze. Blind panic was not quite what he experienced but it was close. His mind blanked. This was a *jaw dropping heart-stopping* moment needing coolness and a calm response. Somehow it did not seem right. Having had sex with her daughter he was now confronted with her mother minutes later. Mack could not help feeling bad.

"You must be James," she said in a soft voice. "Effy's young man."

"Er, yes, that would be me."

"May I come in? Jane asked me over to wait for their return with Grace from Manchester." Her lilting Irish accent, he learned later, was typical of South Dublin. Right now it hinted at tearful sadness.

"Of course, Mrs Halloran. I'm sorry. You caught me by surprise." With pants down and Effy naked in bed. "Please, do come in."

Mack ushered her in. Having taken her coat he invited her to come into the living room where the fire was burning.

"Can I offer you a tea or coffee?"

"Tea would be lovely." She smiled, a hint of sadness and tiredness in her eyes. "Where's Effy? I would like to see my daughter if I could."

"She's in her room doing her homework." Mack found himself telling a white lie that made him feel uncomfortable. "I'll go and get her when I've switched the kettle on."

281

Once in the kitchen he washed his hands and then filled the kettle. Tasks completed, he dashed up the stairs and entered Effy's room. "It's your mum. She's downstairs and wants to see you."

"Is she now?" Her voice sounded frosty.

"Effy, please. She is your mother and honest, she doesn't look good. She looks terrible. My mum's invited her here to wait for Grace's return. I know you'll treat her right. I'm making her a pot of tea – do you want some too?"

Effy nodded.

Mack prepared a tray, hoping as he did so that Effy and her mother would not start arguing in some horrendous fashion. The last thing he wanted was to act as a referee. On returning to the living room he saw Effy with her arms round her quiet tearful mother. Placing the tray on the coffee table, he asked, "Would you prefer if I left you alone for a little while?"

"No, please stay," Effy answered in a subdued voice.

"Yes, please stay," Mrs Halloran implored.

Mack watched as Effy dabbed the tears from her mother's eyes with a hanky. The sight of daughter and mother touched him. Having poured the tea he sat down in his father's armchair. Studying Mrs Halloran, he noticed for the first time she could not be much older than his own mother. There was a familiar weary sadness about her face. Now that he knew why, the truth was so plain to see. She looked older only because she was not as well-dressed as his mother or his aunt. There was no sign of make-up and her hair was not styled, only tied back and greying. Her dress, whilst clean, was shabby. The other unavoidable thing was how she was so skinny rather than slim. For the first time Mack also noticed where her daughters' good looks came from. Mrs Halloran must once have been a beautiful young woman. It was then that the economic reality of life in the Halloran household hit home. Seven daughters, one income, meant financial struggles for the breadwinner. These struggles must finally have reached breaking point for the parents.

Only now did it make sense. Effy's school and day clothing were in stark contrast to the skirts and dresses she had made. Most were well-worn and, on reflection, hand-me-downs. Other items she had bought with hard-earned money from the Saturday job and summer holiday work. Realising he was so much more fortunate in comparison was upsetting.

Could this explain her father's behaviour? Was it seeking refuge in his religion that had taken him a step too far down a troubled version of his beliefs? So did it all hinge on the struggle to cope with the economics of a large family and shaky business? He knew so little about the Hallorans. Effy was reluctant to speak about her parents, most definitely when it came to her father. All Mack knew was what he had once heard his father say about Mr Halloran's work: that he owned some kind of small-scale printing business, much of it devoted to printing material for churches and other religious organisations.

Effy's mother broke the silence. "I always liked coming here to visit your mother. She keeps such a beautiful home."

"You've been here before?" Mack posed the question but his thoughts were racing ahead making sense of it all.

"Oh, yes," she answered. "Many times when you've been at school, and my daughters, too. Jane, your mother, has been such a good friend to me over the years. We're of an age, your mother and I. We made our friendship through the Mothers' Union. I've watched you and your brother grow up as Jane's watched my children do the same. My husband began to change some years ago. Your mother and I decided we had to keep our friendship to ourselves. I don't know how I could have carried on without her support. It's been hard having to keep this friendship secret, and never more so once little Jane was born. I've had to visit Caitlin in secret. Bridget and Jane have ensured I had the opportunities but we could not breathe a word of it lest Sean found out."

Certain things began to make sense. Glancing at Effy, he could see this was news to her as well as to him. The revelations began to flow like waves on an incoming tide. Bridget had been the linchpin of the family in recent years, doing her best to hold everyone together. When she'd left, it was out of despair. Bridget was unable to deal with life in the household any longer. She was having her own personal problems. Mrs Halloran did not elaborate further but it made sense. Mack thought of Bridget and Greg straightaway. Caitlin and Adam? Well, it made more sense but what followed next was by far and away more revealing. His illusions about the secrecy of their relationship fell apart as they listened.

"My daughter fell in love with you when you first came to live in Bradford. I remember overhearing her saying to Grace how much she liked you. How much she hoped you two would get to meet each other one day. I can't imagine you ever noticed how she used to look at you. Of course, your mother and I used to joke about it because you were both so young and innocent. Then, you two somehow managed to come together in spite of

283

everything. We didn't know how it happened but yet it did. It's only through Bridget that we've finally learned some of the story."

The more he and Effy listened, the more it made sense. Sean Halloran had found it difficult to cope as his daughters reached their late teens. Life had become strained within the home for the girls. Caitlin's pregnancy, Ellen's misbehaviour and Effy's rebellion had finally broken him. So had begun the collapse of family life. Her husband had found it a struggle not only dealing with his daughters but also with his business. This had plunged him deeper into an obsessive religious zeal, as Mack had suspected.

When Ellen and Effy had walked out their father had succumbed to a depressive tyranny. As the mother, she was held to blame for her mutinous daughters. She and Grace had become scapegoats for all his problems. Believing her wedding vows were sacred, she had struggled to keep the marriage afloat. But now the strain had proved to be too great. Coping with an obsessive domineering self-righteous man had left her with no choice. She had to abandon him for her own sanity and her remaining daughter's happiness. Deprived of her other daughters, she was distraught, depressed and desolate. Grace's running away had brought her to the realisation her marriage was a wreck. Now all that she could do was to try and salvage the love of all her daughters.

Thankfully, Jane, as Caitlin's mother-in-law, had stood by their long-time friendship. When Ellen and Effy left home Jane's prompt action had saved the girls from ruining their lives.

Mack was more affected by the unfolding tale of woe than he thought possible. He could see the tears welling up in Effy's eyes as she listened to her mother. It was not only the mother's sadness affecting him but also that of the girl he loved so much.

Effy's tears came from understanding why her mother had stood by her father. Her mother had wanted the marriage to work and to do so she made every effort to stand by her husband. Now Effy understood why her father behaved as he did. It was the consequence of trying but failing to cope with daily life. She had never understood this until now. Even so this did not excuse his behaviour in her eyes. Her parents' lives were in stark contrast with those of the MacKinnons. Effy could not blame Mack's parents for their well-off comfortable lives. She reasoned if the MacKinnons had had seven daughters they would have struggled.

Neither Mack nor Effy realised how time had flown as they'd listened to her mother. They heard the front door open. His parents sounded cheerful as they entered the room with Grace in tow.

Mrs Halloran rose up joyous relief replacing the depressed tiredness on her face. Grace looked uncertain, anticipating the worst. The tears flowed. Mrs Halloran hugged her daughter so hard that she squeezed the breath from her body. It was not quite the reaction Grace was expecting: more the one she received moments later. Effy slapped her sister across the face.

"Ow, what was that for? That hurt!" Grace exclaimed.

"That's for hurting our mother. You frightened her and scared the bejeebers out of the rest of us. Oh, and for having Mack make a ridiculous promise!" With those words uttered, Effy hugged her sister, tears of relief running down her cheeks. "God, I'm so glad you're safe, Grace. I don't know what I would have done if anything had happened to you."

The unexpected slap had taken everyone aback.

"I deserved that, I'm sorry." Grace rubbed her cheek. "But couldn't you have slapped me less hard? Heck, it stings!"

Then, hugging her sister back, she added in a whisper, "Effy, you know I wouldn't hurt you on purpose for anything."

"James, would you and Effy make some more tea for everyone?" Jane MacKinnon directed. "Effy, can you make a sandwich up for Grace, please? I don't think she's had much to eat this last couple of days. There's some cooked ham in the fridge, and some Cheddar."

Mack understood his mother's coded message to leave the adults alone with Grace.

Not a word passed between them in the kitchen. Effy dried her tears and proceeded to make the sandwich. Mack decided to break the silence as he finished pouring boiling water into the teapot.

"All in all," he began, "Grace took it like a man. But the slap was a tad harsh."

"I feel so awful," Effy confessed. "I've never hit anyone in my life. I can't believe I did it. What will your parents think of me? They'll think I'm a terrible person."

"No, they won't," Mack reassured her. "They'll understand it was a spur of the moment reaction. Compared to the number of times they had to break up fights between Adam and myself it's nothing."

"Yes, but isn't that what brothers do?" she countered. "Sisters aren't supposed to do that to each other."

"Well, no lasting damage done. She knows she had something coming. Better you than your dad handing out the pain. If I can understand why you did it, I'm sure my parents will."

"My Da would never lay a hand on any of us. I've done something unforgivable, slapping Grace."

Mack put his arm around her shoulder. "Nobody will blame you for what you did. As for unforgivable, I would say what Grace's did qualified for that. So, who's going to be sleeping on the floor tonight? You or Grace?"

When they returned with the tea they remained listening to the grown-ups. Mack learned that Mrs Halloran's forename was Róisín. Later Effy explained it was an Irish name meaning "little rose".

Grace would stay for a day or two with them at her mother's request. Mack suspected it would be longer under the circumstances. It was clear to him and Effy it was a done deal made by the two mothers beforehand. His father was in on it too. This was clear from his expression. Mack had learned to read his dad's face like a well-thumbed book. Meanwhile, Róisín Halloran was intent on returning home to talk to her husband. The thought of leaving her husband terrified her. What would she do when she left him? All she knew was how to be a housewife and mother. Where could she go? Effy wanted to go with her mother but Róisín Halloran would have none of it. This was between husband and wife, and she preferred to deal with him on her own.

Mack's last words to his mum before going to bed were plain. "Time to come clean about what you and Effy's mum have been up to behind our backs."

"I'll think about it," was all that Jane MacKinnon would commit herself to saying. "Goodnight, James."

CHAPTER 60

This Heart of Mine – Jimmy James & The Vagabonds
(Piccadilly 7N.354331 – 1966)

Saturday 19 November 1966

Having two girls in the household was not without its problems. The first few days proved a struggle for both Mack and his dad. Getting to the bathroom first thing in the morning before the girls proved a challenge, more so for Mack than his father who, after the first two mornings, rose an hour earlier to beat the queues. Mack struggled to get up first thing in the morning. Early starts were not his forte so he ended up last in the queue waiting for either Effy or Grace to come out. What the Halloran household must have been like in the mornings he could not begin to conceive. Effy had once revealed it was morning madness with sometimes two occupying the bathroom at once. Ellen usually ended up being last. Mack didn't find this surprising, considering what he knew of Effy's sister. The only slight up side was that his father drove both girls as far as Manningham Park before heading off to the bank. Now Mack had no need to rush, though he missed the extra time with Effy.

Other than the bathroom issue there were major plusses in his daily life. Chores were down to taking the rubbish out, lighting the coal fire and cleaning the car. Effy and Grace seemed only too pleased to be helping his mum with chores. Effy insisted on doing the household ironing as well as assisting his mum in the kitchen. She and Grace also wanted to help with the dusting and polishing in future. Grace had replaced him on tea and coffee duties, becoming the resident tea girl.

His mother had always run a tight domestic ship but it was even smoother now. This was just as well since, with a baby on the way, it enabled her to rest. Effy had even said to Mack that she hoped she could stay on to help his mother when the baby came.

Jane MacKinnon continued keeping them in the dark about what was happening. It was clear that Róisín Halloran was coming up in the daytime when they were at school. According to Ellen, Effy had learned their mother had come to visit Bridget one evening. What their mother was planning to do remained secret. If she was going to leave her husband the unanswered questions remained. When would she do so and where would she go? With Mack's mum holding her own counsel they were none the wiser. Even Ellen was in the dark. If Bridget and Caitlin knew anything they were saying nothing.

By the weekend it seemed as though Grace had always been staying with them. She fitted into the household and was so much more mature than when Mack had first met her. One thing was beginning to seem clear. Grace would be staying a while longer than a few days. The arrival of a new divan bed meant that the attic room was about to get used.

On Saturday afternoon Mack helped his dad move the girls into the large attic. He was then told that on Sunday he would be moving into what had been their room. His would become the nursery for the baby. By the time Effy was back from her Saturday job Grace had already begun to put a feminine touch to the attic room. Effy could not wait to have a bed to herself again. Sharing the single bed with Grace had been uncomfortable to say the least. Later she confessed to Mack her disappointment not to be next door to him anymore. Grace's arrival now meant even fewer opportunities for sex.

The Alan Bown Set was going to be on at the club so they were keen to get off. Effy didn't want to leave Grace on her own. It was only on Grace's insistence they set off. Grace was planning to help Jane MacKinnon with some sewing. According to Effy, she was quite the genius seamstress. She could make smart outfits even without commercially bought patterns. Grace could draw her own patterns to fit anyone. As skilled as Effy was when it came to making a dress, Grace was her superior.

Meeting up with everyone in the square was a time to put the week behind them. Tom had already whisked Ellen over. They were busy in conversation with a large group including Angie Thornton. The debate was raging about stopping and seeing the Alan Bown Set. The alternative was going to the Twisted Wheel in Manchester to see The Coasters. Some were in favour of chancing it and trying to see both acts.

Angie struggled to make a decision. Torn between staying and spending some time with Effy or going, she was in a quandary. Their planned girls' get-together had gone on hold given the events of the past week. Tom and Ellen were keen to go over to Manchester. Linda, having found herself a new boyfriend, was keen to stay. It was out of the question for Mac and Effy to go to Manchester. As much as Angie liked Tom and Ellen she didn't fancy ending up being a gooseberry. As luck would have it, two girls she knew had planned to go over on the last bus and were only too pleased to go with them.

In the end Angie decided to go, making arrangements to meet Effy as planned.

The club had packed with Mods early on. Anyone trying to get in late had no chance. This was a top band that drew a full crowd. Few realised as they watched that Alan Bown was the trumpet player. Most assumed it was the lead singer, Jess Roden. Still, it made no difference to the music they played, which was slick and soulful. Most of the numbers performed were covers like *Headline News*. *Emergency 999* was the nearest to a chart hit and it went down a storm with the regulars. Even Mack, who could be supercritical, gave it his thumbs up. Best record of the night was Chubby Checker's *At The Discotheque*. Mack had searched and searched for a hard-to-find copy for weeks without any luck.

They made a relatively early return home. Effy was worried about any developments involving her mother and father. Robert MacKinnon was asleep in the armchair, with the television still on but showing static. Effy went straight up to the attic bedroom while Mack woke up his father. There was no news, although Mrs Halloran had called in to see Grace. She would return tomorrow.

Róisín, as Jane MacKinnon now called her, returned and closeted herself with Effy and Grace. Mack suspected matters must be moving towards a conclusion. Later, when he was alone with Effy and Grace, he asked what was happening. Effy said her mother had told them nothing other than that they were not to worry. She'd said she was fine and that she would tell them what was happening when there was something to tell. But her appearance contradicted what she'd said. Rósín Halloran was definitely not in a good way. The sisters had serious concerns about her state of mind and physical wellbeing. Whatever was going on between her and their father, they were not privy to it. Bridget and Caitlin might know but if they did they were saying nothing.

CHAPTER 61

It Keeps Rainin' – Fats Domino (London American 45-HLP 9374 – 1961)

Tuesday 22 November 1966

They left Mack to "babysit" Grace when Effy went with the MacKinnons to the parents' evening. After finishing her homework, Grace brewed some tea in the kitchen. Mack joined her a few minutes later to take a break.

"You know something, Mack? I'm the right girl at the wrong time. I was born too late, like the song." Grace sounded serious.

"What do you mean by that?" Mack could not believe what he was hearing. Those words from her lips were startling. Grace was not joking.

"Effy's not the only one who fell for you. I did too. You and I could have been an item if our ages were different. Don't take this confession as an attempt to get off with you. Even if I dared, which I never would, I could no more replace Effy in your heart than I could grow wings and fly to the moon. Confession is good for the soul, so they keep telling me. That's why I've said it. I needed to get it off my chest. If you ever changed your mind about Effy don't imagine I'd come running. I wouldn't, because I love my sister too much to ever hurt her and that includes replacing her. There, I've said it."

"I'm flattered," replied Mac, taken aback by the revelation. "That must have taken so much courage to say. Thanks for telling me. It couldn't have been easy. I'll respect your confidence forever, though I don't know what else to say."

Grace looked him straight in the eyes with a wan smile. "There's nothing else to say."

Pouring tea into his mug, she giggled and swept her coppery mane from her face. "You might as well know. El had a bit of a crush on you, too, when she was younger. Don't ever mention it to her or she'll skin me alive, and I doubt Tom would appreciate knowing it. Neither would Effy."

"What's so special about me that you Hallorans get a crush on me?" he couldn't resist asking.

"I wish I knew," Grace replied, smiling and taking a sip of her tea. "If I ever found out I would bottle it and make an absolute fortune. You have a way with us Hallorans. But it's not only us. I know for a fact you'd be able to work your way through most of my friends at school given half a chance. You have quite a few admirers at St. Jo's."

"Gee, thanks for the info! Does that mean I need to wear a safety hazard notice? 'Girls beware! Love machine!'"

"Don't let it go to your head. I can't imagine your dad being too thrilled widening all the doors so you could get through them."

"Ha, ha! Funny, as if. I'm cracking the whip. Back to work. Don't think you can slack 'cos you're stopping here."

"I've finished my homework so I'm going to watch some television."

An hour later Effy and Mack's parents returned. They sounded cheerful.

"I take it that it went well?" Mack asked, not looking up from the equation he was working on.

"Effy, it seems, is a bright young woman. They all agree she's university material." Robert MacKinnon added a barb for him. "Which should spur you on to do as well."

"All A grades, then?" As if Mack needed to ask. "So no pressure on me, eh?"

"Seems so," responded his mother. "Where's Grace?"

"She finished her homework. Got fed up with me babysitting her and went to watch television. I've got this last equation to finish. Won't be a mo, then you can let me know what a clever lass Effy is – as if I didn't know already."

It was 9.30 when the telephone rang. Mack's father answered. They could not hear what the conversation was about but he returned with a grave expression. The telephone call was from Róisín Halloran. She was at the Royal Infirmary. Sean Halloran had suffered a heart attack and was in Intensive Care.

CHAPTER 62

What Becomes Of The Broken Hearted – Jimmy Ruffin
(Tamla Motown TMG 577 – 1966)

Tuesday 22 November 1966

Róisín Halloran greeted her two daughters and the MacKinnons outside the side ward, looking pale, drawn and gaunt. Effy couldn't remember her mother looking so strained before. On top of all the suffering her mother now had to deal with her husband's heart attack. As much as Effy had come to detest her father, tears rolled down her cheeks. She felt in part responsible for his condition. Had her words and actions over time triggered the heart attack? Another side of her laid the blame on his intransigent zeal. He had brought it on himself. It was his own damned fault. Somehow, this did not sit true with her either. She could never feel free of guilt because of her defiance.

What would become of them if he died? How would they deal with the emotional loss? Despite everything they would all feel his loss.

Robert MacKinnon asked if he should fetch Caitlin and then go and get Bridget; they would surely want to be by their mother's side. But Róisín Halloran did not know how to respond, so Effy made the decision on her behalf. Caitlin could wait until the morning because of her baby daughter. It would be wrong to drag them out at this late hour. Bridget would feel hurt and upset if she did not know. Without a telephone there was no other way to contact either of them. Rob MacKinnon agreed and set off to fetch Bridget.

Mack entered the College building conscious that all eyes were on him. It was still early and it had to be his first stop today before going up to the Grammar. Even so, pupils were beginning to arrive at this early time. He recognised some of the Sixth Formers chatting in the corridor. Young men were never seen on the premises but Mack was already a familiar sight. His celebrity status was greater than he realised. Within seconds two girls claiming to be in Effy's tutor group accosted him. Exuding politeness, he asked if they could show him the way to the school office.

"You must be Fiona's boyfriend," observed one of them, introducing herself as Chloe. "I'm in her tutor group and English Lit class."

"A pleasure to make your acquaintance, Chloe," Mack responded, head inclined in a slight formal bow, tongue planted in cheek. Having read a little of Effy's Jane Austen set book he laid it on a bit thick.

"The pleasure's all ours. Is something wrong with Fiona?" asked the other, not volunteering her name.

"Nothing to concern yourselves with ladies. I'm sure she'll return tomorrow feeling considerbly improved," Mack responded in his best George Knightley manner, tongue firmly in cheek and smiling.

"Please let her know I asked after her and I hope things work out well for her family. Tell her that Chloe Johnson asked after her."

"I will," he promised, little knowing that Chloe Johnson would be a part of his and Effy's circle of friends in the future.

Coincidence seemed to plague his life. Handing over absence letters for the three sisters he found himself accosted again. This time it was Effy's form tutor who happened to be in the office. Mack found himself having to explain about her father's hospitalization. Her form tutor knew about him and his relationship with Effy, which left him confounded. Then, when she said, "It was a real pleasure to meet your parents last night," Mack had had enough.

There was more to follow from her before he could make good his escape. "They are such charming people and it's so good of them to take on the responsibility of looking after Fiona. Especially given all the present difficulties in her family life."

Mack thought he had managed to get away until he was introduced to Ellen's form tutor. At least they spared repeating the details. Making a polite though rapid departure, he hoped he never had to experience doing this again. As he went out of the doorway he muttered, "The things we do for love. I must be crazy."

On returning home in the afternoon he found Effy and Grace looking exhausted. They had refused to leave the hospital until they knew the extent of their father's condition. The heart attack was not as severe as first thought.

Sean Halloran would pull through, although he would need to take it easy for a while. Mrs Halloran had gone with Ellen to the printing workshop. There they asked his second in charge to take over the running of the business until he was fit to return. Ellen turned out to be a great help, even staying with her mum until her father returned.

At the weekend Tom stayed over at Mack's, wanting to be there for Ellen if she needed him. All the daughters wanted to be on hand when the doctor judged their father well enough for visiting. But Effy and Ellen were still angry with him. They didn't plan to see him as Aileen and Bridget did. Caitlin did not expect to see him but even so she hoped he might want to see little Jane.

Mack asked Effy to invite Angie to the house rather than to meet in town. This only struck him as bizarre when both were in his house. Even more bizarre was the way his mother took to Angie. That was uncomfortable, too. What would his mother have thought if she knew the truth about him having had sex with both of them?

After his mother had been introduced to Angie, she had given her son an odd look – not one he was happy to receive. There were so many times when he couldn't help wondering if his mother was a mind reader. It was unlikely and it was impossible but he did wonder. Angie took Effy down to the city centre for an hour or so before returning her home.

On Saturday Angie came over. All five went to the cinema, taking Grace along with them. One weekend missed down at the club wasn't going to be the end of the world. *Seconds* was X-rated but Grace got in without anyone challenging her age. The makeup artistry applied by Ellen and Angie had something to do with it. She looked eighteen after they had finished. It was then that Angie confessed the truth, stunning them all.

"Sorry, everyone. I've been lying about my age. I'm not quite as old as I've pretended. My eighteenth is on New Year's Day and you're all invited to my birthday bash. I feel so bad about this. You're all such good friends of mine I couldn't bear to keep on deceiving you all," she blurted out when they least expected it.

When asked why she'd misled them all, Angie admitted it was for a reason. "I wanted to keep guys the same age as me from pestering me and trying to get off with me. By pretending to be older I put most of them off. Apart from that, it's easier getting served in pubs, especially The Vic Lounge and Upper George. Word got round that I was older, which was why no barman ever challenged me."

Grace found Angie fascinating and said she would be trying the same trick in future. Pretending to be older was, in her words, "A cracking good idea". Effy and Mack exchanged worried looks. Knowing what Grace was like they could both see potential trouble ahead. Their worst fears surfaced when she made it plain she wanted to go over to The Plebs with them.

294

"When I'm fifteen next year please take me with you. I want to go where the action is."

Rósín Halloran came to see Effy and Grace on the Sunday evening. Much to Mack's astonishment, she asked him to join her and Effy in a private conversation. What she told them left both with some serious thinking to do before arriving at a decision. They thought long and hard about it, discussing the matter for over an hour. Mack was steadfast in refusing to let Effy go alone. In the end they agreed: come what may, they needed to go into this together. Besides, Mack was curious as to why her father had invited him to come along with Effy.

If it had not been for Róisín Halloran's persuasive appeal they might have refused. As it turned out the sisters agreed to see him each in turn. Sean Halloran's special request was that Effy and Caitlin should see him as couples. Mack could not help wondering, why the two of them? Adam and Caitlin he could understand, but Effy and himself? Well, that was a teasing puzzle. Her mother kept repeating there wasn't going to be a scene if they went. For the family's sake they needed to go.

CHAPTER 63

Treat Her Right – Roy Head (Vocalion V-P 9248 – 1965)

Sunday 4 December 1966

Neither Mack nor Effy had anticipated a priest meeting them as they walked towards the side ward. Fr. Jumeaux was not quite what they'd expected. Mack guessed he was about ten years older than his father, judging by the amount of greying hair. Róisín Halloran introduced him in a low voice.

"Fr. Jumeaux has been our counsellor, acting as a mediator between myself and Sean. Since we first spoke he has spent a considerable amount of time with your father. We needed someone for both spiritual guidance and psychiatric help. Fr. Jumeaux will tell you more about himself, I'm sure. In view of what has happened these past few years I felt we both needed help. You must understand, Effy, I believe in the marriage vows I took. I believe in the sanctity of family life – though not in the way your father has corrupted it in his madness. You must understand, Effy, leaving your father would be the last thing I would want for the two of us. He was and still is unwell but he remains the love of my life. I made my sacred vow promising to stand by him in sickness and health. It's a vow I want to keep. I had no idea how unwell he was becoming. Your father needs to find himself again. He has lost his way and is in need of spiritual and medical guidance. With Fr. Jumeaux's diagnosis and help we may see change. Please listen to what Fr. Jumeaux has to say about your Da. It's best if he does so rather than myself. I'll meet you both afterwards."

"Let's go somewhere a little more private," Fr. Jumeaux suggested.

They found a small visitors' room where Fr. Jumeaux went into considerable detail. He had taken holy orders late in life, having worked as a qualified psychiatric doctor for many years. Combining his work as a priest and doctor he now helped those with severe mental issues. This was the case with Effy's father. He had spent the last two days conversing and praying with him as well as acting as his confessor. Sean Halloran was a troubled man who had tried without success to manage a stressful life. Over time he had become a chronic depressive. This manifested itself as overly zealous behaviour contrary to the Church's teachings. Trying to be the breadwinner for a large family as well as managing a printing business had brought it on.

Fr. Jumeaux further explained. Living alongside a depressed person life could become hard, demanding and stressful. Family and friends suffered due to the challenges presented by someone with chronic depression.

Men had to be strong and resilient. The expectation was that men had to be capable of dealing with any demands placed upon them. The truth was this was not true of all individuals. Yet because of these expectations many men were unlikely to seek help. To do so would be to appear weak. Men had to appear to be strong when confronted by challenges and adversity.

It was of vital importance that family members understood that chronic depression was a serious illness. Family members had to play their parts in the treatment and care of a loved one. In such instances, marital and family therapy was often required. It wasn't all doom and gloom. There was good news that came twofold.

First, the doctors treating Sean Halloran informed them this wasn't a heart attack: at least, not in the true medical sense. It was a condition they called "stress cardiomyopathy". Intense emotional or physical stress caused a severe cardiac dysfunction. This mimicked a myocardial infarction. Rest and recuperation in a stress-free environment were vital if Sean Halloran was to improve. Plans were in place to ensure that would happen.

Second, as part of the restorative treatment he had to understand what was wrong. Until he understood why his daughters had turned against him, he would not be able to progress. But Fr. Jumeaux was confident that this had already happened. Sean Halloran confessed that it had been like a fog clouding his mind and judgement. Once clarity had begun to return, his mental fog had dispersed. He had realised what had been happening to him and to everyone around him. A full recovery would take time and medication but the most important thing was his immediate response. Sean Halloran wanted and needed reconciliation with each of his daughters.

It was his request that Effy should be the first he should see, and also that she should bring along her young man. Fr. Jumeaux emphasised they should not fear seeing him. It would not be an ordeal or anything they should dread.

The priest was right. It could have been an ordeal but in fact it was far from it. Mack had never spoken with Effy's father in all the years he had seen him in church on Sundays. When he and Effy entered the room, they found a tired, quiet, pale man: not the ebullient person Mack remembered from Sunday mornings outside church.

"I'm glad you've come, young one," began Sean Halloran, addressing Effy in his Galway lilt. "And I'm glad you've brought your young fella, too." He looked at Mack. "I've seen you ever since you were a lad, but you're a man now."

"How are you, Da?" Effy hesitated before leaning over and giving him a kiss on the cheek.

"It's a long time since you called me, Da, Effy. It's lovely to hear you call me that again. As you see, I've had a bad dose in me head and me chest, but God willing I'll mend."

"You've never called me Effy before."

"Time I did. Everyone else does, so why should I be different?"

"James prefers us to call him Mack," said Effy. "Seems we both prefer to be something other than our given names."

Sean Halloran studied Mack for a moment or two.

"In the Gaelic that means son." After a pause, he added, "We have a saying in Ireland. A son is a son till he takes him a wife. A daughter is a daughter all of her life."

"My mother wouldn't agree with that sentiment, Mr Halloran. I suspect I'll always be her son no matter what."

"Jane MacKinnon. A good, good woman, your mother. A true friend to my wife – and also to my daughter, almost as if she were a member of the family, which I suppose by marriage she now is. It shames me that I couldn't see the truth of it. My wife tells me you're a good young fella, and that Effy could do no better. Is that true, son?"

"I hope so, Mr Halloran. She's special to me."

"He's everything and more, Da. Plain speaking, I love him."

"And you, young fella? Do you share the same feelings as my daughter?"

"Without doubts or reservation. I'm in love with your daughter."

There were a few moments of silence. Effy's father closed his eyes. Then he began to recount the story of how he, Sean Halloran, had met Róisín O'Rourke. Coincidences seemed to rule Mack's life. This particular one was as eerie and as strange as anything he had ever imagined or experienced.

Róisín O'Rourke had set her cap at a young apprentice boy in church. The first time she'd seen him, it had been a Sunday. She was fourteen, and the young man fresh from Galway fifteen. He'd arrived in Dublin to learn his trade as a printer with his uncle. Róisín's younger sister, called Grace, had arranged their first meeting.

On hearing this, Mack and Effy exchanged wide-eyed open-mouthed looks.

"So, that's where Grace got her name from? Mum has a sister called Grace?" Effy couldn't resist interrupting the flow of the tale.

"She *had* a sister called Grace. The dear girl passed away when you were small, before our little Grace was born. She was the sweetest person you could ever have wished to know."

As Sean Halloran continued the story of his courtship, Effy and Mack learned that it had not been easy. Róisín's parents had been exceedingly strict and didn't approve of him in the least. When their attachment came to light her father had tried to end their relationship. Both had refused to do so, marrying in secret and escaping to England where they had lived in Liverpool for a time.

Telling the story of how his and his wife's romance had begun in adversity seemed to cheer Sean Halloran. Reminiscing brought a smile to his face. Mack couldn't remember ever seeing him smiling with such warmth. It was as though it made him feel better about himself, and for a moment Mack saw a young man much like himself experiencing true love, rather than a middle-aged man haunted and burned out by life's difficulties.

Turning to Effy, her father confessed, "I'm truly sorry, with every fibre of my being, dearest child. I've been such an awful father to you for so long. I have failed you. Failed your sisters. Failed the love of my life, your dear mother, and I've failed myself."

"It wasn't always so, Da. We didn't realise how difficult you were finding it looking after such a large family. We never understood what a responsibility you were carrying as we grew up," Effy replied, tears welling up in her eyes.

"There, there, little one, no need for tears. You were always my little mouse in the house. Always the one who seemed overlooked. Not the youngest, not the oldest, but the one who seemed to miss out the most on everything. I tried to love you all in the same way but somehow you were always a little more special to me. It will take you time but I hope you'll find it in yourself to forgive me for all the wrongs and ills I've done you. When I remember those terrible things I'm ashamed of myself. I begin to see, thanks to Fr. Jumeaux, how lost I had become and how now I must begin to find my way back onto the right track.

"We have a saying in Ireland. *If God sends you down a stony path, may he give you strong shoes.* The shoes he gave me weren't strong enough for my stony path. I hope the Good Lord will see fit to give me another, stronger pair to last out the journey."

Plans for Sean Halloran's recuperation were soon in place, and arrangements almost finalised. He and his wife would be staying with family in Ireland.

In his absence Sean Halloran had offered his foreman a junior partnership. The young man had worked for him from his apprenticeship onwards, he accepted the offer without hesitation. According to his wife, Sean Halloran had treated Dick Shepherd as if he were the son he'd never had. Shepherd would take over the running of the place until Sean Halloran returned. Bridget would oversee things in her father's absence. Mack's father had agreed to keep an eye on the finances of the business by overseeing the accounts.

A convalescence of at least six months was recommended. Fr. Jumeaux would continue to have sessions with Sean Halloran until he left. Caitlin would be coming in later in the day, along with her daughter and husband, to see her father. Effy was so pleased to hear that Caitlin and her father would reconcile that she burst into tears. Her father would finally meet his granddaughter, Jane. If he had accepted Mack, she hoped he would also accept Adam as his son-in-law.

Before she and Mack left, Effy, tears streaming, hugged her father with all her strength. She never actually said that she forgave him but words weren't needed. The forgiveness was in the tears and the hugs.

Sean Halloran's parting words to Mack were man to man, not man to boy. "Prove you're man enough for my Fiona, for your Effy. Treat her right."

CHAPTER 64

Love, Love, Love – Bobby Hebb (Phillips BF 1522 (B) – 1966)

Monday 5 December 1966

Effy came down to birthday cards and presents waiting for her on the kitchen table. There was too little time to open them all, so she made the decision to open the presents in the evening. Except for one special present that Mack slipped into her hand at the door. Sitting in the back of the car she opened the small parcel and let out a tiny gasp. Whatever it was, it was in a Fattorini presentation box. Fattorini's was the most expensive and upmarket jewellers in the city.

Opening it she found a gold bracelet. Not some 9kt. gold-plated bracelet but a solid gold 18kt. wide band bangle. It must have cost Mack an absolute fortune. Months later she was finally able to wheedle the price from him. It had cost a staggering £30, money saved from his summer work at Benny's. Afraid she might lose it if she left it in the presentation box, Effy slipped it onto her wrist. There was a note with the bracelet.

Mack had written down the lyrics from the B-side of a Bobby Hebb record he loved to play. The lyrics summed up his love for her. The day was complete before it had even begun.

When Grace and Ellen saw the wide gold bangle on her wrist they gasped too. The bangle was so beautiful that Effy couldn't help looking at it. She kept it under her blouse cuff, taking care the whole day not to scratch it.

Further surprises awaited as her sisters turned up in the evening, among them a much-changed Deidre back from university for the Christmas holidays. Jane MacKinnon had organised the surprise party to celebrate Effy's seventeenth birthday. It was also doubling as her parents' leaving do. Angie and Tom had even come over from Halifax, to Effy's delight.

The medicated and subdued Sean Halloran was more like the father Effy remembered from her childhood. Her mother seemed happier than she could recall seeing her for years. They were leaving for Dublin on the Thursday. This was their last chance for six months to see all their daughters together.

They had planned to shut up the house. Then they had suggested that Bridget and Ellen could return. That way Deidre had somewhere to come home to during university breaks.

Bridget was reluctant to give up her flat. According to Ellen, following a conversation with Greg she changed her mind. She would keep the flat on but would move back into the house as a temporary measure. Ellen doubted Bridget would spend every night at the house. If she did, Mack wondered, how often her friend Greg would come visiting? Mack could almost see Tom mentally rejoicing on hearing the news. His prospects for staying over with Ellen looked better than good.

Mack's parents made it clear they would like Effy to stay with them. His mother was especially fond of her. They would also look after Grace. In their defence, Mack knew their offer to do so was genuine. Given Grace's age, the MacKinnons would be better caring for her. Mack also viewed the matter from a different perspective. He suspected that his mother's motive was to have Grace around to stop Effy and himself from getting up to no good.

Effy kept her bracelet covered but could not resist showing it off to Angie.

"Wow! God almighty!" Angie exclaimed. "Cover it up quick before I'm blinded!"

"What do you think?" Effy was bubbling with excitement.

"What do I think? What I think doesn't matter. What do you think?"

"He shouldn't have."

"But he did. Live with it. I would in your place. Show me it again. That's beautiful and I if I'm not turning green then I ought to be. I have to find me a fella like Mack."

"Why haven't you?"

"Finding someone like Mack is harder than finding a pot of gold at the end of a rainbow. I've more chance of winning on Littlewoods pools."

"I feel mean about what I got him for his birthday. What should I get him as a thank you?"

Angie joked. "How about a ball and chain?"

"No. Be serious. Besides, he's got me already. What do you suggest I should I get him for Christmas?"

"How much can you afford?"

"Not much. I've six sisters to buy for, and the MacKinnons."

"Remember my Grandma's advice?"

302

"Yes." But Effy sounded unsure.

"Do I have to spell it out, girl?" Angie paused, looking at Effy. "Let me put it this way, Eff. If Mack were my guy and gave me a bangle like that, I'd shag him senseless so he'd never forget how much I loved him. I would even give him a blow job."

"A what?"

Angie whispered the explanation in her ear.

"Women do that?" Effy asked in a quiet shocked voice, flushing at the thought. "Have you ever... you know?"

"No. Not yet because I've not found my perfect fella," Angie replied.

"What are you two gassing about out here in the hallway? Come on, Effy, it's your birthday do. You should be with the rest of us," Mack called from the doorway.

"We'll be in a minute," Angie answered. "It's girl talk."

CHAPTER 65

Love Makes the World Go Round – Deon Jackson
(Atlantic AT 4070 – 1966)

Saturday 17 December 1966 – Shotgun Express

Rod "The Mod" Stewart was every bit as superb as Mack and Effy had heard. Shotgun Express was a tight musical outfit. Beryl Marsden's uncanny resemblance was such she could have doubled as Angie's older sister. It didn't escape without comments. As a singer she was impressive, her voice powerful and driven with soulful emotion. That was everyone's consensus. The drummer was a standout on account of his height. He was a giant bloke whom Mack identified as Mick Fleetwood from photos in the weekly musical press.

The disappointment came when the band didn't perform their recently released single. Mack and Effy had hoped to hear *I Could Feel the Whole World Turn Round*. Instead they heard the usual Eddie Floyd, Wilson Pickett, and Sam & Dave covers. Good as these cover versions were, they were not in the same league as the originals. It was another great night, with The Plebs packed solid as usual.

Afterwards, in George's Square in the cold night air, everyone enjoyed a good laugh. It was late, but no one was ready to go home yet. A couple of police constables standing outside the main Post Office looked on.

Tom had persuaded his parents to let Ellen stay over until the morning. This was fine as long as he slept alone downstairs. Mack and Effy would have to ride back to Bradford, which was a pity. Angie offered to let them doss down in her parents' front room. It was an offer they wanted to accept so they could spend time cuddled up together. Having promised to be back in the early hours Mack and Effy believed they had to honour their promises. Tonight everything seemed right with their world. A new year was looming, heralding more changes that would affect their lives.

They were young, they were in love, they were together as fate had decreed: two hearts, one love. Nothing else mattered. For Mack and Effy, love did make the world go round..

[The End of Book 1]

304

Acknowledgements

My loving thanks to my wife Julie for her patience during the many hours I spent writing the novel as well as for her comments and advice. Also my grateful thanks to all the following. Ven Cooke for being the first to read the rough draft and for her encouragement to keep writing. To my sister-in-law Helen for her encouragement. Many thanks to my old friends from those days: Paul Foster, Colin 'Bill' Graham and Brian Warner who agreed to allow me to mention them in the novel. Also to the memory of my 'cuz' Ryk Arkulisz aka 'Acky' who never lived to see the novel completed. Ryk was instrumental in getting me into the Mod scene as a teenager. These turned out to be some of the best years of my life for which I owe him an unrepayable debt. If you went to Halifax's Plebeians Jazz Club or Manchester's Twisted Wheel between 1965 and 1968 thanks for helping to make them such exciting places. Without you it couldn't have happened. To all the wonderful Soul singers and R&B bands who created the music and played at these venue I am deeply grateful. Your music inspired a generation of youngsters like myself with an abiding love and passion for Soul and R&B.

About the author

John Knight was born in Halifax, West Yorkshire, in 1949. Now retired and living in Cheshire he divides his time between the UK and Spain. A Mod from the age of sixteen he believes that *once you're a Mod, you're always a Mod*. He is working on a series of novels set in the Sixties following on from *Jimmy Mack* with others that will have parallel interweaving storylines.

305

Lightning Source UK Ltd.
Milton Keynes UK
UKHW040600090119
335256UK00001B/44/P